MAP

THE GENDER GAME

BELLA FORREST

DEDICATION

To my readers, for every kind comment, email and review.
I would not have come this far without you.

PROLOGUE

My sweating palms slipped against the handles of my bike as I cycled at a pace I hoped would not look suspicious. I tried to fix my eyes ahead on the perfectly even road and not keep glancing over my shoulder at the makeshift wooden trailer I was pulling behind me.

As the uniform townhouses on either side of me grew sparse, so did the light. By the time I arrived at the edge of town, the sun had set.

I had been lucky so far. I hadn't passed anybody I knew, and nobody had halted me to ask where I was going.

I slowed to a stop once I reached the end of the last concrete road on this side of the city. Catching my breath, I wiped my palms against my blouse. My lower back felt sticky with sweat. And I had run out of water.

But I was almost there now.

I repositioned my throbbing palms on the handlebars and my feet on the pedals of the bike when a voice called behind me.

"Violet? Is that you?"

I froze.

I knew that voice. It was one I'd grown accustomed to hearing every Monday, Wednesday, and Friday. Ms. Dale, my defense trainer.

What was she doing in this part of town at nightfall?

I forced a casual expression to my face and twisted around.

The fluorescent street lamps illuminated the tall, lithe brunette standing on the sidewalk outside Georgette's Laundry. She was clutching a bundle of white sheets.

"Good evening, Ms. Dale," I called back.

"What are you doing out here, Violet?" she asked.

My jaw twitched as she left the sidewalk and approached me.

"Trashing Ms. Connelly's old china," I explained, a response I had thought up long before leaving my room this morning.

"Oh, I see," she said, her eyes moving from my three-wheeled trailer and returning to my face. "Wish I had someone to run *my* errands." She grimaced at her laundry.

I managed a half-smile.

She lingered a few seconds longer before glancing back at the launderette. "Right, well… you'd better be on your way. You know the junkyard gets creepier the later it gets."

"Yeah," I murmured.

"See you Monday."

She turned on her heel and I let out a slow breath. Gritting my teeth, I faced forward again, my eyes focusing on the narrow cobblestone path that branched off from the end of the road. I cycled for another fifteen minutes down the winding route, past the suburban cottages and misted greenhouses until I reached a pair of corrugated iron gates— the junkyard's entrance. Pulling the gates open just wide enough for my bike to fit through, I rolled it inside. I gazed around the sea of color-coded trash containers, wide-eyed. Nobody was around. *So far, so good.*

The overpowering smell of artificial mint filled my nostrils as I wound around the containers toward the back of the enclosure. The chemical the hygiene department sprayed in here helped to mask the odor of trash, but had the tendency to cause a dull headache.

Arriving at the last row of trash containers lining the back wall, I stopped. I grabbed the handles of the container directly in front of me and slowly eased it forward to reveal the brickwork behind it. I hurried to the wall and sank to my knees on the ground. My fingers fumbled along the bricks, feeling for the tell-tale gap. Finding it, I gained a firmer grip and coaxed it out of place. Then I worked on the previously weakened bricks behind it and above it until I had created a hole just large enough for my frame to squeeze through.

I had to be quick now. Quicker than ever. If someone spotted me here like this, all my days of preparation, all my sleepless nights, would be in vain.

I darted for the wooden trailer hooked to the back of my bike and, clutching the clasp that was holding the lid securely shut, I unfastened it. My heart was hammering against my chest as I opened it.

Curled up in the cramped wooden crate, knees drawn to his chest, eyes tightly closed, was my eight-year-old brother, Timothy.

My eyes moved over the mark etched into his right hand. The mark of a black crescent.

The mark that had changed our lives forever.

It took a few seconds for him to unglue his eyelids and realize that it was finally time to climb out. His black hair clung to his moist forehead as he raised his head to look at me. His gray eyes shone with fear.

I leaned over and wrapped my arms around his midriff, helping him step out. He winced and groaned against me. It killed me to think of how much time he'd been holed up in that box.

But it wouldn't be long now.

It wouldn't be long.

"Come on, buddy," I breathed. "Cad will already be waiting for us."

I pointed to the dark gap in the wall. He glanced at me uncertainly before lowering to his hands and knees. He scurried through. I followed immediately behind him. A chill stole through me as we emerged on the other side.

I swallowed hard as I gazed around at the seldom-frequented surroundings. At least, what I could see of them. We were standing amid a slushy marshland, pale and glistening beneath the strip lights that lined the exterior of the wall. Fifteen feet away flowed Veil River, above which hung a dense gray mist. The river was wide, so wide that the opposite bank was a blur even in the daytime when the mist was thinner.

We crept as quietly as we could through the sludge, toward the edge of the vaporous water. I continued to reassure Tim in whispers that Cad would be waiting in his rowboat, just like he'd promised. Only a little further up... but as we reached the river's border, neither Cad nor his boat were anywhere to be seen.

"Where is he?" Tim gasped.

"He... He's got to be along here somewhere. Let's move up the bank a bit more."

I led Tim further up the river through the marsh, knowing how much danger we were in now. My whole plan had revolved around Cad being here, waiting for us, so that Tim could immediately board his boat. We shouldn't be roaming in the open like this. Wardens could spot us at any second and the consequences would be catastrophic.

"Oh!" Tim hissed, making me jump. "There's a boat!" He jabbed a finger toward the river as Cad's competitive rowboat came into view.

Warm relief washed over me. *Thank God.*

Cad closed the distance between us, an apologetic look on his unshaven face.

"I'm so sorry," he whispered, as he bumped the boat against the bank. "I had some, uh, unexpected complications. You know, with Margot. She started asking me where I was going and… Let's just get this done."

I turned to my brother and bent down. Wrapping my arms around his thin waist, I lifted him up. But before I could pass him to Cad, he struggled against my grip, forcing me to replace him on the ground.

"Wait, Vi!" he breathed. Tears moistened his eyes. "When am I going to see you again?"

My voice caught in my throat. How could I answer a question like that? What could I tell him? I didn't want to lie and say that I would see him next week, next month, or even next year. Because once he reached the other side of the river, I didn't know if I would ever see him again.

I cupped his face in my hands and planted a firm kiss against his forehead, his nose, then his cheeks.

"We'll see," was all I could think to whisper.

My chest ached as I thought of returning home to the orphanage tonight to sleep alone in my room. And tomorrow, waking up without him. How I would have to maintain complete ignorance as to his whereabouts to everyone in the city.

I pushed the thoughts aside.

"I love you, Tim," I said, hugging him tightly as I buried my face in his hair. "Don't forget it."

"I love you too, Ma," he whispered.

Ma. How I despised it when he called me that. *And now of all times…*

Gripping him firmly, I pried his arms away from my neck and rose to my feet.

"You need to go," I choked.

Tears streamed down his dirty cheeks as he finally let me pass him to Cad, who hauled him onto the boat.

Even as Tim left my grasp, every part of me remained holding on. As Cad sat Tim down and, with a grim nod of his head, began to row away, I couldn't let go.

My eyes stung as I gazed through the mist at their retreating shadows.

I had already imagined this moment in my head long before tonight. I'd pictured myself standing on the muddy bank, staring out over the water and waiting until the mist engulfed the boat. Until I lost sight of them completely.

But now that it was happening, I couldn't handle it. It only made Tim's departure seem all the more final. All the more conclusive.

I turned and began wading back across the marshland, but after barely five steps, I stalled.

Three hunched shadows loomed near the wall. Three large, black dogs. Sniffers. And behind them, two tall, broad-shouldered women in deep green uniform. Wardens patrolling on their nightly rounds of the wall's perimeter.

I dropped down, flattening myself against the wet ground, the panic in my chest almost suffocating me.

It was too late.

They had seen and sensed me. Growls ripped from the dogs' throats as they closed the distance. But it wasn't the end of the world if I was caught out here. As long as—

"Watch out, Violet!"

Tim's scream.

My blood ran cold.

Stupid boy. Stupid, stupid boy!

The dogs' and wardens' attention instantly shot to the water, where the outline of Cad's boat was still visible.

Losing all interest in me, the five of them dashed to the water's edge. One of the women pulled out a whistle from her pocket and blew it before barking a command to the dogs.

"No!" I cried, stumbling after them.

In spite of its toxicity, the dogs leapt into the water, their powerful legs navigating the current twice as fast as Cad's oars as he attempted to speed up and escape.

Two of the animals reached the boat and leapt onto it, causing Cad to topple into the river. One of the dogs closed its jaws around Tim's shirt and tugged hard, pulling him over the edge and into the water.

My vision became tunnel-like. All I could see was Tim being pulled through the water, back to the bank. I attempted to swoop in and grab him as the dog arrived at the shore, but one of the women leapt at me. Tripping up my already shaking legs, she tackled me to the ground.

"Violet!" Tim screamed again. I gazed helplessly as the second warden locked his inflamed arms behind his back and began dragging him away.

Back toward the wall.

As the woman straddling my hips drove a tranquilizer dart into my shoulder, that scream would become the last memory I ever had of my brother: A marked boy.

CHAPTER 1

Eight years later...

"*Merrymount Mill*," read the sign hanging above the entrance of the graystone windmill. "*Facility for Convicted Juveniles.*"

I wrinkled my nose, flexing my fingers around the handle of my tattered suitcase.

I had no idea why it was called Merrymount. There were no "mounts" around here, or anywhere in the flat land of Matrus—mountains were a luxury enjoyed only by our neighbors in Patrus. And nothing about this towering brick building, or the shriveled brown fields that surrounded it, could be described as *merry*.

But I ought to start getting used to it. This was to be my residence for the next two years, assuming I behaved myself.

This would be my third home—if a detention facility could be called that—in five years. A textiles factory deep in the countryside, about twenty miles from here, had been my first, and a sewage plant on the other side of the city, by Veil River, had been my second. A flour mill certainly beat the latter.

If I managed to keep myself in line here for the next two years and successfully complete my seven-year incarceration period, I would be on track for reintegration into the city a few days after my twenty-first birthday... whatever life the Court expected a girl with no family to live after having spent her adolescence locked away from society.

And I had better not slip up. I'd already rebelled against the Court at the age of eleven by committing obstruction of justice, and after being convicted of womanslaughter (albeit involuntary) via the use of a weapon (even if it was a dinner fork) a few years later, there would be only one fate left in store for me if I didn't get through these next two years without first-degree infractions. It would be straight to the city labs, where I would be put painlessly to sleep without further trial or consideration.

There would be nobody to miss me, I supposed. I no longer had my younger brother. He'd been flagged as "excessively domineering" in the matriarchy's screening lab when he was eight and consequently deemed an unfit member of Matrus' peaceful society. A score of five out of five for both aggressive tendencies and insubordination was essentially the kiss of death for any Matrus-born boy. Tim was a slave in the coal mines in the Deep North now. Or so I'd been told. I hadn't seen him since the day I'd failed to smuggle him to Patrus.

After I'd been caught and sedated by the riverside, I'd been forced to spend the next two weeks in isolation—my first taste of imprisonment. The more I begged to be sent to the mines with my brother, the more I was ignored. I even tried to locate the aircraft that transported the boys to the North once I got out, but I was caught near the hangar and thrust back into isolation with the stern warning that if I stepped out of line again, I would be locked up long-term.

Over the years, I'd eventually managed to see the futility in pursuing Tim, but the day I gave up looking for him was the beginning of a steeper downhill slide. A slide that I still struggled to find reason to fight against. And my anger simply fueled my rebellion.

But I had to fight it now, and keep my head down, unless I truly did have a death wish.

My aunt, uncle, and cousin Cad might miss me if I was gone, though I almost never saw them as they lived on the other side of the river in the patriarchy of Patrus.

Then there was the owner of my old orphanage, Ms. Connelly. She had always been kind to me, though she'd probably be senile by now, assuming she hadn't died already. The few childhood friends I'd had would have moved on with their lives. None of those friendships had been deep.

"Keep moving, Ms. Bates," my escort said to me, nudging me in the shoulder. She was a green-uniformed warden armed with a crossbow; a stocky woman nameless to me and about half a foot short of my height.

The warden ushered me through the doorway and we emerged in a small reception room whose walls were lined with lockers and hanging white aprons. An oval desk stood opposite the doorway, behind which sat a plump middle-aged woman with cropped brown hair and horn-rimmed glasses.

"Violet Bates," she said, glancing up. Her lips, lined with plum-colored lipstick, pursed. She rose to her feet with a black registry book and wound around the table to approach us. She paused a few feet away, eyeing me shrewdly. "Nineteen years old."

I nodded curtly.

"Almost a clean record for the past four years," she went on. "Two minor incidents of violence against fellow inmates, involving punching."

I nodded again, swallowing. Those punches had been well-deserved.

She furrowed her brows before concluding, "Right, I know where we have space for you. Follow me. My name's Ms. Maddox."

Ms. Maddox led me through a back door and we arrived in what I could only assume was the main place of work in this mill, a vast circular room filled with aisle upon aisle of grinding and sifting machinery. I sneezed. Everything in here was dusted with white particles.

She led me across the room to a staircase. By the time we'd reached the top, my calves were burning and Ms.

Maddox was positively wheezing. I'd counted eight floors in total.

"You're right at the top," Ms. Maddox explained, panting as we turned into a dim, worn gray-carpeted corridor lined with wooden doors. She stopped at the sixth door to my right and turned the handle. She pushed, but the door didn't budge. She huffed in frustration. "Josefine!"

There was a span of silence before a vague voice replied, "Yeah?"

"You have locked your door again! Were you not reprimanded just last week for this?"

A bed creaked. Light footsteps sounded. A chair scraped and the door slowly drew open.

A waifish girl who looked no older than nine stood barefoot in the doorway, wearing a checkered brown dress. Her face, splashed with freckles, was round and framed by a ginger mop of short, yet wildly curly hair. The apples of her cheeks were high and plump, her small lips pursed and heart-shaped. She had a look of righteous indignation in her large—almost bulbous—green eyes.

Her fingers flicked to the chair at her side. "It wasn't *locked*," she muttered, scowling.

"Obstruction of entry to dormitories is forbidden," Ms. Maddox countered. "I do not want to have to remind you of that again."

The girl rolled her eyes exaggeratedly and retreated into the room. Ms. Maddox led me inside. The windowless room was square-shaped and held very little, save for a bunk bed which Josefine had just climbed onto, the chair, a rickety table, and a chest of drawers.

"Well, this is Josefine Rankin," Ms. Maddox explained.

Josefine scrutinized me through the jungle of her low-cut bangs as she perched on the top bunk.

"Hello," I said, offering her a small smile that she didn't return.

"The bathrooms are situated to your right when you walk out the door, at the end of the hallway," Ms. Maddox explained. "Meals are served at eight, two, and seven-thirty. Work finishes at seven p.m. each day. Lights out at nine-thirty p.m., no exceptions. You should be asleep by ten p.m. Wake-up call is four a.m. You have thirty minutes to get up, get washed, and be downstairs in the work room."

I grimaced. Wake-up call here was one hour earlier than even the sewage plant.

"I trust that Josefine will answer any questions you may have," Ms. Maddox ploughed on. "At four-thirty a.m. tomorrow, you'll be given a briefing of your tasks. It's ten to eight now, so you'll have to wait until tomorrow morning for food."

My stomach was rumbling after the long journey to get here, but I was used to skipping meals.

"You'll find that most of the same rules apply here as they did at Divedun Sewage as well as at the textiles factory," Ms. Maddox continued. "Wardens roaming the building night and day, routine searches when entering and leaving the dining room, etcetera, etcetera."

"Right," I muttered. I'd been searched before embarking on the journey to Merrymount, too. Nothing sharp was allowed in my suitcase, not even nail clippers. That was why there were never mirrors in the dormitories of these facilities, only in the bathrooms, which were monitored by wardens.

"I'll see you tomorrow morning," Ms. Maddox concluded. She backed out of the room and clicked the door shut behind her.

I turned slowly to the bunk, resuming my focus on Josefine. I cleared my throat. "You, uh, sleep up there, I assume."

Josefine nodded.

"Okay…" I heaved a sigh before dumping my suitcase on the lower bunk. I sat down, spreading my palms over the mattress and gauging its softness. A little softer than my previous bed. Not that this was saying much.

I removed my boots and rolled off my socks, stretching out my legs and toes. I sat there for a few minutes in silence, staring at the blank wall opposite me. Then I glanced at Josefine, who was still sitting in the same position, knees drawn up against her chest, arms around her shins.

"Going to the restroom," I murmured, before leaving the room and taking a right turn down the corridor.

The bathrooms were clearly marked at the end and I moved inside to find a showering area and a row of sinks and cubicles. I stopped in front of one of the sinks to splash my face and caught my gray eyes in the mirror. I hadn't slept much last night and it showed. I looked like crap. My skin, lightly tanned by the sun, appeared dry and lackluster, and my black shoulder-length hair, normally dead straight, was crimped and escaping in all directions from my pony tail. I shook it out, running my fingers through it, before heading to a stall to relieve myself.

When I returned to the sinks, another girl had entered—a girl I recognized instantly. Her features were ratty, with thin lips, a protruding upper jaw and lanky brown hair that clung to her scalp like a helmet.

Vera Sykes. A girl who had almost caused me to gain a third infraction over the past five years due to a run-in I'd had with her back in the textiles factory. I had not seen her since.

She looked just as surprised to see me, her eyes widening a fraction as she stared. But then she turned away abruptly, deciding to ignore me. She washed and dried her hands before sweeping toward the door. Though, as she brushed past me, she moved a little too close—managing to nudge me in the back. Then she sped up, hastening through the exit.

Idiot.

I couldn't stand girls like Vera. Girls with neither brain nor backbone. Her way of surviving the facilities was by becoming the full-time ass-licker of whoever she deemed the toughest person in the block… or the toughest person who could stand to be around her. She'd been friendly with me for a couple of days before I'd started avoiding her. After that, she'd gone behind my back and revealed her second face.

Though in fairness, I wasn't good at getting along with people my age in general. I struggled to connect and was often labeled a loner. Not that I minded. Making friends in facilities like this wasn't encouraged. It wasn't supposed to be a social club and that was one of the reasons girls were uprooted and made to rotate the facilities.

I returned to my room to find Josefine lying on her back, staring up at the ceiling. She didn't look at me as I entered, though she addressed me for the first time. "What's your name?"

"Violet."

"And… how did you wind up here?"

I sat down before turning my mind heavily back to that fateful day at school. It had been a sticky Monday afternoon. I'd been fourteen years old when a girl two years my senior, whom I'd had a history of discord with, had picked a fight with me in the dining hall because I'd objected—in no timid words—to her jumping the line. We'd started with bare hands, and would have continued that way if she hadn't scooped up a fork. I'd reciprocated to ward her off, not to plunge the fork into her throat. But she had launched at me at exactly the wrong moment, and at exactly the wrong angle. She'd died in the hospital a few hours later.

After that, my life became one of slavery to my country. Waking up at the same time every day, being carted from one chore to the other. And trying to stay out of trouble. I'd gotten into a few fights—only two of them recorded—but I had been careful to avoid the use of actual weapons. Weapon usage by anyone other than an authorized warden was strictly prohibited throughout Matrus; it was one of the most basic commandments of our monarch, Queen Rina.

I didn't feel like spilling all this history to Josefine now. So I just replied, "I got into a fight with a bully... What about you? And how old are you, by the way?"

I took a seat in the chair so that I could see her as we talked. She'd positioned her head closer to the edge of the bunk and was looking at me now.

"I'm eight and a half... I'm only supposed to be here for another two weeks," she replied. "Mom was taken to the Drewsbury Center while I got stuck here. We got caught."

I frowned. "Caught?"

"Caught without permission, trying to return from Patrus. We wanted badly to move back here—it's our home. I was born here and so was Mom. But the Court was telling us we'd have to wait two weeks for approval. We couldn't wait that long. Mom was going mad, and she was going to get into a lot of trouble if we didn't leave Patrus right away. So she traveled back with me in my uncle's rowboat… We left Dad."

It was disturbing that Josefine should be put in a facility like this one, which was filled with girls convicted of far worse crimes than premature migration. Her crime had not even been hers, but her mother's. But this was common of the Court's decisions. They were known to make statements, however harsh, to discourage the public from even considering infractions. Matrus' government frowned upon residents who decided to move to the patriarchy in the first place, so making it difficult for them to return ensured that they thought long and hard about their choice.

"How come you went to Patrus to begin with?" I asked, although I hardly needed to. There weren't a lot of reasons that women who were born and bred in Matrus would migrate to Patrus.

"Because of my dad," Josefine responded grimly. "He was born there. He moved to Matrus because my mom asked him to. They married here and he took her name. But he couldn't survive here. He begged Mom to let him take us back with him."

"… And your mom couldn't bear it in Patrus," I finished. Just as marriages only usually lasted in Matrus if Matrus was all the man had ever known, the same was true of marriages in Patrus; women born there were conditioned to the ways of life in the patriarchy. They didn't suffer from culture shock as Matrus-born women did.

A woman in Patrus had about as many rights as a pet animal. She couldn't legally reside there without being owned by a man, and even with a husband she was limited. She couldn't go out by herself, she couldn't work, drive, or own money or property. I'd even heard that their physical appearance and clothes were dictated by the man, if he so chose, and arguing was completely taboo. Women were dependent to a humiliating degree.

I'd spent the last five years of my life as a Matrian prisoner, but even so, I was sure that I still held more dignity than I would in the patriarchy. I had never crossed the river to Patrus, as I suspected no self-respecting Patrian man would want to cross to Matrus, either (unless it was on business).

Things weren't a lot easier for men here. Any Patrian male wishing to migrate to Matrus had to first undergo a full background check to shed light on any potential disruptive tendencies. Only if the man was deemed to be a low to moderate risk (it was rare for any Patrian male to be considered a "low" risk) would he be allowed to be coupled with a Matrian woman and adopt her last name. Retaining his ego was out of the question. No matter what qualifications he might have arrived with, he would be relegated to an occupation of repetitive manual labor— only sons of the Court were allowed to pursue the sciences or other intellectual professions. They weren't allowed to own property or assets, although they were allowed to drive and roam by themselves. This extra leniency shown toward them was made up for by the harshness of Matrus' legal system — there was little male-committed crime in Matrus for a reason.

Such differing upbringings between Patrian-Matrian couples were all but impossible to reconcile in the long term. Veil River was known colloquially as Suicide Stretch, and there had been more than a few incidents of couple suicides over the years.

Hook-ups between the nations usually only happened if one of them had an occupation that required them to spend time on the other side of the river, like trade officials, or negotiations ambassadors. The majority of women in Matrus either chose a Matrian partner, or opted to be without a partner completely and conceive in an insemination center. My mother had chosen the latter to have my brother and me. And if I ever decided I wanted a child, I would do the same.

I didn't need a man in my life—not even a Matrian male—and from all that I'd been told by my mother before she died, I was better off without one anyway. *Better to remain always self-reliant. Self-reliance means you're in control. Don't ever think you need a man for happiness.*

Besides, even Matrian husbands were a headache with all the accompanying paperwork and responsibility they came with. These days I had a hard enough time being responsible for myself.

Josefine shuddered, horror swimming in her irises. "You don't know how bad it is in Patrus for us girls, Violet…"

From the few papers I'd managed to get a glimpse of in the communal areas of my last facility, the situation wasn't about to get any better. The newly ascended King Maxen was proving himself to be a more ruthless monarch than his recently deceased father. He was rumored to be pouring a staggering amount of resources into the development of a new pharmaceutical drug that anesthetized emotions while sharpening logic and intellect—hardly the makings of an empathetic people. Reporters feared this would make Matrus' dealings with the nation only more strained in the years to come. Patrus' emphasis on drug development worried them especially, as Matrus' thus-far unrivaled expertise in the fields of biology and medicine was the one thing Matrus truly had to offer Patrus in exchange for water and fresh crops from the verdant mountainous region. Matrus could survive without Patrus' trade, but it would make life more austere for all of us.

Things hadn't always been this way.

According to our history books, centuries ago, Matrus and Patrus didn't even exist. They were one group of people, one band of survivors of the Last War that toxified vast swathes of the great land once known as America. The troop discovered a small haven amidst the wasteland of Appalachia—a haven that was the stretch of mountainous land now occupied by Patrus. All the survivors used to live on that side of the river, men and women. It was only after they began the work of building a new civilization that political divide struck. It started with a party of women protesting against the colony's quickly forming male-dominated leadership. The party believed that if men were allowed to prevail again, they were simply creating a replica of the former testosterone-driven regime that had led everything to ruin. They argued that if they were to learn anything from the past and stand a chance of building a better future, women must finally take the reins.

But the men in power refused. No satisfactory headway was made after countless meetings and protests. Thus, the female party had a choice: stay and essentially bite their tongues, or leave and put their beliefs into practice elsewhere. They opted for the latter after discovering that the land on the other side of the river, while not as conducive for living as their current side, was still habitable compared to everywhere else they had searched. And so began the split. It wasn't only women who chose to follow the female party in founding Matrus— a percentage of men agreed with their manifesto and followed them too. Similarly, a portion of women chose to remain under male rule. The most outspoken of the female party was put forward to lead Matrus as queen—Queen Daphne the First—and soon after, the first king was appointed in Patrus (whose name slipped my mind).

To say that both nations had come a long way since their founding must be an understatement. We had so many structures and amenities and rules and restrictions in place now (not to mention the increase in population) that I found it hard to imagine what it must have been like in those pioneering days, hundreds of years ago. Certainly there hadn't been as many rules so early on—though, if I remembered my history correctly, the screening of "violent" boys was instituted by Matrus' politicians pretty quickly, as well as the building of aircraft that were used to discover the mines in the Deep North...

Josefine was quiet. Her expression had turned somber, distant.

I left the chair and sank into bed where I began rifling in my suitcase for my nightclothes.

"Do you have any brothers or sisters?" she asked. An innocent change of subject.

My throat tightened. "No." I lied.

"Me neither," Josefine murmured.

I was glad that she didn't say anything more after that.

After changing into my pajamas, I rummaged in the side pocket of my suitcase until my fingers ran over a thin smooth square and my mini-flashlight. I dimmed the ceiling light before crawling beneath my blanket.

I switched on the flashlight, illuminating the most precious item I possessed: a faded photograph of a boy with eyes and hair like mine. My brother, at five years old, three years before he'd failed the screening. It was a picture of him on a swing, a broad grin splitting his chubby, mud-smeared face. A snapshot from a time when our life was happier.

The photo had a bit of tape still attached to the back from where I had fixed it against my bedpost in my previous room. I stuck it against the wall now, level with my pillow, and stared at it long into the night. Far past ten o'clock. I replayed the months, weeks and days before his capture over in my mind and wondered if there was anything I could have done differently.

I didn't think so. My brother was what he was. A fault in Matrus' system.

Surrounded by Josefine's snores, I switched off the flashlight.

CHAPTER 2

I felt like death when a blaring alarm sounded the next morning at exactly four a.m. I'd have to face the consequences of falling asleep so late for the rest of the day.

Josefine leapt out of bed and I clambered groggily after her. Gathering up our clothing, we moved to the showers which, thankfully, were separated into stalls.

After washing and dressing, Josefine and I followed the crowd milling down the hallway, heading for the staircase. I spotted Vera up front, standing next to the largest girl among us. The girl's hair was so short and her build so wide, one could have easily mistaken her for a man from behind.

I kept my eyes down, avoiding people's gazes, as we piled down the long staircase. On reaching the ground floor, we entered the work room and lined up in front of the machinery. At four-thirty a.m. on the dot, Ms. Maddox entered the room, holding her black registry book. One by one, she called out and ticked off our names.

Facility registers were usually in chronological order, rather than alphabetical, which meant that the girl who had been called out before me—the troll of a girl I'd spotted earlier, Dina Bradbury—must've arrived just shortly before me.

"All right," Ms. Maddox said, snapping her book shut. "Work begins."

Everyone began moving to the machinery, while Ms. Maddox approached me and explained my responsibilities. I understood and quickly got the hang of the grinding machine she was asking me to monitor. It wasn't a difficult task.

The hours blurred into one another, as I was used to them doing, and I stopped looking up at the clock.

Finally, it was time for breakfast; we exited the mill and trudged along a pebble path toward a bleak brick building a quarter of a mile away which served as the dining hall. A buffet was already laid out. I'd lost sight of Josefine in the crowd, so I lined up with the rest of them and piled my plate with hot food. We were only allowed one plate per meal, so everyone filled it to spilling point.

I was still looking for Josefine as I turned to search for somewhere quiet to sit. Then I caught a glimpse of her fiery red hair on the opposite side of the room. She stood with her back against the wall, while Dina loomed in front of her.

I couldn't spot any wardens around; perhaps they were outside the door, waiting until the crowd in here settled down.

Forgetting all about finding a quiet spot, I dumped my plate and cutlery down on the nearest table to me and weaved through the crowd toward them. My eyes trained on Josefine as she picked up one of her bread rolls and handed it to Dina. Before she could do the same with her second roll, I stepped between the girls and gripped Josefine's arm, guiding the roll back to its rightful place on her plate. My gaze was steely as I glared at Dina. Although we were actually almost the same height and roughly the same age, physically, she was much larger than me. This was the first time I'd seen her face up close; her eyes were small and spread too far apart to be attractive, their color dark brown, almost black. Her forehead hung low, and metal braces glinted against her teeth.

"Who are you?" she asked, her eyes narrowing.

"I'd like to ask the same," I replied calmly.

My eyes fell to the roll on her plate that belonged to Josefine. Before she could react, I snatched it up and returned it. Clutching the young girl's shoulder, I pulled her out of the corner Dina had bullied her into and stood in her place.

"I suggest you keep to what's yours," I whispered.

Dina's broad cheeks flushed and a muscle in her jaw twitched. Anger glinted in her eyes. Her disposable plate creaked in the tightening grip of her meaty hands. But then she backed down, as I'd known she would, and turned on her heel and steamed away. I knew a coward when I saw one.

Dozens of eyes were on me as I escorted Josefine to the table where I'd left my plate and cutlery. Nobody had touched it.

I pulled up a chair for Josefine next to me and we both sat down.

"You make sure you stay away from that girl, okay?" I told Josefine as I dug into my porridge.

The girl looked shaken as she picked up a piece of apple. She glanced nervously at Dina, who, having taken a seat across the room from us next to her new crony Vera, was glaring daggers our way.

"And don't look at her," I said. "Giving her attention makes her think she has power over you. Ignore her."

Josefine resumed her focus on her plate. She took a bite of everything but the two rolls, which were the most substantial food she'd collected. So I gave her my untouched sandwich. "Eat this. It hasn't been contaminated by Piggy Hands."

That brought a smile to Josefine's face. "Thanks," she mumbled. She accepted and began munching.

We spent the next fifteen minutes in mostly silence as we finished eating, and then a bell warned us that breakfast was drawing to a close. We had to get a move on.

Josefine and I picked up our plates and left the table to get in the line leading up to the trash cans. After I dumped my plate in the waste, someone brushed into my right side. I turned to see that it was Vera. She had a comically solemn look on her face as she leaned back against the wall and crossed her arms over her chest.

"Mind where you're going," I muttered, before taking Josefine's hand and leading her away.

"You really shouldn't mess with Dina, you know," Vera called after me. I didn't give Vera the satisfaction of turning around and asking why, but she offered it herself. "I'm serious, Violet Bates. I share a room with her... You don't know where she's come from."

Oh, please.

I sped up with Josefine and exited the dining hall, Vera's irritating voice fading out in the crowd.

I asked Ms. Maddox if Josefine and I could share a work station after lunch and she agreed. She allowed us to choose one in the far end of the room, as far from the other girls as we could be. After an hour or so, Josefine seemed to put thoughts of the incident with Dina behind her and became chatty. She asked me more questions about myself; particularly, she was interested in my parents. I told her that I didn't know who my father was and that my mother had chosen to conceive my brother and me in the city's insemination center. She had died from complications during my brother's birth.

"So you do have a brother?" Josefine asked.

"Not anymore."

"What happened to him?"

I hesitated before replying, "He failed the test."

"Oh, I'm sorry," Josefine said, subdued.

She understood that there was only one kind of test that a boy could fail in Matrus, and it had nothing to do with education. Other than the basic ability to read and add up numbers, boys weren't given an education like girls were, just an apprenticeship in manual labor.

The same was true of the girls in Patrus who weren't allowed to attend school like the boys. The only semblance of training they received was domestic.

I was grateful when Josefine redirected the conversation. Talking about Tim was painful. She asked what my favorite subject at school was and I immediately thought of my defense training. My lessons with Ms. Dale had been the highlights of my week. Ever since I could remember, my dream had been to become a warden when I grew up. There was something about their toughness, their strength, that I had always admired. I had never pictured myself pursuing any other occupation.

That had lasted up until the age of eleven when Tim had been captured.

A lot of things had changed in me after that. I'd found myself getting into fights easily and had visited the doctor for medication to ease my bouts of anger. Once Tim had gone, all of the attraction becoming a warden had previously held for me evaporated. After my brief spell of imprisonment for trying to smuggle a marked boy to Patrus, I'd still continued my defense training because, well… it was the only thing I really knew how to do well. And Ms. Dale had encouraged me to continue. She'd told me I had a natural instinct for fighting and that it would be a shame to let it go to waste. Maybe when I got older, I'd change my mind. I didn't think so, but I followed her advice.

Although it had been a long time now since I'd had any formal training, my instinct had never really left me. And over the years of incessant manual labor, my body had kept fit and strong. Plus, I'd grown in height.

"I wish I could be brave and tough like you," Josefine sighed wistfully as she dipped her hands into a trough of flour.

"You can be," I told her. "It's about your mindset. Refuse to be browbeaten. Like this morning. You didn't have to hand over your bread rolls. You could have refused, pushed past her, and gone outside to look for a warden."

Josefine nodded. "I suppose I could've," she mumbled.

I took my turn in asking her questions—her own favorite subjects, her dreams and aspirations. She told me she wanted to be an environmentalist like her mother. She wanted to help improve the soil in Matrus so that we could produce more natural foods and import less from Patrus. A noble career. I wished I had such a strong vision for my future once I got out of here. I still had two years ahead of me, but Josefine's focus made me feel I ought to start thinking more seriously about what I was going to do with the rest of my life.

By the time it was time to stop work, I had developed a thorough liking for the young redhead. Perhaps it was just her age, but she reminded me of my brother—not the timid and shy side of her, but the fiery, feisty side that bubbled to the surface on occasion. I hoped she wouldn't lose that as she got older. If she received the right training and diet, she'd make a good fighter. Unlike my brother, she wouldn't be penalized for her boldness. Unless she started doing stupid things like brandishing dinner forks in a fight.

We hung up our aprons in the reception room and headed back to our room, where I picked up my night-clothes before heading out again to take a shower. My hair badly needed a wash and I was feeling dusty in the most unexpected of places from having spent the day in the mill.

I stood for a while in the shower, relishing the warm water gushing down my back. Showers, like rain, always had a way of calming me. The pitter-patter beat, the incessant contact. Nothing made me feel sleepy faster. But my shower turned lukewarm too soon—an unpleasant quirk of detention facility bathrooms. Wardens didn't want girls dawdling— they never wanted girls dawdling. I hurried to finish washing my hair before it could go ice cold. Then I dried, dressed, and left the bathrooms.

My eyes were beginning to droop as I returned to our door and I wanted nothing more now than to climb into bed and lose myself in sleep, even if it did mean skipping dinner. But my pleasant daze was disturbed as I arrived to find our door ajar. That was unlike Josefine, and I was sure that I'd left it closed.

When I pushed the door open, I saw Josefine trembling on the floor, her right eye bruised and puffy. Surrounding her were the contents of my suitcase, scattered all over the room. My gaze shot to my most prized possession. Tim's photograph had disappeared from my wall. And on my pillow... lay a pile of shreds. The only relic I had left of my lost brother, destroyed.

"Dina?" was all I managed to breathe.

Josefine whimpered a "Yes."

That photograph had survived with me through a lot of shifts and upheavals. The thought that it should be ripped from me like this, by that... that animal...

I wanted to both scream and cry at once. But instead, I surrendered to an emotion I had gotten to know all too well, and felt all too often, over the past eight years.

Anger. My fury consumed me and every fiber of my being felt like it was burning up.

I couldn't even bring myself to care if what I was about to do would prolong my sentence by months. Feeling my fists connecting with that monster's face would make it all worthwhile.

My chest heaving as I attempted to regain some semblance of control, I thundered out of the room.

That girl is going to regret ever crossing paths with me.

CHAPTER 3

I stopped the first girl I came across in the hallway—a rotund fifteen or sixteen-year-old—and gripped her shoulders. "Which room is Dina Bradbury's?" I demanded of her in a menacing whisper.

"I-I don't know," she stammered, trying to shrug away.

Cursing beneath my breath, I let her go before moving on to the next girl, and then the next. The fourth girl I stopped knew which room Dina resided in, and the moment the answer left her lips, I hurtled there.

Arriving outside the door I burst in, my fists balled so tight my short nails dented my flesh.

Dina was standing on the opposite side of the room with her back toward me. I couldn't see what she was doing exactly, but as she twisted around, her eyes bulged. I had found her alone, with nobody to obstruct my path to her.

I lunged forward and grabbed hold of her shirt. Swinging a leg behind her knees, I sent her crashing to the floor.

I leapt on top of her, pinning her down. Then I began pummeling blow after heavy blow against her face.

She groaned, her large form struggling beneath me as I straddled her hips. Her head shifted from side to side, trying to avoid my beating. Then she raised a hand and managed to catch the next punch before it could connect. Her grip closed around my fist and I fought to maintain my dominance as she twisted forcefully beneath me. She managed to dislodge me with a speed I hadn't been expecting, getting me on my side. She thrust her knee upward to collide with my groin, but I shielded myself with my shins. We broke apart, scrambling to our feet. Her nose was already bleeding. Next, I would squash it flat.

I was about to close in on her again when, to my confusion, she reached into her mouth. When she withdrew her hand, she was holding the top and bottom layers of her braces.

Removable braces.

She'd managed to keep them from the wardens.

My pulse raced as I realized what she was doing. She quickly broke off the smooth rubber seal at the end of each of the wires, leaving them bare and pointed. Then she held a brace in each hand, positioning the wiry ends between her fingers so they stuck out like claws.

As she lashed out with her right arm, I swiped it with mine, knocking it away from me.

She has weapons. I can't get caught up in this. I need to get out of here, my brain was telling me, and yet my mind and emotions were dictating a different thing entirely.

I hadn't hurt her enough yet. I wanted to break her nose. Give her a black eye. Split her cheekbone. I wanted to give her some kind of permanent scar so that she would always have something to remind her of what she had done to me.

She swung out at me again, this time with both hands. I ducked, but not fast enough. She managed to catch my right shoulder, splitting the fabric of my shirt and etching a stinging cut into my skin.

And then she launched all her weight toward me at once, crushing me against the floor as I had done to her. She raised both hands and attempted to bring them down against me, wires pointed downward. I gripped her wrists, stopping them a few inches away from my body, using every muscle in my arms and shoulders to keep the wires from plunging into me. Catching the glint of malice in her eyes came as a wake-up call. I realized in this moment, she was as crazy as I was.

Neither of us are thinking straight.

Even though my rage was still running wild, this was just stupid. Really stupid.

So she ripped up Tim's picture. I can try to piece it back together again. But I can't get involved in this.

What the hell am I doing?

As I strained beneath her weight, I struggled to slip out of the lock she had me in.

I had made my bed, and now I was forced to lie in it.

If I'd had longer nails, I could've dug them into her flesh in an attempt to loosen her grip. Instead, I had only my bony fingertips to use to press down hard against her pressure points. I managed to make her left hand release its hold on the brace, but with this hand now free, she used it to clamp around my neck, crushing my windpipe.

As I gazed into her dark eyes and fought to breathe, I wondered if she would actually go so far as to kill me. Maybe Vera had been right in her warning. Maybe Dina was insane.

My vision started going hazy, and I couldn't even yell out for help. I scooped up the brace she dropped, but every part of me was screaming to not go down that road. Not to even cut her arm in an attempt to free myself. That slope was far too slippery. I was already on my last warning.

I wriggled wildly, forcing her to reposition her body in order to maintain her dominance. And as she did, I was finally able to put my legs to use. I slid both knees upward in one forceful thrust, causing her to jerk forward. Her hold on my neck loosened.

I gasped, heaving oxygen back into my lungs. My instinct was to immediately brace myself for another attack… but it didn't come.

Then I realized that my right hand—the hand that had been clutching her second brace—felt moist. In fact, my upper chest and right shoulder felt moist, too. A trail of moisture.

My eyes refocusing, I scrambled to sit upright, heaving her weight off of me.

Harrowing déjà vu washed over me as I stared at Dina, lying on the floor while choking and clutching her throat, blood spilling from her neck and pooling around her.

The door shot open behind me.

A scream erupted. Vera Sykes's scream.

"OH, MY GOD! VIOLET'S KILLED DINA!"

I haven't killed her! I thought to myself in a panic. *She's still alive! She just... She just needs to get to the hospital, dammit!*

But the amount of blood that was spilling from her throat... As Vera raced away, shrieking for the wardens, I already knew what would happen next.

CHAPTER 4

Footsteps pounded outside. Five wardens spilled into the room—Vera and several other girls looming behind them.

I was in a daze, still not believing what had happened. My sodden hands were trembling as two wardens flipped me over and pinned me against the floor. The other three picked up Dina and rushed her out, before dragging me to my feet and pulling me into the hallway after her.

My blood pulsing in my ears, everything around me was a blur. As we approached Josefine's and my room, I managed to catch a glimpse of her terrified face, but they pulled me right past her. They wouldn't bother to stop to collect my things. What use would they be to me now?

We arrived at the stairwell and my feet dragged and tripped as we wound our way down the steps. Reaching the ground floor, we moved through the work room and the reception where Ms. Maddox was sitting. I didn't even get a chance to witness the expression on her face. I was forced forward as the wardens escorted me out of the mill.

We came upon four more wardens here. Two of them raced off around the side of the building, returning in two trucks. Dina was loaded into the back of one, myself into the other. As they slammed the doors shut behind me, I was plunged into darkness — the nightmare replaying over and over in my mind. Those few seconds before Dina's end. My knees thrusting upward. The moistness of her blood. Her choking.

The vehicles trundled down the long track that led to the city, but it sounded like they parted ways as they reached the end — mine split to the right, Dina's to the left. Both headed to different destinations. Very different destinations. I clutched the base of my seat as beads of sweat formed on my upper lip.

The road was bumpy. My elbows and the back of my head banged against the walls, but I could hardly make an effort to hold myself still. It was as though the life had been sucked out of me already. Everything seemed pointless.

I'd imagined this moment a number of times since claiming my first life. I'd imagined this journey, across the bumpy outskirts of Matrus, blending into the smooth roads of the city, where the labs were situated. A small part of me had always known that my anger would get the better of me again.

Closing my eyes, I lost track of time.

Finally, the doors opened, letting in a stream of street-light. Hands grabbed me and pulled me out and I found myself standing on a sidewalk, my surroundings not what I had expected them to be. I was not outside the labs, but the gates of Frenton, another detention center—the most central to the city. Then I reminded myself that this should not be surprising. It was nighttime and lab technicians didn't work at night. Of course, I would spend the night in a cell and be taken to the labs tomorrow morning.

The wardens led me to the main rectangular gray build-ing and into a reception area where they picked up a set of keys from the woman behind the desk. Then we walked along a hallway before moving down a stairwell, down, down, down, until we reached what had to be the lower-most floor. We arrived at the end of a hallway lined with cells, all empty. They stopped outside the third one on our left and thrust me inside.

After locking it, they strode away, leaving me to the deathly silence.

I wasn't sure what to feel. Somewhere within me still blazed my perpetual flame of anger, indignation, and resentment. But deeper than that, there was more. There was abandonment. There was betrayal. There was a hollow sense of grief. For years, I'd been grasping at straws in an attempt to find meaning to my life, purpose to my days. As much as my country had been the cause of my darkest depths of depression, it had also picked me up from them. It had forced me to keep going in *some* direction, even if it wasn't what I would have chosen for myself. In many ways, being imprisoned had been the best thing that could have happened to me. It had taught me to stop feeling and to simply concentrate on *doing*. We were worked hard and weren't given time for much else. Days were comfortably numb.

But now, as I sat here alone and taskless in the gloom, I didn't know how to still my mind. Almost decade-old feelings resurfaced, clawing at my chest and heart, threatening to overwhelm me.

Through it all, questions broke above the surface, surging like bellows in the wilderness.

What am I?

Why am I here?

Where did I go wrong?

When and how did I become a person unworthy of living?

Do I truly deserve to die?

So lost was I in my mind's tempest that I didn't notice when the prison doors finally opened and the wardens stopped right in front of my cell.

I gazed up at them, my vision focusing. These women were different wardens from the ones who had dropped me off here. They escorted me out of the holding cells, up the staircase, and back to the ground level. I gazed through the windows. It was still dark outside.

Where are they taking me?

The air had a certain feel to it—a crispness—and the crows had started cawing, indicating the imminent daybreak.

Perhaps they wanted me to be first in line.

We crossed the courtyard and approached a different truck than the one I'd arrived in. They locked me inside before piling into the front and starting the engine. We drove away from the compound, the quiet, neat streets lined with pastel-colored townhouses bleeding away on either side of me. I hadn't visited this part of the city for years and we passed places I hadn't seen since I was a child: the Racelle Art Gallery with its luminous mural-clad exterior, the multi-columned, whitestone Krisler Theater, the pebble-dashed City Library. I'd forgotten how pretty Matrus City was.

The sky was clear as I looked up. The stars glistened down on me, as if taunting me. It was a beautiful morning to be my last.

My heart palpitating, I tried to focus on the road. We met a crossroads, and I expected the driver to turn left down Wester Road, which was the most direct route to the labs. But she didn't. Instead, she carried on straight ahead, deeper into the center of the city.

"Where are you taking me?" I couldn't help but ask. My voice sounded scratchy. It'd been hours since I had last spoken.

Neither of the wardens bothered to answer.

The situation only became stranger when I realized we were nearing the royal quarters… The palace.

I wondered if there had been new labs set up recently that I wasn't aware of. But as we continued to make a beeline toward the royal quarters, it became clear that we were heading to none other than the palace compound itself.

What is happening?

We glided down the final road that led to the high wall surrounding the majestic tower which served as the queen's and her courtiers' residence. Constructed from white stone and dotted with tall windows, it loomed over thirteen floors. The queen was reputed to live at the very top, occupying the highest two floors with her daughters.

Upon our arrival at the cast-iron gates, we were searched before they allowed us inside.

I had never been on this side of the gates before, I had only seen the occasional photograph in the papers, and my eyes struggled to take in the incredible sight. Surrounding the tower were geometrical gardens whose lawns were almost too green, flowers almost too large and vibrant. Ornamental fountains spiked with stone fish gushed out water. Quaint stone paths wound through the grass and flora, leading up to the main entrance of the tower: double shiny steel doors.

"Why am I here?" I asked again.

"Just follow," the warden holding my right arm replied.

Arriving at the steel doors, the wardens knocked. The doors whined open seconds later. A chambermaid wearing a starched white dress appeared on the other side as though she'd been expecting us. She led us across a luxurious lobby to a rug-clad sitting room before taking her leave. The wardens sat me down on a silky padded chair, then assumed positions on either side of the door.

As we waited—for what, I could still only muse—the only sound to distract me was the ticking of an old oak grandfather clock in one corner of the room.

Then I heard more footsteps. The doorknob twisted and clicked and a man stepped inside the room, a man I recognized. His hair was light—almost white—blond, and his face sported a thin goatee. His eyes were powder blue, his skin sallow. His features were altogether so fair and pale, he looked washed out. I had seen his face in the papers before; he was the only male consultant to Queen Rina's Court—a scientist whose name was Alastair Jenks, if I remembered right. Born and bred in Matrus, he was the son of a member of the Court, and a distant relative of scientist Ianto F. Jenks, who had pioneered the methods of screening boys—the same methods that were still used today in the matriarchy.

I felt a biting pang of resentment. If it weren't for Alastair and his family, Tim might have never been taken and I might not be here now. We might still be living in the orphanage, or maybe I would have taken a job and started earning enough to become his official guardian, and for us to move into our own home. Tim might have begun an apprenticeship.

Why has this man come to see me?

He had entered armed with a crossbow and a shoulder bag. I eyed the bow's loaded tip. Perhaps I had been right about the wardens not wanting to wait until the main labs opened. Perhaps he was going to finish me off sooner: now. I had no idea why a man of such high status would do it personally though, and he didn't move any closer. He strode to a chair near the clock and sat down, his weapon resting casually on his knee. Then he let out a subdued cough, clearing his throat.

"I have some news for you, Ms. Bates," he said, his voice nasally and off-puttingly high-pitched. "Ms. Bradbury passed away in the hospital about an hour ago."

My heart stilled.

"I also have a proposal for you," he went on. "A proposal that I suspect you will not refuse." He paused for a moment, scrutinizing me. "A situation has led Her Majesty and the Court to find use for a person with… your type of background. We have been watching the detention facilities, waiting for the right young woman to whom we may offer this opportunity."

"Opportunity?" I managed.

"You took defense lessons with Ms. Dale up until the age of fourteen, did you not?" he asked, as though I hadn't spoken.

I nodded.

"The opportunity involves embarking on a mission which, if successfully completed, would suspend your sentence. It would allow you another chance to redeem yourself and reintegrate into society. Your previous crimes would be erased from your record. Forgotten about. You would essentially be starting from a blank slate…" He raised his almost nonexistent brows. "How does that sound?"

My anger had given way to bewilderment and I couldn't stop frowning at him. What mission could be so important to the Court that it would cause them to erase two counts of womanslaughter from my record? I felt shocked that they would even consider compromising their principles in such a gross manner.

"What mission?" I asked.

"Before I explain," Alastair replied, "I will warn you that after receiving this information, you will need to make an immediate decision. Take up the challenge, or not. And if for some reason you decide the latter, you will receive your due injection without delay… This room will be the one that you die in." His voice lowered. "Think carefully, Ms. Bates."

In spite of my bias against the scientist, I wasn't sure that there was anything to think about. This mission would offer me the chance of a new life and freedom from detention facilities. Maybe the rules in Matrus would even change someday and allow the boys in the North to see their families. Maybe I would discover happiness.

Besides, however dangerous this mysterious mission could turn out to be, anything was better than death… *Wasn't it?*

CHAPTER 5

"I understand the choices you have laid out," I told the scientist stiffly. My voice had dropped several tones deeper than normal. "I accept the offer. Tell me the details."

Alastair's mouth twitched. I guessed that was the closest he would get to a smile. "Very well," he said, putting down his crossbow for the first time. He began to pace the room slowly. "Recently we had a break-in at the Court's labs—*my* lab, specifically. Some valuable items were taken. Specimens. After a thorough investigation, we discovered who the thief was. Unfortunately, we had a snitch in our midst. A double agent, bribed by Patrus. She has been caught and reprimanded"—*put to death, without a doubt*—"but the damage has already been done. There is, however, one specimen that we believe is still salvageable. The most vital of all of them. It is the result of thousands of hours of experimentation and research." Alastair paused to drag a small table in front of me. Then he placed a hand into his bag and pulled out a tightly rolled-up piece of paper. He dropped it onto the table and unfurled it, revealing a map of Patrus.

He moved a forefinger over the paper, resting it atop the city to the far west, where the mountains were located.

"Fortunately, we, too, have somebody on the inside," Alastair went on. "An agent of our own who has infiltrated Patrus' high society. He resides several miles away from King Maxen's palace and their newly renovated laboratory, which he has discovered is where the specimen is being kept... Now, this is where you come in. He wants assistance to recover it."

My stomach clenching, I leaned over the map. "What is this 'specimen'?" *And what makes you so desperate to get it back?*

"What the specimen is," Alastair replied, "is of no consequence to you. The only thing you need to know is what it looks like." He moved again to his bag, drew out three photographs and planted them on the table next to the map. The pictures depicted a strange silver object in the shape of an egg. It was perched on a stark white table, supported by a transparent glass tripod.

"This silver egg," Alastair said, "is what you need to retrieve. It's hard to tell its size exactly from these pictures, but it's not too large to carry. Its length is about that of my briefcase, its width a bit narrower." He raised his bag up for me.

"What would I have to do, exactly, to recover it?"

"That will be made clear soon enough," he replied. "Once you reach the other side of the river."

My chest constricted. *The other side of the river. They're going to cart me off to Patrus.* Out of one prison and into another. For there was no way a self-respecting Matrian woman could describe Patrus as anything other than a prison.

Alastair still hadn't made it clear why they had been waiting for 'someone like me' to come along and assist with this task—a convict who had no experience in matters of robbery or espionage. I could only assume that this mission wasn't something a lot of people would volunteer for. People with lives, family, and choices.

"You said that other items were stolen," I said through a dry throat. "Other specimens that are pointless to reclaim. Why then is it not too late for this one?"

"The silver egg's shell is a protective casing," Alastair replied. "It's designed to self-destruct if forced entry is attempted. But, regrettably, that is a matter that's up for contention. Although I am in possession of its only key, the casing technology is still in the early stages of development. The inventor cannot guarantee that Patrus will not find a loophole if they work long and hard enough… hence, time is of the essence. We must retrieve the egg soon."

I glanced again at the map. "But how can I go to Patrus on such short notice? Wouldn't I need to go through immigration procedures? Or apply at their General Hall for residence? I would need to wait for—"

"Our contact can speed up the entire process to three days," Alastair replied, cutting me short. "He's able to pull a few strings… Getting there expediently will not be an issue. The issue for you will be *staying* there—and safely. Staying there in a way that you can execute the mission without hindrance. Which brings me to my next point: you must marry our contact."

"What?" I thought I had misheard Alastair.

"You must marry him, Violet," he repeated, with unmistakable enunciation.

"M-Marry?"

"Yes," he replied bluntly. "Marriage is the only way a Matrian woman—or any woman for that matter— can have an existence that's even semi-worth living in Patrus. Our insider will sort out your papers, and when you arrive, he will marry you and take you under his wing. Then he will provide you with the details you require to execute the mission."

My voice was still trapped in my throat, but my mind raced with questions.

Who is this man? What is his occupation? What does he look like? How old is he?

"Do you have a picture of him?" I asked.

"Yes," Alastair replied. "You'll need to recognize him once you arrive at the dock."

He retrieved a photograph from the side pocket of his bag and handed it to me.

I found myself staring down at a clean-shaven man with a smart, trimmed crop of black hair, thin lips and a narrow, triangular jaw. His exact eye color was hard to make out from the photo. Somewhere between gray and blue. He looked perhaps in his mid-twenties. I found him neither attractive nor repulsive, though I wasn't used to judging men in either respect. Heck, I wasn't used to judging men at all. Other than Tim, I hadn't had significant close contact with males and didn't think I'd ever need to. I sure as hell never thought I'd end up coupled with one.

"His name?" I rasped.

"That isn't required yet," Alastair replied.

I swallowed, my eyes boring into the man in the photograph, as the word swirled around and around in my head like a nightmare:

Marry.

CHAPTER 6

After showing me the photograph of my soon-to-be husband, Alastair was done answering questions. He took the photograph back from me, telling me that he would give it to me again when it came time for me to leave. Then, after replacing the map and photograph in his bag and gathering up the crossbow, he led me out of the room. Two wardens were still waiting outside the door.

He turned to one of them and said, "Take her to a guest room." Then he addressed me. "While preparations are underway, you should be using your time productively. I will solidify your schedule for the next three days and have you notified after eight a.m."

I barely even had a chance to nod before Alastair strode away.

The wardens flanked my sides and escorted me down a winding hallway till we stopped outside a door that revealed a small suite containing a single bed, a bathroom and a kitchen area.

The wardens remained outside, closing the door behind me. I moved to the bed and slumped down on the mattress. My limbs were exhausted. I should try to sleep, but I couldn't conceive of attempting it. I was still struggling to wrap my head around my meeting with Alastair.

Less than an hour ago, I'd been preparing myself for certain death and now here I was, on the verge of entering a marriage.

Being thrust into the land of Patrus.

I recalled the fear in Josefine's eyes as she had spoken of the state of the patriarchy these days.

Will it really be worse than my current life? I couldn't see how it wouldn't be. Even though I was a Matrian prisoner, I was still respected as a person in my own right. As an independent entity. As a woman. In Patrus, I would be deemed incapable of being anything but some man's shadow. An accessory. A pet. No rights. No voice.

I couldn't imagine anything more daunting.

Even though I wore sweaty, soiled clothing, I curled up beneath the blanket and nestled my head deep into the pillow. Doubt and fear still swirled in my mind as dawn arrived sooner than I was comfortable with. I remained in bed until someone rapped against my door at eight-thirty a.m.

I stumbled toward the door but it opened before I could reach it.

It was Ms. Dale.

Her appearance in the palace was both surprising and comforting. It felt like an age since I had last seen her, though it had only been five years. Her face displayed more creases than I remembered it having, and her hair was visibly graying. Her physique, however, looked as tight as ever. She was shouldering a large backpack.

She cracked a small smile at me, which I couldn't help but return.

"Violet," she said, moving inside. "How are you?"

I shrugged. What did she expect?

"Mr. Jenks sent me. He informed me that you are to embark on a confidential mission to Patrus and over the next few days, he wants me to help you brush up on some skills."

"Oh."

Defense skills.

What exactly does he have planned for me in Patrus?

"We're to start now, so I guess you should get ready."

"Okay." I turned away from her and moved to the bathroom.

"Also," Ms. Dale added, "I brought these for you." She slid the backpack off her shoulders and withdrew an outfit that filled me with a sense of nostalgia. Sturdy shoes, long pants and a top made of durable, stretchy black fabric that was almost impossible to tear. I remembered her lending me a couple of uniforms just like this during my early teenage years.

I flung the clothes over my shoulder. "Thanks."

"And… I should also mention that Mr. Jenks's preference is for us to go to The Green to train."

"*What?*"

"Yep," she replied.

The Green was the dense forested region that ran across the entire northern border of both Matrus and Patrus. The river that separated the nations also ran through it, and that was one reason why its water was so toxic.

The Green's biosphere was not deemed safe to take up residence nearby; the trees and vegetation were noxious. But it was also avoided for another reason: the wildlife that lived there.

"Why does he want us to train there?" I asked. "What's wrong with your training rooms? Don't you still have them?"

"I do," Ms. Dale replied, almost apologetic. "But Mr. Jenks said that training in The Green will make it more of a… high-stress scenario. Apparently, that's something you're going to have to get used to."

My jaw tensed.

"The Green won't kill us," Ms. Dale went on. "We'll only be there for a few days during the daylight hours."

I felt nervous that this mission might turn out to be more dangerous than I'd thought. Though, given the stakes and the weight of the prize I had been promised should I succeed, it would be naïve of me to think it would be easy or of moderate risk.

It was with a tighter throat that I entered the bathroom. I hurried to brush my teeth and take a shower. After drying myself off, I bound my hair into a tight knot atop my head before slipping into my new clothes.

Ms. Dale was waiting patiently for me on the edge of the bed. Her brown eyes rose to meet mine.

"Your breakfast was delivered." She pointed to the bedside table, where a tray of sandwiches had been placed along with a jug of water. I picked at and drank as much I could stomach before returning my focus to Ms. Dale.

"You ready?" she asked, cocking her head.

"Yeah," I muttered, even though I felt anything but.

Two wardens followed us as Ms. Dale led me out of the palace, across the gardens, and toward the main gates of the compound. Reaching them, she turned to me and said, "Wait here with the wardens. I'll fetch my truck."

She returned about a minute later driving the same old truck she'd owned five years ago. The wardens escorted me through the gates and piled into the backseat, sandwiching me between them before giving Ms. Dale the go-ahead to leave.

I had been hoping that I could be alone with Ms. Dale for the next three days; that she would be deemed enough security. But apparently the wardens still considered me too much of a threat—to what, exactly, I wasn't sure.

The streets were all but empty as we rode through them, which meant our journey to The Green passed faster.

Soon the outline of the forest and its halo of greenish mist began to creep into view. A wiry fence was all that separated the mass of trees from the countryside, because there was nobody to keep out. Nobody ventured here, just like nobody ventured into The Outlands either—the desolate wilderness beyond Matrus' eastern and southern borders.

Well, almost nobody. There had been cases of rebels venturing north particularly; usually mothers of marked boys who were mad enough with grief to think they could find their son if they just walked far enough. They paid no heed to the impossible size of The Green.

As much as Matrus' leadership made efforts to emphasize that every law and restriction instituted was for the sake of our nation's — and womankind's — long term peace and well being, and that it was only because of a long history of misbehavior by men that we were in this position to begin with, their assurance wasn't enough for a minority of women whose lives had been touched by the screening. Whenever I thought of my brother, it still wasn't enough for me. But I hadn't lost my mind. At least, not yet. I had learned enough about the world outside from Ms. Connelly and almost every teacher I'd had in school—nobody who tried to escape came back.

Their words still haunted me now as we closed the final distance. The truck stopped in a meadow, a quarter of a mile before The Green started. Ms. Dale slipped out and trudged around the vehicle, opening up the trunk. She pulled out two breathing masks and handed one to me while placing the other on herself.

She addressed the wardens. "I'm sorry. I thought I had a couple more masks back there."

They frowned as Ms. Dale took my arm and guided me out of the truck. Without a backward glance, she began traipsing across the field of brittle grass toward The Green, pulling me along behind her.

I sensed that she didn't want the wardens shadowing us, either.

In any case, the two women had no choice but to wait in the vehicle unless they wanted to risk getting sick.

"Stay within earshot," one of the wardens called after us.

"We'll do our best," Ms. Dale replied. "But I must go wherever is most conducive for training…"

I could feel the atmosphere intensifying the closer we drew to The Green. The temperature also seemed to spike, though perhaps that was just me working up a sweat. I found myself wishing that my clothes weren't so tight, that my shoes were made of a thinner material.

As the mist pervading the trees began to touch us, Ms. Dale stopped and reached into her bag again. She pulled out a gun from the back compartment and two pairs of gloves from a mesh side pocket. She handed one pair to me and we both pulled them on before continuing.

We reached a narrow door in the fence. Ms. Dale drew out a key, unlocked the door, and pushed it open. My breathing sounded labored as we stepped through it and entered the first line of trees. From the outside, I never would have guessed the mist was this thick. I could hardly see more than ten feet in front of me. We wouldn't have much warning if an animal came charging for us.

We had entered a world of low-hanging trees bursting with green sap. Moss-covered boulders, purple mushrooms, and dead wood littered the deep, moist undergrowth. Slimy vines that resembled snakes hung down from the canopy of leaves—a canopy so thick, it was rare to catch a trickle of sunlight. The lighting was gloomy and altogether surreal in its greenness.

Ms. Dale strode a step in front of me, her gun at the ready. Sweat trickled down my forehead behind my mask as we ventured deeper.

After thirty minutes had passed, I was sure we'd traveled well out of the wardens' earshot. Ms. Dale was obviously not afraid of me. Not only did she have the skills to easily overpower me, I doubted she truly believed I'd become the criminal the wardens made me out to be.

She stopped abruptly. I followed her gaze straight ahead through the trees.

"Do you hear that?" she whispered.

"What?" It was a struggle to hear much other than my own harried breathing beneath this heavy mask.

"Listen closely," she said.

As I strained to hear, I realized what she had noticed—a low buzzing, coming from somewhere in front of us, in the distance. A buzzing that was growing louder.

My heart skipped a beat. "Red flies?" I whispered.

"Sounds like it, doesn't it?" she murmured grimly.

Ms. Dale began scanning the ground around us. She darted with me through the trees until she located a hollow trunk. She pulled out another object from her backpack, an aerosol container, and sprayed the hollow. Shiny black centipedes the length of my hair squirmed out, worming themselves into the brushwood. Then Ms. Dale pushed me inside. I cramped my body up as small as I could to make room for her to crawl in next to me. There was enough room for us to sit side by side while still having a view of the outside.

The buzzing was hard to miss now. It thrummed in my ears.

Ms. Dale sprayed the aerosol again, through the opening of the trunk and into the forest's atmosphere. She acted just in time. A few seconds later, a blur of brown zoomed through the undergrowth with a dense red cloud moving at an alarming speed close behind. It was a wild boar, running for its life from a swarm of huge blood-colored flies. It darted out of sight, the flies maintaining their close pursuit.

I could only be grateful that it was the animal they were chasing, rather than us.

Ms. Dale and I waited stiffly until the buzzing faded, then climbed out of the hollow and straightened.

"So, Violet," Ms. Dale muttered, brushing off her pants. "Now you've seen it for yourself. The flies do exist."

"Yeah," I said, my throat hoarse. Those flies were supposed to be vampiric. They attacked in swarms and if there were enough of them, they could drain an animal or even a person to the point of death. But I was already facing certain death by execution if I failed this mission, and I trusted that Ms. Dale was trained to deal with this environment.

"Let's continue," she said curtly. She handed me the aerosol can. "You carry this for now."

During the next stretch of our journey, the occasional squawk of a bird made me jump, and I was introduced to yet more insects—jumper bugs and rope leeches—as well as a silver python that looked large enough to swallow me whole. But Ms. Dale deftly guided me onward.

She stopped again as we arrived at the first clearing we had come across since entering The Green. Taking the aerosol container from me, she roamed its perimeter and sprayed generously. It was some kind of pest repellent, evidently, but it also had a side effect of clearing the mist, making our vision a little clearer.

Then she moved over to a fallen tree whose carcass was thriving with new life. She scraped away the weeds and moss from its surface, then placed her gun atop it, along with her backpack, opening the bag's zipper.

"Come here, Violet," she said.

I approached and stood next to her as she began to empty the bag's compartment of... more weapons. Guns—large and small. By the time she'd finished, her backpack had shrunk to a fraction of its previous size.

My eyes met hers. "You're going to train me to use... weapons?" I whispered.

"Yes," she replied. "At the request of Mr. Jenks."

My eyes trailed over the assortment of guns. Only wardens, authorized warden trainees, or professionals like Ms. Dale were allowed to handle weaponry. All of my defense training to date had consisted solely of physical contact.

Now I couldn't help but suspect that putting me into a "high-stress" situation wasn't the scientist's main motivation for wanting me to train in The Green. He probably wanted to keep all this undercover as much as possible, and the primary appeal of this location was its isolation.

"So I have just three days to perfect my skills?" I asked.

"I don't expect you to be perfect," Ms. Dale replied. "But I do expect you to become proficient. Once you're in Patrus, as a woman, it's highly unlikely you'll find an opportunity to train or practice... You'll be lucky to get hold of a gun at all."

"Then what's the point of training?"

"Because it will push your comfort zone—something you need to get used to for your time in Patrus. Moreover, it's what Mr. Jenks wants, so let's start."

She set up a target—a rotting log—before picking up the nearest weapon to her, a handgun. She began demonstrating how to stand, aim and fire. She hit the target dead in the center, several times over, before passing the gun to me. It felt cold and heavy in my gloved hand. And so very foreign.

I spread my feet apart as she instructed, assuming a firm stance before taking my aim. I missed wildly.

She made me try again and again, until I got closer to the target. It took me all of two hours to hit the exact center.

"Good," Ms. Dale said. "Let's move on to something larger."

Great. Larger and probably noisier.

I had been on edge the whole time, constantly glancing around the clearing, afraid that our noise would draw unwanted attention from the creatures of The Green.

Ms. Dale picked up the gun with the longest barrel and handed it to me after a brief explanation of the differing mechanisms between this and the previous firearm. Then she allowed me to fire. It didn't take me nearly as long to succeed in hitting the target with this. I was warming up, I supposed.

She made me try out a third gun, and then a fourth. By the time three p.m. struck, I was famished.

"We'll continue practice after lunch," she said, taking my gun from me and resting it on the dead trunk along with the others. "Let's head back. There's food in the trunk."

As she placed the backpack on her shoulders without the guns, I frowned.

"You're just going to leave those here?" I asked.

"Yes," she said. "They'll be here when we return. It's not like there are thieves roaming around in this place."

We traipsed back the way we'd come and returned to the truck. The wardens looked thoroughly bored. Judging from the bag of dirty napkins on the floor in front of the passenger's seat, they'd found something to eat already.

It was a quick lunch and we rested for another fifteen minutes before returning to the clearing for our afternoon session.

We resumed where we had left off, and by the time darkness began to close in—which was as early as six-thirty due to the denseness of The Green—I had worked with every single weapon Ms. Dale had brought with us. I'd definitely had my comfort zone pushed, but once I'd gotten the hang of the technique, it wasn't nearly as difficult as I'd envisioned. Wielding a gun had started to come naturally to me. That didn't make me any less afraid of the weapons, though—not so much of being shot at as afraid of the damage I could inflict with them myself. I had a hard enough time controlling my fists.

We packed everything up, headed to the truck, and journeyed back to the palace. It was late by the time I arrived in my room. We'd hit rush hour on the way back and been delayed. Ms. Dale told me she would greet me at nine the next morning.

Except for a chambermaid to bring me some dinner, nobody came to see me that night. I'd thought that Alastair might, but perhaps he wouldn't bother until the papers were ready—supposedly in two days.

With my arm muscles sore and body aching, I slept far more easily that night, though my slumber was punctuated with a nightmare involving echoing gunshots, red flies, and silver snakes.

The next two days passed in much the same manner as the first, except that Ms. Dale varied the weapons she taught me to use. On the second day, we focused on crossbows and knives, and on the third, she brought along a sack full of more common objects. Every day items that could be turned into weapons, like pens, rope, and hair pins.

We met with a few more scares from the wildlife—like a pack of wolves Ms. Dale warded off with an explosion of gunshots, and a horde of venomous spiders raining from the trees. But otherwise, thanks to her experience in this environment, things went as smoothly as I could have expected them to go.

I could have sworn, though, at one point, that I actually saw the shadow of a person darting through the trees—or some other kind of creature that stood tall and upright. But it vanished quickly, before I could even point it out to Ms. Dale, leading me to conclude it was the mist playing tricks on my eyes.

At the end of the third day, we finished half an hour early and sat together on the log, steeling ourselves for the journey back.

I sensed melancholy in my trainer. Melancholy that I shared. Neither of us knew when, or if, we would ever see each other again.

She gazed down at her gloved hands, her feet grazing the soil.

"I saw that you were a disturbed girl," she said quietly. "But I never thought it would come to this."

I stared at my own hands. "Neither did I."

"I wish I could have done something to help keep you out of trouble. I know you cared about my opinion."

"I doubt there's much you could have done," I muttered. *I was on a collision course.*

I was beyond wanting to explain the details of the murders I'd committed to Ms. Dale, because the details didn't matter. All Matrus saw was that I had claimed two lives.

"Maybe encouraging you to pursue the occupation of a warden was a mistake on my part," she said, as though she hadn't heard me. "Maybe you should have been channeled into something tamer, though it would've been a waste. You were my best student."

I dug my nails into the log. She was speaking as though this second lease on life I'd been granted by Alastair was hardly much better than being put down.

"Ms. Dale... Did Mr. Jenks really not tell you any details about the task ahead of me? Nothing at all?"

My trainer hesitated for a moment, then shook her head. "He didn't give me specifics, because he said they were not required... I will say one thing, however." Shifting on the log, she twisted to face me. Her expression was serious, her brown irises glimmering in the pale evening light. "Once you reach the other side of the river, trust no one, Violet. Do you understand me?"

Swallowing, I nodded.

CHAPTER 7

After Ms. Dale returned me to my room, I was left to wait alone. I didn't know when Alastair would come for me. The papers were supposed to be ready, but it was possible they could be delayed.

There was nothing I could distract myself with; no books or newspapers. I ended up taking a long shower to wash my hair free of all the gunk that had accumulated in it from The Green. When I emerged in the bedroom in my bathrobe, I was surprised to find a chambermaid waiting for me. I hadn't heard her enter through the noise of the shower.

"Mr. Jenks wishes to know if you are ready for a reception," she said, her voice a tad monotone.

"Uh, yeah. I will be in a minute."

She nodded and exited the room.

Grabbing some fresh clothes that had been placed in the closet for me during the day, I quickly dressed and draped my hair in a towel.

I moved to sit down, but my nerves would not allow it. This was it. My last night in Matrus. Wringing my hands, I paced up and down the far end of the bedroom until footsteps sounded outside the door. There came a polite yet sharp knock.

"Come in," I called.

The door glided open. In stepped Alastair sporting a deep blue suit and carrying his crossbow again, followed by... I could not believe my eyes.

Queen Rina.

The queen of Matrus herself.

I hardly knew how to react. I stared, rooted to my spot and gaping at her as she glided into the room after Alastair, who closed the door behind them.

She wore a long, brown, padded-shoulder dress that clung to her tall, slender frame. Her appearance was striking, but not beautiful. Her features were too severe for that. Her face was long, the apples of her cheeks sharp. Framed by thin, slanted brows, her eyes were narrow, their color almost black—like her short bob of hair.

"Your Majesty," I murmured. I should've fallen to my knees before her immediately and kissed the back of her right hand. But I couldn't physically bring myself to do it. The same stinging resentment I'd felt toward Alastair surged up in me and I remained standing, holding her gaze.

I had all but forgotten about Alastair until he dropped a gray folder onto the bed in front of me.

"Everything is lined up," he said. "Your papers have been filed with the immigration department. After Her Majesty and I leave you, go through this folder carefully. You will need to memorize all details contained within it. Not only memorize; you must live them and breathe them. The photograph of our contact is also in the folder—keep it safe. You should be ready to step out of this door at midnight tonight. I will come to collect you and drive you to the port, where you will take a late ferry to Patrus."

"O-Okay," I said, my eyes returning to the queen. As if mirroring me, consciously or subconsciously, she, too, had remained standing, even though there was a seat only a couple of feet behind her. Her gaze was still on me, and I suspected that it had never left. It was hard to read her expression though—what she might be thinking. How she might be judging me. Her face was stoic, quite devoid of clues. If she disapproved of my reception of her—or rather, lack of it—she wasn't showing it. Neither was Alastair. He appeared too busy with the matter at hand to think of much else.

"I must also impress upon you one more thing, Ms. Bates," Alastair plowed on. "Something that, really, should be obvious to you by now, since you seem to be a sharp girl.

But it's important for me to emphasize all the same." He stepped back from the bed and stood level with the queen. "Matrus cannot risk a war. Our nation is founded on peace. The type of mission you are about to undertake is, admittedly, not orthodox. But sometimes drastic actions are necessary, especially since we are simply reclaiming what is ours. Even despite this fact, if King Maxen got wind that you were sent on our bidding, if you somehow caused yourself or our contact there to be outed, the consequences could be crippling not just for you and him, but for your entire country. Patrus would see it as an affront— at a time when relations are already strained. Hence, you cannot be too careful. Pay close attention to everything our man tells you."

I stared at the scientist as he finished. Even if I was successful in retrieving this mysterious egg, how would Patrus not suspect that Matrus was behind it? I didn't understand what would be stopping them from finding out, and then probably tracing everything back to me— the newly arrived Matrus girl with magic papers.

The Court must have thought this through though. They weren't stupid. I supposed things would become clearer once I reached Patrus, but this truly did seem to be a tricky situation.

Both Alastair and the queen exuded an air of tension as they studied me. I found myself considering again how curious it was that they should select me for this task out of all their citizens. Couldn't they have waited for a more suitable—and experienced—person? I would have thought that a man would be better suited. He could in theory blend in better and move about freely. *They must be desperate to get the job done.* The thought came with a feeling of empowerment—something I hadn't experienced in a while. *If they're as desperate as me… then they need me, just as much as I need them.*

The queen stepped forward, closer to me, and rested her hands against the bedpost. Then she spoke for the first time.

"Ms. Bates," she said, her tone deep and commanding. "You may not understand the full implications of this mission now. I do not expect you to. You are young. But if you keep your courage, if you pull through this with strength and determination, you will go down as a hero to your people. In spite of your past, you are still a child of Matrus. And now you must fight for her. You must bear this responsibility with tenacity. With enthusiasm and passion. You have a nation behind you, Ms. Bates. During whatever trials you may face, always remember that."

She let her words hang in the air before pursing her lips and giving me a firm nod. I supposed that she expected me to feel roused now. Raring to go. Honored at the opportunity to put my life on the line. It was my home that I was fighting for, after all.

But I didn't feel anything like this. Instead, my mind was ticking.

"Your Majesty," I said, bowing my head just a touch. "I understand the weight of this responsibility, and what is at stake should I fail. For this reason, I believe it would be wise on your part to give me an extra incentive… an extra personal incentive. This would ensure that, on both a conscious and subconscious level, I will be making my best effort at all times."

As her brows rose, I could practically hear the question pass through her mind: *What could be more personal than serving your homeland?* But she didn't shoot me down.

"My proposal is simple," I dared continue. "If I succeed, allow me to visit my brother, Timothy Bates, who was transported to the coal mines eight years ago."

Her nostrils flared slightly as she breathed in, her eyes moving fleetingly to Alastair's. She hadn't been expecting me to attempt to get something out of this deal above having my own life spared.

She gave it a minute of thought before a smile cracked her porcelain face. "All right," she said. "If you succeed, and return with the egg without creating trouble for Matrus, then you shall visit your brother the very next week."

It was as though a light switched on inside me. My heart swelled with joy and an anticipation I could hardly contain. When I'd taken a shot at setting my own terms, I hadn't dared to hold much hope that the queen would bite. But my suspicion had been correct: both she and her Court were as desperate as me.

Tim. He would be sixteen now. How would he have grown? How would he have changed? I felt jittery at the thought of seeing him again. It would be unreal. A dream. It still hadn't quite sunk in what I had just negotiated for myself.

I bowed before the queen this time, and in spite of all the obstacles I knew were up ahead of me, I smiled more fully than I had in years.

"I will succeed, Your Majesty."

CHAPTER 8

I didn't have long till midnight. After the queen and the scientist took their leave, I sat cross-legged on the bed and opened the gray folder. Along with the photograph, it contained a three-page letter of recommendation signed by a Mr. Lee Bertrand. As I continued to read through the letter, I soon realized that Lee Bertrand was the man I was to meet on the other side of the river. The man I was to marry.

He was recounting in small, neat handwriting how he and I had first met, three years ago during one of his visits to Matrus to inspect lab equipment. How, in spite of our distance, we had maintained a relationship all these years, him visiting my home whenever he frequented Matrus. He explained that I was an orphan who had received little education and had worked in a bakery for all of my adolescent life. I was "one hundred percent clean, with no history of disease or promiscuity". And, as one could note from the picture they'd received of me—*what picture?*—I was "more than pleasant to the eye". He would marry me posthaste and take full responsibility for me the moment I set foot on their side of the river. He ended with the assurance that I would make "an innocuous addition to the society of Patrus".

My mouth had dried out by the time I had finished. I sat there, staring at the pages.

I wasn't sure whether to feel insulted, intimidated, or relieved that Lee had thought all these details through for me, leaving me only to memorize them. I brewed in a mixture of all three for the next half-hour as I read the letter over several times to ensure I didn't miss anything. I wasn't used to this—having things done for me. Least of all by a man. I had never relied on a man before in my life, for anything. But if I wanted to stand a chance of seeing my brother again, it looked like I was going to have to get used to it.

Time passed quickly. I managed to force myself to sleep for an hour and a half, and then it was time for me to get ready.

Alastair arrived at midnight precisely, carrying a small, yet completely empty suitcase. I frowned at him as he handed it to me.

"You will be provided with everything you need once you reach Patrus. But it will look odd if you arrive carrying nothing at all."

I slipped the folder inside the case to give it some use, and then the two of us departed from the palace. Alastair hadn't bothered to bring any weapon with him this time, at least not that I could see. He seemed to have gained confidence that I wasn't going to try anything. Of course I wasn't now. He'd be an idiot to think I might.

He led me outside the royal compound's main gates, where a long white car with tinted windows was waiting for us. He opened the door to the backseat and held it for me as I slid inside, before slamming it shut and seating himself next to the driver. The car moved forward.

I gazed through the tinted panels at the quiet city as we sped away toward the dock. I lost track of time, and soon, direction. My eyes glazed over as I attempted to mentally steel myself for what was to come. A risk-filled mission whose details were still a mystery to me, and marriage to a man I'd never even met. I'd never felt more unprepared.

My stomach grew tighter as I lowered my window to let in the air. It was becoming colder, sharper, and moister. My eyes refocused on the streets of modest townhouses. We were almost at the water.

Soon, we were driving through the steel gates that led directly to the road that lined the misty dockland. There was only one ferry operating at this time, its round lamps gleamed through the fog of the river.

I climbed out of the car and Alastair led me to the narrow rope bridge connecting the jetty to the ferry. We stood stoic for a moment, holding each other's gaze.

"How are you feeling?" he asked. He looked tired and anxious.

I didn't want to admit that I was afraid. My feelings were none of his business. I just nodded stiffly.

"All right," he said, dropping his voice to a whisper. "Remember everything we've told you. We are depending on you, Ms. Bates. Don't forget that."

I doubted I would.

He gave me a twitch of a smile before walking away.

I found it a bit disconcerting that there had not been any talk at all about how I would return to Matrus after the mission. That was a bridge they apparently weren't willing to cross until we came to it.

As Alastair returned to the white vehicle and the driver pulled away, back toward the safety of the city, I crossed the rope bridge and boarded the boat.

Other than the captain, who sat in the control cabin with her head buried in a newspaper, there was only one other person on board—an elderly woman wrapped in a woolen shawl near the back. I sat a few rows in front of her and gazed out of the window, my eyes scanning the dark, vaporous waters.

If only my brother could have boarded one of these, I couldn't help but think. *If only he could have made it to Patrus and been accepted there...* It would have been relatively easy to arrange clandestine visits with him if he'd resided just across the river—compared to not knowing his whereabouts at all.

I pulled my thoughts back to the present. Reality. *Focus.*

"What's bringing you to Patrus?" The old lady behind me spoke up.

I twisted reluctantly to face her. "I'm, uh, moving there."

Her eyes bulged. "Are you really?"

"Yup." *Really.*

"Who's the man?" she asked.

"A scientist."

"What kind of scientist?" she asked, rising from her seat and moving to a row closer to me.

I wished that she would have stayed where she was. I wanted to sit in silence, mentally prepare for my arrival, not be hit with a barrage of questions. But I supposed that this would be good practice for me. A test run, to see how well I had memorized, and how naturally I could spout off, all the lies.

"I can't say, to be honest," I replied. "His work is high-level. He's not even allowed to tell me the details."

"I see," she murmured.

Then she fell quiet. Though I could practically hear her thoughts. Because the same thoughts ran through every Matrian's head whenever they came across a woman making the move to the other side.

Poor thing.

What a waste.

She'll never last.

She offered me a weak smile. "You must really love him."

Yeah...

I fixed my attention firmly out of the window to make it clear that I was done talking. When the ferry left the dock five minutes later, we were still the only two passengers. I watched the bank grow further and further away, until the mist became too dense for me to see it anymore. I stood up and walked to the opposite end of the boat. Being a warm night—or morning— it was unpleasantly stuffy inside. None of the windows could be opened, to prevent spray entering the boat. I had never touched the river water directly, but I had seen its effect on other people, and if you ingested too much, it could be fatal. I hoped my brother hadn't swallowed much when he fell into the river that night he'd been ripped from me.

The ferry sped up, forging its way through the mist. Due to its thickness, when Patrus' bank finally manifested, it came with little warning. I witnessed Patrus' dockland in clarity for the first time. Warm orange lights glittered along the lengthy wooden jetties, illuminating a myriad of boats that looked quite different from those you'd find in Matrus. Most of them appeared to have been constructed primarily with leisure in mind rather than mere functionality, with shiny, attractive exteriors, spanning several floors and complete with open rooftops protected by transparent shields. There was also a bay reserved exclusively for competitive rowboats—like my cousin Cad's.

Our ferry slotted into an empty bay and stopped. I let the elderly woman walk ahead of me, though she stopped to chat with the captain, leaving me to step out alone onto the empty jetty.

I breathed in, scenting the atmosphere as a gust of wind caught my hair. It was breezier on this side of the river.

I cast my eyes around, trying to find my bearings... and my host. Lee Bertrand. He was supposed to be waiting for me.

Clutching my suitcase, I moved away from the vessel. There was a road beyond the docks, and behind that was a towering wall, just like we had in Matrus. No overwhelming difference between the lands so far.

Lee had to be around here somewhere. I caught sight of shadows moving near the cargo ships, further along the shore. But I was apparently alone...

Then I spotted movement to my right and a man wearing a dark brown coat appeared from behind a lamp post. He sported a tartan cap that shaded his face.

I was hardly breathing as he closed the distance between us. The breeze carried his fragrance, sharp and citrusy, and stopping a couple of feet in front of me, he removed his cap, allowing the dock lights to illuminate his clean-shaven face.

"Ms. Bates." His voice was deep and low.

"Mr. Bertrand," I whispered, my grip tightening around the handle of my suitcase.

His narrow lips formed a smile that reached his eyes—eyes that were more blue than gray.

He looked younger in person and there was a slight boyishness to his features, which I found kind of comforting.

I reached out to shake his hand, but he instead closed his fingers around mine and held it gently.

"Let's go," he said beneath his breath. "We'll talk later."

He remained holding my hand as he reached across me to remove my suitcase from my grasp and carry it. He pulled me away from the river, toward the road. We reached the sidewalk and stopped in front of a black motorcycle that leaned against a lamp post.

He attached my suitcase to a holder at the back of it before lifting up the seat to reveal a hidden compartment which stored two helmets. He handed me one, which I proceeded to strap to my head while he did the same.

He pushed the seat back down. "After you," he said, patting it.

I straddled it, moving as far back along the seat as possible. Clutching the handles, he positioned himself in front of me. I felt embarrassed and uncomfortable to place my hands on his shoulders, but as he coaxed the engine to life, I had no choice. We rolled off the sidewalk, slipping onto the deserted road where we picked up speed. The chill of the morning amplified, my skin tingled with goosebumps.

We drove close to the gray brick wall for about two miles before Lee eased our pace. An opening emerged: a pair of wide, gold-plated gates. As we passed through them and reached the world on the other side, my jaw slackened.

Sprawled on either side of us were vast artificial lakes, exploding with fountains made to glimmer in the darkness by brilliant underwater lights. The tall spurts of water shot up to varying heights, swaying in the wind as if in a dance. Droplets sprayed the road and touched us.

I had seen pictures of these lakes before, but the photographs did them little justice. The expanse of clear, shimmering water felt almost like a taunt to their neighbors—Matrus couldn't even conceive of such waste.

But Patrus could afford it, just like they could afford other extravagances, thanks to their fertile mountain region. I glanced there now, toward Patrus' peaks. Their majestic outline loomed closer, and I felt an unexpected rush of anticipation to see them up close.

As soon as the lakes and fountains ended, towering apartment blocks began. They spanned ten floors, and each block was separated by lush lawns and illuminated gardens. The buildings were beautiful to look at. Their smooth steel exteriors gelled with dark wooden panels that lined the balconies. Each block boasted a terrace garden, vines spilling over the rooftops like hair. Being situated on this prestigious entry road to Patrus, of course, only the affluent could afford to live here.

The broad road led us past miles of this development until the blocks gave way to a different kind of architecture and we arrived in an expansive community of large two-story houses. These were clearly family homes—many of the front yards contained swings and other playground equipment, and they had garages large enough to fit three vehicles.

As Lee sped up, I held him tighter. This was the first time I'd been on a motorcycle. He could probably tell from the pressure of my fingertips against his shoulders.

We joined a highway and to the left of us, more suburbs slipped away. To our right was apparently the beginnings of Patrus City— a halo of orange light overhung a sea of densely-packed buildings. Buildings, tall and short, wide and narrow; shops, arenas, eateries, offices, houses.

Then Patrus' famed Crescent River came into view. It acted like a moat for the king's residence, a magnificent five-turreted stone palace built against the cliffside of a mountain. The river set the king's home aside from the rest of the city, on its own little island.

Lee forged onward and began a route that led us into the foothills of the mountains. We wound upward, higher and higher, and began to pass more residences, albeit at longer intervals. These houses were all very different and more extravagant than any I'd seen so far. Spanning four levels, they were stark white and triangular-shaped, their walls more glass than brick. Racing cars and powerful motorcycles filled the driveways.

Higher and higher we climbed, until we had gained a bird's eye view of the ground: the glittering city to the north, the eastern and southern suburbs… and Veil River, so far away now in the distance.

Finally, Lee pulled into the empty driveway of a triangular villa identical to all the others that lined this mountainside. The only distinguishing factor about his was a neatly trimmed row of flower bushes lining the ground floor.

As Lee stalled the motorcycle, he slid off and I stepped off after him, steadying my knees as the gravel crunched beneath my feet.

His crop of black hair was mussed from his helmet and draping down near his eyes. He slanted a glance at me, then gestured to the front door. "Shall we?"

We approached the entrance and barking erupted from behind the door, making me jump. As we stepped into a dark hallway, a large shaggy brown dog leapt up at me, front paws against my waist. I patted the dog's head awkwardly. I didn't have much experience with animals. The canine's tongue wagged, swiping at my wrists.

"Come on, Samuel," Lee muttered, slipping a hand through the dog's collar and pulling him into an open doorway before shutting him inside. "Sorry," he said with a roll of his eyes. "He doesn't get visitors very often."

He switched on a light, and led me through to a spacious open plan kitchen-dining room. The floors and ceiling were wooden, as was the kitchen table. A beam hung over it, dangling half a dozen pans. A granite counter stretched the length of one wall, immaculately clean and tidy. White blinds were drawn against the wide windows.

Lee removed his jacket and hung it over a high-backed chair, revealing his true physique. It was slimmer than his bulky coat had made him out to be, but I guessed fairly attractive.

I wasn't wearing a coat. Just a plain, long-sleeved top and black pants. I sure hoped that he *did* have clothes sorted for me. I didn't even have a change of underwear.

"Can I get you something to eat or drink?" he asked, drawing up a chair for me.

"Uh, a drink, please. Just water."

He filled up a tall glass from a crystal canister and handed it to me. His lips curved again in another fleeting smile. The thought that he might be as nervous as me about this whole situation brought me a thread of comfort.

I had to remind myself that he was not like the other men in Patrus, even if he pretended to be to the outside world. He belonged on the other side of the river, my side. He was a Matrian male. He should understand what I was going through in coming over here.

"So," he said, breathing out. "Welcome, I guess."

"Thanks," I said, letting out my own stifled breath.

With both of us sitting opposite one another beneath the bright kitchen spotlights, perhaps he felt as bare as I did. As awkward and exposed.

"How was the journey?" he asked, pouring a glass of water for himself.

"It was fine…" I struggled to embellish my answer.

"Do you have my picture with you?" he asked. "And my letter of recommendation?"

"Yes."

"Okay. You may as well hand those back to me. You only needed to carry them in the unlikely event that you were stopped by someone before I met up with you on the dock."

Lee had placed my suitcase on the floor near my feet. I stooped down and retrieved the gray folder, handing it to him.

"Thanks." He glanced briefly inside it before stowing it away in one of the kitchen drawers. He resumed his seat and placed his hands on the table, twisting his silver watch. "So, I'm sure you want to know more about me."

"Um, yes."

"My full name is Lee Desmond Bertrand. Named Lee by my father, Desmond by my mother. I am twenty-five. On paper, I'm native to neither Matrus nor Patrus. In fact, I was born in the middle of Veil River. Literally. My mother was fleeing from Patrus to Matrus to give birth to me, but timing was not on her side."

He paused to sip from his water.

"Why was she fleeing?"

"Her relationship with my father was a tumultuous one. She had wanted to move back to Matrus even before she fell pregnant with me, but my father forbade it. He wanted me to be born in Patrus. Being a migrant and a woman, there was nothing she could do at the time except go along with her husband's wishes, obviously. But she plotted an escape the night she went into labor, a plot that went horribly wrong... I was lucky to have survived."

"Did she survive it?" I wondered.

"Yes. She died a few years back."

"Oh, I see. So... you have no true nationality?" I posed.

"I have allied myself officially with Patrus, though my loyalty has always been with Matrus, like my mother's was. My mother was spotted on the river by a Matrian the night she gave birth, and she and I were taken to the city hospital. I managed to spend the first ten years of my life in Matrus—and they were my happiest years—before my father reclaimed me. But in the strict sense of the term, yes, you are correct...I have no true allegiance to any nationality."

"And how did you become... this?" I asked.

"Let's just say I was still young when I came here, and my father's position was of great benefit to me... Honestly, the less you know about this particular subject, the safer you and I will both be."

I pursed my lips. "I see."

He glanced around the kitchen. "I've been in this residence for the last three years. I live alone with Samuel, with no siblings or family in general to bother us. My father died a year ago... My duties are down in the lab, near the palace. It takes about half an hour to commute by motorcycle, depending on the time of day. I will be out a lot during the week, sometimes also at the weekend."

"What sort of work does a scientist in Patrus do, exactly?" I asked. "I read about a pharmaceutical King Maxen has commissioned development on…"

"Yes. Patrus is trying to become as proficient as Matrus in the fields of biology and medicine. King Maxen wants to catch up, become as competent in them as Patrus is in architecture and engineering… But the new king has no intention of playing fair, of building from scratch based on their own research and merits. He wants a head start. Upon his ascendance to the throne, infiltrating Matrus' lab was a logical first step. He wants to reverse-engineer what was taken in the raid and work out how to recreate it… Of course, he knows that there's not much Matrus can do to fight back; he uses Queen Rina's reluctance—and practical inability—to start a war to his advantage."

I lowered my brows. "In all the years you've been under-cover, what sort of missions have you been on for Matrus?" I couldn't help but ask, even though I suspected that he would be reluctant to answer.

"Never a mission, per se," Lee replied. "So far, the neces-sity hasn't arisen. I have been Matrus' eyes and ears, report-ing back what I see and hear from the higher levels of the patriarchy, so they can plan and take action according-ly on their side. That's why you're here to assist with the task ahead, because I cannot do everything on my own.

And I can't be caught. My presence here and the trust the authorities have in me are extremely important to Matrus."

He lapsed into silence, his blue gaze still on me. I wondered whether he wanted me to talk about myself a bit, though I was sure that he'd already been told everything about my history.

"I-I understand... Will there be some sort of test by the authorities for how well you know me?" I asked. "Or how well we know each other? Before we're allowed to, uh..."

"Marry?"

I was glad that he spared me the word. "Yes," I managed, heat creeping to my cheeks.

He shook his head. "Sometimes it is required. But it won't be in my case." He swallowed the last of his water, surprisingly cool about the subject. I ought to be like that, too. This wasn't a real marriage. It was just an arrangement. An arrangement that would allow me to stay safely in Patrus, and that would be annulled as soon as our job together was done.

"I noticed you didn't shake my hand, back on the dock," I said, changing the subject. "Is that something you don't do here?"

"It's not something that's done between the sexes." He heaved a sigh, pushing his glass aside. "There is a lot that you're going to need to pick up on while you're here... This is going to be a long discussion. Are you sure you don't want something to eat?"

I was feeling less nervous now than when I'd first come in. I realized that I was hungry. I definitely could stomach something. "I'll eat," I acquiesced.

He rose to his feet with a smirk. "And that brings us to another 'don't': Don't ever tell anyone that I've cooked for you."

CHAPTER 9

Lee's dinner was delicious — no doubt the freshness of the produce contributed a lot to the flavor. The food was simple, with basic herbs and spices, and the core ingredients were enough to make it take off.

I ate more than I had intended to and after I finished, I found myself leaning back in my chair, holding my stomach.

He eyed me with amusement, setting down his own fork. "Had enough?"

"Yeah. Thanks."

He hadn't wanted to talk much over dinner. Maybe because he hadn't wanted to ruin my digestion, but now his mood became more serious.

"There are a lot of rules you're going to have to absorb. A lot to bombard you with at once. But I plan to keep you under my wing as much as possible. You'll learn the ropes as we go about our activities. You'll never go out alone, and when I'm gone, you'll stay in the house with Samuel and not answer the door to anybody."

It sounded like what I was used to: a prison life. I wondered how different my days would end up being on this side of the river, after all.

"Tomorrow we will have a tight schedule," Lee went on. "In the morning, I'll need to take you shopping. In the afternoon, we have an appointment in the marriage hall. We will sign the papers and be wed. Then, in the evening, I'm going to take you into the lab to meet my associates and, most importantly, show you around."

My head spun. A tight schedule was an understatement. "Your associates… you've told them about me already, I assume?"

"In brief," he replied. "I told them the same day I found out you were coming over here. It wasn't really a surprise to anyone that I should keep it a secret; I'm not exactly known to be a talkative person when it comes to my personal life… Anyway, don't worry about them. They won't be very interested in talking to you. Men don't talk much to women here — they'll ask a few polite questions, and that will be that."

"Won't they be suspicious that you're bringing a Matrian girl into the lab?"

"We won't stay long enough to cause suspicion," he replied. "We'll do a quick walkabout and then head off. But it'll be enough to give you a bearing on the place."

After another pause, he stood up. "Wait here," he said.

He headed out of the room while Samuel padded inside. The dog wagged his tail and nuzzled his head against my knees before slipping it onto my lap. He sat down in front of me, and I stroked his ears until Lee returned.

Lee was carrying a red folder, which he laid on the table. One by one, he pulled out what appeared to be profiles of a dozen men, each sheet containing a headshot along with personal data.

"These men will be obstacles in retrieving the egg from the lab." He tapped a finger on the photograph in the center of the table in front of us, a photograph of a young man who looked more beast than man compared to the others who, although tough-looking, were fairly well-groomed. His dark brown hair draped down to his shoulders in waves. His forehead was low and wide, his face rough and unkempt. But he struck me as handsome in spite of his roughness. I was instantly attracted to his physical appearance—something I couldn't say in the case of the other men scattered over the table, or Lee for that matter. His deep-set eyes radiated a fierce green even in the photograph. "Viggo Croft" was his name.

"These are the wardens in charge of security surrounding the labs and the palace," Lee said. "They have received the highest level of training Patrus has to offer. They are the best of the best when it comes to protection around here. You'll often spot them roaming the border of the Crescent. Especially Viggo. He's the chief coordinator and very little gets past him… He resigned from the force about a year back, due to 'irreconcilable differences' with the man who was chief at that time—he clearly has a strong independent streak—but got himself into a spot of trouble with the law while he was on leave. At the time, King Patrick struck a deal with him that if he returned to the force to work for the next four years without pay, the infraction would be expunged."

"What was the infraction?" I asked, feeling a spike of curiosity.

"Obstruction of justice," Lee replied.

That had been my first infraction.

"Anyway," Lee continued, "the point is, he's not managing the security by choice at the moment. It's a service that he's forced to perform in order to avoid jail."

He paused, eyeing the papers. I wasn't sure how Lee's "point" was actually relevant to the task at hand.

"So… guards are always around? Day and night?" I asked.

"More or less."

"Then how exactly do you plan to retrieve the egg if they're constantly stalking the place?"

Lee sat back in his chair. "With difficulty… But we'll take this one step at a time. Tomorrow in the lab, I'll show you the location of the egg, and then we'll discuss the next step."

His response didn't sit right with me. I didn't like being fed information in dribs and drabs. "I'm not a Patrian woman," I reminded Lee while keeping my tone polite. "I'd like to know the full extent of my role in this mission."

Lee breathed out. "I understand that, Violet. But I'm saying this for your own sake. I don't want to overburden you with so much information now. You've just arrived."

Hm. Maybe he was right that I ought to give myself a bit of landing time. I needed to know more about the mission, more about the risks and the dangers that I was about to be thrust into, but if he told me everything that was on his mind now, I doubted I'd get a wink of sleep, and I needed to be fresh for the day ahead.

Deciding not to press, I glanced back down at the profiles. "Are you on speaking terms with these men?"

"Yes," Lee said. "Though I try to stay under their radar as much as possible, in case you haven't gleaned that yourself by now."

"Have you ever met King Maxen?"

He nodded darkly. "Yes, a few times. I've been summoned to visit him before along with other members of the board."

"What's he like?"

Lee grimaced. "He's everything that you've read about in the papers. Ruthless and fiercely intelligent, with a demeanor personable enough to influence people and get things done. A deadly combination."

We lapsed into another stretch of silence as I gazed through an open window and down at the mountain.

Samuel let out a snore. He had fallen asleep with his head still on my lap.

"Maybe that's our cue." Lee chuckled.

I slipped myself out from beneath the dog, lowering his head to the carpeted floor against his paws before heading out of the sitting room with Lee.

So far, Lee had given me no reason to feel uncomfortable around him or think that our relationship would be anything but businesslike and perfunctory, the same as if he'd been a woman. In fact, his personality struck me as rather flat and bland (something that was not uncommon among Matrian males).

But even in spite of the ease I'd come to feel around him, my heart couldn't help but quicken as we climbed the staircase to the next floor.

He's going to give me my own bedroom, right?

Thankfully, as we arrived on a landing, he took a right turn and led me to what was clearly a guest bedroom, containing a single bed. The view from here was prettier than downstairs. I even spied a stream flowing near the road that I hadn't noticed before.

"There's a single outfit for you to wear tomorrow in the cupboard, along with a night dress and underwear," Lee told me, pointing to a mahogany chest of drawers in one corner of the room. "Hopefully they'll fit. Tomorrow, we'll equip you properly."

"All right."

"Well, I'm heading to bed," Lee said, backing out of the room. "See you in a few hours."

After we bade each other good night, he closed the door behind him. I moved to it instinctively, searching the back of it for a lock. There wasn't one.

Although I felt almost guilty for it, I found myself dragging a chair to the door and barricading it… taking a page out of Josefine's book.

CHAPTER 10

I woke up to the sound of drilling drifting up from somewhere beneath me. I was in a daze as my eyes shot open
and I took in my strange surroundings. Then I remembered. *I'm in Patrus.*

My head ached dully as I headed to the bathroom. I'd
eaten too much last night and I felt dehydrated. I drank
from the cold water tap before washing and looking at my
outfit, which turned out to be a modest blue dress that
stopped just below my knees, and a light gray woolen cardigan. I rarely wore dresses even before I was incarcerated,
but this one wasn't too bad. The bra was too large, however.
I strapped it on anyway before pulling on the dress and
buttoning up the cardigan. Lee had also helpfully provided me with a watch, made of silver like his.

I padded out of the room and into the corridor, which
was almost blindingly bright. Sun streamed in through a
skylight in the ceiling, warming my skin.

Amidst the drilling, I heard the clinking of cutlery and I headed down to the kitchen to find Lee already dressed. He sat at the table looking clean-shaven and bright-faced, in front of a bowl of what looked like oatmeal. He wore a smart gray suit, his black hair combed neatly back.

"Hi, how did you sleep?" he asked.

"Pretty well, thanks."

"Good. I was going to come and wake you up in ten minutes. You should eat some breakfast." He gestured to the stove, where a pot of warm oatmeal sat. On the counter next to it were a bowl of deep pink berries and a jar of honey. I helped myself and took a seat opposite Lee at the table. The berries were the sweetest, most succulent I had ever tasted, and the milk was creamy and rich. Much better than my usual breakfast.

Lee was watching me as I finished, his expression thoughtful. "I suppose I've been in Patrus too long to appreciate the food like you do. I've forgotten how good it tastes compared to Matrus."

Although much of Matrus' fresh produce was imported from Patrus, they gave us the worst of their harvest, always keeping the best for themselves. Not that I could blame them. Matrus would do the same if they were in Patrus' position.

"Where's that noise coming from?" I asked as the drilling continued.

"I have someone down in the garage fixing my third motorcycle," he said. "Hope it didn't disturb you."

"Not really."

I found it funny that he had three motorcycles when there was only one of him. It wasn't like I'd be able to ride it; Samuel would sooner be granted permission than me.

I finished my breakfast and noting that I was done, Lee straightened before speaking. "Right," he said, glancing at his watch. "It's time for us to head off. Are you ready?"

"Yes."

"Okay, wait here. I'll be down in a minute."

I roamed the kitchen as he left and stopped at a window that was slightly open. Even though I was feeling nervous about the day ahead, the beauty of the landscape lifted my spirits a little. The luscious greenery. The fresh air, fragrant with morning dew and the scent of pinewood. The swallows, chirping and soaring over the treetops.

I supposed I could better understand the lure of Patrus for even a Matrian woman now that I was here. If you could ignore everything else that went on in this place— the lack of rights, and the fact that you were basically a prisoner of your husband—the land was beautiful. Vibrant, verdant, closer to nature than Matrus was, and maybe ever would be. There was little to no feeling of shortage on this side of Veil River. The population being smaller than that of Matrus probably helped. There was more wealth and resources to go around in general. The quality of life in a purely material sense was superior even for a woman. I had yet to witness real Patrian society for myself, but so far, I wasn't feeling as daunted as I'd expected.

"Okay," Lee said as he descended the stairs and entered the kitchen. I turned to see him holding a brown wallet, which he slipped into the side pocket of his pants.

"Let's go."

Samuel followed us to the door before Lee shut and locked it. His motorcycle was where we had left it, in the center of the driveway and the gravel crunched beneath our feet as we approached it. Lee handed me a helmet and then the engine roared. We headed out of the driveway, slipping onto the winding road that led down to the city.

It was quite surreal how different everything looked in the daytime. Seeing everything in color, I gained a whole different perspective of the mountain road and the triangular villas that lined it.

We soon began to pass vehicles rolling up the mountain, and as the slope lessened and we arrived on flatter ground, we joined a highway that hummed with many more—at least half of them motorcycles.

I found myself peering into the windows, curious to glimpse the passengers. I spotted some families—wife and husband in the front, kids in the back—but mostly, the vehicles were occupied by lone men. On the way to work, I guessed.

The sky was almost cloudless overhead as we neared the city. Lee branched off the main highway onto a narrower street filled with restaurants before we arrived in a communal parking area.

I got off, steadying myself as I gazed around. The parking lot was practically empty.

"Now is the best time to go shopping," Lee said. "While most men are at work. Early morning and evening are when it gets most crowded."

"So how come you're not at work?" I asked as we drew away from his motorcycle.

"My hours are more flexible than most," he said with a half-smile. "Besides, I have a day off today — I'm getting married, remember."

His hand closed around mine as he led me out of the parking lot and onto the street of restaurants. His leading me like I was a child felt weird, but I understood that Lee had to behave differently while we were out. All of the restaurants were closed at this time, except for a couple of cafeterias.

The streets were immaculately clean, and I had to say that this aspect of Patrus reminded me very much of Matrus—their attention to hygiene. Even the exteriors of the buildings were well-maintained, many of them appeared recently repainted.

He led me down a narrow alley and we emerged onto another road that was populated with shops that catered specifically to women. Clothes boutiques, hairdressers, and salons surrounded us.

Lee's brows furrowed as he glanced over my hair and nails. "We'll pay a visit to Ciantro's first." He pointed to a storefront that appeared to be a beauty and hair salon combined.

My hair was the same as it had always been: long, dry, and unstyled. And my nails… well, they were what they were. Given the environment that I had been living in for the past several years of my life, there had hardly been any point in putting effort into them.

We crossed the road and entered Ciantro's, catching the attention of a tall, skinny man with a perfect coif of blond hair.

He smiled as he looked from me to Lee.

"Morning," he said jovially, moving to the reception desk. "And what can I do for you today?"

Although he was inspecting me, he was clearly asking the question of Lee.

"Just a wash and style for the hair," Lee said. "And"—he gestured to my hands—"a… whatever you call a hand treatment."

"Manicure," the man replied with a grin.

"Yeah," Lee said. I glanced around the pristine white salon. We were the only ones here.

Lee offered me an encouraging smile before nodding toward the man, indicating that I follow him.

The man led me to a chair in front of a sink and after telling me his name—Tyler—began washing my hair. He didn't talk as he worked—just the odd question about my usual "hair routine", which warranted a very short answer. After cleansing my hair, he dried and styled it.

Staring at the finished result in the mirror, I was glad that Lee hadn't told him to do anything drastic. I still looked like myself… just shinier.

Then he took me to the opposite end of the salon where he worked on my nails for the next forty-five minutes—a process that I found tedious. I was relieved when he finally was done, and allowed me to return to Lee, whose head had been buried in a newspaper most of the time.

Lee smiled warmly, his eyes lighting up as he looked over the finished result. He pulled out a platinum card from his wallet and swiped it against the machine on the counter. Then we said thanks and goodbye, and left the salon.

Next, we headed to a clothes store a few doors along. When Lee asked me what sort of thing I liked, I admitted I wasn't really sure. I'd grown up on mostly hand-me-down pants and shirts in the orphanage, and detention facilities didn't exactly provide the opportunity to develop a sense of style. The attendant—another perfectly groomed and extremely knowledgeable man—ended up helping us out. After trying on dozens of outfits, we ended up with two bags full of clothes —mostly dresses, but a fair amount of pants and shirts too (which pleased me). Lee said that dresses were advisable for me to fit in with the general dress code of women in Patrus, though I could wear fitted pants and shirts occasionally (and obviously I would wear whatever I wanted when I was in the house).

I knew a lot of women adored shopping—in Matrus, too—but I wasn't one of them. The first hour was a novelty, but after that it became rather dull to me, like watching someone poking at my nails had.

I hadn't been paying attention to the prices, since Lee hadn't, but I suspected it would've cost him *a lot* of gold. The materials were all organic and high quality, unlike what I was used to wearing.

Since we weren't having a proper ceremony, Lee told me that a traditional wedding dress was not required, but that I still needed something elegant. We ended up choosing a well-tailored long indigo-blue dress that, according to the attendant, made my eyes "pop". Whether they did or not, I couldn't deny that it looked nice. Not me, but nice.

By the time we left the shops, it was nearing one o'clock. We headed back to Lee's motorcycle, where we offloaded the bags. Then he turned to me. "So, we don't have time to return home before the appointment. You can change into the dress and shoes we picked out for the marriage now."

We dug into the bags and retrieved the items before he led me to a building of public restrooms nearby. As I moved into one of the shiny, steel-gray stalls to change, my throat went dry and I started perspiring more than I should have on a day of such a moderate temperature. I had to remind myself that there was no need to feel nervous. *This marriage is fake. It won't mean anything.*

After pulling on the dress and slipping into the shoes, I stepped out of the cubicle and stared at myself in the mirror. My hair hanging down my shoulders in soft waves, the blue dress hugging my frame at the most flattering of places, I didn't remember the last time I'd felt so feminine. Perhaps when I'd tried on my mother's makeup as a kid.

Drawing in a deep breath, I tore my eyes away from the mirror and rejoined Lee outside.

I kept my gaze on the ground as he offered his arm to me, though I could feel his eyes pass over me in polite admiration.

"You look perfect," he said quietly.

An odd feeling swirled inside me. That was the first time I'd been complimented by a man. I wasn't sure whether I liked the attention or not.

Lee cleared his throat. "Right, so, uh… we're not far away. About five to ten minutes' walk. It'll be easier to go by foot from here."

I held his arm a little harder than I had intended as I focused on keeping my walk steady in my new shoes. We first returned to the motorcycle to drop off the clothes I'd changed out of, and then, leaving the street of women's boutiques, we wandered down another narrow alleyway. We passed several more streets after that—streets with barber shops, men's clothing stores, as well as other shops retailing furniture and food. We didn't exchange a word as we walked for the next ten minutes, until we finally arrived outside a tall, red-brick building with a sharp, protruding spire.

"Central Matrimony Registration Office."

We stopped outside the entrance. Finally, Lee and I met each other's eyes as he straightened his jacket.

"Okay." His Adam's apple bobbed. "In we go."

He pushed open the door and held it for me as we stepped into a sterile reception room. The lighting was white and bleak, the carpets a dull shade of green. A wide desk lined the wall opposite us, behind which sat three men in black suits. The man in the middle—a middle-aged bald guy with a heavy goatee—stood as we approached. A perfunctory smile spread across his lips.

"Good afternoon, Mr. Banks," Lee said, holding out a hand for him to shake.

"Afternoon, Mr., and soon-to-be Mrs., Bertrand," he replied.

My hand instinctively moved to shake his, but I caught myself and instead gave him a brief nod, which he returned.

"Do follow me."

Mr. Banks led us through a door to our left and guided us into an office. Here, he circled around a black wooden table and sat down, while he gestured for us to do the same in the two seats positioned in front of us, opposite him at the table.

He ducked down and opened a drawer, reemerging with a pile of papers, which he placed in front of Lee, and handed him a pen. Then Lee began to sift through the pages, signing and dating multiple sheets. Once he was done, he handed the papers back to Mr. Banks.

Then Mr. Banks withdrew a single sheet of paper and passed it to me. "Read it and sign, please," he requested of me.

My eyes trailed down the page. What I was reading was a declaration of oath to give up every freedom a woman took for granted in the land of Matrus, for the sake of my "husband". The language of the document didn't bother to soften the blow as it concluded:

"I hereby declare my full dependence on and submissiveness to Lee Desmond Bertrand, who will take responsibility for my speech and actions, as well as ownership of any possessions previously deemed my own."

It was like a deliberate affront to Matrus-born women. The document was designed to intimidate. As if a Matrian's transition to Patrus wasn't already difficult enough. Even coming from being a prisoner to my homeland, I found it an affront to my identity. Gritting my teeth, I scribbled my name and the date in the same manner one would strip a bandage from a wound. I would have been hurting a lot more if I'd been a regular upstanding Matrian citizen.

Mr. Banks slid the paper back to his side of the table and glanced over it briefly before nodding. "Good," he said. "Now…" He dipped behind his desk again, opening another drawer, before appearing this time with a small black velvet pouch.

He handed it to Lee, who opened it and drew out a single golden ring, then Lee twisted in his chair to face me.

"Do you, Violet Bates," Mr. Banks spoke up, "accept Lee Desmond Bertrand as your lawfully wedded husband?"

My voice caught in my throat as I stared at the ring. I realized that it was engraved with a name. *"L. D. Bertrand."*

It became clear to me in that moment that Mr. Banks would pull out no second ring. There would be no exchange of vows, either. Just a single vow. A single ring.

A single leash.

This ring means nothing, I reminded myself again firmly. *I'm not actually getting married. Lee won't be my husband. We are business partners and this is all just an act.*

I gulped before answering: "I do."

CHAPTER 11

After Lee placed the ring on my finger, our business in the marriage office was done. On exiting the building, we both took a moment. As I stood on the sidewalk, the fresh air against my skin was soothing. I couldn't wait to get out of this dress. Out of these shoes. Out of Patrus.

I had to keep my mind on the prize at the end of the tunnel: my brother—seeing him again would be all the reward I needed.

Lee gestured to my ring and said in a low voice, "Whenever we're out of the house, you should wear it. It's important that you have it on you at all times in case something happens—in case you get separated from me. You will be safe with that ring."

I narrowed my eyes on him. "What do you mean by 'safe'?"

He began to walk me away from the building, back to the alleyway at the other side of the street. "Let's just say there are some less-than-gentlemanly men here in Patrus."

Okay...

"I don't mean to worry you," Lee went on. "Most men here are decent, albeit different from what you're used to. Just keep the ring on your finger, eyes to the ground, and you'll be fine... Now," he said, looking straight ahead at the street we were about to emerge on—the street filled with women's shops. "I suggest we head home for lunch. By the time we eat, we won't have long before we have to return to the city for our lab visit this evening."

I'd hardly spent any time in Lee's house so far, but it was already feeling like a haven compared to the rest of this disconcerting place.

Lee and I changed into more comfortable clothing when we got home. He had cooked a lot the morning before and frozen the leftovers, so we ended up finishing them off for lunch.

As we sat at the table, I couldn't stop thinking about the marriage office, keenly aware of the new weight on my finger.

"Patrian marriages," I said, chewing slowly, "do they all take place in an office like that? Are there no proper ceremonies, like we have in Matrus?" *Are they all so per-functory?* was what I was curious to know.

"No," Lee said, dabbing the sides of his mouth with a napkin. "There are traditional ceremonies here, too. Some men opt for lavish arrangements, while others prefer to keep it low-key. It just depends on the man... and how much he takes into consideration the preferences of his bride."

"I see," I muttered. Whatever weddings took place in Matrus were almost always accompanied by ceremonies. Even if they weren't grand or lavish, efforts were made to hold a small gathering at least.

"Well," Lee said, finishing his meal and standing, "I'm going to take Samuel out for a walk and then we can head off. In the meantime, feel free to do whatever you want around the house. Make yourself at home and maybe freshen up for this evening. I suspect we'll end up going to a restaurant for dinner, so we could be out fairly late."

My eyes followed him as he moved across the room to drop his plate in the sink and then headed out of the kitchen. He called for Samuel and led him to the door.

Finishing my food, I rose from the table and moved to the window, peering through the blinds as they left.

I glanced furtively at my ring again before walking to the sink to wash up the few dirty dishes.

Make myself at home. That was something I'd had to try to do a lot over the last decade, though I hadn't had a true home since my mother died.

I headed to the bathroom and after splashing cool water on my face, I decided to wander around the house a bit. I found myself roaming the stories of the triangular building, gaining a better understanding of Lee in the process. He really didn't like clutter, we were alike in that sense, and there were hardly any ornaments or decorations, except for the odd abstract painting on the wall. His own bedroom—bigger than mine but hardly containing more—also held a single bed.

There was an exercise room on the second floor, containing dumbbells and several large pieces of equipment, and next to it I discovered a library. Its walls were lined with tall glass bookcases, and I noticed he had an awful lot of books on guns, explosives and other weaponry, a lot more than he had about biology, which was supposed to be his primary occupation—this kind of unnerved me. Then there was a whole shelf dedicated to psychology.

I picked a book up—one about the history of arms development in Patrus, which listed every single gun invented by Patrian natives—and sat down with it in an armchair. A few of them were familiar to me from my training with Ms. Dale. Although I was sure the weapons I'd trained with had been produced in Matrus (it would be rather hypocritical for Matrus to import goods as destructive as guns from Patrus) the design was practically identical.

I paged through the dusty pages until Lee and Samuel returned, both panting as they moved inside. Apparently their walk had turned into a jog.

Lee headed to his room to take a shower and get ready for the evening—something for which he only needed fifteen minutes. Then he was downstairs again, looking crisp and fresh as ever, wearing a new suit—deep burgundy in color.

Leaving the house, we rode back down the mountain to the city, while the sky darkened overhead. On arrival at the lab—a seven-story building whose walls consisted entirely of shiny, dark-tinted glass—Lee punched a code into a number pad and the gates drew open, allowing us inside. After parking and removing our helmets, Lee took my right hand and planted it firmly around his arm before leading me through the revolving doors.

My heels clacked against the sleek floors of the reception area. There was nobody behind the long white desk, even though a phone was ringing. Lee moved to it and, leaning over the counter, picked up the phone.

"Hello?" he answered, frowning. "Oh, Viggo. Yes, Lee here. Nobody's behind the desk. Why were you calling? Maybe I can help. Huh. Okay, yes." Lee moved behind the desk and examined a computer. Then he read out a string of numbers. "Did that work? Okay."

Lee hung up and looked at me. "That was Viggo Croft," he murmured, moving to my side. "The code to the back gate was changed, he was calling in for it. He'll be heading here—"

A door creaked from some distant part of the building. Then footsteps grew louder. A door opened to our left and in stepped a tall, handsome man with a mane of dark brown hair. Wearing a trench coat and heavy boots, he looked less unkempt than in his photo, with just a little stubble darkening his thickset jaw, though he had a scar across his right cheek which I hadn't noticed in the photograph. His olive-green eyes swept over the room and landed on us. They paused on me for but a second before he gave Lee a brief nod and headed across the room to another door.

"Viggo." Lee spoke up before he could reach it. He took my hand and led me toward the warden. "This is my new wife, Violet." My attention was drawn momentarily to Viggo's hands as we neared; his knuckles were red and raw, like he'd punched someone or something one too many times without adequate protection.

Viggo's eyes returned to me, his right brow raising a fraction. He nodded, his expression remaining stoic. I nodded back just as curtly.

Then his focus resumed on Lee. "Good evening, Mr. Bertrand." He turned and left the reception.

The room went quiet, still, in his absence. As though his presence had brought with it an aura of tension.

"Well," Lee whispered, blowing out softly. "That was quick…"

"Yeah," I said dryly. "He didn't seem to approve of me."

Lee chuckled. "There aren't many people he does approve of, apparently. He's a loner. Lives in a cabin by himself up in the mountains."

Lee fell silent, his eyes narrowing like he was straining to listen to something. Then he said, "Do you hear that?"

I strained to listen and nodded. I could just about make out voices murmuring somewhere in our vicinity.

"My colleagues, a few rooms away. The work day is over, but they often hang around in the evenings... Anyway, let's take a look around."

We moved to an elevator and Lee punched the button for the seventh floor.

"There are seven levels in total, as you can see," Lee said, trailing a finger over a map of the facility that hung against the elevator door. "The lab is huge with hundreds of rooms. It's recently been renovated and expanded," he explained. "It was less than half the size only last year."

That would explain why everything looked so new and shiny.

Arriving on the seventh floor, I realized why Matrus ought to be afraid. I wasn't a scientist, but the apparatus contained within these labs looked sleek and sophisticated. The building itself seemed to be almost as large as the city lab in Matrus. That was saying a lot, considering that Matrus' lab was also used for routine euthanasia of criminals. In Patrus, from what I knew, they didn't bother with all that hassle. If somebody committed a serious crime like murder, they were publicly hanged.

"Are you aware of everything they're developing here?" I asked Lee in a whisper as we moved along the wide hallway and peered through open doorways of the labs.

"Not everything," he said. "But a fair amount. A lot of time and resources are going toward developing the 'smart drug'. Its official name is Benuxupane," he added. "The drug has already been formulated and deemed fit for consumption. Several scientists in this lab are going to take it within the week."

"Will you?"

He shook his head. "No."

"Do you know the real reason they're developing it? What exactly do they plan to do with it?"

"Matrus' news channels have basically got it right," Lee muttered beneath his breath. "Emotions are a hindrance to King Maxen's plans."

Before I could ask anything more, we turned a corner and arrived outside a closed white door, next to which was a screen. Lee swiped his thumb, and the door opened.

We emerged in another lab, the largest I had seen so far, with row after row of tables lined with microscopes, Bunsen burners, and specimen racks filling the room from wall to wall. Around the edges were glass cabinets, some containing books, others piles of folded lab coats… but as we roamed the lab, one in particular caught my eye. Lee noticed where my attention had flown, and it appeared that this was where he was leading me.

"You've spotted it, haven't you?"

It was hard not to spot. One of the glass cabinets was unique from the others. It didn't have shelves, and the glass looked much thicker, even reinforced. Perched in a tall, black metal tripod was a silver egg. *The* silver egg. I moved up to the cabinet and stared at it. I couldn't believe it was just here... visible to anyone entering this lab. Just a few feet away from me.

I turned to Lee in confusion. "So this is definitely it?" I asked.

He nodded. "This is the egg."

"Can't you open this case?" There was a number pad next to it.

He grimaced. "No. I'm not high up enough to access the code."

I dared reach out and touch the glass. "But it's just... glass. Couldn't it be broken easily?"

Lee reached for my hand and pulled me back. He began leading me to the other side of the lab. He didn't answer until we'd exited and returned to the corridor.

"We ought not linger in that room," he whispered as we made our way to the elevators. "As for the glass, yes, it could be broken if enough force was applied. You're talking about explosives, though. That glass is tough as hell. It wouldn't be so simple as smash and run... and then"—we moved into the elevator and he hit the button for the ground floor—"of course, you'd have to escape Patrus… Trust me, if it was simple, I would have done it already. Remember also that we cannot get caught—neither you nor I. If one of us was, they would quickly place the blame on Matrus."

I was mired in confusion. We had to retrieve the egg from the glass cabinet, but at the same time, nobody could suspect that it was us? What about when we suddenly went missing? Even if Lee didn't come with me, but stayed behind, what about me? I'd had these doubts before, and Lee still had not clarified them.

"You'd better start giving me details," I said irritably, no longer able to hide my frustration. I was fed up of being led blindly along.

"I will," he said. "Tonight, when we get home."

The elevator reached the ground floor and we stepped out. "For now," he said, his tone raising and brightening, "I ought to take you to briefly meet my colleagues." He glanced down at me, an artificial smile on his lips, clearly indicating that I assume the same. "We got married today, remember?"

Right.

He led me across the reception area toward a pair of double doors. Before pushing open the door, Lee whispered, "The head scientist of this lab is in here. My boss, Richard. He's the overweight one."

He replaced my arm through his and walked me inside.

A group of ten men were gathered around a billiards table, all of them older than Lee—I suspected in their mid-forties—except for one, who looked about the same age, perhaps in his late twenties.

My eyes lingered on the short, rotund man with blond hair and a thick mustache. Richard.

"Lee!" the youngest man cheered.

"This is your girl?" another man spoke up. "Violet, did you say her name was?"

"Yup. My wife," Lee said through his plastic smile. He displayed my ring finger to them.

"Good man," the younger guy said, patting Lee on the back.

"Thanks, Simon," Lee said.

Richard and the others weren't nearly as informal as Simon. They nodded politely and murmured, "Congratulations."

Lee took a seat with me on a couch, accompanied by Simon and three others who abandoned the game. Richard also strolled over.

"How many more days of leave will you be taking?" Richard asked Lee, his voice rich and throaty.

"Oh, I'm not entirely sure, Richard," Lee replied. "As you can imagine, Violet and I have a lot to catch up on and a number of things to adjust around the house."

"I understand. Let me know once you have a date."

"Of course."

Lee fell into five minutes of small talk, throughout which nobody bothered to address me. If I wasn't a guilty spy on a hazardous mission for Matrus, I would have been annoyed by that. As it was, I was relieved that the attention was kept off me and Lee tackled all the questions.

Lee stood up. "Well, we're off to have dinner," he concluded. "I'll catch you around."

"Where are you going to eat?" Simon asked.

"Uh…" Lee said, slipping a hand into his pocket. He bobbed thoughtfully on his feet.

Before he could reply, Simon suggested, "How about The Red Boar? We were planning to go there ourselves tonight. I'm pretty starved now, in fact. You could join us."

Lee hesitated, but apparently struggling to find a polite way to turn Simon down, replied, "Okay. Sounds like a plan."

Other than Simon, four others accompanied us: Luke, Frederick, James and Rocco. The others remained in the billiards room, except for Richard, who headed home.

Lee pulled back with me as the men exited. "The restaurant's not too far from here," he said beneath his breath, "about twenty minutes by car. Though it's in an area I'd hoped to avoid. Not the end of the world though, as long as you stick with me."

On exiting the lab, we headed to the parking lot where Simon offered to drive us in his vehicle. I sat in the back, while Lee sat in the passenger's seat next to Simon. We drove out of the lab compound and passed road after road that was teeming with life. Men with their wives and children populated the sidewalks, milling in and out of shops and restaurants. These were the same streets that had been almost empty earlier in the day.

I sensed us approaching the river that encircled the palace by the subtle change of atmosphere, the breeze seeping through the car windows becoming crisper. We reached a parking lot at the end of a long promenade, beyond which were the river's gushing currents and the tall, well-lit walls of the palace. On our side was a long line of bars and eateries. I immediately noted the lack of women and children in this area.

"There's the place." Lee pointed it out to me. A bright red sign depicting a muscly boar hung above a large, dimly lit restaurant, outside of which was an open-air enclosure of tables. Our group managed to secure a table from a group who'd just finished eating as we arrived.

I didn't have an appetite as we sat down and eyed the menus. I always felt tense around strangers, and particularly these men who were potential obstacles in accomplishing my mission. I told Lee to order me whatever he was having before leaning back in my seat, half in and half out of the conversation sparking up among the men around me. I'd hoped that, as uncomfortable as the meal might be, it would at least prove to be interesting; that they'd talk about their work, and the types of experiments they ran all day in that monstrous lab, but apparently work talk was reserved for work hours. Their primary topic of conversation became a major event that was due to take place soon, a cage fight between two of Patrus' most skilled professional fighters.

I found it endlessly strange to listen to them talk about fighting as a sport, something that people watched for entertainment, when in Matrus any sort of physical combat was discouraged to the point that even a punch could have somebody reprimanded.

Violence was taboo in my world, as much as women getting jobs was in theirs.

"What are your hobbies?" Simon turned to me and asked as the food arrived.

Oh, someone's deigned to ask me a question.

Hm. Hobbies? What hobbies would be deemed acceptable here in Patrus for a woman? Cooking was the first that sprang to mind. Ironically, I actually couldn't cook to save my life. Lee was a better cook than I could ever hope to be.

It felt like the only thing I knew how to do well was fight.

I was glad when Lee helped me out. "Other than being a bread artisan, Violet is a painter. An *excellent* painter."

I scoffed internally.

"Wonderful," Simon replied, sipping from his glass. "Next time I come to visit Lee, I'll have to take a look."

Yeah... Good luck getting yourself out of that one, Lee. He'd have to go hunting for some unsigned paintings to brighten up his walls, though it shouldn't come to that. I was still holding out hope that this mission would only take a matter of days (then I could see my brother again as early as next week!)—though I'd been given no reason to hope this. Nobody had mentioned a timeframe yet, neither Alastair nor Lee.

"What are *your* hobbies?" I returned the question to Simon, hoping to divert the attention away from myself.

But as Simon began to answer, I hardly heard him. Something—someone—caught my eye across the tables.

It was my cousin, Cad. Cad, whom I had not seen in years.

He was with two other young men I guessed were friends. The three of them were moving toward our eatery, already scanning for a seat among the outside tables. He hadn't spotted me yet, but that wouldn't last long if I didn't get the hell out of here. Being surrounded by Lee's colleagues, I didn't have the time or ability to explain anything to Lee, of course. I immediately turned my back on Cad while lowering my hand beneath the table to grip Lee's knee. I held it firmly, hoping to instill in him my urgency.

"I-I'm sorry, Simon, you'll have to excuse me... Lee, where are the restrooms?"

Lee looked confused, but nodded toward the entrance of the restaurant. "At the back, near the bar. I'll come with you."

"It's all right," I murmured, biting down on my lower lip. "Stay here. " I feared the two of us standing at once would attract more attention our way. Cad might even think that we were a couple freeing up a table.

There was a moment of hesitation in Lee, when I feared that he would insist on coming with me all the same. But it was just the back of the restaurant. That could hardly be considered leaving him—could it?

I tore away from him, trying to make my retreat as undramatic as possible, even as I was forced to walk sideways so that my face remained obscured from Cad, who was nearing closer and closer with his friends.

The restaurant was huge. It had four main entrances, and I could hardly see through to the back of it as I stepped inside because of all the men moving around. I spotted the sign for the ladies' restrooms at the back, but to my dismay, they were closed for maintenance. *Closed. How could they close the restrooms?* The men's were open on the other side of the bar. *Dammit.* I was still the only woman in this place that I could see, so I supposed they'd hardly had any complaints.

I backed into the shadows as best as I could while trying to keep a tab on Cad's movements, which was hard with all the bobbing heads. I caught a glimpse of him entering the building with his friends—obviously having failed at finding a table outside. They were making a beeline for the bar, which meant I needed to move again and fast, but I had effectively backed myself into a corner. There was only one path I could take from here to the main aisles that led to the doors, and that would mean crossing straight in front of Cad.

If he saw me now, it could be a disaster. He would cause a scene and demand not only that I explain myself, but also that I go to see his parents. I wouldn't be able to shake him off and he wouldn't believe the lies that I'd fallen into a romance with Lee. Cad would know that it was impossible. And if any of those scientists heard him talking or discovered we were related… it would be far too much of a footprint for me to leave in Patrus.

My palms were sweating as I kept my gaze trained on the out of service sign on the restroom door and their conversation floated in my ears above the rest of the noise in the pub. They were talking about rowing, Cad was, apparently, as keen a boater as ever.

It was strange to hear my cousin's voice again. Strange, yet comforting. I felt a bittersweet twinge in my chest, wishing I could greet him. But I couldn't stand where I was much longer without looking seriously odd. I sensed that a waiter would be the first to ask me if I was all right.

I twisted ever so slightly, just enough to glimpse the nearest exit. If I moved tactfully, I could slip around the back of Cad and his friends' chairs while they weren't looking. Then I could get lost in the crowd and make my way back outside. I could rejoin the dinner and tell Lee that I was feeling sick and that we needed to leave.

But before I could even begin my attempt to move around them, Lee spoke up behind me.

"Violet?"

He'd come to see if I was all right. And he either had not been informed about my cousin or simply hadn't seen or recognized him.

I was already picturing Cad turning to Lee, and then following Lee's gaze toward me. I didn't have time to think. My gut instinct took over and I found myself darting forward, past the out-of-order sign and into the ladies' bathroom.

My heart raced as I gazed around the stalls. I spotted a window above the line of sinks and, kicking off my shoes and hanging them over one wrist by their straps, I climbed onto the sink and pushed it open. Gripping its frame, I hauled myself up to find myself above a trash yard around the back of the building.

Swinging my legs over, I leapt and landed on the roof of a trashcan. I slid off, tearing the hem of my dress in the process, and landed on the puddle-strewn ground. I quickly slipped my shoes back on before hurrying toward the gates that marked the exit of the yard. Thankfully, they weren't locked. I rushed through them while trying to tidy my hair and straighten my dress. Taking a deep breath, I leaned back against the yard's wall.

Lee would probably go barging into the ladies' room after me and suspect that I had climbed through the window. I guessed he would climb through, too. I would wait here for him to emerge, and then the two of us could roam back to the tables before taking our leave.

I couldn't help but wonder what was going through his head right now, though. He might be doubting me, thinking that I'd decided I wanted to get out of all of this and tried to escape while I thought I could. If I hadn't had a reunion with my brother dangling ahead of me as a carrot, the notion of running away would probably be tempting, but even that would require a level of insanity I didn't possess. I'd be caught, and probably thrust into jail... And jails in Patrus were rumored to be a woman's worst nightmare. I would be better off in a Matrian detention center any day.

As for Cad, I'd gotten out of the building before he had been able to see me properly. The most he would've seen of me was my back. Although Violet was not a very common name, I had to hope that he'd write it off as a coincidence and not think any more of it.

I clasped my hands together, waiting tensely. The street was dark, except for a single strip light a few hundred yards away. It cast eerie dancing shadows on the brick work surrounding me.

Where was Lee? Why was I still waiting for him? It occurred to me that maybe, rather than climb through the window, he might've gone around the front and would be making his way to the back alley now.

I started moving toward the crowded street that ran perpendicular to the alley. I'd feel easier waiting where there were bright lights and people, but as I had almost reached the busy sidewalk, a group of men turned the corner. Big, heavy-set men with identical tattoos—a solid black square beneath the left ear. They had the rough appearance of farmers or manual laborers: sun-tanned skin, windswept hair, baggy clothes, and clunky boots.

Almost colliding with me, they stopped abruptly, their eyes raking over me curiously. Balling my hands into fists, I kept my eyes firmly on the ground while attempting to dodge and slip past them. But one of them—a man with a pockmarked face and a jungle for eyebrows—apparently wasn't done looking at me. He moved directly in front of me, blocking my path.

"What are you doing alone?" he asked.

"What business is that of yours?" I said through gritted teeth. He clearly wasn't a warden.

I moved to push past him but again he obstructed my way, taking a step closer to me this time.

"She's too well dressed to be a stray," one of his companions muttered.

I glared into the eyes of the man looming over me, refusing to be intimidated. I could have flashed my ring to show him that I had a guardian, but I wasn't a Patrian girl. And I wanted him to know it. He couldn't just push me around.

I could tell that my stand aggravated him. His arm shot out to grab my wrist, but I had already predicted his movement and with a sharp chop of my right hand, I knocked his arm aside and jerked backward.

His eyes lowered to where I had struck him, which would soon show bruising, and then raised to me again in disbelief.

I hadn't been sure why Lee had been hesitant to come to this part of town, but perhaps men like these were the reason. The man surfaced from his surprise and lurched forward, giving me no choice but to remove my stupid heels again and hurry back. I was feeling angry and frustrated enough to get into a physical fight with him, but I wasn't quite that stupid. Even if I outsmarted him, which, judging by the slowness of his reflexes, wouldn't be all that difficult, now more than ever I had to control my temper. Plus, he wasn't alone.

As I ran, the voices of schoolchildren chimed in my ears. *Violent Violet, Violent Violet.* My nickname at school. I'd become notorious early on in my life for finding trouble. But if I didn't stop now, I would only be digging a deeper grave for myself.

The man, and now his companions, pounded down the street after me. I wasn't sure what he intended to do if he caught up with me. Beat me for my insolence? They were apparently on the lookout for "strays", a term I hadn't heard before, but I could take a good guess as to what it meant. Women who, for whatever reason, found themselves living in Patrus with no male to act as a guardian. No guardian in this country equated to less than zero rights. Unsupervised women became like lost children, wandering the streets at risk. According to my knowledge, this was one of the reasons why polygamy was allowed in Patrus—to give Patrus-born women plenty of options, and ensure they never had to be without a man.

But even though I was aware of all this, my pride wouldn't let me flash my ring at my pursuers and my hands remained tightly balled. The guy would only take my show of a ring as fear, weakness on my part. And there was nothing I hated more than giving a bully what he or she wanted.

Reaching the end of the alleyway, I glanced behind me. There was still a fair distance between us. Though my speed had been hindered by running in bare feet over the coarse concrete, I had gotten a head start.

I looked left and right, sparing a couple of seconds to figure out which would be the most direct route, before hurtling to my right. I'd been in such a rush, I hadn't noticed a man crossing my path at exactly the same moment and I found myself slamming into a hard chest. I staggered back, gazing up at a familiar face. Not Lee's. But Viggo's.

Based on the surprise on his face, he hadn't been sent to find me by Lee. He was obviously just doing his regular evening rounds. Next to him was another man, a warden I recognized from the profiles Lee had shown me the night before.

My pursuers' footsteps behind me stopped short, and I twisted to see them do an almost comical abrupt about-turn and head off in the opposite direction.

"What are you doing without your husband?" Viggo asked me in a low, disapproving tone.

"I'm on my way to him now," I replied tersely. I considered turning the guys who had been chasing me into Viggo and his companion, because I was sure that harassing a woman the way that guy had was against the law. Even though females were supposed to never be unsupervised, it couldn't be *legal* for men to prey on "strays".

Viggo gripped my arm firmly. His palm felt rough and warm. He pulled me out of the darkness of the alleyway and into the bustling street.

"Where is your husband?" he repeated.

"I last saw him in The Red Boar," I muttered.

"You are not supposed to be alone," he said tersely, glancing at my ring, which was visible now that I'd unclenched my fists. "Surely your husband has told you that?"

"I'm not alone," I said, probably too snappily considering I was talking to a warden now. "He's just around the corner. We accidentally got separated in the crowds."

Viggo retained his grip on me as we headed down the street, but I shrugged him off when we turned a corner. *I'm not a damn child.* I had already put up with Lee holding me earlier, I didn't see a reason why I had to put up with Viggo when he wasn't even my "husband". I didn't bother to check Viggo or his partner's reaction to my assertion of independence. But although he stayed close, he didn't try to resume his hold on me.

We walked in steely silence until we reached the restaurant. Lee was bouncing on his feet near our table, looking bedraggled with worry while speaking into a phone. His eyes gleamed with relief as he noticed us approach. Relief, but also doubt and disturbance. A dozen questions must have been roaming his mind, but he would have to wait until later for an explanation.

"Violet," he gasped, taking my hands and pulling me to his chest.

Viggo cleared his throat. "With due respect, Mr. Bertrand, I would keep a better eye on this one... She has a rather adventurous mind for a bakery girl."

Viggo's green gaze rested on my face once more. Then he turned on his heels, his long trench coat billowing in the breeze as he and his companion stalked away.

CHAPTER 12

Lee was understandably shaken. The others looked confused, too and I was forced to address all of them, even as I looked around for Cad, praying that he hadn't come back out here.

"I'm sorry," I said. "I, uh, I needed to use the restroom but it was out of service. I found a back door and went through it. I hoped to find another restroom nearby, but I got lost." Here I turned to Lee, and tried to look apologetic. "I'm sorry, it was stupid of me. I guess I'm still getting used to the rules."

Lee slid an arm around my waist before facing his colleagues. "I need to get my girl home, gentlemen. I apologize. Enjoy the rest of your evening."

To my relief, he led me away from the restaurant, and firmly out of Cad's potential view. We returned to the teeming sidewalks, where Lee stopped to hail a cab—one of the dozens of blood-red cars roaming the roads at this hour. It was of course too risky to discuss anything meaningful in the back of a cab. We waited until we arrived back at the lab, where we had left Lee's motorcycle. Only as Lee started the engine and we rode off did he speak.

"What just happened?" he asked. I could feel how tense his chest was as I gripped it.

"I'm sorry," I breathed. "I spotted my cousin, Cad Thorne, and there was no way I could think to warn you. I had to get out of his sight."

Lee let out a deep sigh—of relief, I could only assume. "Well, I'm glad that was the reason," he muttered. "I honestly thought you might've tried to do a runner."

"No," I reassured him.

"You'd be a fool to attempt it," he said.

"I know." *For more reasons than you might be aware of.*

I told Lee about the men I'd encountered in the alleyway, looking for "strays".

He tensed up again. "God, Violet. Alleyways are the absolute *worst* place for you to stand at night. Especially in that part of the city. Guys like the ones you ran into are known to snatch even married women. They take females away from the city and surrounding suburbs, deep into the mountain region. There are a number of scattered towns in those harder-to-reach areas which are inhabited primarily by peasants, though frequented by city men more than the state would like to admit… Let's just say they're not places you'd enjoy visiting."

I took the hint. Men seemed to be able to get away with using women for their own dark deeds here in Patrus, unlike in my homeland. Any untoward approach by a man toward a woman in Matrus would be the last thing he ever did. It virtually never happened.

"Did you show them your ring?" Lee asked, rounding a corner and joining the main highway that led to the foothills.

"Yes," I lied. It was easier to lie than attempt to justify why I had not.

As he lapsed into silence, I recalled the last unsettling words Viggo had spoken. He had already guessed something wasn't right about me.

"What did you make of what Viggo said?" I dared ask.

"Well, obviously, getting into trouble the day after your arrival wasn't the smartest idea. *Especially* not with Viggo." Lee sounded pissed off.

I blew out a breath. "Look, I'm sorry, okay? If Cad hadn't arrived, I wouldn't have left you. How does Viggo even know about me being a bakery girl?"

"I told the guys in the lab," Lee said through his teeth. "I guess he overheard the conversation or was privy to office gossip."

We spent the rest of the journey in silence; a silence that was broken only by Samuel as we entered the house.

Lee headed straight to the staircase after locking the door, without a backward glance at me.

"So what now?" I asked, hands on my hips as I stared at his retreating back. "You said you would finally tell me the actual plan."

Lee paused in his ascent, but didn't turn around. "I know," he muttered. He hung his head, reaching to rub his temples. "But as I said, it's unfortunate it was Viggo who found you... Just give me a bit of time to clear my head and consider if anything needs to change. I'll still tell you the plan this evening. I promise."

I watched in annoyance as he disappeared up the stairs, while I was left with a slobbering Samuel.

I moved to the kitchen, and, since I hadn't actually eaten anything for dinner—I suspected Lee hadn't either—I rummaged in the fridge. We had already finished all the leftovers, and there were no other precooked items here that I could see. I ended up grabbing a slab of butter and some bread from the cupboard over the sink. Pulling up a chair at the table, I buttered a slice and chewed glumly.

Whatever was ahead of me, this sure hadn't been the best start.

When Lee came back downstairs, I was still sitting at the table, paging through an old newspaper I'd spotted on one of the seats. It was actually extremely interesting to see the way Patrus presented the news. Their excited tone when reporting their advances was so at odds with that of

Matrus when covering the same news. And the types of advertisements that appeared in between the pages were also… interesting. I struggled to find a single one that didn't feature a scantily clad girl. *Modeling is apparently one profession that is excusable for women here…*

I set the paper down as Lee took a seat opposite me.

I raised my brows expectantly.

"I've thought about it," he said, leaning back in his chair and rocking slightly. His demeanor was calmer now. "Tonight could have been worse." His expression softened as our eyes met. "I'm sorry if I was harsh earlier. You just have no idea how stressful it was not knowing where you went. When you ran, I honestly did believe you'd lost your senses and were trying to escape… So…" Pressing his hands together, he sat forward. "Now you've seen the egg. You know where it's located, and hopefully could find it in that lab in the dark if you had to… In a few weeks, the city lab's ten-year anniversary will take place. A banquet will be held to commemorate the occasion. It is not a widely-publicized event; it's reserved specifically for the scientists who work in the lab, and members of the king's council have also been known to attend. The night of this banquet will be the perfect time for us to strike."

Weeks. My stomach plummeted—I had hoped this would be over in days. The thought of staying in Patrus for so long terrified me. If tonight's mini-fiasco was anything to go by, I was sure to mess up again. My nature wasn't designed to handle this environment.

I stared at him, frowning. "I don't understand. On a night when so many important people are together in a room, wouldn't security be higher than usual?"

"Yes," Lee replied. "But that shouldn't hamper anything, if all goes to plan… Give me a minute."

He retreated from the room and returned a minute later carrying the same folder he'd brought in yesterday, along with a second green-colored folder. He opened the latter and pulled out a map. Unfolding it, he spread it out on the low table in front of us. It was a plan of the lab, each floor and all its rooms clearly marked.

He pointed to the lowest level, a few doors along from the reception area. "This is the events hall, where the banquet will take place. What's required is a big distraction that will keep everyone's attention on the ground floor, leaving the highest floor"—his finger traveled up the map and rested on the large laboratory that held the egg—"unwatched," he concluded. "We won't need long to do the deed anyway. Just a few minutes."

"What kind of distraction do you have in mind?" I asked.

"Explosives," Lee replied. "In the weeks to come, my plan is to install them inside the building near the hall so that when triggered, the blast will be so destructive, security's immediate occupation will simply be attempting to get everybody out alive."

I realized that I had stopped breathing. "So, you're saying it's probable that some of the diners will lose their lives in this?"

Lee nodded and I swallowed the lump in my throat. Having committed womanslaughter twice, claiming lives shouldn't be anything to make me flinch. But of course, those incidents had been accidents. These would be cold, premeditated murders. I wasn't a murderer. I was a girl with a difficult temper. "And the egg?" I asked. "I don't understand how—"

"I'll figure out the distraction, while you will take care of the most important business: the egg."

"I'd need explosives to blow the glass."

"Yup," he said. "We'll have to work on equipping you with some. Then you will seize the egg—setting off a hot-wired alarm in the process, which will be ignored for a good while due to the commotion downstairs—and make your way up to the roof." He traced my route on the map. "There is a stairwell near the egg's lab, which leads up to the rooftop."

"The roof? Assuming I actually manage to get that far, what happens once I get up there? And won't the building itself be shaken to its core from the explosions at its base? Won't it be alight and crumbling?"

"I'll be careful in my choice of explosives," Lee replied. "The building will be burning, of course, but you'll be quick. Your focus will be extricating the egg and getting to the rooftop… I will meet you up there, and we'll have pre-arranged transport for the two of us."

I glanced back down at the map. *Transport for the two of us.* I could only think that meant that Matrus would be sending an aircraft to carry us both back over the river to safety…

"I still don't understand how we wouldn't be instantly blamed though," I said. "Especially if we were absent from the dinner and—"

"First," Lee said, "we won't be absent from the dinner—we'll need to discuss the specifics of this nearer the time. Second, I also won't stay away from Patrus for long in the aftermath. Once we've returned the egg to Queen Rina's palace, I'll come back discreetly, and reintegrate myself into the scene. As for your absence…" He grimaced. "Trust me when I say it's not difficult for husbands to hide their wives in Patrus. Most wives hardly go out anyway. There was a murder case last summer where it took five years for the man to be convicted, simply because nobody noticed his wife's absence."

My jaw dropped.

"It can be that bad," he assured me. "Especially if the woman is from Matrus. She typically has no family over here. Another option could be to say that you died in the blast. That might be a better way to play things… Then as for the issue of *who* will take the blame if not us…" He looked me in the eye. "Who do you think could be used as a scapegoat?"

Used. I didn't like that word. Still, I racked my brain. "Um… Well, it would need to be someone with regular access to the building. Someone who knew it well, and… if the bombing was to make any sense, it would have to be done by somebody who had a reason to hold a grudge against Patrus. Someone who was discontented with their life here." My voice trailed off as Lee nodded. "Who are you thinking?" I asked him.

Slipping out the red folder, he spilled the wardens' profiles out on the table before his forefinger settled on a single one.

Glaring up at me was the rugged face of Viggo Croft.

CHAPTER 13

"Viggo?" I clarified as I stared down at his picture.

"Yes," Lee said. "He fits the bill excellently for a potential anarchist. Let me explain to you a bit more about his background and it should be clear why... I told you that he got into trouble with the law for obstruction of justice."

I nodded. *Just like I did.*

"Well, the circumstances surrounding that are rather interesting. Viggo used to be married—to none other than a Matrian woman. She was an emissary at the time they met. She tried to move over here but, you guessed it, found the adjustment to Patrus' culture extremely difficult. As the official story goes, her and Viggo's relationship had been tense for months. One night they got into an argument, after which she stormed out, alone. Although Viggo went out after her, she managed to shake him off and lose him. She wandered the whole night as an act of protest and, as the early morning hours drew in, she came upon a couple of drunks who had less than noble intentions.

"Fortunately for her—or unfortunately, depending on how you look at it—she had been trained in self-defense by Viggo. She stopped their assault and escaped, but she ended up killing one of the men in the process. Given that there were no neutral witnesses—only she, the victim and his accomplice were present at the scene—she had no way to prove that she had been acting in self-defense. Viggo found her in the morning, stumbling back toward their home. After she told him what had happened, he tried to cover up her crime… obviously knowing what would ensue for her. He made an attempt to ship her back to Matrus, but failed. She was taken before the judge, and—given that she was already guilty of having left her husband and roaming the streets unsupervised at night—there was little sympathy for her in the trial. Long story short, she ended up being sentenced to hanging."

Hung for acting in self-defense. The sheer injustice caused the blood to drain from my face.

"Viggo was to serve four years in jail for his act of dishonesty. But, given his skill and the value he added to the city's security force, jail time was deemed a waste for him. He was made a special offer: resume his position as a palace warden and serve without pay for four years… He's in his second year now. His wife's death has obviously scarred him. He moved away from the city and set up in a cabin in the mountains a few weeks after the hanging.

He's never been the most approachable of guys, but since he lost her, he's notorious for being tightly strung—as you may have noticed."

Lee rose to his feet and paced in front of the window.

"So, in sum, we have a man with a clear grudge against the state, who has lost his wife, and is now leading a life that's been forced upon him... Men have snapped beneath lesser burdens." He caught my eye. "But just as important as all of this," he went on, "is that he was made chief coordinator. He has access to the lab... It would honestly be hard to think of a more suitable person to lay the blame on."

My stomach tensed. *An innocent person.* We would be framing an innocent man, who had obviously already been through hell and back. This didn't sit right with me. At all.

"There must be some other way we can pull this off," I breathed. "I can't believe that laying the blame on someone else is the only way. What if it we didn't set this up as a terrorist attack but instead... I don't know, some other kind of explosion in the building? It's a laboratory, Lee. Surely there are other exploitable options?" *Options that don't involve a beating heart.*

Lee shook his head. "I've thought this through, Violet. I've thought this through for days. I understand your hesitation to frame an innocent person—of course I understand. I feel as uneasy as you about it. But this is the only way we can convincingly pull it off without laying the blame squarely on Matrus. Remember, Patrus stole the egg from Matrus in the first place. We are only retrieving what is ours."

'What is ours'. You mean what is the queen's and her army of scientists'. An object whose contents I still had no damn idea about.

I pursed my lips, my stomach continuing to churn.

"So," Lee continued, his voice becoming more subdued. "The next question is, how exactly would we go about setting the man up as an anarchist? How would we make it convincing? How do we make sure that he's at the right place at the right time?"

I didn't feel like offering any more suggestions. Lee had apparently already thought all this through, anyway.

"The first issue," he said, "is that we need to be able to track his movements, and understand his day. We need to be aware of when he's doing his rounds by the Crescent, when he's at home, and when he's at the gym or in the cage."

"Cage?" I interrupted.

"He's a professional cage fighter. That's what he does for money these days. Takes as many fights as he can while off work."

"Oh. I see." I recalled the conversation Simon and Lee's other colleagues had regarding the sport's popularity here in Patrus. "How would we track him?"

"Come with me," Lee said, gesturing to the door. I rose and followed him to his bedroom where he sat down at his desk in front of a computer monitor before pulling open a drawer and lifting out a ball of metal foil. Within it was a semi-transparent gel-filled capsule that I almost didn't notice because of its minuscule size. In the center of it was a black dot. I leaned closer. Some kind of… square object? My eyes weren't sharp enough. I would need a microscope to be able to describe it better.

"What is it?" I asked.

"An ingestible tracking device."

My eyes shot up to meet Lee's.

"Are you *serious*?"

"Yup," Lee said. "Swallow it down with some water, and it will embed itself in the gut—staying there for up to three weeks."

Ugh. "Where did you get this thing?"

"It was developed in Matrus, actually," he said. "I picked it up from Alastair during my last visit to the queen's palace. It's so tiny, you wouldn't even notice it gliding down your throat when swallowed with a gulp of liquid. He'll never know it's inside him, and it'll pass through naturally on its expiry."

"H-How would you actually make him swallow this?"

Lee refolded the foil around the capsule and placed it in my hand. "The question is, how will *you*?"

CHAPTER 14

"**S**lipping Viggo this tracker will be your first task,"
Lee explained. "And it needs to be done as soon as
possible. He has a fight tomorrow night on the outskirts
of town. I'll drop you off there, and you'll need to figure
out how to do it."

Lee opened up his cupboard and pulled out a stiff shirt
and an even stiffer gray suit. The shirt and jacket were
padded around the shoulders. A man's outfit.

My lips parted.

"Try this on," he said.

As I pulled the costume on over my clothes, it was
surprisingly lightweight and comfortable. I looked in the
mirror. My chest, which didn't bulge much anyway, could
easily pass as a man's. The shirt was amply bulky.

"This is a temporary measure," Lee said, eyeing me
over. "I have a body suit for you, too." He rummaged in
his closet and pulled out an actual skin-colored male body

suit, complete with bulges in all the right places. "But I figured that'd really be throwing you in at the deep end. This gray suit will be enough for tomorrow."

He replaced the body suit in the cupboard, and then drew out a wig of curly black locks and strips of facial hair.

"This is insane!" I said.

Lee looked half amused as he applied my wig and then the facial hair with a thin, transparent adhesive. By the time he was done, I was a black-haired man with a mustache and a generous beard. The facial hair helped to cover the softness of my jaw. I would have laughed in disbelief at how realistic it looked had I not been so tense.

"However you figure out the logistics, this task shouldn't be too difficult," Lee said. "Remember, it'll be nighttime. I'll give you this, too." He brandished a cap and planted it on top of my head. "Oh, and lenses, to be doubly sure…" He left for the bathroom and returned with a rectangular silver packet, as well as a narrow white and blue box. He split the packet open and told me to tilt my head back while he applied the lenses. I hadn't expected the application to be so uncomfortable, but he managed it. When I looked back in the mirror I had dull brown eyes. My eyeballs had gone reddish with irritation, my tear ducts working overtime.

"Your eyes will get used to them," Lee assured me.

"And shoes," I murmured. "I guess I can wear the ones I arrived here with. They're unisex. But then there's the matter of my voice. What if I need to speak?"

"You should try to avoid speaking at all costs," Lee said. "But in case you can't…" He held out the small box so that I could see the front of it. Bold, jagged black letters stamped across the packaging announced the product as "*Deepvox.*" He opened the box to reveal it was stuffed with tablets.

"You're kidding me."

"Nope." Lee laughed. "This is actually a thing here. Swallow one of these and it'll deepen your voice for up to twelve hours. Designed for men who aren't happy with their natural tone."

"*Go deeper. Last longer,*" was the brand's slogan.

"What are the side effects?" I asked, dubious. I squinted at the tiny, almost illegible print on the side of the box.

"Your throat might get sore," Lee said. "But that's nothing that can't be solved with some warm honey and ginger tea. You should get used to it after a while, anyway."

How many times was I going to have to swallow these things? How many excursions would I have to make before leaving Patrus?

For the sake of my sanity, I figured that it was best to only look one step in front of me at a time.

"I should test the product now to see how well it works on me," I said. "And how quickly it will work."

We headed to the kitchen where I helped myself to a glass of water.

I swallowed one of the small round pills gingerly and waited with bated breath. Nothing happened at first, other than my heart pounding. Then I began to feel a constricting, tingling feeling at the back of my mouth. It wasn't strong enough to hurt, just enough to be unpleasant.

"Say something," Lee said.

"Hello." A noticeably deeper voice blurted from my lips. Not quite deep enough to pass me off as a man, though. I consulted the product's description; it said it could take up to an hour for the pill's effect to fully come into play.

"I suggest you take three tomorrow evening to be safe," Lee said. "Otherwise, I guess you're ready."

Lee had to go out early the next morning, which left me alone in the house with Samuel. As I washed up after breakfast, I already knew the wait for this evening's excursion was going to be tedious. Tedious and nerve-wracking.

I ended up gathering a pile of books from the library and sitting out in the garden; the mild temperature and mountain breeze helped to calm me. I took a seat in a deck chair and tried to forget about the time for as long as I could, until I could no longer ignore Samuel's whining. I finally acquiesced to his requests to play ball and remained busy with him until lunchtime. I brought food outside for both of us so we could sit in the sun and eat, and then spent the rest of the afternoon indoors. I had roamed every room in the house by now, but I still had not set foot in the basement. On heading down there, however, I discovered the door was locked.

I huffed and returned upstairs.

I had deliberately eaten until I felt stuffed again, hoping to make myself feel drowsy so I might be able to get some solid sleep before Lee's return. I had been awake most of the night before, tossing and turning and worrying. The food was beginning to take its toll and I slipped into my bed and managed to pass the rest of my alone time in slumber.

I woke up to the sound of the front door unlatching, and Samuel's barks as he scurried to the door.

Yawning, I staggered out of bed, splashed my face with cold water, and headed downstairs.

A black canvas bag was waiting by the doorway, filled with some kind of heavy, rectangular weight. The door was open, and I caught sight of Lee crossing the drive and returning with an identical second bag.

He quickly closed the door and turned to me, rather out of breath.

He planted down the second bag next to the first and reached into his pocket. He rummaged and pulled out a square piece of card: a ticket to the event at Brunswick Arena. There were to be four fights that evening; Viggo and his opponent, "Seamus Vanguard", were up first.

"Keep this ticket somewhere safe," Lee told me. "And don't forget to bring it with you."

I stowed it in my pocket, my focus returning to the bags. "What are they?" I asked.

"Explosives," he replied over his shoulder as he descended to the basement. Then he changed the subject. "By the way, we should leave in less than an hour."

I sensed his unease. As a Matrian male, Lee wasn't a naturally aggressive person. Less aggressive than me, I was sure. I doubted any of this came instinctively to him.

"Okay, I'll start getting ready." I dragged my feet up the stairs to Lee's room. Opening the cupboard, I pulled out all the parts of my costume and quickly slipped out of my clothes and pulled on the shirt and suit. I decided to leave the whole facial hair thing to Lee, but did make an attempt to apply my wig.

Lee arrived a few minutes later, carrying the lenses and the pills. Once he finished my cosmetic appearance—leaving my eyes feeling sore and watery again—I took the pills. After ten minutes, my voice had deepened enough to be passable as a man's, even if a slightly effeminate one. But by the time we arrived at the Arena, it should have deepened further.

I stuffed my ticket into the jacket pocket while Lee equipped me with a pager and, of course, the all-important ball of foil. I was also sure to remove my wedding ring.

As we were about to step out of the house, Lee's phone rang.

"Hello?" Lee answered. His expression went serious. "Yes. Yes. It's going according to plan. Yes."

After a few more *yeses*, Lee handed the phone to me. "It's Alastair," he whispered.

Alastair? I took the phone and pressed it to my ear. "Mr. Jenks?"

"Ms. Bates?" he replied. It was strange to hear his voice again. He felt like another universe away.

"Uh, yeah. It's me. I just took some Deepvox pills."

"I see. How's everything going?"

"Okay, I think." I replied, frowning.

"How are you finding Patrus?" he asked.

How does he expect me to answer that? "Uh, not exactly pleasant." *Not that Matrus' detention centers were pleasant, either.* But at least there my sense of worth wasn't constantly being affronted, and I wasn't under so much stress.

"Okay, well, I won't keep you," he said. "I'll check in with both of you again soon."

With that, he hung up. My eyes turned to Lee in confusion. "What was that about?" I asked.

"Wanted to verify for himself we're both still on the job," Lee replied. "Make sure I hadn't lost you." He opened the front door and we strode out into the night. "Anyway, I think you should start focusing now," Lee said as we donned our helmets and climbed onto his motorcycle. "Visualize what you need to accomplish tonight in your head."

Lee drove me through the tail end of rush-hour traffic to the outskirts of town—suburbs to the south that were noticeably rougher than the city or any other areas I'd passed so far. The streets were not as well cleaned, the buildings shabbier, and the men roaming around looked generally more unkempt. I was still unable to spot a single woman amidst them.

Lee parked the motorcycle in a bay on the sidewalk opposite a tall, round building, the first two floors of which were occupied by a noisy, smoky eatery. He led me across the road and around the side of the building where we stopped outside a set of open, peeling, red double doors. I poked my head through to find a stairwell leading downward.

"The arena is through there," Lee whispered. He backed up against the wall of the building and glanced nervously to the left and right. "As you can see from the ticket, we're a bit early. Not a problem, though. Just go through those doors and show your ticket."

"What time will you come to pick me up?" I asked.

"Viggo's up first and his fights rarely go past one round. Let's say… giving time for any possible delays… eleven."

"That late?"

"Well, you shouldn't just leave straight after Viggo's fight. It's considered discourteous and you might draw unwanted attention to yourself."

"Okay," I said. "Where exactly will I meet you?"

"Where I've left my motorcycle now," he replied. "I'll be hovering somewhere in that area and watching for you."

I nodded again, my palms and forehead breaking out in a sweat.

"What happens if I get caught?" I asked.

"You've just got to make sure you don't."

Great.

Lee lingered for a minute longer, readjusting my fake hair, which had gotten disheveled after the motorcycle ride. My eyes still felt irritated, but since he didn't remark on them, I assumed they didn't look too odd. I doubted teary eyes was a great look for a Patrian man.

Drawing in a deep breath, Lee took half a step back and gave my left shoulder a reassuring squeeze, then turned and headed back to the main road. I didn't wait to watch him disappear from view. I hurried through the double doors and down the staircase. I had work to do.

The door awaiting me at the bottom was open and unguarded. Stepping inside, I found myself surrounded by an arena that was smaller than I had expected. It could probably fit about three hundred people, which wasn't exactly tiny, but not grand like I had imagined the venue of a national sport would be. Not much pride had been taken in the aesthetics either. The seats were made of garish red plastic, and the walls and ceilings were rough and unpaint-ed, the brickwork clearly visible. But maybe this was all intentional; I supposed that it added to the atmosphere.

I turned my mind back to the conversation I had over-heard with Lee's colleagues, when they had been excitedly talking about a fight that was to take place in a few days' time. I couldn't remember the name of the arena where it would take place, but it hadn't been Brunswick. I was sure of that. Maybe Viggo's career hadn't taken him to the big leagues.

In the center of the room was a cage in the shape of an octagon. It had two entrances and the mesh walls were constructed from thin malleable metal, and the edges of the cage's floor itself looked painfully sharp. Their ridges were pointed; if someone slipped against them with the right amount of force, they could easily cause serious damage. Probably even hospitalize someone. I guessed this was deliberate though—making their environment as rough and treacherous as possible to up the stakes and keep the men on their feet at all costs.

I roamed around the arena, mulling over my task, until voices came from the door near one of the back rows of seats. Two men strode into the arena carrying lighting equipment and two small foldable tables.

I moved back into the shadows and took a seat, trying to remain as inconspicuous as possible while they set up the lights. They unfolded the tables in front of each of the entrances. Then more men came in with more paraphernalia. Some carried chairs and boxes of food, while others carried towels and first-aid equipment. Finally, I spotted something interesting—a man carrying in two containers of water. He set one down on the tables at either entrance, where two flasks had already been placed.

More banging and commotion ensued while they rigged up all the final lights, and then everyone retreated through the back door. I wondered if anyone had noticed me at all yet, or whether they'd just chosen to ignore me.

Either worked for me. The main thing was that the room had become empty again. This was my window of opportunity—a window I had to grab with both hands now that the fight was drawing so close.

I left my seat and made a beeline for the nearest cage entrance. The flask on this side was helpfully labeled with the name of Viggo's opponent. I sped around the cage to Viggo's side. Glancing over my shoulder, I hurriedly opened the flask. It was already filled to the brim. I retrieved the foil ball and unfurled it, dropping the transparent gel capsule into the water. It blended in so well that I had to make an effort to search for it. It floated on the surface, too, which meant he'd likely swallow it in his first or second gulp.

Footsteps sounded in the stairwell. Replacing the lid, I jerked back from the table and resumed my seat.

I exhaled slowly, wiping my palms against my pants. *Okay. It's done. The worst is over.* Now, hopefully, all I had to do was wait.

Twenty minutes before the fight seemed to be the magic time of arrival—the arena began filling quickly and within a matter of fifteen minutes, every single seat had been taken, leaving many forced to stand. With five minutes to go, the main doors were closed.

The excitement in the room was palpable, and I was surprised to see many women accompanying their husbands.

Dressed to the nines, in front of me sat three of them in a row, sandwiched by their husbands.

In between flicking their perfectly coiffed hair, they were gushing about the fight that everybody else seemed to be so breathless about: Croft versus Vanguard.

In spite of my nerves, I couldn't deny that I was excited, too. Attending this event was unique—an adventure. Something I'd never imagined myself doing in my whole life. I suspected this would be the high point of my stay here in Patrus, so I probably ought to make the most of it.

The lights dimmed, leaving a single spotlight to blast down in the far right corner of the room. Boos erupted as a tall, sculpted man stepped out, bare from the waist upward. He was bald, and every visible inch of his bulging physique was etched with green-ink tattoos. His face reminded me of a shark's—angular, with a broad, flat nose and a cruel, crooked mouth.

Wearing yellow shorts trimmed with gold, 'Seamus "Sharp" Vanguard' made his way to his entrance and climbed into the cage. He skipped around the enclosure— bowing in four directions while gnashing his teeth and beating his chest—before retreating into his corner.

Then the spotlight sped to the far left corner of the arena. Cheers erupted before Viggo even came into view. When he did emerge beneath the glaring beam, the crowd went wild.

"There he is!" gasped one of the women in front of me through the deafening applause.

He wasn't introduced with a nickname like Seamus. Just Viggo Croft.

Viggo looked quite different in his role as a fighter. His hair was tied back, revealing the full breadth of his jawline. His physique was muscled, but in a more understated—and, in my opinion, very attractive—way compared to his opponent. Although their weight must be even, Viggo was taller, leaner, and I suspected more agile. His knuckles were tightly bound in bandages, and his shorts were plain black.

I found my butt sliding to the edge of my seat as he prowled down his aisle and swept into the cage. He didn't offer the audience any introductory performance like Seamus had; he simply planted himself immediately in his corner.

A man sporting a blue shirt and white gloves moved to the center of the cage and beckoned both fighters forward. After he informed them that they were to obey his commands without exception, a bell rang. The commencement of the fight was announced by the booming voice of a man whom I was sure must have popped a Deepvox pill or two. *Nobody's voice is that deep.*

The two men circled for a few seconds before Viggo drew in. He aimed a front kick at Seamus's chest, causing him to stagger toward the edge of the cage. Seamus, trying to regain a central position, threw a flurry of punches, but Viggo blocked them deftly before counteracting with a powerful right hook that knocked Seamus to the floor.

The crowd erupted.

"He's got the takedown!" one of the women in front of me squealed.

Viggo pounced on the man before he could rise, pinning him down and raining punches. Seamus held up his elbow, attempting to block them, but Viggo was too overpowering. He came in with blows not only to the side of Seamus's face and ears, but also against his kidneys. Seamus, daring to come out of pure defense mode, shot up a punch toward Viggo's face, but that only opened himself up. Viggo hammered down a punch so hard I found myself wincing, and the next thing I knew, Seamus had gone still and the referee was calling a stop to the fight.

My eardrums ached from the cheers.

Viggo rose to his feet. Although he had won, there wasn't the slightest trace of victory in his expression. He barely even made eye contact with the crowd. He looked uncomfortable, forced into the situation. I knew that feeling.

Everybody stood and clapped. Whistles ricocheted around the arena.

I watched with bated breath as he was handed his flask by a man in a black shirt. He swallowed a few mouthfuls before handing it back. That should have been enough for the capsule to glide down. I guessed Lee would know soon enough.

Viggo didn't hang around to soak up the adoration. As soon as the referee announced him as the official winner, he swept out of the cage as swiftly as he had arrived, strode down his aisle, and exited the basement.

As everybody settled back down to wait for the next fight, I tuned into the conversation the women in front of me were having.

"When is that guy going to move on to bigger things?" a blonde was saying. "He doesn't belong in this dump. Such a waste of talent!"

"He's been approached by the big league a bunch of times already, Vanessa," a man, presumably her husband, replied. "He turns down their offers again and again. He doesn't want a bigger spotlight."

"He's twice the man most big-league fighters are," a brunette chimed in. "Cruz. Rosen. Croft would knock them out. He'd be top of his division!" She shook her head sadly. "He'll fade away if he doesn't move up in this game."

"Maybe that's what he wants," a second man retorted. "Whatever he's doing this for, it's clearly not legacy."

The conversation died down as the next fight was announced. The lights dimmed, and once again the spotlight shone on the far right corner of the arena. This was to be a "middleweight" fight. Terrence "Trump" Wilson versus Bernard "The Beast" Hill.

As the two opponents made their way to the ring one after the other, I was shocked to see a huge chunk of the audience get up and leave the arena. They really had just come to see Viggo, only they weren't adhering to the etiquette Lee had advised me to follow.

I understood why so many left. Professional fighting was still a complete novelty for me, but even I found the second fight slow and plodding. Neither had the skill or agility of Viggo to make it an interesting match. It went on for five rounds, and by the time the winner was announced, three quarters of the arena had left.

I felt bad for the fighters as they bowed, and clapped harder in a feeble attempt to make up for the lack of noise.

But those women were right. Viggo didn't belong here.

I checked my watch. Lee was due to collect me in ten minutes. I made my way to the exit before the next pair of fighters could enter the room and climbed up the stairs, out into the open air. I headed to the main road and crossed to wait by the bay to make it easy for Lee to spot me when he arrived.

After a couple of minutes, a familiar figure exited the bustling eatery. Draped in a long trench coat, hood pulled up over his head to shadow his eyes, Viggo was carrying a bottle of water and a bulging paper bag. I realized he was heading right for me. Or, rather, the motorcycle bay, and I moved discreetly backward, trying not to stare as he approached a beetle-black motorcycle.

He seemed too intent on leaving the arena to even notice me standing nearby.

A part of me was tempted to congratulate him for the fight just for the hell of it, but I bit my tongue. Of course, that would be a stupidly unnecessary thing to do.

He stowed his items beneath the seat, swung himself onto it and roared away down the road, in the direction of the mountains.

When Lee arrived at eleven on the dot and asked if I'd placed the capsule, there was a lump in my throat as I replied, "I did."

CHAPTER 15

After I gave Lee details of how I'd planted the tracker, he asked, "So how was the fight?"

I couldn't deny that I had enjoyed it. "It was good."

But I didn't feel good about what we were doing, in spite of Lee's assurance that we were doing nothing wrong—that we were simply retrieving a stolen object. But Viggo hadn't stolen it, he was just a foot soldier. Someone just trying to survive, like me.

I wished that the banquet was sooner, not only so I could see my brother sooner, but so that I would not have to carry around my guilt for so long.

I realized that the only way I could get through this would be to stop thinking about what I was doing. Adopt tunnel vision. Do everything required to ensure things ran smoothly so that I could get out of here, see my brother and then, assuming I couldn't wrangle a way to stick with him permanently, reintegrate myself into some form of existence back in Matrus… and try to move on with my life. I'd probably look to move somewhere far away from everybody—like Viggo had done—to reduce the odds of getting into trouble again.

Numbing myself shouldn't be too much of a challenge. My years spent in detention facilities had made me good at that. Blinders on, head down, same routine day in and day out. Just get through the day. I had to see this mission involving Viggo Croft like everything else: threading needles, sifting flour, or shoveling crap.

This was all simply another detention, where I had no choice but to do as I was told.

Once I adopted this mindset and stopped considering consequences, I felt lighter and I was better able to engage in Lee's conversation.

"Viggo knocked out the other guy in the first round," I told him.

"Yup." Lee smirked. "No surprise there."

I wished that professional fighting was a thing in Matrus. If it had been, I might not have ended up in so much trouble with the law. I'd have had other ways to let off steam.

"If I was a man," I muttered, "that's what I would be doing." This was probably the first time I'd ever truly considered what it would be like to be a man.

"Fighting? It's not all it's cracked up to be," Lee said. "It's a hard, hard life."

Yeah, well, life is hard whatever you do.

Reaching the foothills, we let the quieter atmosphere halt our conversation: the gentle mountain winds, the fragrance of the soil at the end of a warm day.

Samuel was asleep when we returned to the house. We headed immediately to Lee's bedroom and drew up chairs at his desk. He switched on the monitor and pulled up a detailed map of Patrus. Roaming it, I spotted four flashing red dots. They were all stationed near the city center.

"You're tracking other people, too?" I asked.

"Yes," he replied. "There are a few whose help I've needed, and I've had to keep an eye on them. There's Viggo," Lee said excitedly. He pointed to a red dot that I hadn't even noticed yet. It was up in the mountains, some distance away from Lee's home. While we were situated on the southwest side of the palace, he was northwest.

It seemed that he had already reached his home by now, as his dot appeared stationary.

"So," Lee said, leaning back in his chair, looking relieved. I reached up to peel off my mustache. "Step one is completed," he said. "You successfully tagged him and we can now monitor his movements in real time."

"Next, I suppose we need to figure out his schedule," I muttered, pulling off my wig and removing the rest of my scratchy facial hair.

"I agree. We need to know what, if anything, he plans to do on the night of the banquet. This should be easier than what you did tonight. Viggo has little time to vary his schedule. When he is not working as a warden, he's typically either fighting or preparing for a fight. He trains at a gym in the city, and behind the reception desk is a schedule of all the booked sessions, as well as each of its members' upcoming fights. You'll likely need to hang around for a bit and wait until the receptionist goes for lunch, but the arrangement would be similar to tonight. I'll drop you there and give you about half an hour—I'm sure within this time you'll find an opportunity. There's usually only one receptionist behind the desk and since we'll be arriving just before lunch, he'll have to take at least a short break to fetch his meal… We'll do it tomorrow—leave here at eleven-thirty in the morning, okay?"

Okay… Another risk for me. But I understood why; Lee was more valuable than me in Matrus' eyes.

I sat with Lee a little longer, staring at the map and watching the red dot that was Viggo.

Then I left his room and headed to my own. Entering my bathroom, I removed the suit, took a quick shower, and changed into my nightclothes before climbing into bed.

As I drifted off to sleep, I returned to the Brunswick Arena. The electrifying atmosphere flooded my mind: the bright lights, the roaring of the crowd… The mass celebration of physical prowess.

That night, it was me in the cage instead of Viggo, and opposite me, a stocky blonde female inked with green tattoos, whose face uncannily resembled a shark.

CHAPTER 16

I decided to wear the full-body suit for this lunchtime's excursion to Viggo's gym. Since I would be roaming in the daytime, rather than lurking anonymously at the back of a shady arena, I figured that I would feel less nervous with it on.

Lee donated three outfits to me: jackets, shirts, and pants, and I spent the morning tailoring them so that they would fit me properly. I pulled the pants' ends up by a few inches before adjusting the jacket and shirts. My time working in the textiles factory had been useful after all.

As for my shoes, I decided to wear my own again, the same as last night. They were kind of scrappy, but they'd do.

I also took four Deepvox tablets two hours before we were due to leave.

By eleven-thirty, I was ready to leave. My voice had sunk deeper than the night before, not fight-announcer deep, but deep enough to pass as a real man.

I couldn't stomach a lot of brunch, and it seemed neither could Lee. He was just as nervous as me.

Lee headed upstairs briefly to check on Viggo's location, and returned to report that Viggo was near the palace, as expected. He also placed a small red rectangular object in my hand, and a miniature notepad and pen in my pocket. I stared at the red object, turning it over in my palm. On one side was a blank screen.

"It's an advanced pager. Smaller and less conspicuous than a phone, it will vibrate when I trigger it"—he drew out an identical red object from his right pocket—"and a message will pop up on that screen. You can also send a message to me if you need to. As for the notepad, use it to note down the dates… So, are you ready?"

I nodded.

"Then let's go."

The gym was fancier than I'd expected it to be. It was a stylish steel structure spanning four floors, perched right on the bank of Crescent River.

Lee dropped me off one street away. "I'll be back in about forty-five minutes, but I'll send you a message when I arrive."

"Okay."

I strolled casually across the road, keeping my eyes firmly focused on the ground. Reaching the building, the glass doors opened automatically and I stepped into a cool reception room with slate-tiled walls and black marble floors. A minty hue hung in the air.

I dared to raise my eyes and gaze around the room. To my pleasant surprise, it was empty. Perhaps it was lunch break already. This meant I had to be fast; I had no idea when the receptionist would return.

Withdrawing the notepad, I planted it down on the table while leaning over and scanning the desk for the big ledger Lee had spoken of. It was one of the first things I spotted—just to the left of me. I reached down a hand and lifted it up before paging through it. Indeed, Viggo's schedule had been marked there, and it was a busy one. His heart might not be in the fighting, but nobody could fault him for his dedication to the sport.

I kept a keen ear out for sounds of the receptionist returning, but I had time to flip through the schedule a second time to be doubly sure that I had not missed any pertinent dates or times. He wasn't booked in for anything on the night of the banquet. That was the day we were most concerned about.

I replaced the ledger on the table, careful to reposition it exactly how it was, and ambled away from the desk.

Glancing up at a clock that hung above the main entrance, I still had loads of time. Only five minutes had passed. Not wanting to hang around in the reception area, where I would likely have to engage with the receptionist when he returned, I took off down the corridor to my left, deciding to explore the gym a bit. There were no signs indicating special permission was required, and the doors at the end of the corridor leading deeper into the gym were wide open, so I assumed that nobody would object.

The corridor's walls were made of glass, allowing me to peer into hall after hall of cages as I walked. Each hall contained two or three cages, and the walls were lined with lockers and benches.

I stopped at the fifth hall, where two fighters were going at each other in a cage. I watched as they grappled on the floor, each trying to wrestle the other into a choke hold. The loser eventually tapped the floor, and his opponent released him.

I continued exploring, passing more halls, until I reached the end of the building. I stopped and turned around, but wasn't willing to retrace my steps to the reception so soon. I didn't want to return there until I had to leave the building.

I entered an empty hall. I was better off sitting in here and waiting, rather than roaming around where I was more likely to run into trouble.

I moved to one of the benches closest to the back wall and sat down. My eyes traveled all around the room, taking in every detail with interest. There was a line of punching bags hanging from a thick metal rack on the opposite end of the room.

Another ten minutes passed as I waited for Lee's message.

Retrieving the pager from my pocket, I punched in a message and sent it to him. Just two words: *I'm done.* It took him about a minute to reply, *"OK. Stay where you are. I had to head to another part of town. I'll be there ASAP."*

I sat back on the bench, blowing out a breath. I was not great at waiting.

My eyes returned to the punching bags. Slowly, I stood up and made my way over to them. Balling my fists, I landed my first punch against one. It was heavy, barely budging. The outer fabric was also rough, as though specifically designed to cause calluses and harden skin.

Glancing around the room again to check that nobody had entered without my noticing, I landed a harder punch in the center of the bag, causing it to sway away from me before swinging back. I punched again, and then again. My knuckles weren't used to this abrasion, and they were already feeling sore, but it was in a therapeutic way. I continued punching, though when I sensed my skin was about to break, I switched to kicking. Luckily, the clothes I was wearing were not too tight. I removed the jacket, since it was making me hot and stuffy, and began attacking the bag with kicks. Back kicks, front kicks, side kicks. I practiced everything I remembered from Ms. Dale's training sessions.

It felt good, really good, to awaken muscles I'd forgotten about, feel the stretch, the burn in my thighs as I pushed myself harder. Although I did keep an ear out for the sound of the pager vibrating in my jacket pocket, I got carried away and stopped checking the entrance to the hall as often as I should have.

When I glanced up a few minutes later, it was to see a couple of fighters had entered and were heading my way. I stopped kicking, turning to face them, suddenly extremely conscious of the fact that I had discarded my jacket. I felt grateful I had worn the body suit.

The fighters, I soon realized, weren't heading for me, anyway. They merely glanced my way briefly before climbing inside a cage much like I'd seen at the Brunswick arena. Strapping fingerless gloves around their fists, they began to fight.

They didn't seem to mind my presence, so I refocused my attention on the punching bag and continued.

When the pager finally went off another ten minutes later, I was expecting it to be a message from Lee, telling me to hurry outside and meet him on the street. But instead, he'd sent a message informing me that, "There's been a delay. Will be at least another thirty minutes. Sorry. Keep yourself out of trouble."

I wondered what had happened and hoped nothing had gone wrong. I returned to my kicking, albeit with less focus than before.

I got distracted by the fight going on to my left and kept glancing their way. I found myself predicting who would win, even though they had barely started. I figured it would be the shorter one, the man with a mop of ginger hair, who was showing more initiative and daring than the other. As the sparring went on, I became more and more sure of my prediction. And then the ginger managed to trip the other up and pinned his arms behind his back, holding him until he grunted in defeat.

I tried to keep myself looking busy—I didn't want them to think that my attention was on them, and the last thing I wanted was them watching me. I was dressed very differently to them, but at least the clothes I was wearing today were casual - the shirt was loose, as were the pants.

After five more minutes of sparring, there was an audible yelp. I could have sworn that I heard the crack of bone. The ginger had injured his friend during a particularly frenzied takedown. The friend's right ankle looked bent out of shape—probably broken.

The ginger apologized before helping his friend out of the cage and taking him down the hall, no doubt to get medical assistance.

Once again by myself, I was feeling a bit tired of nonstop kicking by now. I took a pause and approached the cage the guys had been fighting in. I moved closer to it, standing on my tiptoes and peering through the mesh. The ridges of this cage were not as nasty as the one I'd seen the night before in the Brunswick Arena, but they still weren't padded. Not something you'd want to fall on.

My breathing quickening a touch, I felt the urge to climb inside it, to see what it was really like on the inside. I climbed into the cage, my feet slipping slightly over beads of sweat.

I moved around its circumference, running my fingers over the mesh. I imagined what a thrill it must be to enter a cage like this on the night of a fight. To be surrounded by crowds chanting your name. What a rush would come with looking your opponent in the eye and having full freedom to make them submit to you.

The pager in the pocket of my jacket, which I had brought in the cage with me over one arm, buzzed again.

"Still delayed. Will keep you posted."

Resuming my focus on the room around me, I heard footsteps outside, moving along the corridor. I hurried out of the cage and made my way back to the punching bags as someone entered the room. The same man returned without his injured friend and headed to the same cage they had sparred in.

He began throwing air punches, flexing his limbs on his own.

He caught me staring at him this time and stopped punching to address me.

"Haven't seen you around here before," he remarked. "You had a good kick going on there…"

I felt my cheeks heat. Now was the moment of truth, the moment to put Deepvox's claims to the test… "Thanks." My voice boomed across the hall, a little louder than I had intended.

"Just joined?" he asked.

"No, actually," I replied. "But I'm considering it."

He tightened his gloves. "How's your punch?"

I shrugged.

"Want to spar?" he asked. "I've got a fight coming up next week and could really do with a partner."

I glanced down at my watch. There was still time, but seriously? Was I about to say yes? I supposed I could exchange some calculated punches with him, but there was no way I could get hit in the face, or start grappling or wrestling with him on the ground. My disguise wouldn't hold up under that sort of strain.

"I'm recovering from an injury myself," I told him. "Lower back. Can't move so fast and can't afford to be knocked down … I'll throw a few punches, as long as it's not near the face."

I didn't sense danger in doing that with this guy. He didn't strike me as the talkative type; the only reason he'd struck up a conversation with me to begin with was because he'd lost his sparring partner… He might not even bother to ask me my name.

"Okay, cheers," he replied, holding the door to the cage open for me.

I double-checked the pager one last time to verify no message had arrived from Lee without my noticing, and since it was still blank, I left it with my jacket at the foot of the cage steps. Then, flexing my wrists, I stepped into the cage.

A spare pair of fingerless gloves like this guy's were hanging from a hook. He offered them to me, and I quickly bound them around my knuckles, which were already red and sore from my assaulting the punching bag earlier.

Then, knocking my gloves together, I faced him.

"Not gonna take off your shirt?" he asked.

I shook my head. I wasn't planning to roll up my sleeves, either.

"All right… let's box."

We met in the middle, and I realized that he was more or less the same height as me, our arms about the same length. He swung the first blow. I dodged and returned one. We danced around the cage, neither of us connecting much, until I seized a small opening and knocked him— perhaps a little too hard—in the gut. He staggered back, taking a few seconds to recover before we went at it again.

"How did you learn to fight?" he asked, eyeing my fists with more wariness than a minute ago.

"Self-taught."

I upped my pace, keeping him distracted so he'd stop asking me questions. He caught my shoulder with a right hook, though I was careful to keep my face protected. As our sparring progressed, a realization dawned on me. This fighter and I might just be two people in an empty hall, but the fact that we were man and woman made this moment feel suddenly epic, sweeping, groundbreaking. Nobody in the world might know it—not even my male accomplice—but we were making history. I doubted any man and woman had ever stood on such equal ground before since time began in Patrus and in Matrus. The male in front of me was looking me in the eye without prejudice, without bias or discernment—as I was looking at him. The thought filled me with such euphoria that I found myself quite breathless, in a daze; so much so that I almost missed blocking a punch.

If only more people could experience this, was all I could think to myself.

I didn't want this sparring match to end. I wanted Lee to leave me alone for at least another half-hour so that I could continue immersing myself in this feeling… but then the pager buzzed.

I dropped my fists, my heart dropping along with them like a heavy weight.

"I'm sorry," I managed, stooping to my jacket and retrieving the device.

"I'm outside", said the message.

I turned back to the fighter, whose name I still hadn't asked, and shook hands with him. "I've got to go," I said before hurrying out of the room, although a piece of me remained in that ring with him.

As I moved along the hallway back toward the reception, my fingers reached up to check that my facial hair was all still in place. Now that hard reality had returned to me, I was afraid that I'd gotten too carried away and all that dancing around might have loosened it. Maybe the mustache was slightly less firm than before, but altogether the hair felt okay. Nothing was going to drop off during the time it took me to return to Lee across the road.

As soon as I stepped through the door, I kept my eyes on the ground and hurried forward, not even glancing to the reception desk, though I sensed someone there.

I let out an internal sigh of relief as I reached the main exit. Out of view of the receptionist, I threw caution to the wind and raced up the twisting stairs. But as I turned the corner to climb up the final flight, I almost collided with someone. I staggered back too quickly, and before I could find my footing, I tripped down several steps until my back hit the stairwell wall.

It was Viggo.

Standing in his trench coat and looking more imposing than ever from his elevated position five steps above me, he had stopped in his tracks and was gazing down at me.

What was he doing here? He couldn't have been here for training—his schedule had made no mention of it.

I straightened and averted my eyes to the stairs, attempting to recover and act as though nothing had happened.

Indeed, I expected Viggo to also continue descending right past me, but to my horror, he stayed exactly where he was. And when I reached his level, he reached out a hand and gripped my upper arm. I found myself being scrutinized by his hard stare, his face inches away from mine.

Crap.

I stopped breathing as his right hand moved to my face. The next thing I knew, I felt a tug on the skin above my upper lip, and then his hand was drawing away again, clasping my fake mustache between his fingers.

I swore in my head. What were the odds of me getting caught as I left the building? And by Viggo of all people?

Viggo seemed to have a penchant for turning corners at the most unexpected of moments.

His frown deepened. "Would you like to explain this?" he asked, his voice dangerously low.

Viggo was one man who definitely had no use for Deepvox.

My mind went into a panic. *What do I tell him?*

My angst was hardly helped by my pager going off again. Lee must be wondering where I was. *Dammit.* I was so close to Lee. And yet I was stuck.

As Viggo's eyes lowered to my beard, I realized there was no point in concealing my identity any longer. He seemed to have already detected that my beard was fake, too, and once that came off, there would be nothing to hide the softness of my jawline. He might even recognize my bare lower face. He'd seen me twice already.

As my mind raced for what explanation I could possibly give him, I realized that it ought to just be as close to the truth as possible. That was the best way to lie.

"I'm sorry," I whispered.

"Sorry for what?" His face contorted.

"I-I'm not a man." The words sounded weird coming from my deep throat.

Glancing nervously up and down the stairwell, I gripped one corner of my beard and stripped it off like a piece of wax. Next, I reached for my wig and unclasped it, letting my long hair fall down my shoulders.

All that remained now were my lenses. But Viggo didn't need me to remove those.

"Mrs. Bertrand."

"I'm sorry," I repeated, my voice constricted. "I've been having a tough time getting used to the ways of Patrus. It's hard never being able to roam by myself. I just wanted a little freedom. To roam the city without my husband holding my hand... My husband approved of this. He thought it would help with the transition."

Viggo's eyes widened. "He approved of you masquerading as a male and roaming the city by yourself?"

"How else do you think I got hold of this costume?" I replied. "He gave it to me. But I am *not* by myself," I added quickly. "My husband has been following me around from a distance, to make sure I don't get myself into trouble.

He's just on the other street. I can take you to him now if you don't believe me."

"I will have to take you up on that offer," he replied darkly.

Stuffing the facial hair into my right pocket along with my notepad, pager and pen, I moved past Viggo and hurried up the staircase. My pager buzzed again. Lee was getting nervous.

"That's my husband," I explained to Viggo as we surfaced on the road. I pulled out the pager and glimpsed the latest message.

"*?????*"

I showed it to Viggo, who grunted.

"What were you doing in the gym?" he asked me.

"Well, I wondered what was in that pretty glass building. I watched some fighters training, roamed around… Fighting isn't a sport, you see, in Matrus. I've worked in a bakery all my life, but I always wished I could've become a warden."

Viggo's expression soured. I could practically read his thoughts. *You're not missing much,* I imagined him thinking. He made no attempt to hide how much he hated his job.

We reached the other side of the road. I led Viggo round a corner until we arrived at the end of the second road along, where I caught sight of Lee waiting. He was standing next to his motorcycle, glancing up and down the street and clutching his pager in his hand.

"There he is," I murmured, pointing to him. "He lost track of me after I went into the building," I explained. "I should have told him I was going inside."

Lee soon noticed us, and instantly froze. I imagined him cursing in his head as he hurried forward, closing the gap between us.

"Violet?" he asked, his voice strained with confusion. "What's going on?" His eyes flitted to Viggo.

"Lee, I'm sorry," I said, moving to him and clutching his arm. "You told me not to wander into any buildings, but I did. The gym on the river bank."

There were undercurrents of confusion in his eyes, but he was quick to play along. Admirably quick.

Viggo didn't need to say anything. He just stood there, glancing from me to Lee in cold disdain.

"Dammit, Vi." Lee exhaled sharply. "I take risks and go to all this trouble to give you a sense of freedom, and this is how you repay me? Doing the first thing I forbade you to do?" Lee's grip around me tightened. "This'll be the last time I trust you." He turned to Viggo. "I understand of course if you need to report us, Viggo. Mark it as an infraction on my name. Even though I was following her, we were stretching the rules, no doubt about it. But I do promise you this will not happen again... We've just been having a difficult time with her adjustment. I hoped keeping her on a longer leash would help us make things work."

I prayed that would get to Viggo. If it didn't, I didn't know what would. He had experienced firsthand the difficulties of a Patrus-Matrus marriage, with his own wife struggling with the constraints Patrus' laws put upon its female residents. I hoped there was a place of compassion within his heart that he would draw on to not judge us so harshly.

Viggo's gaze remained sharp as it continued to roam my face. But then his jaw clenched, resoluteness setting in. "I'll let you off this time, since you were nearby. But if I do witness it again, I'm sure you understand I can't be so lenient..." He cleared his throat and averted his eyes, settling them on some distant point at the end of the road. "As you know, here in Patrus, rules are rules."

CHAPTER 17

After Viggo strode away, both Lee and I let out a long, slow sigh.

"God," he muttered, turning his back on the warden and rubbing his face in his hands. "That was not something I *ever* want to repeat." He glanced at me. "What on earth happened?"

My relief gave way to mild irritation. "What happened to *you*? What took you so long?"

"I had to go pick something up." He gave me a meaningful look. I guessed that meant more explosives or some kind of other equipment necessary for our mission. "But things got delayed. How did you wind up with Viggo?"

"I was hanging around the gym," I began. I decided to omit the little sparring match I'd had. I didn't see the point in mentioning it. It would only make him more nervous. "I tried to keep myself away from the reception area, to avoid awkward questions. I ended up roaming around the training halls. When I finally got your text and was making my way back up to the street, I bumped into Viggo. Like, literally bumped into him. My mustache got knocked off and he noticed. I figured it was best to just come clean after that—as clean as I could."

Lee nodded as he raised the seat of the motorcycle and pulled out our helmets. "You did the right thing. It's likely he's seen this trick played before. I'm certain we're not the first couple to think of it."

I found the idea quite revolutionary as we mounted the motorcycle and Lee kicked us off down the street. That this could be an old trick played by women who found themselves in Patrus but wanted more freedom hadn't occurred to me. Where had Lee actually gotten such a realistic costume? Had he really made it all himself, or had he purchased it? I guessed there must be some kind of underground market for them and I wondered how many women I'd mistaken for men since arriving here in Patrus. Especially at night, when streets were packed and it was far easier to go unnoticed.

Maybe some Patrian females aren't all that different from Matrian ones after all.

Maybe others, too, have experienced the rush I did back in that gym.

As we traveled back through the city toward the mountains, I found myself eyeing everyone on the sidewalks, examining the faces of the men and trying to spot any slight hint of femininity. But then Lee started traveling too quickly and I could no longer continue with that game.

"Anyway, none of this is the end of the world," Lee said as we entered the house. "In fact, we could twist this to our advantage."

"What are you thinking?" I asked, removing my shoes at the doorway.

We entered the kitchen and sat down around the table.

"Where's your notebook?" he asked.

"Here," I said, digging a hand into my jacket pocket and handing it to him.

Lee stroked his jaw as he paged through it, leaning back in his chair. "Hm. Okay. Interesting… And good. So far, he has nothing booked the night of the banquet. As you know, we can't have him having an alibi that evening…"

"How do we turn my collision with Viggo today into an advantage?" I asked again.

"Well, I was actually surprised that Viggo was so lenient with me. He isn't the type to dish out leniencies." Lee paused, glancing up from the notebook. "As hardened as he seems on the outside, he obviously does have weaknesses… I think he has a thing for Matrian girls."

"Well… he married one, so I guess he'd have to…"

Lee sat forward. "I think our strategy from now on—at least in regards to you—has become a lot simpler."

"What do you mean?"

"This further development of… rapport… between the two of you, shall we say, could be used to bridge the gap between him and us more."

"Bridge the gap? Why would we—?"

"We'll need to find a way for you to keep him isolated on the night of the banquet. To keep him away from anyone else's eye. In order to do that, you're going to have to make him go somewhere… Don't ask me where yet—that's something we'll have to figure out. But for any of this to happen, he's going to need to trust you. Gain his trust, and we have more control over him when the night arrives."

I lowered my brows at Lee. I would hardly describe what had happened today as "further development of rapport".

"Of course, another thing that works to our advantage in all this," Lee went on, "is that he needs money. That's the reason he fights in the first place; it pays well compared to other jobs…"

I crossed my arms over my chest, waiting for him to tie all his threads together.

He stood up and moved to the kitchen counter. Planting his palms down on the surface, he turned his back on me. He fell quiet for about a minute before drawing in a thoughtful breath and turning round again. His blue eyes rested on mine with a gleam of optimism—enthusiasm, almost—before he said, "Let's meet Viggo again tonight. I have a proposal to discuss with him..."

CHAPTER 18

After Lee revealed his plan to me, we spent the rest of the day at home, monitoring Viggo's movements. According to the gym schedule, he wasn't due to visit the gym tonight, nor did he have any fights going on. Which meant he would in all likelihood head straight home after work. As evening came around, we watched his red flashing dot make its way toward the mountains, straight from the city center. Once he'd entered the foothills, Lee was confident enough about his direction for us to leave ourselves.

I didn't need to wear a suit this time. We rode out of the driveway on Lee's motorcycle, but instead of taking the usual route down to the city, we headed further upward, higher into the peaks.

It got chillier as we ascended, and I found myself grateful Lee had suggested I wear a jacket. It was silent up here too and soon we came to the end of the residential area and entered a long, deserted stretch of winding road that led us northward toward Viggo's territory.

It was a pity that the sun had gone down, as the verdant landscape sped away on either side of us. I imagined this place would have looked stunning during the day, with brooks bubbling beneath bridges, lots of trees. We reached an open plateau, allowing us an unrivaled view of Patrus beneath us. It was a fairly clear night, and beyond the glittering sprawl of Patrus City, I could make out the deep black stretch that was the river and then, beyond, the hazy glow of Matrus' borders. I couldn't say that the sight made me feel homesick. Anxious to get back, because of the prize that awaited me, but not homesick.

Lee thundered the motorbike forward at a speed that made me nervous. "How much longer?" I asked him. My deep voice hadn't worn off yet.

"Maybe ten minutes."

Ten minutes proved to be about accurate. A bungalow—which was really not much more than a glorified log cabin—came into view at the end of a dirt track. A familiar beetle-black motorcycle was parked outside its porch, next to a three-wheeled trailer that I guessed he used to transport larger objects. The building looked like only a one-bedroom, with perhaps enough space for a small living room, a kitchen and a bathroom. The large square windows were closed off by shutters, though a spill of warm light glowed through their cracks.

As Lee killed the engine and we got off the motor-bike, we stood in silence for a few seconds, taking in the peaceful atmosphere. It was like another world up here. The middle of nowhere. The closest houses were settled nearer to the foothills, miles beneath us by road.

Lee reached for my hand, giving me a reassuring squeeze before the two of us approached the front door.

Lee knocked three times and my stomach clenched as I caught the sound of a door clicking, then heavy footsteps moving toward us.

A bolt was drawn, and then the front door creaked open. My lips unconsciously parted as Viggo towered before us in the doorway, bare-chested. He wore a pair of loose black pants, and clutched in one hand was a roll of cotton wool, in the other some kind of medicated ointment. His bare knuckles were red and glistening.

"Mr. Bertrand?" Viggo said, his eyes widening as they swept from him to me.

"Viggo," Lee replied calmly. "I do apologize for intruding like this. I won't take up much of your time, but I would like to speak to you about something."

Viggo paused, still frowning, before allowing us inside.

We stepped into a narrow hallway lit by a hanging gas lamp, its walls and ceilings made of logs. A rough wicker carpet lined the floor, and the hallway opened up to four different rooms.

Viggo led us through the first door to our left, into a sitting room. A fire crackled in the hearth and before it sat one sturdy armchair. That was the only piece of furniture in the room, save for a low table upon which sat a metal jug and a damp cloth. Viggo set down his bandages and ointment on the table. He grabbed a shirt which hung at the back of his armchair and pulled it on before turning back round to face us.

"It's about Violet," Lee said, his arm moving to my waist. "We're trying to figure out how to make things work in the long term. As you noted, she has an adventurous mind. Even though her work was domestic, she still of course has the spirit of any Matrian woman... My days will become much busier soon. I will have to return to work, and I will not have time to accompany her places... But our meeting earlier got me thinking, and I have come to you with a proposal."

Viggo's gaze froze on Lee, his right brow lifting.

"You spend the most part of every day in the city," Lee said. "I would like to appoint you as Violet's second guardian and have her accompany you for at least a few hours every day, when it's convenient. It will get her out of the house on a regular basis, and I would pay you, naturally, for the service."

Whatever Viggo might have been expecting Lee to say, it sure wasn't that.

"What do you mean, *accompany me*?"

"I mean just that," Lee replied. "Let her walk with you. Be your shadow. It will allow her to explore the city, as she's itching to do, and gain a greater understanding of our culture and residents."

In other words, it'll be like walking a dog. As my husband, Lee had full right to appoint guardianship of me to any other man, with or without my consent.

Viggo's green eyes rested on me, his expression serious. At least he appeared to be considering the proposal.

"I'm not sure this would be approved by head office," he said.

"I doubt you'll have trouble," Lee said. "It's not breaking any laws to bring a girl with you to work."

"Hm… How many hours exactly?" Viggo asked, resuming his focus on Lee.

Lee shrugged. "It can vary. I'm sure we could come to an understanding. Though it would make sense if she came into the city with me in the morning, for work; I could bring her to you, and then either you could drop her back home during lunch break, or you could bring her back to the lab and I could drive her home with me at the end of the day… Whatever works; I'm flexible. As for payment," Lee went on, "I'll pay you the same hourly rate you ought to be receiving as an inner-city warden. Just keep a tally of the hours and let me know."

That ought to be an attractive proposition for Viggo.

He leaned against his chair, glancing down at his knuckles, falling into thought. Lee and I waited patiently.

Finally he looked up. "All right," he said. "I'll accept the offer, but understand that I will back out at any time if things get... complicated."

"Naturally," Lee said, a relieved smile spreading across his face. "Assuming things do go smoothly though, I would say this arrangement could go on for at least a few months, depending on how long Violet takes to adjust to our culture... And could we start tomorrow?"

Viggo rose to his feet, slanting me a glance. "I suppose."

"Great," Lee said. "I'm planning to go back to work in the morning, so I'll drop her off with you on my way to the lab if that suits you. Where do you plan to be at, say, eight-forty?"

"Head office," Viggo replied.

"Perfect," Lee said, rubbing his hands together. "Now, we won't eat up your evening any longer. Thanks again for your time. I hope this can be an arrangement that benefits us both equally."

Viggo merely nodded before shaking Lee's hand. I instinctively reached mine out too—forgetting that this wasn't something done in Patrus. But before I could withdraw it, to my surprise, Viggo accepted my hand and shook it firmly. *Beneath his layers, maybe he's a rebel like me.*

Our gazes locked for three tense seconds.

Then Lee took my arm and led me to the exit.

CHAPTER 19

The next morning, I washed and changed into pants and a shirt and opted to wear my flat shoes again, since I'd likely be doing a lot of walking.

I couldn't deny that the idea of spending hours with Viggo was daunting. I didn't know what we'd talk about. I imagined us spending time in awkward silence. But that wasn't how it was supposed to go. I needed to try to make him warm to me. To even become his friend, if that was possible. Viggo seemed to guard himself against everyone, a friend only to himself. But there had been that handshake. That little crack in his exterior I might just be able to widen.

Lee and I made our way through rush hour and into the city. We passed the lab and he drove me to a tall gray building with a pointed roof near Crescent River. This was the wardens' head office, apparently. I didn't get to see much of it though, before Viggo appeared, waiting for us.

"Thanks again," Lee said, reaching for the small of my back and pushing me closer to Viggo. "You have my number, right? Just let me know if you decide to drop Violet back at lunchtime, or if she'll stay with you until the end of the day. See how it goes."

Viggo nodded.

"See you, then," Lee said before returning to his motorbike and riding away.

Viggo and I stared at each other.

"So, uh..." He nodded up the road, to our right. "My transport's that way."

My mouth dry, I followed him up the busy road to where he'd left his motorcycle. He had me sit on the seat first, and I was relieved to feel my fingers curve around a metal bar at the base of the seat, meaning I didn't have to clutch Viggo for dear life as we roared into the road.

We wound our way deeper into the center of town—not far away from the alleyway where I'd bumped into him the other night—and he parked on a street lined with shops.

"This way," he muttered, jerking his head further up the road.

He stalked forward, and I hurried to match his pace. After allowing the two of us a couple of minutes of silence, I asked, "So what does your day actually consist of as a warden?" I was genuinely curious. I wondered what the similarities were between the jobs of wardens here and in Matrus.

Viggo's eyes remained straight ahead of us. "Various things," he said vaguely. "During the daytime, there aren't usually a lot of incidents. It's on night shifts when things tend to get more… disordered."

"Disordered in what way?" I asked him.

"This city is at a junction with the mountains. There's a whole mix of guys who pass through, many of them of the opinion that they are above rules. We watch mostly for thieves, illegal substance dealers, traffickers, and of course… potential strays." Here, he glanced my way.

"What do you do with 'strays' if you find them?" I asked.

"It's our job to keep them off the streets," he said, turning a corner. "Those we find are taken to Gerter House—a shelter on the other side of town—before reintegration is attempted. Having them roaming the city merely makes it a target for the exact kind of men we work to keep out."

"Which are…?"

"The dregs from Porteque, basically." He seemed to sense my questioning stare as he added, "A spread of towns in the mountains, further west."

"Oh." *Gerter House.* I hadn't known they had an official shelter for women. I guessed they had to put them somewhere though, especially if Matrus didn't accept them— the Patrus-born females. "What causes women to become strays in the first place?"

"They're mostly runaways."

"And how are they reintegrated?" I ventured. I was aware that we were skirting a sensitive topic.

He paused as we approached a road. He looked left and right before herding me across it to the other side. "The first step is to find out where they came from, who their guardian is. Once that's discovered, a team identifies the reason for their wandering. If they ran away like most, they're returned with a cautionary warning. If the issue is more complex, like abandonment, then... well, some women grow old in Gerter House," he finished with a grim clench of his jaw.

That was depressing.

We lapsed into silence as we continued Viggo's route through the city. His eyes were sharp as a hawk's as he glanced around. I noticed the way others responded to his gaze, quickly averting their attention and continuing about their business. Though many of them lingered on me a little longer. Maybe they thought I was a stray who'd been caught.

With Viggo's popularity in fights at night, and his constant appearance around the city during the day, I imagined he was kind of a celebrity here in Patrus. As childish as it was, it made me feel kind of special to be walking with him.

"What made you want to be a warden?" I asked.

"It matched my skillset," he replied shortly.

He was probably wishing I didn't talk this much.

"Like I told you, I fancied myself as a warden back in Matrus," I went on regardless. "Even sneaked to a few defense lessons when I was younger, and when I had the time. Just never got the opportunity to follow through on the dream."

"I've never set foot in Matrus," he replied, "but in Patrus, the novelty soon wears off."

"Why's that?" I asked, recalling Lee's story that Viggo had retired from the force even before his wife had been sentenced.

"It's called life," he replied dryly. "Things lose their shine when you get too close to them."

I sensed there was a deeper resentment over his work as a warden than he was letting on. But I let it go.

"So… you've never visited Matrus, not even once?" I asked.

"The furthest I've ever gotten is its dock."

"And you've never been curious to visit?"

"No."

I blew out. "So… you're working a job you don't like. You apparently live by yourself in the mountains… What's your game plan?" I asked.

"Game plan?"

"What are you working for? What gets you out of bed in the morning?"

"I have obligations," he replied curtly.

"Do you have any family?"

He shook his head. "None to speak of."

"I guess I wonder what motivates you to take on extra work," I dared say. "My husband told me you're also a fighter."

He grimaced. "If you must know, I'm not getting paid for my time as a warden, nor will I for the next two and a half years. I earn my money through fights. As for my 'game plan', once the years are up I plan to buy a larger patch of land, further away from the city."

He was obviously expecting me to ask next why he was acting as a warden without pay. I avoided the subject, since that was too close to his wife for comfort, and I already knew the answer.

"Why do you want to live so far away from everyone?" I asked.

"I just do."

His answers were becoming increasingly short, so I figured I'd give him a break from questions. I didn't want to annoy him too much.

I realized we were nearing the street where I had come to get my hair and nails done, and gone shopping with Lee—the street consisting entirely of women's shops.

As we passed the hairdresser, Viggo asked me a question of his own. "Do you regret coming to Patrus?"

I was surprised not only that he'd asked a question, but also by the directness of it.

"No," I lied. "I mean, it's been difficult leaving behind my old life and entering one so very new, but I don't regret it. It was the only way I could be with Lee."

He went quiet for a few moments before remarking, "You don't strike me as a girl who'd be happy here long-term. It's pretty easy to spot the ones who'll last and those who won't... For women, curiosity isn't a quality that's rewarded here."

"Yes, I know..."

"Hey, Viggo!" a voice chimed from across the road.

Two men were standing there, wardens in long coats and heavy boots. I found it interesting that, although all wardens in Patrus wore a similar style of clothing, there appeared to be no official uniform. Perhaps they used that to their advantage; they could sneak up on unsuspecting suspects more easily.

The men crossed the street and approached us, their eyes glued to me.

"Who's this?" the blond man asked.

"Mr. Bertrand's new wife," Viggo replied. "I've been appointed as her temporary guardian."

They looked rather confused as to how that could have come about, but they didn't ask further questions. One of them retrieved a piece of paper from his pocket and handed it to Viggo.

"Back gate of the lab's code has changed again. Here it is."

Viggo nodded in appreciation.

Then the men parted ways with us, continuing down the road in the opposite direction.

"So do you roam the streets all day?" I asked. "Don't you get tired?"

"No to both questions," he muttered.

"Then?" I cocked my head to one side.

"In about ten minutes, I have an appointment with the owner of an arms store, one of the largest in the city. There was an attempted break-in yesterday—while the store was closed. Nothing was stolen, but I need to examine the site, as well as discuss precautionary methods to put in place to keep it from happening again."

Attempted break-in at an arms store, earlier yesterday.

I wondered, could that have been Lee? The reason for his delay in picking me up from the gym? He'd seemed pretty tense.

"Is there a lot of theft around here?" I asked.

"No," Viggo replied. "The state's punishments are severe. We're talking about dismembered limbs, or in some cases, hanging."

In Matrus, criminals were treated differently—at least, the women were. If a female committed a serious crime, even so far as murdering someone, she was given a second chance. A thorough period in detention facilities, to see if she was capable of and willing to redeem herself. Matrus' men, on the other hand, were not treated with such leniency. If they murdered or plundered, it was immediate euthanasia. Indeed, from a male's very birth they were subject to close scrutiny. They were regularly monitored in their early years for traits that went against Matrus' culture—a domineering temperament, with a strong inclination toward violence and aggression—and between the ages of eight and ten, they were put through the ultimate test to decide whether they were fit to reside in Matrus. The screening employed a combination of genetics and psychology to determine which boys would be forced to leave Matrus and flown off to the mines in the north.

I didn't know what went on during the tests or how exactly they worked. They were usually conducted in the lab near the queen's palace and the details weren't public knowledge.

All I knew was that my brother had come out shaking, and bearing the mark of a black crescent on his right hand. His virtues had been deemed too close to those of Patrus. And of course, the queen and her council didn't want boys like him piling into Patrus. It wasn't in Matrus' interest to help increase their neighbor's population of strong-willed men.

"There isn't much theft in Matrus, either," I told Viggo. "More serious crimes are also rare… Do you know about its justice system?"

Viggo scowled. "'Justice' hardly seems the right word."

I bit my lip. I couldn't exactly argue with that.

"But yes, I'm aware of the ins and outs," he added. "Euthanasia versus hanging, corrective detention for females, jail for males, pseudoscientific screenings, murdering pre-pubescent boys, etcetera, etcetera."

I stalled, my hand shooting to Viggo's arm. "*Murdering?*" I breathed, gripping him hard. "Where did you hear that?"

Viggo rolled his eyes. "Come on, what do you think they do with all those boys? You really believe they're carted off to mines? Do you have any idea how large and organized they'd have to be to contain the increasing number of males, year after year?"

He shrugged me off and continued walking. It felt like a steel ball had materialized in the pit of my stomach.

I dragged my feet forward to keep up with him.

"Do you have any evidence?" I choked. "Any evidence at all? Or is it only a suspicion?"

Viggo was eyeing me curiously now, apparently not prepared for or expecting such a strong reaction from me. "It's a suspicion," he admitted. "Of course, I have never traveled to the Deep North to verify whether the boys are actually there. I don't have access to an illegal aircraft, nor would I have reason or permission to fly there in a legal one."

I let out a breath. I'd truly feared for a moment that Viggo might have evidence. But that would make no sense. Queen Rina had promised me a reunion with my brother. Would she really have lied about that? I didn't want to consider that question. I couldn't start thinking that my brother might be dead. Not after my hopes had been raised sky-high about seeing him again in a matter of weeks. He was alive, in the mines in the North. Just as the queen and the Court said he was.

And yet a niggling doubt still managed to worm its way into my brain. Viggo's words had struck too close to home. On more than one occasion in the past, I, too, had wondered if Matrus could be lying about the boys' destination. The fear had plagued me on and off over the years, but I'd always tried to bury it. After all, how would any of us verify it? All we had to go on was the word of the Court because the only safe way to travel the depths of The Green in order to even have a hope of reaching the elusive North was by aircraft, and flying was illegal for all except the Court.

"What do you think Patrus would do if they had evidence of what you suspect is happening to some of Matrus' boys?" I managed.

Viggo shrugged, his eyes forward again as we turned down another road. "I don't know," he muttered. "Everyone is still trying to understand the mind of our new king... But if his father were still reigning, he probably wouldn't care—unless there was a particular political advantage to be gained by caring, if you understand what I'm saying."

"Not exactly."

"Then never mind," Viggo replied briskly, before pursing his lips.

Would Matrus really have attempted such a mass-scale lie, so confident that nobody would ever find out or let the truth slip? Because if the bubble ever burst, the queen and her courtiers would be decried as hypocrites of the worst kind. What difference would there be between our country and Patrus? We would be considered no better than them, just as prone to corruption, lies and bloody-minded leadership. What role would Matrus' national motto, "Freedom in Peace", play in all this?

Stop thinking.

Matrus wouldn't murder those boys. It's Viggo's biased speculation.

My brother is ALIVE. And I'm going to see him again, if I can just keep my act together.

Being so consumed by our conversation, I had lost track of our surroundings, and noticed we were heading to a large store at the end of the road. Dashner's Arms. The parking lot in front of it was empty. Arriving outside its reinforced entrance, Viggo knocked.

A short, balding man wearing a smart tweed suit opened after a minute and, eyeing me in confusion, he beckoned us inside.

Viggo didn't bother to explain my presence. He simply moved forward with me, following the bald man through a giant warehouse stacked with guns and ammunition, toward a pair of double doors. He opened them up and pointed out a dent against the metal, near the locking mechanism.

Viggo stepped outside into a messy backyard, piled with empty crates and boxes. He inspected the area, walking around the circumference of the yard, looking for what exactly, I wasn't sure. Then he returned to us, his arms crossed over his chest while gazing up the high back wall of the building. "The culprit has left no obvious tracks, but I'll send some colleagues round with dogs later today... I take it you don't have any canines guarding this place, Mr. Crighton?" Viggo asked the bald man.

"No," he replied.

"Then I suggest you get some."

Mr. Crighton nodded.

"I'm also surprised," Viggo went on, "that you don't have a better surveillance system in place. You need more cameras out here." He ran a hand over the dented doors. "And these doors are outdated. You're asking for a burglary without the latest technology."

"Okay, sir," Mr. Crighton replied. He pulled out a pad of paper and began jotting down notes.

Once Viggo finished giving him his analysis on the doors and the yard, we headed back into the building. We ended up spending a while in here—Viggo examined every other exterior door and window. Before we left he also had to commission some new weapons for his division. By the time Viggo was done, it was well into lunchtime.

He returned to where I'd been waiting—in a chair outside Mr. Crighton's office—and reached down a hand for me to take. I couldn't help but notice an odd tingle running down my arm as we touched. It remained for several seconds after he'd pulled me to my feet and let go of me.

Mr. Crighton thanked us and then we left the building, crossed the parking lot, and returned to the road.

"Let's get some lunch," Viggo said.

He stopped with me at the first eatery we passed, a small bakery. When we moved inside, it was empty except for two couples sitting together around a table by the window.

The man behind the glass counter grinned as he looked from me to Viggo.

"Good to see you again, Viggo. It's been a while!" he said. "And who's this? New girl?"

"Mrs. Bertrand," Viggo said tersely, before ordering two large sandwiches. "What do you want?" he asked me beneath his breath.

I opted for a slice of savory pie.

After paying, Viggo carried the tray to a table for two at the back of the bakery. We sat opposite each other—him with his back to the room—and dug into our food.

About halfway through Viggo's sandwiches, the couples by the window rose from their table and made their way over to us.

"Looks like we've got visitors," I whispered as they approached.

Viggo turned.

"Hey, Mr. Croft. I'm sorry to disturb you," one of the men said, eyeing the two of us tentatively, "but I wondered if we could have your autograph?" He held out two white napkins. "We were there at your fight two nights ago. Spectacular performance."

Viggo looked like the last thing he wanted to do was entertain the request, but he acquiesced, if only just to get rid of them quickly. Taking a pen and the tissues from the man, he scribbled his initials on each of the tissues and handed them back.

The men stowed them away appreciatively and Viggo returned to his food. I guessed they were going to leave us alone now, but then the second man said, "I wanted to ask one thing…"

Viggo was once again pulled from his meal.

"Do you ever plan to fight in the big league? You'd smash your way to the top!"

It would probably be physically impossible for Viggo to pull a more unenthusiastic expression. He merely shook his head.

At this, the man backed away, and the group took the cue to leave.

Viggo and I continued eating. Though I couldn't help but ask, "Why?"

Viggo groaned. "Why what?" he snapped.

"Why do you keep yourself at a level you're clearly above?"

He stopped chewing, eyeing me. "What makes you think I'm 'a level above'?"

"Well, it's the way people talk about you. These strangers who just came up to you, and Lee has also mentioned your abilities."

Viggo continued chewing. He waited until he had swallowed a mouthful before answering, "My current level serves its purpose. It pays me the money I need without the lack of privacy... Believe it or not," he added, "there are some things in life that aren't worth giving up for money."

"People already seem to know your name though," I said.

"Exactly," he countered. "And it would be ten times worse if I rose up in the game."

I paused, dragging my knife across the plate, before daring to go on. "I guess to me... it seems a waste. If I had the opportunity, I would go all the way."

His gaze leveled with mine briefly before averting to the table surface. Since he offered no leeway to continue the conversation, I dropped the subject. But I didn't drop thinking about it—my lack of opportunity versus Viggo's lack of desire. I wished in some fantastical twist of events, Patrus would establish a league for female fighters. That would probably be enough to tempt me to stay here permanently or at least try to visit frequently if I could be involved. But Patrus allowing female fighters seemed about as likely as Matrus suddenly halting their weeding out of "high risk" boys.

After Viggo finished his sandwiches, we left the bakery.

In the hours that followed, we didn't talk as much. We passed several other wardens as Viggo roamed the inner city, "making his presence felt," before he began leading me back to his office. He said he had some paperwork to attend to, but we never made it that far.

A sudden buzzing emanated from Viggo's right coat pocket, where he retrieved a phone.

"Okay," he said, his eyes glued to the device. "There's been an incident. An unusual one for this time of day."

Without further explanation, he grabbed my arm and began racing with me toward where he'd left his motorbike. He seated me first before leaping on himself and kicking off down the road.

"What happened?" I gasped as the lurch knocked the breath out of me.

"A kidnapping," Viggo replied.

"Who got kidnapped? By whom?"

"You'll see."

As we careered through the city, a blaring noise erupted from the back of Viggo's motorcycle—a siren. It caused all large obstructing vehicles to quickly clear the roads and let us pass.

As we arrived at the outskirts of the city, I caught sight of six wardens standing around in a huddle on the edge of the road. Viggo stopped next to them and leapt off the bike.

"We recovered her," one of them informed Viggo.

I slid off the bike and followed Viggo, trying to make out exactly what they were all huddled around. Then I heard a low groaning, and a whimpering. It sounded like someone was curled up on the ground. Viggo, who'd pushed his way to the front of the group, was staring downward. I reached for his arm and pulled myself to him, gaining as good a view as him.

Lying on the street was a thin woman wrapped in a lambswool shawl. Her right eye was swollen and bruised, her upper lip cut. The sight made me wince.

"Did you detain him already?" Viggo demanded.

"No," one of the men replied. "He's being pursued as we speak."

"*Where?*" Viggo pressed, his tone bordering on aggressive.

"Southwark Street, moving toward Lumber Avenue. A red car. Keep your phone on loudspeaker."

Viggo stepped away, pulling me back to his motorbike. He touched the screen of his phone before stowing it into his pocket. We both leapt on the motorbike. He pushed away so quickly this time that I didn't have time to find the handles beneath my seat; both nervousness and excitement filled me as I grabbed hold of his firm shoulders and we whizzed off.

Sirens from other warden vehicles blared around us. Reaching a junction, we took a sharp right turn, passed a line of stalled vehicles, and did a U-turn onto a parallel street.

"Brody Street." A voice crackled in Viggo's pocket. "Heading south."

Viggo hit the brakes so hard I almost went flying off the bike. He reversed into a road to our left and roared down it. He showed no signs of stopping at the next junction, but then, in a blur of red and shattering glass, a car came smashing through a shop front and skidded out onto the road directly in front of us. If Viggo hadn't had reflexes fast enough to make another emergency brake, we would have gone crashing right into it.

"Hey!" Viggo shouted. "Stop!"

There were apparently only two men in the vehicle, one in the passenger's seat and one in the driver's. They paid no heed to Viggo's warning and frantically revved the engine to pick up speed and continue driving in the opposite direction.

"Hand me a gun," Viggo called to me over his shoulder. "In my belt."

Reaching my hands through the folds of his trench coat, I felt his belt for a gun and yanked it out. I raised it to him and he took it with one hand. I was tempted to offer to help him, but I was still so new to handling guns, let alone shooting one at a speeding vehicle.

Clutching the motorbike's handle with his left hand, he unleashed bullets at the tires with his right. His aim was sharp. The tires punctured, causing the vehicle to slow.

As we had almost caught up with it, the doors opened and two men leapt out, revealing their full appearance for the first time. They looked unkempt and were dressed in similar rough fashion to the men I'd had a run-in with the night I ended up in the alley in my effort to avoid Cad. And they also had matching tattoos, only they weren't squares on the neck. They were small black triangles etched beneath the right eye. The square and the triangle must have been symbols of two different gangs.

Viggo stopped, leapt off the motorbike and raced after the men. "Stop where you are!"

He shot a bullet into the ankle of the shorter one, causing him to yelp and stumble. Before I could witness the fate of the other, a click sounded just in front of me. The trunk of the car pushed open and out climbed… two more men.

They took one panicked look at me before slipping round the side of the vehicle and darting off in the opposite direction.

I wasn't sure what possessed me, but the next thing I knew, I was darting down the street after them. "Hey!" I yelled.

They shot glances over their shoulders, eyes widening as they realized a woman was on their tail.

"Violet!" Viggo yelled behind me, but I was already turning a corner and chasing the criminals down another road. A dead end, the three of us realized. They stopped short and did a one-eighty, running back in my direction. They obviously thought they could just push past me.

After quickly verifying that their hands were devoid of weapons, I went charging at the nearest one to me. Diving for his knees, I floored him. He thrashed as he landed on his back, attempting to grip my throat. I grappled with him, twisting myself until my legs were in the perfect position to stretch out his arm and trap him in an arm bar. I tugged hard, tightening my hold and straining his ligaments. He grunted in pain.

Footsteps bounded down the street toward us. I glanced up to see Viggo's stunned face.

"There was another one!" I shouted. I hadn't managed to witness where exactly he'd run.

Viggo raised his phone to his ear while he continued to stare at me. "Need backup on Sullivan Street. Three detained criminals by the junction, and another one escaped on foot."

He slid the phone into his pocket before lowering and grabbing the man beneath me. I untwined my legs from the criminal and released him so Viggo could stand him upright, at which point he'd stopped attempting to struggle.

A sense of euphoria filled me, not so different than what I'd felt during my secret gym fight. I'd taken down a criminal—a male criminal, in Patrus. I'd looked him in the eye and shown him that I could match him. I could barely even bring myself to wonder what the consequences of this act might be. I was sure none by the law, since I was under Viggo's watch and guardianship.

Even as we escorted the criminal back to where Viggo must have cuffed and left the others, Viggo remained gazing at me.

"I feel like there's something you're not telling me, Violet," he muttered as we turned the corner.

I feel like there is, too.

CHAPTER 20

As backup arrived, both of us fell quiet. We returned to his motorcycle and headed to the lab, where we found Lee waiting in the parking lot.

Lee's face brightened. "How did everything go?" he asked. He must've been wondering why we were late.

"No doubt your wife will tell you," Viggo said. He nodded his head, his eyes flitting from Lee to me, where they lingered for a few seconds more before he revved his engine and sped away.

After Viggo was out of sight, we mounted Lee's motorcycle. "Why are your clothes torn?" Lee asked.

It was my knees—my pants had gotten frayed. "We, uh, got into an altercation on our way back here. There was an attempted kidnapping. Viggo went chasing after the guys involved and, well, I ended up helping a bit."

"Are you serious?"

"Yes," I said, a tad hesitant in spite of being proud of what I'd done. I wasn't sure how Lee was going to react.

"How did you help?" he asked.

"I tripped up one of the guys. Just held him down until Viggo arrived."

"And how did Viggo react to it?"

"He didn't really say much. I already mentioned to him that I took a few defense lessons in Matrus when I was younger, just like a hobby thing."

"Hm," Lee murmured, looking worried. "Then I guess it worked out okay... But getting involved the way you did was risky. Unnecessarily risky."

"I don't plan to do it again," I assured him, although I would like to, if the opportunity arose. "It was a spur of the moment thing; Viggo had brought me along on his motorcycle anyway, right into the heat of the scene, so helping him hardly seemed like a big extra step."

"Hm," Lee said again.

He went quiet and focused on the road for the rest of the journey. When we arrived back home, we cooked and ate dinner together, and then I retired to bed.

The next day, I awoke to the sound of drilling for the second time since my arrival here. I groaned, sitting up in bed and rubbing my face. *Lee's darn mechanic.*

After brushing my teeth and showering, I headed downstairs to the kitchen to find Lee awake and eating breakfast at the table.

"Viggo called," he said, as I took a seat beside him.

"What did he say?"

"He can't take you today until the afternoon," Lee replied. "He said that he'll pick you up during his lunch hour."

"Oh. Okay." I felt disappointed. This meant that I was going to have to find something to do with myself for the entire morning.

"Also," Lee added, "he's got a later shift tonight, so you can stay with him for that if you want. He said he'll drop you back afterward, say, around half past midnight."

"Okay." *Late night with Viggo.* I couldn't deny that this prospect excited me.

"Mr. Bertrand?" a man's voice called from outside the kitchen.

"Yes, Chris. In here."

A gray-haired man in scruffy blue dungarees arrived in the doorway. He met my eyes briefly with a polite nod, before turning his focus to Lee.

"So looks like I'm done for now," he said. "I trust you'll call me if you detect any problems."

Lee was already standing up and heading to the door.

"Excellent," Lee said, planting a hand on Chris's shoulder and leading him toward the front door. It clicked open and footsteps moved outside.

I fetched myself a bowl of oatmeal before wandering to the window. The two men were talking in the drive. Lee handed Chris a small black pouch, which I assumed contained his payment. They shook hands, and then Chris left through the gate.

I continued gazing out the window as Lee returned to the kitchen. It was a beautiful morning.

"So, what are your plans for today?" I asked Lee.

"I've got to go out again," he said. "I need to leave in five minutes."

He swallowed down the rest of his food before dumping his plate in the sink and heading to the entrance hall. "I'll see you later this evening," he called, before shutting the door behind him.

Okay...

And thus began my wait.

I ended up actively seeking out Samuel—who had been lazing around in the sun outside in the back garden—and recruited him for a game. I couldn't help but be entertained by the enthusiasm he showed for his ball.

But I was getting tired of playing with him in this confined backyard. He'd probably appreciate a change of scenery, too.

I gazed around at the trees enclosing the garden. Beyond the back fence was a road—you could hear the occasional car driving by. That was the same road we'd taken when we'd traveled to Viggo's cabin.

Most men were at work during the day, according to Lee. And women weren't allowed out. I couldn't imagine that there would be many people roaming these mountain roads. And if I wore my disguise…

Although I knew it would make Lee uncomfortable, I decided to head out anyway. I wouldn't go far. I would stay within ten minutes of the house in case I had to run back for some reason. But it would give my head some space and help make the time pass more quickly.

I changed into the male costume before returning downstairs to Samuel. I put on his leash and, grabbing a set of spare keys, headed out. Samuel didn't seem to notice that I was a different person to the one I had been just a few minutes ago. His tail wagged excitedly as we crossed the drive and slipped out of the gate.

We took a right and began strolling up the pretty mountain road, past the crystal-clear stream that ran nearby. I peered into each driveway as we passed, glimpsing the triangular-shaped buildings identical to Lee's.

Turning a corner, I felt the stretch in my calf muscles as we began to ascend a steeper slope.

What I would have really liked, in that moment, was to get away from everyone. Escape into nowhere, like Viggo wanted to do. I wished there was a footpath leading off into nature, away from all man-made constructions and other signs of civilization. But the only path was this road.

Samuel jerked forward, almost making me lose balance. He had spotted a squirrel scurrying across the road.

Gripping his leash more tightly, I reined him in.

We had walked more than ten minutes away from the front of Lee's drive by now. Probably more like fifteen or twenty minutes. My shirt had started to cling to my lower back. The morning sun, pleasantly mild against my skin when we had stepped out, was beginning to feel uncomfortable.

I sighed. We should probably head back now.

"Come on, boy," I said, tugging on Samuel and herding him back down the mountain.

But as we reached the corner and were about to wind our way back around it, the sound of a woman screaming made me stop still.

It had come from somewhere behind me… the house behind me. Number thirty-two.

Then it came again. Another scream. It drifted through one of the open downstairs windows.

"Stop it!" the shaking female voice cried. "Stop!" It grew more ragged, more desperate. "Don't pick that up!"

I heard the sound of smashing porcelain. There was a cry of pain, followed by a door slamming. Then all went quiet.

Barely breathing, I felt my consciousness return to the sunny world around me. To Samuel, tugging at me impatiently. But I remained staring at the house. The silence was more disconcerting than the screaming.

Viggo couldn't arrive soon enough.

Feeling shaken, I returned to the house with Samuel and waited indoors for the rest of the morning and early afternoon. Viggo ended up arriving just before three p.m., later than I had been expecting him.

I had been waiting near the window overlooking the front of the house and as soon as he pulled up on his motorbike, I hurried outside to meet him.

The first thing I did was inform him of what I had witnessed earlier at number thirty-two.

"You need to go and investigate," I concluded.

Inhaling, he ran a hand over his face before saying, "I can't."

"What? Why not?"

"That's not how things work here. Wardens can't just go barging into citizens' private homes like that. The first thing I would have to do is file a report at head office, prompting one of our people to summon the man for an interview. He would be asked questions about what was going on that afternoon, and if it is different from your report—i.e., if he denied anything happened—then they would move on to the woman for questioning to get to the bottom of it. However, because you are a woman, none of this can happen. Women can't be witnesses... especially not women who were out roaming illegally by themselves at the time."

His gaze sharpened.

I pursed my lips.

Lee was at work, so of course, Viggo knew that I would've gone by myself. Perhaps I had allowed myself to get a little too comfortable around Viggo already in assuming that he wouldn't report me.

"What would be required in order to launch an investigation," he went on, "would be for a man to witness the noises. Then something could possibly be done about it."

I sighed heavily. "Okay."

I felt his eyes on me as I looked down at my feet. Then he said, "Hop on," apparently choosing to turn a blind eye to my disobedient wandering after all.

I climbed on to the bike behind him and this time didn't bother gripping the handle beneath my seat for support. Instead I held Viggo as I'd done for the first time the day before, since it was more comfortable.

"Could we just drive past there now?" I ventured. "Number thirty-two. Maybe the cries will have started again."

"Okay." We pulled out of the driveway and took a right, further up the mountain.

We stopped outside the house and waited beneath the shade of a willow tree… But nothing happened. After five minutes of waiting in silence, Viggo started the engine again and we rode back down the mountain.

"So what if a woman witnessed a murder?" I posed, mulling over this particularly absurd rule. Men had a lot of disadvantages in Matrus, some arguably worse than the women in Patrus. But this particular law grated on my nerves. "If she actually witnessed, for example, one man attacking another man. Hacking his head off. Are you telling me she wouldn't be able to testify in court? That nobody would take her seriously?"

"She would need to have gained solid evidence somehow," Viggo said. "Like a videotape or an audio recording. But you are correct, her word alone would not be enough."

I exhaled in frustration. "*Why?*"

"You could ask that question about a lot of things," Viggo muttered.

He was right. I was asking the question more out of frustration than anything else. Not only would a male have to witness the noises, but he'd also have to be willing to testify. The idea that whatever was happening behind that door could continue happening indefinitely disturbed me to no end. I had been half-tempted to barge in there myself while in my costume—or rather, knock on the door—if only to disrupt whatever suffering that woman was going through.

But I guessed that this was just another thing that was best not to think about. Trying to make sense of rules that didn't make sense was rather a losing proposition.

That didn't stop me wondering whether things might change someday. Whether some queen and king might eventually ascend to the two nations' thrones and put an end to rules like this. Though I knew it was a dream. We had lived like this for centuries and it seemed that, as the years passed, both governments were only coming up with more enforcements to keep us ingrained in our ways. I didn't see why anything would change.

At least not in my lifetime.

Viggo parked outside Head Office. I followed him as he swept up the granite stairs, through the steel-gray reception room, and headed directly for an elevator. He punched the button for the sixth—and highest—floor. The doors shuddered and pulled closed. The cables creaked as we ascended and we listened to the sound of each other's breathing until the doors dinged open.

Viggo stepped out into an empty corridor and led me down to a room at the very end of it, a large room with windows that spanned the length of an entire wall. Drawn to the windows, I stared out at the view of Crescent River, the city on one side and the palace on the other. We still weren't high enough for me to be able to see beyond the walls of the palace, though it was the closest I'd ever gotten to the building. I gazed at the windows, and spotted the occasional shadow moving behind them.

I remained standing while Viggo took a seat behind his table and began sifting through a pile of papers. I gazed outside a while longer before joining him. Pulling up a chair opposite him, I took a seat.

I picked up a shiny black pen from a holder and tapped it against the table surface while my feet fidgeted.

"Anything I can help with?" I wondered.

"Nope," he said, not looking up.

I leaned back in my chair, stretching out my arms. Then I took another turn about the room.

"What sort of money do you get paid as a warden… assuming you were getting paid?"

He glanced up at me, raising a brow.

"What?" I asked.

He shook his head and returned his eyes to the papers. "That's not a question you should make a habit of asking around here," he said. "It's not considered appropriate for a woman to ask a man about his earnings."

I narrowed my eyes on him. "So you're not going to tell me?"

The shadow of a smile crossed his lips. Viggo's rebel smile. "If you really want to know, it works out to about four ounces of gold per month."

"And that's considered, like, good pay?" I asked.

"It's, uh, about the highest pay you can expect to receive as a warden."

"I see…" Admittedly, his answer didn't mean a lot to me. I'd never really had a chance to earn income. I'd been locked away too early in my youth. I just remembered getting the occasional silver piece thrown my way by Ms. Connolly when I'd done chores around the orphanage. I'd stored it in a tin box I hid beneath my bed. I wasn't even sure where that was now.

"So you earn double that as a fighter," I went on, leaning against the desk and gazing down at his papers.

"Yeah."

"Hm." I sank back into my chair. Removing my shoes, I lifted my legs and laid my feet to rest on the table.

Viggo looked up again.

"What?" I asked, feigning innocence. "Is this not considered ladylike either?"

At this he chuckled, shaking his head in mild disdain.

Well, I was comfortable like this, and Viggo didn't *actually* mind, so I kept my feet where they were.

In spite of the warden's hardened and usually brooding demeanor, I picked up on a leeway with him that I doubted existed in many other men here. The only way I could think to explain it was the fact that he had been married to a Matrian girl. Marrying her must say quite a lot about him. That he liked a woman who could think for herself. A woman who could challenge him. One whose nature wasn't to be a doormat.

"Do you have any friends?" I found myself asking, interrupting his work again.

"Depends on what you define as a 'friend'," he replied.

"Well, someone you can trust, I guess. Someone you feel comfortable around. Someone you know has your back."

There was a beat before he answered, "Does that really matter to you?"

I shrugged. "Nope."

He clenched his jaw. "Then I'll ask you to keep quiet while I finish this paperwork."

I stopped annoying Viggo at his request. I moved to the window and sat down cross-legged on the floor. I gazed out at the city and what I could see of the palace for the next half hour. When I got bored with that, I took the liberty of helping myself to a few spare sheets of paper and a pen. Resuming my position by the window, I sketched the city out of boredom until Viggo announced that he was done.

As we headed out of the building and returned to Viggo's motorbike, the sun was on the verge of setting. He stuffed a couple of papers he had carried with him from the office into the compartment beneath the seat before retrieving two guns and stowing them into his belt. He covered them with his trench coat and then set his sights on the parking lot exit.

"We'll walk from here," he said. "There's a major fight on tonight. A 'big league' fight," he added, using air quotes. "So there may be some accompanying rowdiness."

"Where does the fight take place?" I asked, thinking back to Lee's scientist friends' conversation outside the restaurant. I didn't recall them mentioning the venue.

"Starkrum Stadium. We'll head there now."

We headed to the river bank and walked along the promenade before turning into a street and winding our way toward a giant dome-shaped building. Its walls were white, and at its base was a long set of glass doors, outside of which was a square where a crowd of people had already gathered to wait in line.

"*Rosen versus Cruz*" was the headline fight, according to the poster that hung above the entrances.

"How often are there big events like this?" I asked Viggo, my eyes running over the long line of people.

"Sometimes as many as five in a month," he said.

Approaching the building, Viggo led me around its wall, away from the crowd. We stopped outside a back entrance, a single, solid metal door. Viggo pressed a button on the intercom board and a voice crackled through it a few seconds later.

"Your name, please?"

"Croft."

"Okay. Come on in, sir."

The door clicked open and we moved inside. A staircase stood directly in front of us, which took us up to the first floor of the stadium. Surrounding us on either side were row upon row of red seats. I wasn't even sure how to start guessing how many were in here. The stadium held seven such levels altogether.

We moved to the barrier and gazed down toward the center of the building, where a huge cage was fixed. Employees in blue shirts ran about the floors like mice, scurrying to make final preparations before the doors opened. There were food vendors set up strategically, causing a scent of frying oil and fresh bread to pervade the arena.

According to the poster I'd spied outside, the fight was due to start in about fifty minutes. So I guessed that meant people should start being allowed in right about now...

Sure enough, the sound of heavy doors drawing open drifted up from downstairs, followed by thundering footsteps and chattering. There were large groups of men, but also a fair number of couples and families.

I remembered I had to be careful not to make myself too visible, in case Cad was here. I reached into my jacket pocket, where I found the cap I'd been wearing earlier while in my manly disguise. I pulled my hair into a bun before placing the hat on my head and tucking my hair beneath it. Then I lowered the cap so that it shaded my eyes.

Viggo noticed, and gave me an inquisitive look. I didn't need to explain my every action. I let him go on wondering...

He soon repositioned us so that we stood directly opposite the main entrance. I imagined he looked quite intimidating from the ground, in such clear view of everybody entering… this big, towering figure, face stern, eyes sharp, like some kind of presiding deity of the cage.

After about half an hour, Viggo moved us again. He led me down to the ground floor, where he moved with purpose, his eyes fixed in one corner of the room, near the men's restrooms. The next thing I knew, he was running forward toward a bearded man in a faded brown coat, who also suddenly sped up.

The man yelped as Viggo's hand closed around the back of his neck and shoved him up against the wall. Viggo's hand dove into the man's right coat pocket where he pulled out a black wallet.

"I don't think this belongs to you, does it?" Viggo asked, his voice dangerously low. He opened up the wallet, revealing cash and an identity card which, indeed, pictured an entirely different man.

The thief's eyes bulged.

Retaining his grip on the man, Viggo pulled him away from the bathrooms and back toward the exit. Two other wardens were waiting outside the doors. Viggo shoved the thief toward one of the wardens and said, "Thief." He held up the wallet. "Take him downtown."

The warden nodded grimly before taking charge of the man.

Viggo returned with me to the building and headed straight to the front row, where he stopped in front of the man who matched the photo in the wallet. Viggo cleared his throat to get his attention.

"Oh!" the man said, leaping to his feet and patting down his coat disbelievingly. He took the wallet. "I didn't even realize it was missing. Thank you, sir!"

Viggo nodded curtly before turning away and heading back down the aisle to stand at the end of it, where he continued his perusal of the room. Dozens of people eyed Viggo and whispered among themselves, obviously having recognized him. This made me feel even more so that Viggo's excuse for not fulfilling his full potential as a fighter was a load of bull. He was already recognized practically everywhere he went. I couldn't imagine that moving up a league would make that much of a difference in his life when he was already used to being spotted and stared at. There was a deeper reason for Viggo's reluctance to fight, but I knew better than to bring up the subject again.

I turned my thoughts back to the thief. I hated to imagine what lay in store for him. One thing was certain, he wouldn't be going pickpocketing again in a hurry.

Finally, the main doors closed. The lights dimmed, and the spotlights shone down on the cage in the center, as well as two aisles on either side of the stadium where, presumably, the fighters were soon to emerge. Large magnifying screens that I hadn't even noticed before lit up around the arena.

Stirring music blasted from speakers and the screens mirrored the two brightly lit, yet still empty corners of the stadium. Not empty for long though. The first fighter, Rosen, stepped out to a round of cheers. He was dark-haired, six feet tall, and wearing bright red shorts. He beat his fists together, protected by stiff fingerless gloves. He stalked down the aisle, climbed into the cage, and bounced around, flexing his jaw and baring his tooth guard as he waited for his opponent.

Next was Cruz's entrance, to a much lesser welcome than Rosen. Half the crowd booed as he made his way down to the cage. His skin was tanned, and he was also about six feet tall. As the two fighters leveled with each other in the cage and the fight began, I looked discreetly in Viggo's direction. His jaw was set firmly, his expression stoic as he watched the fight begin. Though his eyes still roamed the audience, he was obviously interested in watching the fight.

I wondered what he was thinking. Not even the slightest bit of longing? Of reconsideration?

Who knew? His expression wasn't letting on, so I resumed my focus on the fight.

Cruz, the underdog, was already proving himself to be a very worthy opponent. As the first round progressed, he dominated at every turn, sending Rosen spiraling into defense mode. I found myself clenching my fists as I yelled out instructions to the losing fighter (in my mind). *Come on, get out of the corner! Watch his leg! No! He's going to—*

At the beginning of the second round, Cruz took Rosen down, where they began grappling.

I became so wrapped up in the fight, I only realized Viggo had been closely watching me at the end of the second round. As our eyes met, I felt an odd flurry in my chest. It was the idea of him taking interest in me enough to study me, when until now, his general instinct had been to look anywhere but at me.

His expression was curious, with a hint of amusement, his olive eyes reflecting the bright lights. "You really like all this, don't you?"

I nodded, grinning in spite of myself.

He went quiet as the third round began—Cruz still dominating—though I couldn't help but keep glancing at Viggo to see if he was still watching me. He stopped, or at least, didn't get caught by me again.

By the end of the fourth round, Cruz scored a knockout. The stadium erupted in cheers, claps and whistles. Cruz had won himself some new fans.

"Do you want a drink?" Viggo asked me, flexing his shoulders.

"Yeah," I said. The atmosphere was hot and tense.

We moved over to one of the food stalls, where the vendor handed Viggo two bottles of water, free of charge. A perk of being a warden here tonight, apparently.

The water was deliciously cool as it glided down my throat. I breathed out in satisfaction as I downed the whole bottle in less than a minute. I scrunched it up in my hand and aimed it at a trash can. Viggo was slower in finishing his bottle. Now that everyone had a break before the next contenders entered the cage, he was alert again to monitor the crowd.

I joined him in examining the audience… and that was when I noticed a child. A girl wandering down one of the aisles by herself. She looked no older than five. Her blonde hair in bunches, she was clutching a stuffed bear to her chest and looking quite frightened as she gazed around.

I nudged Viggo with my elbow, drawing his attention to the girl as I began to move toward her.

Approaching, I bent down to her level before Viggo could, as I figured she'd take my advance better than his. "You okay?" I asked. "Where are your parents?"

The corners of her lips turned downward at my question, tears filling her eyes. She shook her head, clueless.

"Okay," I said, picking her up. "Come with us."

"We'll have an announcement made," Viggo said, leading me down the aisle. We circled the outskirts of the ground level until we arrived at a wide desk, behind which sat two men in smart black suits.

One of them picked up a microphone and made an announcement for the child, his voice filling the entire stadium. About three minutes later, a young couple came racing toward us, their faces glowing with relief.

The mother, a pretty blue-eyed blonde, looked at me with gratitude as I handed her the child.

"Thank you!" she breathed, before the three of them headed back to the seats.

I could guess what she must have been feeling because I knew what it was like to lose a child.

Five minutes later, another announcement was made for the commencement of the next fight. Everybody settled down and Viggo and I resumed our previous watching position, near the glass doors.

By the time the last fight was over, it was deep into the night. I wondered if Lee had intended for me to stay out this late. He had said that I could stay on with Viggo, though, so I guessed that he must have been aware of how long these events could last

I had a spare key in my pants pocket, anyway, so I wouldn't need to wake him in case he had fallen asleep.

Nothing else noteworthy had happened in Viggo's policing department since we'd spotted the lost child. The two of us waited by the doors until the crowd had piled out and we were alone in the arena except for a few employees tidying up. All the other wardens had left already.

Viggo sighed, his eyes raking over the seats on the ground floor one last time, before turning to face the main entrance. "We're done," he said.

His green eyes were glassy and he looked tired. I pitied him. He not only had to drive me back to Lee's, but then he had his own journey to make to his cabin in the mountains.

I wondered if on nights like this he ever regretted insisting on living so far away from everyone.

We left the stadium and emerged in the square. It was still busy out here. The crowds were dallying, standing, and talking excitedly about the fight, while others were piling into eateries that lined the adjoining street.

As we crossed the open plaza, a trio of men caught my eye. They were sitting squarely in front of the stadium's entrance, on one of the benches. They wore boots and their general scruffy demeanor reminded me of the men we'd chased yesterday. On examining them closer, I realized that they even had the same triangular tattoos beneath their right eye.

And they were staring right at me.

As they rose to their feet, I tugged on Viggo's coat sleeve. I tried to point them out to him discreetly, which was difficult, considering their focus was zoomed in on me.

"Those guys," I whispered, raising myself on my tiptoes to get closer to Viggo's ear while turning my back on them. "You see their tattoos? They're from the same gang who was involved in the kidnapping yesterday."

"Yes," Viggo said and stopped still to meet their gaze. His fists clenched and then he began walking toward them, with me trailing along after him.

He cleared his throat as we approached. "Evening, *gentlemen*," he said tersely. "What might you be staring at?"

It was unsettling that their attention remained on me, even as Viggo addressed them. *Why me? What's so interesting about me?*

Their focus ought to be solely on Viggo, and getting the hell out of here before getting themselves into trouble with him.

"Something wrong?" Viggo pressed.

The man in the middle with scraggly black hair looked steadily back at Viggo, not appearing the slightest bit intimidated.

"Is there a problem?" he asked coolly. "Is it a crime to sit here?"

"No," Viggo replied. His eyes raked over their tattoos. "But considering that you belong to the same gang as your friends who were arrested yesterday, I suggest you not get too cocky around here…" Viggo's glare intensified. "Know what I'm saying?"

"Not sure what you mean by 'gang,' sir," he replied. "You have no evidence that we belong to anything."

Viggo didn't bother arguing with him. These guys were gutsy. Used to living on the edge of the law, pushing its borders as hard as they could.

All three men's focus returned to me once more, their eyes dark and threatening, before they stalked off.

Viggo drew in a shallow breath as they turned down an alleyway. Then he glanced down at me, a slight look of concern in his eyes… Concern which, in turn, unsettled me.

"Why didn't you, like, arrest them or something?" I asked. "Isn't the tattoo evidence enough that they belong to the same gang?"

"It's not solid enough evidence. I can't simply arrest someone for having a tattoo. Or sitting and staring."

"So you're just letting them go," I murmured. "Letting them wander off into the city…"

"You seem to forget that I don't make the rules around here," Viggo reminded me pointedly.

"And why were they looking at me?"

"We can only speculate, can't we?" he said, before closing his hand around my wrist and leading me away from the square. We headed to the street that led back to the promenade. "We didn't manage to catch that guy who ran away," Viggo explained. "The escapee likely told his friends about the wardens who got involved in the kidnapping—and no doubt also mentioned you. It's not every day that a woman takes down a man in an arrest. In fact, I bet it's never happened in all of this nation's history—at least, certainly not the way you did it."

His grip tightened on me as we entered the crowded street, as if afraid I might slip away somehow. He remained holding me just as firmly until we had left the bustling promenade and returned to the parking lot where he had left his motorbike.

He opened up his seat and lowered his guns into the compartment.

"So…" I blew out, leaning against one of the bike's handles. "What's happening tomorrow then? Will I see you in the morning?"

He shook his head. He refastened the seat lid before meeting my eyes. "No. I have a day off tomorrow."

"A day off, huh? I guess that means you'll be fighting then?" I recalled a fight noted in the schedule I'd peeked at in his gym, but since he had already told me he spent his spare time in fights, this was hardly an amazing guess on my part.

"Yes, actually," he said. "I'll be at training throughout the day and then in the evening, I have a fight."

"Where?"

"Brunswick Arena."

Same small place as last time.

"I see." I wet my lower lip. An awkward span of silence descended between us. Suddenly neither of us were sure what to say—or, apparently, do—next. We stood, just looking at each other. Then, with equal awkwardness, we started speaking at once.

"I would—"

"You could—"

We both stalled, sharing a smirk.

"Ladies first," Viggo said, his eyes warming with his expression.

"I was just going to say that I, um, wouldn't mind tagging along with you tomorrow, if *you* don't mind."

He glanced down at his hands. "Yeah, I, uh… Seeing that you like fights so much, I was gonna say you could come to see my fight in the evening. If you wanted to. I could pick you up at about seven."

My smile broadened. *It's a date.*

CHAPTER 21

Viggo sped me back to Lee's home and stayed on his bike watching as I approached the house and made sure that I got inside okay.

Lee was still awake. He opened the door, emerging in his pajamas and carrying a mug of tea. I turned back toward Viggo to wave that he could go, but he was already riding off.

"How did the day go?" Lee asked. We headed to the kitchen. "You hungry?"

"No, thanks. And it went fine. Not much happened. Viggo had work to do in his office, then we headed to the Rosen-Cruz fight. We stayed until the end of the event and then he brought me straight back." I poured myself a glass of water before sinking into a chair opposite Lee. "Oh, and he's off work tomorrow," I added. "But he's invited me to attend his fight in the evening. Said he'd come to pick me up around seven. He's going to get there a bit early."

"Brunswick?" Lee asked.

"Yeah."

"Hm." He sipped from his mug.

"What?" I'd been expecting him to say something encouraging, like it was a good idea that I had accepted the invitation. I was supposed to be getting close to Viggo.

"Nothing," he said. He gave me a furtive glance. "I just, um... I don't want you to get carried away with this task."

"Carried away? What are you talking about?"

He sighed. "I just mean, keep sight of the goal... why you're seeing him in the first place."

My throat tightened. The "goal" in regards to Viggo was something I had to forget. Lee didn't understand. For my, my brother's, Lee's and Matrus' sake, I had to bury our plan for Viggo deep. Otherwise I couldn't do what was required of me.

"As long as you keep that goal in mind," Lee went on, "you'll automatically do and say the right things, and everything will run smoothly."

I nodded, though I knew I couldn't do what he was asking of me. I would pull this off in my own way. I knew myself and how I worked better than him.

I needed to change the subject.

"So what have you been up to?" I asked him.

"Preparing the site," Lee replied, rubbing his forehead. He looked exhausted. "It's not a simple process. A bunch of hoops to jump through, and each step has to be carried out gradually, slowly, and steadily, so that I don't cause suspicion in anyone. The attendees have been almost confirmed, also… even King Maxen might make an appearance this year… There will be a lot of moving pieces when the night finally arrives. A lot of moving pieces indeed."

I nodded briefly again before getting to my feet. "Yeah. Well, I'm going to bed."

"Good night, Violet," Lee said, looking up and offering me a small smile as I moved past him. A smile I couldn't quite bring myself to return right now.

I just wanted to shut myself in my room, throw myself into bed, and lose myself in sleep…

I slept in late. By the time I came downstairs, Lee had left already for the city. I had another empty day ahead of me before this evening.

I didn't want to risk taking Samuel out again. I had already pushed the law enough since arriving here. So, I found myself heading up to Lee's room. I sat in front of his computer, which had been left unlocked, then navigated to the map of Patrus and stared at the five red moving dots. I could guess which one Viggo was—he was already at his gym. I wondered what he was practicing now. Whether he even had a trainer, or if he always prepared for fights on his own. Then I found myself watching the other four dots and wondering who those people were. One of them was roaming the outskirts of the city, while the other three were near the city center, the latter, like Viggo, pretty stationary.

I lost track of how much time I spent sitting in Lee's bedroom. But as afternoon bled into early evening, I returned to the garden, a pile of psychology books tucked beneath one arm. My attempts to focus on reading were shattered, however, when… I heard it again—a woman's cry, coming from the other side of Lee's back yard fence. Number thirty-two.

Dropping my book, I hurried to the fence and listened, trying to catch the words that the upset woman was speaking. I was too far away to hear them. Her speech was muffled.

I ran back inside the house to the kitchen and looked up at the clock. Ten minutes to seven. Viggo should be arriving anytime now and then we could dash around the corner and he could witness the noise for himself. But, fearing it would stop again before Viggo got here, I began looking for some kind of recording device or a camera. I rummaged through all of Lee's cupboards but failed to find anything I could use. *Dammit. I should have asked Lee if he had a camera.* But then I heard a roaring engine entering the front drive of the house.

Viggo had arrived.

I thundered down the stairs and, grabbing a set of spare keys, raced out to him. He smiled faintly on seeing me, but his expression soon turned to surprise as I dashed toward him like I was being chased.

"Number thirty-two!" I hissed. "It's started again…" I went quiet, straining to hear. Yes, I could make it out from the front yard, although it was very faint.

"Let's get closer," Viggo said. "Get on the bike."

I climbed onto the seat behind him. Wrapping my arms around his waist, he tore up the road and stopped on the sidewalk opposite the house.

We got off the motorbike and moved by foot to the other side of the road, where we ducked down beneath a line of bushes. We held our breath, listening as the noise continued. More smashing had started. More pleas. Our faces inches apart, our eyes locked as we concentrated.

"Okay," Viggo said after a minute. "I've heard enough. First thing tomorrow morning, I'll lodge a complaint and have a colleague take the man in for questioning."

"Good," I said, breathing out in relief. Hopefully whatever was going on in there would be stopped sooner rather than later.

"You know, Violet," Viggo said as we began rolling back down the mountain, "you *should* have become a warden."

Arriving at the Brunswick Arena, we descended to the basement and headed through one of the doors at the back of the auditorium. We passed down a narrow corridor and turned through another door into a small rectangular changing room equipped with a punching bag, a bench, a locker, towels, and other items of clothing. I also spotted a second door which led into an adjoined bathroom.

Viggo dumped his bag on the bench before sliding off his coat. Turning his back on me, he removed his black t-shirt. My eyes roamed his chiseled back, watching his muscles ripple as he rummaged in his bag for a pair of black shorts—the same pair he'd worn to his previous fight. He scooped up a towel and moved to the bathroom. "Taking a shower," he grunted. "Helps clear my head before a fight."

Viggo spent twenty minutes in the bathroom before emerging. His hair went straight and almost black when it was wet. The darkness of it somehow accentuated the sharpness of his eyes. His standing there damp and bare-chested made him look like some kind of wild, rugged warrior… and more attractive than I'd ever seen him.

He reached into a pocket at the side of his bag and pulled out a hair tie, fastening his long hair back. Then he pulled out a roll of bandage from his bag and began wrapping it around his knuckles. He used tape to tighten it before standing up and approaching the punching bag. He began to hit it, his punches gradually building in power, until the bag was swinging all over the place, hardly able to catch a break.

"Why don't you wear those thicker, tougher fingerless gloves I've seen the other fighters wear?" I asked him. "Why only bandages? Aren't you more likely to get injured?"

"Yes," he replied. "But it's standard at my level of fighting."

That made no sense to me. "What do you mean?"

"It's what the crowd is used to watching at sub-level. A portion of them prefer sub-level fights for this reason; it's less regulated. More danger involved without hard gloves. More pain."

"Sounds grim," I muttered.

He chose not to comment.

My eyes wandered again around the room. I noticed a pair of flat, cushioned gloves hanging from a hook near the locker. They were apparently designed for a trainer to catch punches. I reached for them and slid them on absentmindedly, as I flexed my wrists.

"Hey," I said, standing and raising my gloved hands. "Want to have a go at punching me instead?"

He paused and turned to me, his expression quickly turning incredulous.

"Why not?" I asked. "Nobody's watching."

He merely shook his head before resuming his focus on the punching bag.

I quirked a brow. "You don't think I can handle it?"

He didn't stop punching to face me this time as he replied through sharp breaths, "I can't throw a punch at a woman."

Hm.

I'd wanted to attempt to recreate the feeling I'd experienced in my gym sparring match with Viggo. But it seemed that wasn't going to happen.

Not wanting to be pushy, I sat down again, glaring at my gloves. Still, I couldn't help but inform him, "I've fought girls as strong as men before." My mind turned back to Dina. Not as strong as Viggo, of course, but he didn't need to know that.

"It doesn't matter how strong you are," Viggo breathed. "I saw how you took down that guy in the street. I know you're skilled. But if you asked me to punch you, it wouldn't be a punch. It would be a nudge, a light jab at the most."

He worked himself up into another flurry of punches until he appeared to be satisfied that he'd warmed up enough. He backed away from the punching bag, tightening his bandages.

"Okay. How about I punch you? " It wouldn't be the same as in the gym, but it would be better than nothing.

Viggo smirked. "That I could allow…"

I rose to my feet, removing the training gloves from my hands and handing them to him. But, on taking them from me, he discarded them on the floor. Apparently, he was going to use his bare palms as my target. *Suit yourself.*

He dipped into his bag and retrieved the roll of bandage. He moved to me, reaching for my hands, but I shook my head. "Come on," I said, rolling my eyes. "We're only going to be at it for a few minutes. You're gonna have to leave for the fight soon."

Still, he looked reluctant. "And what will I tell your husband if you go home to him with bruised knuckles? I already returned you once with grazed knees."

"My knuckles aren't made of flower petals," I replied.

He hesitated a moment more before resuming his position in front of me. "All right," he said, the corners of his mouth twitching in a half smile. He raised a daring brow. "We've got ten minutes. Have at me."

A rush ran through my body as I clenched my fists. Although he wouldn't see me eye to eye, Viggo was still a dream sparring partner. I had been one of the toughest girls in my defense classes; a lot of the other girls couldn't take blows as hard as I could throw them and I'd often ended up partnered with Ms. Dale for that reason. But with Viggo… I didn't have to hold back. He could take anything I threw at him. Plus, I didn't have any facial hair to worry about keeping in place.

I approached him, aiming my first swipe at his right palm, which was rock hard. But the contact felt good. Like scratching an itch. I threw a punch at his left palm, then right again, before moving on to a kicking combination. As my right foot rose to his stomach, he blocked it—firmly enough that I didn't reach him, but not hard enough to cause a bruise.

When I moved to punch him again, he surprised me by catching my wrist. He spun me around, my back against his chest, where he held me in a firm lock. I hadn't expected him to elevate the game. I supposed this was as close as he was going to get in treating me equally in terms of fighting.

Having been trained to get out of this kind of hold before, my next move was wired in my brain. It came as mere instinct for my right leg to slip backward and jerk forward. I caught him at the back of his right knee. He hadn't been expecting that, either. He lost balance, causing the two of us to tumble to the floor. I quickly scrambled to gain an advantage while he lay on his back. Gripping his arms and pressing them hard against the floor, I straddled his hips. I leaned over, my face leveling with his. As our eyes met, we both broke out in a tense laugh.

"Surrender?" I asked him.

I felt his stomach muscles tauten against my thighs. He narrowed his eyes. "Is that what you think this is?"

I didn't get a chance to respond, or see what he'd do next, as a sharp rapping at the door brought reality spiraling back.

Viggo cursed. I leapt off him and he stood up just in time before the door swung open.

Being in Patrus, there wouldn't have been an awful lot of ways a married woman and an unmarried man could have explained that position.

Catching my breath, I smoothed down my top and tried to pretend I'd just risen from the bench when a white-haired man poked his head through the doorway. Surprise registered in his eyes on seeing me here, but he quickly focused on Viggo.

"You're on in twenty-five minutes," he said.

"Yes, I know," Viggo said tightly. I could see he was trying to steady his breathing too. And was there a slight flush to his cheeks? It felt like there might be to mine.

"Good, good." With one last glance toward me, the man backed out of the room.

My cheeks definitely heated as Viggo and I were left alone again. That had been close. I coughed my throat clear and sat back down on the bench. Viggo didn't start punching the bag again. Avoiding eye contact, he moved into the bathroom, where he splashed his face with water and stood in front of the mirror for a while. Then he returned to the room and paced up and down.

I watched him while his focus was on the floor and wondered whether nerves ever bothered a man like Viggo Croft after all the fights he had experienced.

"Have you ever lost a fight?" I asked him. That might not have been the most sensitive question to ask a fighter minutes before he was due to step inside the cage, but Viggo didn't strike me as the superstitious type.

He shook his head.

A grin returned to my face. "Then let's not make tonight a first."

Finally, he looked at me again. His expression was dark, though I sensed a smile hiding somewhere behind it. "I don't intend to."

The next few minutes slipped through our fingers like sand. A round of boos echoed down the corridor. Viggo's opponent must have entered the arena. And then the elderly man was at the door again.

"Time to roll!" he announced excitedly.

I stood up and followed Viggo and the man out of the room. Viggo was my guardian, and even though he'd be in the cage, I was supposed to follow him as closely as possible. When we headed down the corridor, however, and reached the wide-open door to the arena, I had to hang back with the elderly man while Viggo stepped into the spotlight. The audience exploded. I caught Viggo drawing in a light breath before stalking down the aisle. The spotlight followed him, and I was able to move closer to the darkened doorway without worrying about being spotted. Viggo climbed into the cage opposite his opponent—a guy with ebony skin and cropped black hair. Going by appearance alone, they looked a very even match, Viggo perhaps slightly at a disadvantage—his opponent was a little taller.

"May I ask who you are, ma'am?" the white-haired man, who was still standing opposite me by the doorway, asked.

"Mrs. Bertrand," I replied quickly, my eyes reverting to the fight. I didn't want to miss any of it.

"Oh, I see. And how do you know Viggo?"

"My husband appointed him as my second guardian."

The man stopped talking to me after that. My spine tingled as the Deepvox man announced the start of the fight. His voice was almost drowned out by the cheering crowd.

I wished that I could get closer as the two men began to circle each other. I was still worrying about Cad or his parents spotting me. The chances that they'd be at the fight were probably slim, but I couldn't take any risks. I had brought my cap with me, however. If that had been enough to get by at the event the night before, it should be enough here, too.

"Excuse me," I said, taking my leave from the elderly man. I moved down the aisle, approaching the cage.

A security guard stopped me as I reached within a few feet. "Mr. Croft is my guardian," I told him before he could say anything. He let me pass and stand right next to the cage, where the water was kept and the attendants waited.

Up close was more exhilarating than I could have imagined. I could see every detail, every flicker of emotion in their eyes, every bead of sweat.

Viggo's opponent—Rod "Ruin" Ryland, according to the trim on his blue shorts—took aim at Viggo first. Viggo dodged before countering with a right hook which caught the side of Rod's face with a painful smack. Rod skipped back. The crowd yelled. Somehow, I felt that this was going to be another short fight.

Rod approached again, more cautiously, only to quickly swerve backward as Viggo launched a side kick. Viggo took the offensive, Rod backing away further. I could tell that Rod was trying to stay on his feet, jerking away whenever Viggo stooped or stepped closer. Rod clearly didn't want Viggo taking him to the ground. But that appeared to be exactly what Viggo's game plan was.

Viggo advanced, closing in like a panther, until Rod was up against the wall of the cage. Then he hurled himself at the guy's knees, going straight for the takedown. Rod desperately tried to keep his balance, but he only lasted a few seconds before his back went slamming down against the floor, Viggo on top of him. The audience howled and I found myself shouting along with them as Viggo proceeded to smother Rod's defensive punches and catch hold of his arms. "Yes! Come on!" I bellowed. I wondered if Viggo could hear me among the sea of other screams.

Rod proved to be more of a veteran on the ground than I had given him credit for. He squirmed and twisted beneath Viggo like an anaconda, and after about two minutes of intense grappling, to my dismay, he managed to free himself. The two men shot to their feet and resumed circling one another, though Rod was visibly tired by the grappling. His chest heaved and he bought himself some time by distancing himself a few steps. Viggo sensed his weakness. He swept forward and broke through Rod's defense, catching his nose with a hard punch. Rod staggered, then swung back with a flurry of quick, but rather sloppy punches. It did the job of fighting Viggo back a few feet. Then, as I sensed Viggo was about to go in for another flooring, the bell rang, announcing the end of the round.

A smile lit up my face as Viggo stalked toward my end of the cage. He noticed me as one of the attendants handed him a water flask through the bars. Viggo took a swig and I felt a twinge in my chest as his Adam's apple bobbed, the water gushing down his throat.

But I pushed the guilt down. *Down, down, down.* Deep, until it stopped existing.

After handing his flask back to the attendant, Viggo caught my eye again. He gave me the slightest wink before returning to the center of the cage for the second round. Cool as ice, Viggo was.

I hoped that Viggo would finish his opponent in this round. Rod didn't start out nearly as confident as he had in the previous one. Viggo, on the other hand, went in far more aggressively. He forced Rod to the edges of the cage with a slew of well-timed punches before finally opening up another opportunity to sweep Rod to the ground. This time, they fell in a peculiar way, twisting in mid-fall so that Viggo ended up landing on his back, Rod's back against his chest. Rod struggled to twist around to gain the advantage of being face forward and on top, but Viggo was too swift. His arm wrapped around the man's neck, pressing down hard against his throat and strangling him. Rod writhed and attempted to punch Viggo in the head, but Viggo held on tight. Rod even managed to roll over, but Viggo wrapped his legs around his waist, refusing to release his grip on Rod's neck. Rod managed to stand briefly before staggering and falling face forward. Viggo now on top, he served punches with his left hand while choking harder with his right arm, all the while maintaining control over the rest of Rod's body with his expert legwork. And then it was all over. Rod, draining of oxygen, tapped out.

The audience's celebration was deafening. It seemed even louder than at Viggo's previous fight. Viggo stood up, his eyes sweeping fleetingly around the room—over his adoring fans—before he stood by the referee.

Rod's team was hovering over the fighter, along with a physician, checking that he was all right, and then he rose—albeit on shaky feet—to stand on the other side of the referee. The booming voice announced Viggo to be the undisputed winner. The referee held Viggo's arm aloft. The second he let go, Viggo was heading back to his cage exit. He climbed out, his feet hitting the floor in front of me. His skin shining with sweat, he swept past me, catching my hand at the last moment and pulling me down the aisle alongside him toward the exit. This sent the females in the crowd into a frenzy. Wolf whistles abounded, every one of them obviously thinking that I was Viggo's new girl. Thank God Lee and I weren't actually in a relationship. If he'd been watching this, he probably would have been pissed.

I was just glad that I had my back to the crowd and they couldn't see my face. We entered the corridor, the noise of the audience fading a little as Viggo led me straight back to his room.

He shut the door behind us before he approached the bench. He picked up his towel and wiped down his face, chest and torso.

"Good one," I said.

"Yeah," he muttered, not attempting even a smidgen of enthusiasm. He gathered his clothes and shut himself in the bathroom.

After he turned on the shower, there came another knock at the door.

I doubted Viggo had been able to hear it over the running water. I wasn't sure what to do. Answer it, or ignore it? I decided to answer it.

Opening the door, I was expecting perhaps to see the elderly man come to congratulate Viggo. But instead, standing in the doorway was a middle-aged man with sleek brown hair and wearing a smart gray suit. He was holding a black briefcase, attached to which was a badge with black bold letters: "PFL".

"And who are you, Madam?" he asked me. No doubt he'd witnessed my exit with Viggo.

"Mrs. Bertrand. Viggo is my second guardian."

"Ah..." He stole a peek inside the room. "And is Mr. Croft available?"

"He's in the bathroom, but I doubt he'll be long... What do you want to speak to him about?"

The man's brows lowered. Apparently, as a woman, I had just asked one too many questions.

"I'll just... wait inside here, if that's okay?" he said.

"I guess," I muttered grudgingly.

I let him inside before closing the door behind him. He took a seat on the bench, while I found myself standing outside the bathroom door. After five minutes of awkward silence, Viggo emerged, wearing his day clothes. As I was right near the bathroom door, his eyes were on me first. He frowned, and looked like he was about to ask why I was standing in this odd place, when his eyes fell on the... intruder.

I was surprised when the first thing Viggo did was groan. "Mr. Sands," he said, "I told you no."

Mr. Sands stood up, offering a hand to Viggo—which Viggo promptly ignored.

"And I do greatly apologize for the intrusion," Mr. Sands said smoothly, looking apologetic for nothing. "But we last spoke over a month ago. That was quite a few fights ago. I thought there might be a possibility that you changed your mind about joining the Power Fight League since then."

"I haven't," Viggo snapped, throwing his towel against the bench.

"I know you've said you don't want the fame," Mr. Sands bulldozed on, "but surely by now, you have already gained a very large following? After a certain number of fans, it hardly even makes much difference."

My jaw dropped. Mr. Sands was voicing my thoughts exactly!

Viggo shook his head, stubborn as an ox. "No. I'm not interested."

"Would you just take a look at the contract the PFL is proposing, Mr. Croft? I took the liberty of preparing this before coming to your fight this evening. I tried to address a number of the concerns you brought up in our previous talk, and have come up with some creative solutions that might make your rise to celebrity less steep. For example, we could agree not to broadcast the events on television or radio, make your fights only a live event… similar to what you're already used to."

Wow. These people are desperate to have him.

Still, Viggo shook his head.

Although this was really none of my business, I couldn't help but blurt out, "Really, Mr. Croft? They're bending over backward to have you!"

Viggo's scowl deepened as his eyes shot to me.

"You could earn, like, a *ton* more," I went on, disregarding his glare. "And they say they won't even broadcast it so widely." *Plus you'll start wearing proper gloves and not have your hands constantly beat up.*

Now Mr. Sands looked interested in what I had to say.

"Mrs. Bertrand," he said, his face shining with self-serving gratitude, "you truly have a point. Mr. Croft, I implore you to at least read through the contract before rejecting the move to PFL again so swiftly." Mr. Sands held out three sheets of paper.

Viggo dragged a hand down his face. He threw me another hard stare before slipping the contract from Mr. Sands's hands and dumping himself down on the bench to read it.

I approached him tentatively, peering over his shoulder.

After scanning through the three pages, I was nervous about what Viggo was going to do. Reject again?

"The contract's only for one fight," I said.

"Yes," Viggo muttered. "I can read."

"So you could back out of the whole thing easily if you truly hated it," Mr. Sands interjected.

Viggo swallowed.

"I think you should take it," I said quietly.

He perused the contract five minutes longer before he slapped it down on the bench and rose to his feet.

He inhaled, running a hand through his hair. Then he shook his head in resignation. "Okay. One fight… I'll do it."

Yes.

"Fantastic!" Mr. Sands said, positively bouncing on his feet. He was quick to draw out a pen from his briefcase and hand it to Viggo, who moved back over to the bench to sign it.

Mr. Sands didn't stay a lot longer after that. "I won't detain you further now," he said. "You must want to rest after the fight. But I have your number, Mr. Croft. I'll be in touch tomorrow morning."

Viggo nodded, the shadow of a grimace still lingering on his face. As Mr. Sands left the room, he clenched his jaw as if he had just tasted something bad. I let him stew in his own thoughts as he packed up his possessions and donned his trench coat.

"You ready?" he asked gruffly, casting me a fleeting look.

"Yes."

"Then let's get out of here."

I followed him to the door. Instead of taking a left turn which would lead back to the arena, he took a right which brought us to a rusty stairwell. It took us up to a single door, which led out to a quiet street around the back of the building.

He pulled up his hood so that it shadowed his face, while I kept my hat low on my forehead as we made our way to his motorbike. As he stowed his bag beneath the seat, I dared break the silence.

"I have a new name for you, by the way," I said.

He groaned, slamming the seat shut. He climbed on to the motorbike and I slid on behind him, wrapping my arms around his waist.

"Do you want to know what it is?"

"I'm sure you're going to tell me anyway," he grunted.

"Viggo 'The Victor' Croft."

He kicked off and joined the road. Beneath the roar of the engine, I caught him mutter, "You have a nerve, Violet Bertrand."

CHAPTER 22

There was bad traffic on the way back to Lee's. Apparently, there had been a major crash on one of the highways, which caused a ripple effect of solid jams throughout the city. Viggo ended up completely retracing our route, even back past the Brunswick, to take a longer route home. He rode through the city closer to his side of the mountains, northwest of the palace. It was a relief to leave the noise and smoke behind as we climbed the mountains; the fresh air, tinged with the scent of pine, was bliss.

It was a mild night. Viggo got hot beneath his coat at one point; I helped peel it off his shoulders and kept it on my lap so he wouldn't have to stop to remove it, leaving me to feel the muscles beneath his t-shirt as I resumed my hold on him.

Viggo smelled like the pines. Rugged, virile. Maybe it was because he lived out here. The ends of his loosened hair touched my forehead as I rested my cheek against his back. I felt sheltered, safe. Truth be told, I was feeling sleepy now, too, and I closed my eyes for the rest of the journey.

By the time we thundered into Lee's drive, it was later than Lee had been expecting. The kitchen lights were on, the blinds half closed.

I got off the motorbike.

"Good night," I whispered.

"Night," he murmured.

His eyes glinted in the moonlight as I held his gaze a few seconds longer before turning and heading to the house. As Viggo had done the night before, he waited until Lee had opened up before riding off.

Unlike the night before, Lee was still dressed in his work clothes. A navy blue suit.

"What took you so long?" he asked as he closed the door after me. His face was tense.

"A ton of traffic," I said. "We had to go a roundabout way to get here."

We moved into the kitchen. When he offered me dinner, I accepted it. As he went about heating something up, he asked, "So how was Viggo? What did you talk about?"

"He won in the second round," I said. "It was great. I waited right by the cage and watched up close—I wore my cap, of course. And after the fight some agent from the PFL came to see him in his changing room. I've been trying to encourage Viggo to move up to his level, and when the agent offered him a new contract tonight, he finally accepted it."

The spoon Lee had been using to stir a saucepan dropped to the stove with a clatter. He spun around to face me, his expression shocked.

"You *encouraged* him to do that? What were you thinking?"

I stared at him in confusion, my lips parting. "I-I don't understand."

"Why would you encourage him to move up to the PFL? It didn't occur to you that this could mess up his entire schedule? His training, his fights! For heaven's sake, Violet. I warned you not to lose focus!"

I found myself stumbling for words, unsure of what to say. Lee was right. I hadn't given the slightest thought what consequences might ensue if he joined the PFL. His entire schedule that I'd gone to the trouble of noting down could be turned on its head. For all we knew, Viggo might be offered a PFL fight on the night of the banquet.

"As it stood," Lee went on, "that night was completely blank for him. He even had a night off his duties as a warden—I checked. He was to be replaced by someone else that evening. We had this all battened down, dammit!"

Lee sank down in a chair, running his fingers nervously through his hair.

My breathing quickened. What had I just done? Of course, Viggo might've accepted the contract anyway. Mr. Sands and the contract might've been enough to convince him… though I couldn't help but feel that my encouragement had played a part in it. Viggo was a stubborn man. He might not have even heard Mr. Sands out if I hadn't been there encouraging him to listen.

"Oh, this is a mess," Lee breathed. "A complete mess… Did they discuss the next fight in the changing room? Any kind of schedule at all?"

I shook my head. "No. The agent just said that he would be in touch tomorrow morning."

"He might even shift gyms for this. How are we going to figure out his updated schedule?"

"I-I could just ask him when the fight is."

Lee let out a breath, still looking irritated.

The smell of burning filled the room. Whatever Lee was heating up was getting ruined. But he could hardly bring himself to care. I had lost all my appetite now, anyway.

Crap. What have I done?

I sat in my chair, frozen, watching Lee tentatively as he buried his head in his hands. Then, with a deep sigh, he raised his head and looked me. "I'm just… trying to understand how you could have possibly thought that encouraging him was a good idea."

I was thinking of Viggo, of him being paid more and treated better.

"I'm sorry," I said. "I've been trying to make friends with him and I… I slipped up."

"We can't afford slip-ups. And do I need to remind you that my life is on the line just as much as yours is in this?"

"I know," I said through clenched teeth. *Even though I seem to be the one taking on the major risks all the time.* I felt like snapping something back at him, but I held my tongue. I knew I had messed up.

Lee stood up and turned off the heat beneath the sizzling pan before proceeding to throw the food in the trash.

Even though I no longer wanted to eat, I remained in my seat while Lee prepared a second dinner for me. When he placed a plate in front of me, I picked at the food, hardly able to swallow.

I felt like I was losing myself on this mission.

I pushed the food away after I'd eaten all that I could and drank from the glass of water he'd set down for me.

Lee's mood had quieted. "Okay," he said, sighing. "Look, Violet. I know this is hard. Trust me, I do. And we all make mistakes… But you've *got* to stay focused. Everyone is counting on you."

I managed a nod. "A reunion with my brother is on the line, too." I wasn't sure whether he knew that.

Biting his lower lip, he stood up. "Okay. I'm heading to bed." He began moving toward the door, but as he passed my seat, he stopped. He glanced down at me still in my chair, a furtive look in his eyes. Unexpectedly, he stooped. A second later, his moist lips were pressing against the side of my neck, beneath my right ear, in a firm, chaste kiss. And then, just as suddenly, he drew away.

"Good night," he managed, before sweeping out of the kitchen.

I stared at the empty doorway in a daze, my fingers raising to the side of my neck. I felt the skin where his lips had been.

What was that about?

Why would he do it?

I struggled for the next ten minutes to make sense of Lee's kiss. It had come so abruptly. So unexpectedly. From nowhere.

In the end, there was only one thing I could conclude:

Maybe I'm not the only one losing focus.

CHAPTER 23

My sleep was fitful that night. A recurring nightmare plagued me, a nightmare about a young boy sitting in a row boat in the middle of a river, being swept away by a current. The harrowing feeling of being able to do nothing but stand and stare remained with me after I woke up drenched in sweat. I glanced out of the window, whose blinds I'd forgotten to draw last night. The horizon glowed orange with the first signs of dawn. I checked the clock by my bedside. Five-thirty a.m.

I breathed in deeply through my nose. I wished that I could take a pill and forget about everything. Become a robot. I grimaced to myself. King Maxen's Benuxupane pills didn't seem like such a bad idea right now.

I took a hot shower, which helped to calm me. Like with Viggo, running water had a way of clearing my head.

I was no stranger to adversity. I'd been through harder times than this before and pulled through. I'd pull through again now. We didn't have long to go anyway, and then this would all be over.

After finishing in the shower and dressing—I didn't bother to dry my hair—I went downstairs. The kitchen was empty, but I could hear Lee upstairs. His shower was running.

I fixed myself some honey and ginger tea and settled down at the table. Samuel came in to greet me with a groggy woof before allowing me to stroke his head. It was raining outside, the first rain since I'd arrived.

By the time I'd finished my tea, Lee creaked down the staircase and emerged in the kitchen.

The first few seconds of his arrival were the worst. My stomach somersaulted as last night replayed in my mind. He also seemed awkward. He murmured a quick good morning before busying himself by the sink.

It appeared that he was going to act like the kiss hadn't happened.

"So, uh, what's on the agenda today?" I asked him. I was wondering what time Viggo would come for me, though he wouldn't have called yet. It was still too early.

"You're not going to see Viggo today." Lee's answer came.

I stared at the back of his head as he hunched over the sink.

What? Why? I wanted to blurt. But I held back. Why was I so bothered anyway whether I saw Viggo or not?

It was the abrupt reminder of Lee's power over me that threw me off.

"I've already left a message on his phone," he said.

"All right," I replied, trying to sound unruffled. I needed to cooperate with Lee, not fight him, for everyone's sake.

"Instead," Lee went on, "you're going to help me with something down at the lab." He turned away from the sink and sat opposite me at the table with a glass of water, still not meeting my eyes directly. He reached into his right pocket and pulled out a phone. "Alastair is due to make a call in about... one minute."

Barely a few seconds after Lee had spoken, the phone rang. The number flashed up as "Mariana"—apparently a disguise, presumably in case Lee's phone ever got stolen. Lee picked it up and pressed it to his ear. "Yes."

He uttered a few more "yes's" and "fine's", before handing the phone to me.

"Yeah?" I said.

"Good to hear from you, Violet," Alastair's pitchy voice replied.

"Things are going fine," I told him flatly, before he could ask the question. "There's really not a lot to talk about. The banquet is drawing closer and we're preparing for it as best we can."

"Good. Good. We're very glad to hear that." A pause. "You'll be seeing your brother soon, and you're making your nation proud, Violet... Never forget that."

I answered with silence. Alastair requested to be handed back to Lee and I handed back the phone wordlessly for Lee to wrap up the conversation.

"So, about today," Lee went on. "We need to leave for the lab in half an hour. I'll explain more on the journey."

I stayed in my seat while Lee left the kitchen. I heard him open the front door, then came his crunching footsteps in the driveway. The garage door creaked, and then an engine sounded: not a motorcycle. It sounded more like a car.

I headed to the window to see a brown five-seater roll into the center of the drive. Lee killed the engine, got out and hurried back to the house.

I met him in the hallway. "I didn't know you had a car," I commented.

"I rented it yesterday," he said. "Forecast predicted it would be rainy, and we can't afford to get wet today." He eyed me. "If you're ready we might as well leave now... Though we'll need to fix you up with your disguise first."

My curiosity, or rather, apprehension, was growing regarding what exactly Lee had in store for us. I followed him up to my bedroom where my costume was kept. Things felt awkward again as he got up close to put on my wig and help me with my facial hair and contact lenses. But his expression remained businesslike.

I changed into the body suit before pulling on a deep brown suit. Then, after popping some Deepvox pills and checking my appearance with Lee, we left the house.

"You sure this costume is a good idea?" I asked as we got in the car. I felt uneasy about going to the lab dressed like this. People had seen me before as a woman. They might recognize me even in this disguise. Plus, how would Lee explain who I was if we bumped into someone?

"Don't worry," Lee replied. "I've thought about it."

Watching the road slip away beneath us, my eyes glazed over as we rolled down the mountain. I tried not to worry, but failed. I didn't like feeling dependent on anyone—man or woman. In fact, I abhorred it. I hated not being clear on the plan in my own head. But it wasn't worth causing more tension between Lee and me. I had to keep biting my tongue. *This will be over soon.*

"Since it's early on a public holiday—the late King Patrick's coronation," Lee said, "the city won't be crowded. And the lab should be mostly empty. You're going to install one of the explosives we'll need for the lab… The one we require to blast open the egg's glass casing."

My heart skipped a beat. "Are you serious?"

"Quite serious."

"I have no idea how to handle explosives."

"Again, don't worry. I'll advise you what to do."

"What about the other explosives?" I asked him. "Have you installed those already?"

"No, but the others I've figured out how to handle without you. It's just this one you need to take charge of."

Lee proceeded to tell me in detail about where and how to correctly install the explosive device.

Arriving at the lab, Lee punched in the code to get us into the parking lot and parked as close to the entrance as he could. He reached an arm around the back of my seat and removed an unassuming brown bag, which he placed between my legs. Then he handed me a pager, which I stuffed into my pocket.

Now all that remained was action. He gave me a firm nod before stepping out of the car.

I watched Lee hurry to the building through the rain. He let himself inside, and his shadow disappeared behind the glass.

I stared down at the pager. In about fifteen minutes, he should be buzzing me.

I kept watch of the digital clock above the dashboard, my fingers clenching around the handle of the bag. Soon only one minute was left. Thirty seconds. Ten seconds… The pager buzzed five seconds late.

I took my cue to leave.

I pulled on a raincoat that had been stuffed inside the back pouch of Lee's seat, positioning the hood low over my face. I slipped the bag beneath my arm, making sure the overcoat covered it, then exited the car and hurried to the entrance.

Lee was waiting behind the glass doors and after he let me inside, we immediately parted ways—I headed toward the staircase that was located near the elevators, while Lee headed to the room behind the reception desk.

I scaled the stairs as fast as I could, breathing hard by the time I arrived on the top floor. Stepping out into the corridor, I recognized it from my previous visit. I no longer had to keep the hood over my head here. Lee's job during the minutes I'd waited in the car had been to stall the cameras recording in the entrance area, the staircase and up here… Just for fifteen minutes. I had to be fast.

As I reached the door of the lab, I buzzed Lee. A few seconds later, the door clicked open, Lee manipulating it from the downstairs control panel.

Stepping inside, I held my breath and gazed around. The lab was empty, eerily quiet. I let the door close behind me before working my way toward the glass cabinet at the back of the room. Toward the silver egg.

This damn egg. There had really better be something valuable in it.

By using the word "installing", Lee had made this job sound far more complicated than it actually was, at least for today. All I had to do was drop off a package of small explosives and hide them here so that they would be ready for the night of the party. He had advised me where I should put them.

My eyes panned to the light above me. It was wide, flat, and circular and fixed into the ceiling. Sliding a hand into the front pocket of the bag, I drew out a few screwdrivers before standing on a table. I raised my arms and began trying to find the right fit. I found one that slotted into the screws perfectly, though they were tightly fit. It wasn't a quick process to unscrew all the screws, especially since my nerves kept causing the screwdriver to slip in my hands. I feared I wouldn't make the fifteen minutes in time.

I exhaled in relief as the light finally came off. I glanced down at the clock by the door—seven minutes left. I placed the light carefully on the table—the last thing I needed was for it to shatter. Then I dug another hand into my bag and pulled out a foil package. I felt four heavy cylindrical objects inside as I stuffed the package through the gaping hole in the ceiling. I positioned them just by the edge, easy for me to reach in a hurry. Then I stooped down for the light fitting and worked as quickly as I could to reposition the screws. It was depressing to think I'd have to go through this all again on the night of the banquet.

The buzzer vibrated in my pocket just as I had one screw left.

Ugh. Screw you, Lee. I'm almost done...

I had the screw at just the right angle. If I let go, I'd have to start this one again, and I was running dangerously low on time. I spent the next minute refining the angle before leaping down to the floor and tucking the chair beneath the table where I'd found it.

The pager had vibrated twice more since then. When I pulled out the device from my pocket and checked it, my blood ran cold.

"GET OUT OF THE LAB!!!"

My heart in my throat, I grabbed the bag and bolted for the door.

Out of the lab? What does that even mean? Out of this particular lab, or out of the building?

But as I reached within ten feet of the exit, I froze. Footsteps sounded outside. I should have checked the pager the second Lee sent the first message. It was too late now. I was trapped.

I looked frantically around the room for a hiding place. I had no time to even consider whether diving beneath the table closest to me would be the best option. A few seconds after I'd slid beneath the furniture, the door glided open. Footsteps entered.

I clasped a palm over my mouth, trying to stifle my breathing. A man in corduroy pants walked past my table, continuing down the aisle. He was dragging behind him a suction cleaner. Why hadn't Lee known about it? I was trusting him blindly. He was supposed to have thought through all this. *I'm putting my life in that man's hands!*

The intruder walked to the end of the aisle and started up the machine. The room filled with white noise.

My fingers unsteady, I reached for my pager and punched in a message. *"STUCK INSIDE. WHAT NOW?"*

I stared down tensely at the device after sending it. *Come on, man!*

Lee's reply arrived forty seconds later:

"STAY WHERE YOU ARE."

What? For how long?

The cleaner was moving slowly but steadily toward my end of the room. He was cleaning thoroughly, too, making sure that he got every last bit of dirt out from underneath the tables.

He was going to find me.

Just as I was contemplating darting beneath a different table—one further away that would hopefully buy me some more time—the door opened again, and in stepped a second cleaner… also with a suction machine. He started cleaning much closer to me. At the rate he was sweeping across the floor, he was going to reach me in less than a minute.

"*TRAPPED*," I paged.

I clutched the device, waiting with bated breath for Lee's response. It wasn't coming.

The second cleaner arrived within five feet. Then four. Then three. Then…

The suction broom took its first swipe beneath my table, missing my left foot by a fraction. Clutching the bag, I spread myself as flat against the wall as I could, leaving as little of me touching the ground as possible. But it wasn't going to be enough. The machine moved forward again, this time aimed directly at my feet. Like a rabbit caught in the headlights, I closed my eyes, steeling myself for the impact while hoping against hope that he might mistake me for a table leg.

The broom hit me. But as it did, an alarm rang out, so loud it felt like my eardrums would split.

Although the broom had touched me, the guy became too distracted to check what he'd hit. He dropped the machine, and so did his colleague. The two of them rushed out of the room.

I took a moment to steady my breathing, drawing in a long, quiet breath.

Then I moved forward and peered out from under the table. Now I needed to get out while I could.

Making sure that my mustache, beard and hair were still on straight—just in case I got spotted outside—I left my spot beneath the table and headed for the door. But for the second time, it opened before I could reach it. There hadn't even been footsteps to warn me. I didn't even have time to throw myself under a table.

It was Lee and I had never been happier to see that man. He scanned the lab wide-eyed before taking my arm and pulling me out of the room.

The corridor was empty, but he did not head back to the same stairwell that I had come up. Instead we moved in the opposite direction down another hallway, before reaching a red door. As Lee opened it, a damp breeze swiped at my face. It led outside, to a narrow metal staircase scaling the back wall of the building. Lee pulled me outside into the rain and we clambered down the steps as fast as we dared.

Then, as we kept close to the wall and pulled on our raincoats, Lee led me back to the parking lot. Reaching the car, he opened up the front passenger door. I collapsed inside, stowing the bag beneath my knees. I expected Lee to take a seat next to me and immediately drive off, but instead he whispered, "I'll be back in a minute. I have to go back in and restart the cameras."

He swept back to the building and through the glass doors. He didn't take long. Three minutes later he was back in the car and we drove toward the parking lot exit. We both were silent until we were firmly outside of the gate and speeding back toward home.

"What happened?" the two of us demanded at once.

"I'm sorry," Lee replied first. "The cleaners were *not* due in today. They were supposed to come tomorrow. A change in the schedule was obviously made, and whoever was responsible for it forgot to mark it in the works calendar. It couldn't have been prevented." He looked at me sideways. "Did you pull it off?"

"Yes," I huffed. "It's done."

Lee nodded, relief washing over his face. "Good girl."

CHAPTER 24

After we returned to Lee's house, he didn't have any-thing for me to do for the rest of the day, but he pre-ferred not to call Viggo. My voice was too deep to see him, anyway. He suggested that I see him again tomor-row, when my main priority would be to figure out whether his schedule would be changing on the night of the banquet.

Lee drove me to head office in the morning and took me upstairs to Viggo's floor.

"Come in," came a familiar grunt as Lee knocked.

Lee pushed open the door and the two of us stepped inside.

Viggo sat behind his wide desk wearing a dark green t-shirt, his coat hanging from the back of his chair. A small pile of papers lay in front of him.

"All right, Viggo?" Lee asked pleasantly.

Viggo nodded, his eyes moving to me.

"Violet mentioned the contract. Congratulations!"

"Thanks," Viggo replied, monotone.

"Okay, I'd better head off. See the two of you later." Lee turned to me and leaned down to peck me on the cheek before leaving the room. The second kiss he'd laid on me. The first he had laid in public.

Trying not to get too caught up in mulling over Lee's weirdness, I approached Viggo's desk. As our eyes met, a smile spread across both of our faces.

I took a seat opposite him. "How was your day yesterday?" I asked him.

He shrugged. "Uneventful. Yours?"

I couldn't quite bring myself to say 'uneventful', so instead I replied, "Fine. Lee had the whole day free and wanted us to spend it together."

Viggo nodded stiffly, averting his eyes to the table.

"Mr. Sands must've called you, right?" I said.

"He did."

"Well?"

"They want the fight to be sooner than I had expected. Next week."

"Next week? Which day?"

"Saturday."

The banquet was to be held the Wednesday after. I supposed that meant Viggo's schedule would remain the same, if the fight was to be over days before. Any changes to his training routine would in theory take place prior.

"Are you able to get any extra time off from your warden duties to train? It's so soon."

"No extra time off above my yearly allowance," he replied. "I'll figure it out."

"Who are you up against?" I asked.

"They've decided they want to escalate me straight to Cruz."

"Seriously?"

"Yup," he said, rubbing his jaw.

"Are you nervous?"

He shrugged again.

I guessed that meant no.

"So, what's your plan for today? Warden duties until evening?"

"No, I've got the second half of today free. I plan to train a little, but I'll be heading back home. I think your husband is expecting that I take you with me, and then drop you at your house at the end of his work day."

"Okay," I said. This would be the first time I'd be alone with Viggo in his house, so far away from other people. I wondered if it might feel awkward.

Viggo returned his focus to his papers, but said, "By the way, you might be interested to know that the man we reported—or rather, you reported—at number thirty-two will be questioned today."

"Good," I muttered. I'd done my part, now I had to hope justice got served.

Viggo finished leafing through the papers in front of him before tucking them into a drawer.

We spent the rest of the morning outside. The rains of yesterday had given way to a bright blue sky. Viggo had to make another visit to the arms store for a meeting with the manager, which took up a good part of the morning, before returning to head office. He led me to a large conference room on the ground floor, where he met with about fifty other wardens—all of them working under him, apparently.

I sat in the chair by a corner, a little separated from the men. I didn't want to cause waves by taking a seat right among them. Viggo had three things on his agenda: first he informed them of new weapons that the force was bringing in, as well as giving them a demonstration. Next he spoke about new security protocols to be instigated near "Thickets Bridge"—apparently a bridge located somewhere in the mountains that connected a route to Porteque. And finally, he asked for an update on what was happening regarding the man who had escaped from the recent kidnapping incident, the man I hadn't managed to catch. There were no updates in that regard. Apparently he had escaped, well and truly.

After the meeting, everybody piled out of the conference room and headed to the canteen for lunch. Viggo and I accompanied them. As we collected trays and served ourselves a hot meal, I felt eyes watching me. Nobody looked directly at me for more than a few seconds, but I could tell the men were wondering who I was exactly, and why I was hanging around with their chief.

After we'd eaten, we left the building and headed to Viggo's motorcycle. Soon, we were speeding toward his side of the mountains.

We hit an unexpected spell of traffic along the way. I thought that maybe another accident had taken place and was clogging up all the roads again, just like the other night. But that didn't appear to be the case here. I strained my neck to see through the line of honking vehicles.

"Damn," Viggo murmured.

"What?"

"I forgot it was today."

"Forgot what was today?" I squeezed his waist, pressing him for an answer.

"King Maxen is making an appearance just up the road. You see that gold sedan?"

"Uh, yeah. Just about." A shiny golden vehicle was parked up near the sidewalk to our left.

"That's the king's. It's the inauguration of a new hospital… I'm off-duty now, otherwise I'd be there making sure things ran smoothly."

"A new hospital?"

"They say it's going to be the most technologically advanced we've ever had in Patrus," Viggo said.

"Lots of new, uh, technological stuff going on around here," I commented.

"Yeah," Viggo said. "And there will be a lot more to follow in the coming months. Don't ask me for details. I don't make a habit of reading the papers."

Or watching the news or listening to the radio, if his cabin was anything to go by.

I guessed life was a lot quieter that way. More peaceful without the constant bombardment of headlines.

I had lived that way for a lot of my life too—not that I'd had much of a choice in recent years, being stuck in detention centers. It wasn't exactly a priority there to keep the girls informed of current events.

I inhaled deeply as we approached the foothills, once again relishing the crisp, pure air.

"Do you always train by yourself?" I asked.

"Of course not. There are guys I spar with in the gym. But sometimes it's good to be out in the open."

I agreed.

Ascending higher and higher, I finally caught sight of Viggo's cabin as we traveled the last stretch of road. This was the first time I had seen it in daylight.

It really was small for a guy like Viggo. I wondered if he ever felt claustrophobic. Then again, if he did, he could sit out in the open, which I guessed was what the chair on his porch was for…

After disembarking and parking his motorcycle, he led me up the steps to the wooden platform that ran around the cabin, and opened the door.

"Come in if you want," he told me, already heading toward his bedroom. "I need to change."

Closing the door politely behind me, I headed to the sitting room. It looked the same as the night I'd last visited. Even the ointment and bandages were in the same place, although the hearth was not ablaze.

I was left to look out of the window—down at the bustling city—for a couple of minutes before Viggo returned barefoot, sporting a loose pair of pants and a looser black shirt that revealed a flash of his chest.

"Want something to drink?" he asked me. "I only have water."

"I'm okay for now."

We returned outside and I followed him around to the back of the cabin, where he had a sprawling backyard. Most of it was overgrown, but there was a stretch in the center where the grass had been kept trimmed. A makeshift log shelter stood by its border. Beneath it was various exercise equipment. Weights, benches, and other strength training gear I couldn't put a name to.

The view from this side of the house took me by surprise. Viggo's home being on a high plateau, it afforded a view of the *other* side of this mountain. The cliffs and peaks dipped down into a lush valley, through which ran a glittering river. And on the other side, more regal mountain ranges sprawled out for as far as I could see. Some peaks were so high, I couldn't even see their tips. Low clouds hung over them in an otherwise spotless sky.

Viggo's view was unique. Cityscape on the one side. Wilderness on the other.

He caught me staring in awe.

"So, deeper into these mountains is where you plan to buy land, once you quit being a warden?" I asked him.

"Not too deep, but deeper."

I squinted, trying to gauge how far my vision would stretch into the distance. "What's too deep?"

"Certainly no further than Thickets Bridge."

Wherever that was...

Viggo moved over to the log shelter and picked up some weights. I knelt on the grass as he began to warm up, my attention half on him, half on the view that was still taking my breath away. So far, things didn't feel awkward, and I suspected that wouldn't change. He was the same man as he was down in the city... just with a bit more breathing space.

Viggo worked out for the next hour and then retreated into the cabin for water. He brought out a steel jug and two glasses.

"Hope I'm not distracting you by being here," I told him, accepting a glass.

"No," he said, dropping down on the grass next to me. "I planned to give myself a bit of a break today anyway.

Still some days to go before the fight... and I know Cruz's style. Seen it many times before."

He removed his shirt, wiping the sweat from his face, chest and neck.

I stood up and wandered over to his equipment, testing the weight of his dumbbells. They were heavy. Very heavy. I played with a few other items before turning to face him. He was watching me.

I slipped my hands into my pockets, kicking at the ground casually as I asked, "Would you teach me a thing or two about what you know?"

"Teach you what, exactly?"

"I don't know. Some punching and blocking tips. Some grappling techniques. You're like a snake when you get a hold of someone."

He glanced toward the front of his cabin, as if to check no one was watching. "Okay." Putting down his glass, he strode over to me. "Let's start with some blocks... Say I go to punch you like this"—he moved his fist toward me in slow motion—"how would you block it?"

I swiped it aside with a swift chop of my right forearm. Not the most elegant move, but it usually did the trick.

"Okay," Viggo said. "And what about like this?" He came in with a slow round hook. Since there was enough space between us, I ducked down and went for his knees.

"Now I would floor you," I said, hooking the back of my ankles against the back of his.

"Try it," he said.

I jerked my ankles forward, causing him to lose balance. He caught his fall expertly with his arms rigid and palms spread out.

"And now," he said, sitting up and twisting me around so that my back was against his chest, "if I held you in this choke…" He locked one arm around my neck, the other fastening my arms behind my back. "How would you get out?"

Hm. Good question.

This was difficult because neither of us were standing. I couldn't knock him to the ground like I had done back in his changing room when he'd held me from behind.

I tried to maneuver my legs to distance myself and loosen his grip on me, but I failed. I realized that I actually did not know—or remember—how to get out of this.

"What's the answer?" I asked.

"What if I told you the answer is, there's no way out of this one?"

"I'd call bull."

He chuckled. "Then get out of it."

His challenge got my creative juices flowing.

I realized what I would do. My knees were touching the ground, which meant that I had leverage. Due to the nature of his hold, his face wasn't far from the back of my head. I would jerk my body upward suddenly, catching him with a head-butt strong enough to weaken his grip on me for a few seconds. Then I'd slither out.

Obviously, I wasn't going to actually do that now. I didn't want to give Viggo a bloody nose before his fight, so I just explained it to him.

"Hm. That might've worked," he said. "But I guess we'll never know. Now that you've told me your idea, I'll be sure to watch the back of your head."

Still his grip remained on me. "Hey, come on!" I said, grinning.

"There is another way out of this, though," he said. "At least one other way that wouldn't require you to smash my face in. Figure it out."

Viggo was a hard taskmaster, but I liked it.

Another idea came to me, and this time I acted instantly. Using my knees, I shoved all my weight to the right as I leaned backward. The mix of movement and direction was enough to rock Viggo's balance. We both toppled to our sides on the grass. As we made contact with the ground, there was a second where Viggo's hold loosened on my arms. I managed to slide them out in front of me and then break his hold on my neck enough for me to squirm and twist until I was facing him, our noses inches apart. I froze, realizing just how close we'd come to each other. Closer than we'd ever been. I paused for a few seconds to take in the details of his eyes, his dark lashes, every hue of green in his irises and the way they seemed to gleam as he looked back at me. Then, experiencing a flush of bashfulness, I switched back into fighting mode. Curving my right arm around him, I shoved myself further upward until my right shoulder dug into his neck, while I flattened his left arm beneath me. His right arm was still free, but I kept my head pressed close to his, which made it tougher for him to gain control of me.

Of course, if he was actually fighting with me, he would've made things a lot more difficult. But as I released him and we both sat up, there was still a shine to his eyes. He seemed pleased.

We spent the next few hours discussing techniques and putting them into play—mostly grappling, which was what I enjoyed the most, but also some punching and kicking. Before we knew it, dusk was upon us. That was just as well, I supposed. Viggo had worn me out. I was fit from manual labor, but I hadn't done resistance training for years. Of course I didn't have anywhere close to Viggo's lasting power. He could have continued all night.

Although evening had fallen, we still had some time left before Lee arrived back home. Viggo strolled over to the wooden shelter, gripped its roof, and, with one fluid motion that caused every muscle in his back and arms to flex, he lifted himself onto it. He glanced down at me. "Wanna come up here? The view's pretty good."

Heck, yes.

I wasn't tall enough to reach the top of the roof, so Viggo offered a hand and helped me up. We sat down facing the wilderness, our legs dangling over the edge. The mountains glowed orange in the evening light, enhancing their raw beauty to something of fantasy.

I had gained a new appreciation for why Viggo wanted to live up here. The view alone was worth the absence of electricity.

"Thanks for that," I said to him, leaning back, my eyes ahead.

"Welcome."

A span of silence fell between us, but it was not uncomfortable.

I glanced over my shoulder, toward Viggo's second view. The city. My eyes traced the shape of the river, and that of the buildings extending around it; they melded together, forming one giant crescent around the palace. Then I asked a question that had been nagging me for a long time.

"What is the actual meaning of your crescent symbol?"

Viggo followed my gaze and joined me in eyeing the city. "It symbolizes strength and potential. Growth, like the waxing moon."

"Ah," I said softly. "That makes sense."

It was ironic that it was Patrus' crescent mark that Matrus authorities stamped on boys who failed the test, when Patrus was the last place they'd ever be allowed to go.

I turned my thoughts to the symbol on the Matrus flag—a curved grain of wheat. It was fairly self-explanatory. It signified growth and fertility, but it was intended more to be an ode to a society rooted in pragmatism, diligence, and most importantly, peace.

I sensed Viggo watching me as I gazed upon the city, but I didn't let on. I felt that strange flurry in my chest again.

He seemed to hesitate, then asked, "How did… you and Lee meet, Violet?"

I realized that this was the first time I'd heard Viggo use Lee's first name.

"I thought he told you," I said, my jaw tightening.

"Yeah," he said. "He did mention it in passing, I guess… Never mind."

I let him fade into quiet. The less we discussed Lee and me, the better.

But since he'd posed a question about my relationship, it seemed only natural that I should turn a question on him that ran along the same lines. "Have you always been single?"

"No. I haven't. I… I was married. But things didn't work out."

I sensed the discomfort in his voice and immediately regretted asking the question. I didn't want to dredge all those painful memories up for him. Not on such a beautiful evening as this, when his mood appeared to be lighter than it had been since I'd met him.

"I'm sorry," I said and glanced away, hoping to make it clear that I didn't expect him to offer anything more on the subject.

My eyes traveled further over the city of Patrus to its vast surrounding suburbs. Then northward, where The Green began on Patrus' side of the river, extending like an infinite ocean of trees. Then to the river itself, whose hanging mist was tinged with the evening sun… And then beyond that, blurred by the fog, the faint outline of Matrus.

Sitting here with Viggo, it felt somewhat painful to stare in my homeland's direction for long. I'd had enough of the cityscape, anyway. I twisted back around and faced the wilderness. Viggo did the same.

Only a quarter of the sun was visible now above the peaks. Soon we would have to leave. I didn't want Lee getting tense with me again, under more suspicion that I was getting "carried away".

But we still had a few minutes left.

Enveloped by the peaceful atmosphere, on the cusp of light and darkness, a question bubbled up in me.

"You ever wonder if things will always be like this?"

"What do you mean?" Viggo asked, his voice husky.

"Just… how we find ourselves living."

Viggo's gaze lowered to his hands. There was a pause before he replied, "More often than I should probably admit."

Having both been victims of the law in our countries, I supposed we were more vulnerable to wondering. Grief did that to you. It made you wish for a life that wasn't yours. It made you dream.

But dreaming wasn't encouraged in my world. Just like expressing views opposing that of our Queen wasn't. Doing the latter publicly was an offense that led to serious consequences—jail time, or occasionally even banishment.

Criticism of the Court was something that had to be done behind closed doors, with people whom you trusted wouldn't rat you out. I suspected Patrus was similar in that respect, given Viggo's caginess to clarify certain comments he'd made about Patrus' leadership.

My eyes fixed on a family of eagles swooping down upon a rocky cliffside, settling in for the night.

"Do you feel like you belong in Patrus?" I asked him in almost a whisper.

Viggo furrowed his brows. "I s'pose I don't really understand the question. I was born and raised here. I am a man."

I didn't really understand the question either. I'd been born and raised in Matrus. I was a woman. Matrus was where I belonged. Matrus was my home…

"I guess I just wonder what happens to someone who doesn't feel they belong on either side of the river."

Viggo didn't have an answer to that one.

CHAPTER 25

We didn't stay much longer on the roof. Viggo pushed himself off, landing on the grass, and I was about to jump off after him when he reached up to help me. I hesitated, unsure of how this was going to work. Holding his hands at this angle would be silly.

"Hold my shoulders," he said.

His hands positioned on the roof on either side of my hips, he beckoned me closer with a gentle nod. I leaned down to grip his shoulders. As I slid into his arms, his hands engulfed my waist. Warmth flooded through me. My feet touching the ground, I was suddenly acutely aware of my erratic heartbeat. I withdrew my hands from Viggo's shoulders and he let go of my waist, but we shared the same two feet of soil for a few seconds, his eyes reflecting the fading evening light.

Then I staggered backward. I looked toward the cabin, feeling lightheaded. *What's gotten into me? It's this mountain air or... something.*

"Let's go," Viggo said. His voice came as a croak. He left me and strode toward the front of his home; I found my balance and followed him.

Mounting the motorcycle, neither of us spoke as we traveled back to Lee's house.

We arrived well on time. Lee had only just gotten in and he smiled on opening the door to me, before the two of us waved Viggo goodnight.

"Any change of schedule for him? No press release has been made yet involving a date." Lee asked as soon as we were inside.

"It'll be kind of a last-minute fight," I said, my throat feeling parched. "It's been fixed for Saturday."

"Hm. Okay," Lee said, stroking his chin. "That gives us four days before the banquet. I don't see why his schedule would change much immediately after the fight... Everything should still run as planned."

The next few days passed quickly. Almost too quickly. Except for Lee reporting a scare in the lab, where he'd witnessed a group of men huddled around the egg, evidently trying to coax it open, nothing very eventful happened.

Lee assured me that they'd failed to open it, though for all we knew, they might be getting closer to figuring it out. It was a good thing the banquet would soon be upon us.

Lee continued to drop me off with Viggo in the mornings, and when he and I weren't in his office, roaming the city, or in some meeting, Viggo would be in the gym. I watched from the bench while Viggo worked out, sometimes by himself and sometimes with others. The two of us didn't go up to his cabin again.

I had no more 'special' jobs to accomplish for the mission. My next and final task would be on the night of the banquet. The night I was due to leave Patrus. Lee's own prep work was almost done, according to him. It was no wonder that he had been so busy. He not only had to keep up with the demands of his job in the lab, but, on top of that, fulfill his end of the deal for Matrus. He had a lot of weight on his shoulders. We both did. I regretted resenting him for not taking on as much danger as me—although my tasks might be more out in the open and carry more immediate risks, he was still working hard in the background.

I didn't ask Lee for details about his own work, though. I didn't want to know his business, and I was glad that he didn't offer the information.

I was also glad that he didn't make any more advances toward me, though I still felt an undercurrent of awkwardness around him.

I was relieved when Saturday came around. The day of Viggo's fight. It marked a milestone—only four days left to go.

Although Lee was at home, and in Viggo's eyes there was no reason for me to hang around with him, Lee suggested that going to his fight would be helpful. I'd seen Viggo regularly up until now, and I needed to keep the momentum going for the last few days.

The fight was due to take place at night, and since Viggo had a number of other things to do before then—PFL formalities, like final weigh-ins and such—he didn't come to pick me up until the evening. The fight was to be held in the same stadium as the Rosen-Cruz fight. I could only imagine how crowded it would be.

As I hopped on Viggo's motorbike and we headed down the mountains, Viggo confirmed that we should expect a lot of people; the tickets had sold out in record time, spurring the PFL to set up screens around the outer walls of the arena so that people could watch from the square and bordering streets. Although the PFL had agreed not to broadcast the fight on television or radio, broadcasting it to extra people outside the stadium was apparently something that they could get away with in the contract.

Something told me that I was feeling more nervous than Viggo for the fight as we rode around the building to a back entrance. He looked calm and collected as ever as we entered the building. His confidence was something that I admired—he wasn't cocky or arrogant, but pragmatic. He simply knew what he was capable of.

A man in a suit was there to greet us at the end of the entrance hallway. He introduced himself as Mr. Doherty, cofounder of the PFL. He shook hands with Viggo before leading us to a changing room—certainly a step up from Viggo's previous room. It was more than twice the size, everything more luxurious, from the front of the door engraved with his name in gold letters, to the soft, fluffy towels, to the air-conditioning, to the tray of refreshments waiting on a table. My eyes lingered on the padded, fingerless gloves hanging from a hook by the door.

Viggo nodded briefly in appreciation before Mr. Doherty left us alone.

I wandered about the room and approached the frosted window. I opened it just a little to gaze outside at the crowds already forming.

Viggo dumped his bag down and fished out his fighting shorts, also a step up from his previous fights. These were black with gold trim, sporting the bold letters "PFL".

Viggo headed to the ensuite bathroom to shower and change. When he emerged wearing the shorts, he removed the gloves from the hook and sat down next to me on the bench. I watched as he strapped them on. Finally some decent protection for his knuckles.

"Those look good," I commented.

He flexed his fingers in the gloves. "Yeah."

He stood up and began swinging air punches.

"PFL makes a huge fuss about everything," Viggo muttered as he continued to warm himself up. "There must have been over fifty journalists at the weigh-ins. My picture will be everywhere tomorrow." He scowled. "Then there's all the trash you're expected to talk about the opponent… Can't stand hype."

"Well, you don't have to play along," I said to him. "You can do whatever you want. You're Viggo Croft, remember?"

He scoffed.

"What happens after you win this fight?" I asked. I was confident that he would win. It seemed silly to use the word *if*.

"Then I suppose I will wait a week or so to see what the aftermath is like. If the buzz is somewhat bearable, I guess I'll sign up for a second fight. If it's intolerable, I won't."

Someone knocked on the door. Some guy in black PFL uniform, one of the event organizers.

"A gentleman from *The Sportster* would like to have a few words with you in the final lead up to the fight," he said. "Would you be willing to talk to him?"

Viggo's expression darkened. "Is that the same guy who brought Miriam up earlier?" he asked.

"Uh… yes."

"Then you can show him the exit."

The organizer looked disappointed, but didn't press. He backed out of the room.

Miriam.

"Who's Miriam?" I asked, hoping he wouldn't mind the question.

Viggo turned his back on me, busying himself in his locker. "My late wife."

I regretted asking. We both went quiet.

Another interruption came barely five minutes later. As Viggo opened the door, it was another man in black PFL uniform, blond with a scratchy beard and holding a clipboard.

"Sir," he said, his eyes passing me as they swept around the room, "you need to come to meet Cruz now. The referee needs to have his final word with the two of you together."

"Okay." Viggo sighed. He glanced back at me, indicating that I follow, but as I headed with him to the door, the employee objected.

"I'm very sorry, Mr. Croft," he said, "but if your female friend could wait here in your changing room…"

Viggo's jaw twitched in annoyance. Then he exhaled. "Okay. Violet, wait here. Don't go anywhere."

"I won't," I assured him.

He left the room with the man, shutting the door none too gently behind him.

I roamed around the room a second time, stooping to pick up a bottle of chilled water from the refreshment basket. Then I approached the window again and peered through the crack. We were on the ground floor, so I couldn't see the full extent of the crowd, but it had ballooned since the last time I'd looked out just a few minutes ago.

After finishing my water, I needed the bathroom. I locked myself inside, and realized I'd been sweating in spite of the air conditioning. It was the buzzing stadium, being surrounded by crowds of people, the atmosphere wrought with tension and excitement.

But the second I stepped out of the bathroom, a heavy fist flew at me from nowhere and caught me square in the face. I reeled, pain searing through my nose. Stars circled before my eyes. Before I could attempt to defend myself, a heavy weight was flung at me, knocking me from my feet and pinning me facedown against the floor. As I tried to yell, a hand clamped around my mouth, and then a second hand, lined with some kind of pungent-smelling tissue, folded around my nose.

My brain became foggy. I could no longer struggle. And then all went black.

CHAPTER 26

I woke up to a splitting headache and a coppery taste in my mouth. Blood. My own blood. I was lying flat on my back, the floor hard and rough beneath me. And cold. Terribly cold. Prying my eyelids open, I sat upright. Metal clanked and I realized that my wrists and ankles were fastened with chains—chains that were fixed to the wall behind me, immovable, no matter how hard I strained against them. And my clothes were ripped, my hair a matted mess.

I sat in a small, windowless room, whose walls and floor were stone. The only light emanated from a dim gas lantern on the floor.

Where am I?

My heart pounding, I fixed my eyes on the opposite wall, where jagged words had been scrawled in red paint.

"WELCOME TO PORTEQUE."

I stopped breathing.

Attached to the wall, beneath the words were… photographs? I squinted in the gloom. Each depicted a woman, curled up in a fetal position on a floor that looked very much like the one I was currently sitting on. Behind, and looming over her was a man. His body was cut off at the waist, so all I could see were his legs and heavy boots. Just as every woman was different, so appeared to be every man; different leg heights and shoe sizes. Then, as my eyes fell to the lowest photograph on the wall… I recognized the clothes the girl was wearing.

That girl was me.

What is this?

Before I could consider yelling, I heard footsteps.

The heavy wooden door opened and in stepped a man whom I had seen before. He wore different clothes—unkempt, Porteque-style clothing—but I recognized that scratchy beard. It was the PFL attendant who had taken Viggo away and insisted that I stay behind in the changing room.

A second man entered behind him. He had a tattoo beneath his right eye. I recognized him too. He was the man who had seen me take down his friend in the road—the man who'd gotten away.

They moved toward me, their leering eyes raking me over.

Arriving in front of me, the tattooed man lowered and grabbed my throat. I attempted to fight him off, but there was only so much I could do while my hands and feet were bound. I'd never felt more vulnerable and powerless in my life.

He tilted my head upward and gestured to a shadowy corner in the room that I had not paid much attention to until now. Fixed to the wall was a camera, pointed directly at me. They had been watching me.

"What do you want?" I breathed. The men seemed to be deliberately keeping their backs to the camera.

"First," the tattooed man replied, his voice as scratchy as his companion's beard, "to teach you your place."

His right hand balled into a fist. Gripping my hair with his left hand, he dealt me a crushing blow in the gut. Once, twice, thrice. Winded, I coughed and spluttered, clutching at my sides. I collapsed as he kicked me in the kidney, curling myself up into as tight a ball as I could.

"Ada!" the second man shouted, his voice resounding in the chamber.

I dared glance up as more footsteps echoed.

A short woman entered the room; she was bone-thin, with lanky mousy-brown hair. I didn't think that she was any older than twenty-five, yet she had deep lines around her mouth and forehead. Beneath her right eye, she, too, sported a triangular tattoo.

The moment she laid her dark eyes on me, she lurched forward. Her fingers dug against my scalp and ripped at my hair, forcing me into an upright position.

She bent down to my level and spat in my face.

"You know that it was my husband you took down?" she hissed.

I tried to protect myself as she dealt me a stinging slap across the face. Her thinness was deceiving—she had muscles in those arms.

She struck me again and again, her bony fingers like whips against my skin. Then, reaching for a belt around her waist, she clasped at a handle and drew out a knife. Holding the back of my head, she pulled me closer to her.

"Stop," I wheezed.

She ran the tip of the blade against my upper cheek, beneath my right eye socket, in one sweeping crescent motion.

I cried out again, tears leaking from my eyes.

"Stop," I rasped. "Stop it!"

She came at me again with the knife, but before she could make a second contact with the blade, one of the men gripped her by the arm and snatched the weapon from her hand.

"Enough," he said gruffly. "We don't want her so cut up just yet."

Ada, eyes still glimmering with rage, grabbed my neck and forced my head downward, toward the feet of the tattooed man. She squashed my face against his boots, their grime soiling my skin.

"Know your place before a man!" she hissed.

She held me there for five seconds before releasing me and stepping backward.

I pressed my back against the wall in a feeble attempt to distance myself from the men I was left with.

"The second reason you are here," the tattooed man went on, as if there had been no interruption, "is to assist us in sending a message to any other bitches like you who have managed to leech their way into Patrus."

He moved to me and, holding my hair, panned my head to the camera again. "Say hello," he whispered, his mouth inches from my ear. He snickered, reaching into his pocket and drawing out a strip of brown fabric with two holes gouged into it. His male companion produced the same and so did Ada. They tied them around their heads so that the upper halves of their faces were obscured but for their eyes.

Another man entered the room, both of them sporting similar masks… and one of them carrying a hot iron bar.

The man carrying the bar handed it to Ada. She waved it around before my face, taunting me with it, bringing it closer until its heat caused my skin to break out in a heavy sweat.

She gathered a strand of my hair and trailed it over the hot iron, singeing it and producing a sickening burning smell. She waved the frayed ends of my hair before my face, pressing them to my nostrils.

"Imagine what your skin will smell like."

She grabbed my arm and extended it before glancing at the camera. An oily smile glided across her face as she addressed the lens. "This is for every woman out there who thinks it's okay to shout back at her man."

She lowered the iron bar against my sensitive inner wrist.

My skin exploded in agony. A screech erupted from my throat. I was sure that I would pass out.

Still eyeing the camera, the woman went on, "For every woman who thinks she can cheat, or talk behind his back."

Another strike of the iron bar, a few inches further up my arm. Somehow, it was even worse this time, knowing what was coming. Tears spilled from my eyes as I struggled to break away from her grasp.

Still, she went on addressing the camera, "For every woman who thinks she knows better."

Another burn, climbing up my shoulder. My entire body, drenched in sweat, had begun to shake uncontrollably.

"And this," she said, in a lower voice, a terrifying sense of finality to her tone, "is for every bitch who thinks she's equal."

I was sure that the madwoman was going to strike me in the chest, maybe even drive the sharp end of the rod through my heart... So it came as a surprise when she stalled, and instead placed the rod down on the floor.

The runaway criminal standing behind Ada gave me a knowing smile, relishing my fear.

Bastard. I saw your cowardly ass run away from me back on that street.

He bent down to my level and I flinched as his hand gripped the side of my face, his calloused thumb touching my cheek.

"It's a shame," he said. "Look at you—young, blessed with good looks, a nice body… We don't treat all female visitors to Porteque like this, you know. Some of them we even make wives out of, like Ada. We found her at sixteen."

"Why are you telling me this?" I croaked.

He sighed. "I'm not telling you as much as I'm telling the women who will watch this."

He let go of my face and rose to his feet. He addressed his companions surrounding us. "Bring in the table."

One of the men exited and returned a few seconds later, pushing along a rickety steel table on wheels. It had wrist and ankle holds attached to either end of it. Ada manifested a key and freed me from my current chains one at a time. I immediately leapt for the door, but it was a hopeless endeavor. My captors crowded around me, wrestling me into submission. They dragged me to the table where they strapped me down. These restraints were tighter and it felt like they stopped the blood flowing to my feet and hands. Maybe that was the idea.

As they gathered around me, the runaway man spoke: "Cut her."

I writhed as they reached into their belts and withdrew knives. They used the steel edges of the table to sharpen the blades, Ada on my right even gouging me in the thigh as she did so, deliberately careless.

These people are insane.

"Stop!" I begged. "Please, I'll do anything! Just stop!"

That I had resorted to begging these animals cut me to the core, deeper than any knife could. It felt like renouncing any semblance of dignity I had left.

These people needed to be lined up and shot. If only I had a gun. Ms. Dale's last-minute training would've actually been useful.

"How do you want to do this?" Ada asked the runaway. They appeared to have finished sharpening their knives.

The runaway, standing closest to my head, replied, "Same as the last."

His answer brought a dozen nightmarish visions to my mind. As their knives descended on me, all I could do was close my eyes and pray. I thought of Viggo, about the chance I'd never have to see him again, and about the mission and my lost opportunity to reunite with Tim.

As the blades began to press into me, piercing skin, a man yelled outside.

"EVACUATE!"

The door burst open and in stepped another man, face shining with sweat, eyes alight with alarm. "Wardens!" he panted.

The word sent relief rolling through my body.

"WHAT?" the runaway man yelled back. "Impossible! They can't have reached us so quickly!"

"They're here!" he insisted.

Ada and the men surrounding me swore. Shoving their knives back in their belts, they loosened me from the table before grabbing hold of me. The tallest man— the runaway—hauled me over his shoulder, dangling me upside down, while a second man grabbed my wrists and held them tightly together. That didn't stop me from thrashing my legs. As they carried me out of the dank room and up a flight of grimy stairs, the man holding my wrists connected his knee with my face, sending my head into another tailspin.

I could no longer keep track of where we were going or who was around me. All I knew was that their route was dark and bumpy, and then the air suddenly became a lot colder. A chill wind caused my skin to break out in goosebumps. We were outside.

I caught the glare of headlights to our right, and a loud roaring noise in the distance. Then came gunshots. We reached some kind of vehicle and I was shoved into a spacious trunk and locked inside.

I had no idea how much time had passed since I had been kidnapped. But the man had said that the wardens' arrival was quick. I had no idea how the "wardens" had managed to locate me so quickly, given that Porteque was supposed to be tucked away in the depths of the mountains—somewhere even Viggo seemed hesitant to enter.

I was rolled from side to side as the vehicle picked up speed, in spite of the hard bumps in whatever road—or track—we were following. I tried to grab hold of something to avoid more injury, but soon we were traveling so fast, the bumps so wild, it was impossible to avoid getting banged about.

What's going on?

Where are they taking me?

The ground tilted in a slope. I rolled to the other side of the trunk. My stomach dropped. We were going downhill. Fast.

The gunshots grew louder behind us.

The base of the vehicle vibrated, then we shuddered to a stop that sent the back of my head smashing against the trunk's side wall.

The truck bobbed as people climbed out, unloading it of weight, and then the trunk opened. Two hands shot inside and grabbed me, yanking me out, and my feet sank into shallow water. We were in the dip of a wooded area and, as I gazed around wildly, I noticed we were surrounded by a crowd of men—and one woman—and five trucks. I gazed up at the slope we had just descended. Its steepness made me feel nauseated. The gunshots echoing down came from somewhere near the top.

The man, whom I realized was the same coward who had run away, tugged on me, pulling me through the water as everyone else began to cross the stream.

I wouldn't let them drag me further.

The man must've thought that I was too weak to put up much of a fight now. My nose had started bleeding again, and my brain was clouded, but desperation had a way of making you find strength you thought you'd lost.

I dropped all of my weight downward, my backside hitting the rocky bed of the stream. My wrist slipped from the man's grasp and I lurched for his knees, toppling him backward into the water. As he landed, his right hand instantly moved to his knife. But I had already predicted that.

I slid the blade out of its sheath and without a second's hesitation slashed his throat in a fit of fury. His blood drenched my hands and arms and flowed around me as I fought to stand up… only to be instantly struck by a vicious blow to the back of my head. The jolt caused my grip around the knife to slacken and it flew from my hands as I tripped. The upper half of me fell on land, but my legs and feet still trailed in the water.

I cried out as a foot stamped down on my back. Then hands gripped my neck, fingers gouging into my throat. With whatever renewed energy I'd managed to summon rapidly ebbing away, I fumbled around on the ground, searching for a sharp rock. Discovering a stone that felt jagged enough to cut skin, I raised my arms and pressed down hard against the man's hands with one palm, while using the other hand to rip sharply with the pointed tip of the stone where I estimated his wrist was.

Wherever I'd managed to strike, it worked. His hold on me loosened enough for me to gasp for air. I twisted myself around, only to see my latest attacker joined by five other men. They weren't going to mess around this time. They knew it. I knew it. The deprivation of oxygen had made me too weak to stand up anymore. I couldn't even attempt to continue defending myself.

As the closest man leapt for me, all I could think to do was curl myself up in a ball, as if that would somehow soften the pain of the impact.

His full weight crashed down on me, knocking my head back.

But I did not feel the tip of the knife or slash of the blade.

No. All I felt was his crushing weight.

I managed to slither out from beneath him and glanced up to see the other men had stopped in their tracks. Not just stopped, but they were beginning to scatter, racing across the stream and into the woods on the other side.

That was when I realized why the man on top of me had become so… motionless. As I slid out from under him completely, his face thunked against the ground. At the back of his head was a round, bloody bullet hole.

I scrambled backward and tried to stand up, but I felt too dizzy. When I looked toward the slope where the bullet must have come from, my eyes found a tall figure running toward me through the trees. With the silhouette of a long gun in his right hand, his outline was familiar, even in the darkness. Wavy hair. The straight shape of a trench coat.

I almost cried out in relief as Viggo's face emerged, illuminated by soft shafts of moonlight. His eyes gleamed with anxiety as he took in my bloodied state.

"Whose blood is that?" he uttered in a strained whisper.

I looked toward the stream and pointed to the corpse of the man whose throat I'd torn open. Then I spotted the knife, still coated with blood. It had fallen on the ground, not far away.

Shouts of wardens drifted down from the slope. Viggo cursed. Throwing a sharp glance in their direction, he hurried into the stream and dragged the corpse out. Then he scooped up the knife. Wrapping his hands around its handle, to my shock, he drove it back into the dead man's throat.

Leaving the blade erect, he leapt toward me, slipping one strong arm beneath my knees, the other wrapping around my waist. Then he picked me up and began to run with me.

But not in the direction I'd expected him to; not back up the slope he'd come from. Instead, confusingly, he dashed across the stream and reached the opposite side. Shooting another look over his shoulder toward his rapidly approaching colleagues, he hurtled into the woods with me. The same woods the Porteque men were escaping into. The same woods the wardens were firing bullets toward. One hissed past us now, frighteningly close.

"Viggo," I panted. "What—?"

"Don't talk," he breathed, his eyes trained ahead of us.

I clung to him more tightly as the slope on this side steepened. I pulled myself closer against him, my bloodied hands slipping against the skin behind his neck.

My heart hammered as I caught sight of silhouettes of the Porteque gang up ahead.

What is Viggo thinking? Is he going after them? While carrying *me? Has he gone mad?*

As I had become almost fully convinced that he was chasing after the criminals, Viggo's direction diverged from them. He swerved diagonally to our left, while they were moving decidedly right.

The trees became denser as he continued to run, and the bullets no longer reached us. The gunshots grew fainter, and the loudest noises became Viggo's heavy boots crunching in the brushwood and his harried breathing so close to my ear. I could practically feel his heart pounding against me.

I had never witnessed Viggo so tense. For the first time since I'd met him, he showed fear.

I needed first aid. I needed to visit a hospital.

The gushing of water came within earshot. Then a clearing came into view, through which ran a river. Its surface glistened in the moonlight as we approached. Finally, Viggo came to a stop.

He looked down at me. "Can you stand?"

"I-I'm not sure."

He exhaled. "Okay."

Lowering me gently, he seated me at the edge of the bank. He proceeded to remove his coat, belt and gun and hang it on a branch. Then he returned to me, wearing the same shirt and pants he'd worn earlier in the day before the fight. He sat down next to me and swung his legs into the water and the next thing I knew, he'd dropped into it, submerging his upper chest, still fully clothed. Apparently, he was tall—and steady—enough to touch the bottom, even with the current.

He winced. "It's cold. But we have to get you cleaned up. There was no time back in that stream."

I examined myself more closely. It wasn't just my hands, arms and face that had gotten splattered with the blood. There were stains on my neck, upper chest, lower torso and clothes. I removed the torn garments, balled them up, and discarded them in the river. Now I wore only my underwear, which was also stained.

"Come," he coaxed softly.

My body tensed up as I slipped off the bank's edge, into his open arms. My chest constricted, my skin breaking out in goosebumps. I wound my arms around Viggo's neck and pulled my body flush against his, for support amidst the current, and for warmth.

"You're worried I could be punished for killing that man?" I panted against his hair.

I felt him swallow against my shoulder. A pause ensued.

"Do you want to know what happened to Miriam? My wife?" His voice was hoarse.

"What?" I whispered, as my stomach clenched with guilt at the thought that I already knew.

"She was hanged for defending herself in a situation not all that different from this. She killed an attacker without a neutral witness." Viggo's chest heaved beneath me. I sensed an undercurrent of guilt to his tone. *Does he blame himself for her death?* "I… I'm not saying the same insane rule would apply to you. Even the court doesn't care much about what happens to these Porteque dregs. But it's not worth the risk."

He created a few inches' gap between us. His eyes studied my arms before he began to run a palm along them, down to my hands, rinsing me of the blood. The current was doing a good job of cleaning my torso and chest on its own.

"I'll say I killed him if anyone questions it," he continued. "I planted my handprint on the knife."

"There'll be no consequences for you?"

"None to speak of."

"How will you explain both of us being sopping wet when we return?" I asked, shivering as one of his hands ascended to tenderly brush against the side of my face.

"I'll tell them one of the guys split from the group with you, and I found the two of you crossing a river, where I headed him off. He got away, but I managed to get a hold of you."

"You're a good liar."

He gritted his teeth and held my gaze. "Sometimes that's what's required to do what is right in Patrus."

I looked down, experiencing a spike of discomfort.

"Okay. I think you're done." He gathered me to him and moved us back to the bank. Climbing out, he settled me on the ground before heading to the branch where he'd hung his possessions. He retrieved the coat and brought it to me, hanging its heavy weight around my shoulders. The smell of him immediately made me feel safe and pro-tected. "Better remove your underwear, too. Just throw it in the river and keep my coat."

I breathed in. "Okay. "

Viggo turned his back on me while I maneuvered my way out of my bra and panties. I hurled them into the river before pulling on his long coat. I fastened up the zipper to my neck. "You can turn around," I murmured.

He turned and bent down and scooped me up. As he rose and I tightened my grip around his shoulders, I real-ized my hands were trembling. Aside from the cold, I was still recovering from shock.

When Viggo began to run again—gripping me as though he feared I might loosen my hold—my cheek fell against his shoulder. His fear was not unfounded. I fought to maintain consciousness, but exhaustion finally claimed me. I faded out.

CHAPTER 27

I woke to the noise of whirring rotors. I was lying on something soft. Narrow, but comfortable. Someone's palm was pressed on my forehead. I opened my eyes.

Viggo's handsome face hung over me. His hair was wet, and tied back. His dark brows had been deeply furrowed, but became less so as our eyes locked. He removed his hand from my head. I tried to sit up, but he pushed me back down.

We were in the belly of some kind of aircraft. The walls were rounded and lined with metal panels. This was the first time I'd ever been in an aircraft, let alone flown in one. The sensation was unsettling. My ears felt blocked.

I was lying on a cushioned stretcher, Viggo sitting beside me on a stool. Memories of the night washed over me and I relived every terrifying moment. Waking up in the dark and the cold. The lack of control. The fear. The pain. The humiliation. The anger. The relief.

I was still wrapped in Viggo's coat. I felt its inner lining brush against my bare skin; it took the edge off my still-damp hair and body. I reached up to my face. I had a bandage over my nose.

I stared up at Viggo. "How did you find me?"

"Thanks to your husband," Viggo replied. His voice was low, like he hadn't spoken in a while.

"Lee?" I breathed. "Where is he?"

"He's back in the city," Viggo explained. "But he was able to communicate to me your location. The moment I realized you were gone, I called him and he was able to guide me and my team."

"But how would Lee know?"

Now it was Viggo's turn to look confused. "You didn't know that he has you tracked?"

My breath hitched. *No. I didn't know that.*

Since when had Lee been tracking me?

I had looked at his computer only recently to watch Viggo's red dot on the map, and I hadn't shown up there. As I turned my mind back to the last few days, I realized he must have done it the night he got annoyed with me. The night I'd told him I had encouraged Viggo to enter the PFL, and potentially mess up our whole schedule. The night Lee had first kissed me.

Whatever Lee's motives—be they borne out of some kind of possessiveness or not—I could only be grateful now that he had done it. Otherwise, I would have likely died in that dark basement.

"I did know," I lied, rubbing my head. "I just—with everything, I didn't put two and two together."

"As soon as we touch down in the city, I'll take you to the hospital. Your husband said that he will be waiting there for you."

"Okay," I said, swallowing. My mind turned back to earlier. "Hey, what happened with the fight?"

"Forget the fight!" he growled. "I left the arena as soon as I found you gone. It was that damn attendant, wasn't it? The one who told you to stay in the room."

I nodded. "And the runaway criminal, from the other day…" *The man I killed.* I explained to Viggo who else I'd seen, including Ada.

Viggo scowled. "That arena needs better screening as to who gets in and out. As for the others, I still have men back there making arrests… You remember we saw members from that gang, sitting in the square after the Rosen-Cruz fight. They were watching you, probably trying to find a way to get at you then, too. The gangs of Porteque don't take kindly to women rising above their role, God forbid when it's against one of their own. They took your felling one of them as an insult to their entire clan."

"They're insane," I breathed.

"They'd call themselves law-upholding," Viggo said darkly.

We lapsed into a span of silence. Trying to turn my mind away from the horrors of the night, I thought once again of Viggo's missed fight. He had just… walked out.

Abandoning Cruz, the organizers and thousands of fans. Guilt gripped me.

"Thank you, Viggo," I whispered, my throat thick.

He didn't acknowledge my words. He averted his gaze over his shoulder. "How much longer?" he called to an unseen colleague.

"Five minutes," a man called back.

We sat wordlessly for the rest of the journey. On descending, Viggo slipped his arms beneath me, picking me up again. He carried me out of the aircraft and we emerged on a landing strip on top of a towering building. Surrounding us was Patrus City.

"How far is the hospital?" I asked him as he carried me through a door which led to a stairwell.

"This is the hospital."

His answer came as a disappointment, which confused me. I'd been beaten up; I needed to see a doctor and be treated. But somehow I'd been expecting a little more delay until meeting Lee again… until leaving Viggo.

Viggo wound down the stairwell and pushed us through a set of double doors, which led us to a bustling hallway. Doctors—all male, of course—were moving in and out of rooms, pushing carts, speaking with patients. And then we spotted Lee, sitting tensely on a bench at the end of the corridor. He sprang up as soon as he spotted us and hurried to close the distance.

His face was deathly pale. His chest heaved in relief as Viggo transferred me to his arms, Lee's citrusy scent overtaking Viggo's.

"Good man, Viggo," Lee said hoarsely. "Good man."

Viggo merely nodded, his green eyes locking with mine for a second longer, before he turned and disappeared down the crowded corridor.

CHAPTER 28

Lee and I didn't get the opportunity to talk much about what had happened before I was called in for my appointment with Dr. Milman, which turned out to be a lot more intrusive than I had anticipated. In Matrus, all doctors were females (with the exception of just one male who was the son of one of Queen Rina's courtiers). I guessed now I knew what it felt like for Matrus males every time they needed an examination.

Dr. Milman focused on doing everything he could for my injuries—stitched up the cuts, applied a thick white cream to my burns before bandaging them—and after Lee returned to the room, he informed me that I could leave. He equipped us with several bottles of medication and cream along with extra bandages, and said that the best thing I could do for recovery was rest.

The doctor arranged for a wheelchair for Lee to borrow so he didn't have to carry me everywhere. I was still feeling dizzy whenever I stood, but the doctor said that should resolve itself in a day or two.

Lee wheeled me downstairs and outside to the road where he hailed a taxi. Once inside, I found myself rehashing everything that had happened, with Lee asking for every harrowing detail.

I was relieved when we arrived back at Lee's house and once inside he carried me up the stairs, to my room. He laid me down on the bed and tucked me beneath the covers.

"How are you feeling now?" he asked, looking me over with concern as he stood by my bedside.

My eyelids felt heavy as lead. I needed to sleep.

Lee took the hint. "I'll leave you alone," he said. "You have to recover as quickly as possible. We have only four days left… Whatever happens, we can't let this interfere with the banquet."

CHAPTER 29

*T*he banquet.

As much as I tried to put off thinking about it, the time was drawing too close now. As much as I struggled to continue brushing it aside, I couldn't. I could no longer keep it thrust down to the depths of my subconscious.

Only four days left.

Four days, and I will be calling Viggo to the scene of the crime.

Four days, and I will be framing him for an atrocity he didn't commit.

Four days, and I will have ruined his life… Maybe given the Court reason to take it from him.

None of my previous techniques for numbing myself worked anymore. Maybe it was the stillness I was forced to inhabit, the quiet of my room as even Lee left me alone for hours on end.

It was as if every emotion I'd kept pent up since the beginning of this mission came flooding out at once. Overwhelming me. Drowning me.

How could I have ever agreed to do this?

Viggo had rescued me from death and here I was contemplating in only a few sleeps' time, pulling the rug out from under his feet. Stabbing him in the back in the worst possible way. I had made him trust me enough to show his vulnerability: the loss of his wife, his struggle with Patrian society, and his readiness even now to defy the rules. I had become his *friend*. Why else would he have left the fight to save me if he didn't value our friendship? If he didn't like me? He could have informed Lee of my disappearance and then left the rest of his team to look for me. He'd been off-duty at that time, anyway. He hadn't needed to leave the fight for me, nor had he needed to cover up the murder I'd committed. And yet he'd done all this. He'd foregone the mass of money he could have made from that fight, angered thousands of people, and maybe even put his sparkling future career on the line… all for me.

I shook my head as I lay in bed with my eyes closed.

No. No. I can't do this. I can't do this.

The hours slipped away at terrifying speed. Soon night had come around again. Then morning.

Lee's brief appearances to check in on me came as simply blips in time, brief interruptions to my agonizing over Viggo. He informed me that he'd washed Viggo's coat and taken it to the wardens' head office for him to collect.

Alastair called the evening of the third day before the banquet to speak to both of us. Lee told me that it was best not to tell him about the kidnapping—that it would only freak him out.

So I told Alastair that everything was going smoothly, even as I was screaming inside.

I told him that Lee and I would be ready for the banquet, even as I ached.

I didn't know what to do, or what to say—if anything—to Lee. I felt trapped in a web of my own making. Tangled up in knots with no hand to free me.

Although I should be focusing on nothing but my recovery, I was barely even aware of my physical state anymore. I used the cream and medication as the doctor prescribed, mechanically, by rote, barely even bothering to check the progress of my healing in the mirror.

I was too far gone, my mind lost on a different stratum.

Do I tell Lee what I'm feeling?

I feared his reaction, and I didn't want to lay any more stress on him than he was under already, but I finally reached a precipice where I felt I would lose my mind if I kept my emotions bottled up even an hour longer.

So, when I heard him return to the house, I called for him. He came climbing up the stairs and entered my room, sitting on the edge of my bed.

"Are you okay?" he asked, tensing.

I propped myself upright against the headboard and drew in a breath. "Lee..." My voice came out uneven.

"I-I don't know that I can do this." *I can't do this.* I could hardly believe what I was thinking. *I have a reunion with my brother on the line!*

Lee heaved a sigh. He reached out a hand and cupped my knee, squeezing gently. "Violet, I understand your nerves. In spite of my preparation, I still find myself doubting. Can we really pull this off? Will we get out alive? Etcetera, etcetera. You need to stop thinking. We have only two days left, and then there will only be *doing*. Two days, and you should be out of here… back home. Safe. Two days left, that's all. So just… keep it together. Okay?"

"But Viggo," I croaked. "He saved my life. He sacrificed—"

"Violet," Lee said, sterner this time at the mention of Viggo. "Remember what I said. Don't lose sight of the bigger picture. In fact, you should *only* be thinking of the bigger picture. Nothing else. That's all you're here for. Once you keep your mind focused on the goal, all the details become insignificant… just moving pieces on the board. Pawns in the game. You understand?"

I didn't. I neither understood nor agreed with what Lee was saying. I could no longer accept that implicating Viggo was the *only* way. And yet even I could see that there was no point continuing this discussion. As much as I wished I could speak honestly with Lee to release some of the pressure escalating within me, he was a closed book. It was far too late in the game to be bringing up feelings and sentiments. None of it mattered. In Lee's mind, the plan was already chalked out for us, set in stone. After his preparation in the lab, the explosives he'd set up, the destruction they would cause, and the lives they would claim, there was no moving backward.

We were on a freight train with broken brakes.

We had to execute, or die trying.

But as Lee left me to rest again and get an early night, I knew that I had become a different kind of passenger. The kind of passenger to leap from a runaway train. The kind who would not wait until the end.

CHAPTER 30

Once midnight fell, I swung my legs off the bed.

I stood up and didn't feel dizzy.

I walked around the room, my back straight, head up high. Still no dizziness. Then I moved to the bathroom and stared at myself in the mirror. My face was still bruised, of course, and the stitching beneath my eye still fresh. I searched my drawers to check my mustache and facial hair hadn't been removed and found them still there along with the adhesive and my wig.

I padded to the door and opened it a crack. The corridor outside was dark. I poked my head out fully, then stepped out. I couldn't hear any sounds indicating that Lee was downstairs, so I headed to his room and pressed my ear against the door. Deep, heavy breathing. He was asleep.

I hurried back to my room and applied the facial hair and wig in record time, then pulled on a jacket. I didn't need to bother with the bulky body suit. It was nighttime, so hopefully nobody would see me anyway.

Finishing in the bathroom, I approached my bed and stuffed three spare cushions beneath the blanket to make it look like my form was lying there—in case Lee came in for a brief glance during the night. I needed to buy myself as much time as possible.

Samuel was asleep in his basket outside the kitchen, and I hardly dared to breathe as I made my way to the front door. I picked up Lee's chain of keys hanging from the coat rack, pulled on a pair of shoes, and then slowly, carefully, went about opening the door. The metal was well-oiled and the mechanism opened with a soft click. I closed it and locked it behind me before heading round the building to Lee's motorcycle that was leaning against the wall.

Even though I was able to drive whatever vehicle I wanted in Matrus—I had never actually learned. I had spent too much time in detention to have come across the chance. Now, as I rolled the motorcycle out of the driveway, out of view from the house, I felt terrified. I barely knew how to start it—everything I was about to do was based on witnessing Lee and Viggo drive their motorcycles.

But this was the only way I could make it to Viggo's house.

This was the only way.

After strapping one of the helmets to my head and pushing the motorcycle a comfortable distance away from

Lee's house, I dared attempt to start it up at the side of the road. It took a minute before I managed it. It came alive more easily than I expected. Now I had to hope that riding it would come just as smoothly… It didn't.

As I hopped on, I immediately lost balance and my right leg almost got crushed beneath the falling machine. It took a good five minutes for me to feel comfortable raising my feet from the ground again. I revved the engine, causing the motorcycle to jerk forward. I almost lost balance a second time. I feared I might swerve off the road before I ever reached Viggo's.

But there was no time for second thoughts. I couldn't afford to entertain doubts.

I spurred the vehicle ahead, as slowly as I could without having the engine conk out due to the slope we were ascending, before gradually building confidence and rolling faster. I had two advantages at least: first, the roads up here weren't busy, and second, I knew the way to Viggo's cabin fairly well.

So, I found myself hurtling through the night, the road slipping away beneath me.

Framing Viggo wasn't the only way. I knew it wasn't. There had to be other scapegoats we could use. We could pin the whole operation on the men of Porteque. Leave a message behind on a building in big red letters or something, declaring it to be an act of rebellion. They were already anarchists, so this could follow on naturally from their recent kidnapping of me.

Whatever the case, once I'd seen Viggo, Lee and I would have no choice but to scramble around for another solution to prevent the blame falling on Matrus. Lee would be mad at me, but I didn't care. We'd figure out a last-minute alternative, because we'd have to. We both had too much at stake to fail in this mission.

Drops of rain began to fall. Drops which soon multiplied and came down harder and heavier, until I was drenched to my underwear.

Still, it didn't matter.

Almost there now. Almost there.

I was shivering by the time I recognized the turn down Viggo's lane. The rain had become torrential and it was a wonder that I hadn't skidded off the road entirely. I trundled down the dirt track—fast turning to thick mud—and skidded to a stop ten feet before Viggo's cabin.

No gas lamps shone through the gaps in the shutters. Perhaps he wasn't even home.

I had to pray that he was only asleep.

Discarding the motorcycle, I stood, my knees feeling shaky from the journey. The first thing I did was reach for my fake hair and tear it off, shoving it into my pockets. I might not even need it again after tonight.

My blood pounding in my ears, I hurried to Viggo's porch and scaled the steps to his front door. I hesitated to catch a breath, then knocked four times.

No answer.

I knocked again, five times, more loudly.

Still nothing.

Oh, no. Don't say he's out after all.

I left the porch, striding back out into the rain, and circled the building. Shutters covered every window. I couldn't see through a single one of them. Moving back toward the front of the building, I stopped dead in my tracks.

A light had been lit. As I turned a corner, at the bottom of the porch stairs was Viggo, wearing nothing but boxer shorts. His hair was mussed, his eyelids hooded. I had obviously woken him up.

But his expression came to life on realizing his intruder was me.

"Violet!" He gaped. "What are you doing here?" His eyes shot to the motorcycle, his face falling. "Where is your husband?"

I stood rooted to my spot as though paralyzed. "He's not here," I rasped.

Viggo launched forward and grabbed me by the hand, pulling me toward his porch, up the stairs and through to his cabin. He slammed the door behind us, towering over me in the hallway. He turned on me, backing me against the wall, his expression a mixture of alarm and utter confusion.

"You... You *drove* here?" he demanded.

My hands balled up. I nodded, holding his intense gaze.

"What the *hell* has gotten into you? Do you know the punishment you could receive for that infraction? And that's leaving aside the fact that you've roamed across a mountain at night completely on your own—have you forgotten what just happened to you?" He gripped my shoulders in frustration as I merely stared back at him. "Say something, dammit!"

I'd gone over what I was going to say to him in my mind already, but now that I was here, standing in this stupidly narrow corridor, Viggo so close to me we were practically touching, I felt breathless. Claustrophobic.

"I, uh, I need to tell you something," I managed, my voice deeper than it should have been.

His brows rose, eyes widening. "Clearly!"

I couldn't go so far as to tell him the truth, obviously. He couldn't know that I was a spy, that I'd been trying to frame him all along, or anything about our mission. After telling him all that, he'd likely not trust another word I said. Why should he? I had no idea how he'd react or what he'd do, and I couldn't run the risk of losing the chance to see my brother again. A chance I *still* was convinced that I had.

I just needed to make sure that Viggo didn't come anywhere near the lab tomorrow—even if I failed to convince Lee that the Porteque men would be better scapegoats.

Gathering confidence, I looked Viggo seriously in the eye, parting my lips to speak… but before I could utter a word, my jacket pocket vibrated. When I slipped a hand inside my pocket, it closed around my pager. I'd forgotten it was still in there. My throat drying out, I lifted the pager and glanced at the screen.

"SAY ANYTHING, AND HE WILL BE ASSASSINATED."
My blood ran cold.

Lee had woken up and tracked me down. I'd known all along this was a possibility, but I had been hoping against hope that I would make it back in time.

But what is Lee talking about?

Have Viggo assassinated?

Why?

How?

"Violet?" Viggo drew my attention back to him. "What's going on? Did your husband send a message?"

I hurriedly stuffed the pager back into my pocket. My first instinct was to assume that Lee had panicked on seeing me at Viggo's and was now bluffing out of desperation. *Lee doesn't even have those sorts of contacts here, does he?* I thought back to the moving red dots on Lee's computer screen. Lee had told me that they were people whose "help" he'd used. I wasn't sure to what extent that "help" could stretch, or how much he trusted them. Obviously not enough to work with him in directly stealing the egg; otherwise, why did he need me? Or maybe Lee would find a way to pull off the assassination himself.

I supposed it was possible that Lee wasn't bluffing.

But why? Why was assassination necessary? It was as though Lee was assuming that I'd lost myself to guilt and was about to spill everything to Viggo.

"Violet!" Viggo urged.

I parted my lips, on the verge of going through with my original plan. But Lee's message had burned itself into my brain.

Assassinated.

Maybe there were other reasons he (or his mysterious "helpers") would be forced to end Viggo. Reasons I wasn't aware of. Lee had said from the very beginning that Viggo was one of our biggest obstacles... and that was why Lee had sent me in to neutralize him.

Only in the process, I've become neutralized myself. I'd gotten "carried away". Exactly what Lee had repeatedly warned me against.

I tried to forecast Viggo's life in a few days' time, assuming that I went ahead with Lee's plan. Viggo would be facing death on that path, too. The state would offer him no less punishment for the crime. But maybe down that route, there was a chance that he would find a way out. A chance that he would find some evidence to prove himself innocent. Maybe Viggo could convince the authorities to conduct an in-depth investigation into the matter... Viggo would suspect me, having received my call to the crime scene. Maybe he wouldn't even link me to Matrus; maybe he'd think that I'd been traumatized and threatened so severely by the men of Porteque during my time captive there that I was doing their bidding in causing disruption. As I recalled the brainwashed Ada, that could be a plausible assumption.

And perhaps people would assume that I'd burned in the blast, so there would be no wondering where I'd gone.

And I'd be back in Matrus. Maybe even already reunited with my brother by the time investigations came to any conclusion.

As strange as it sounded, letting Viggo face Patrus' judicial system seemed like a better chance of survival for him.

"Violet!" Viggo clutched my shoulders and shook me again, forcing me to look him in the eye. "What did you come to tell me about? What could have *possibly* been so important that you felt the need to travel to me in the middle of the night without your husband?"

In his exasperation, Viggo had moved closer to me still. I could no longer take the pressure of his imposing form in such proximity. Pushing past him, I strode into the living room, clutching my head, my back turned to him.

Now I couldn't think of a single good reason I could offer as to why I had come here. Why I had gone behind my husband's back…

I might have already done irreparable damage by coming here tonight. Piqued his interest in Lee's and my relationship to a point where it should never have been piqued.

Viggo entered the living room after me. His tone had become calmer, quieter—more hesitant—as he said, "Has Lee… done something to you? Did you have an argument or…"

"No," I said, shaking my head firmly. "Nothing like that. We-We're okay." My pitch rose as I repeated, "We're okay."

The floorboards creaked. Viggo stood just a foot behind me now. I could hear his breathing. Breathe in his scent. My heartbeat quickened as his hand closed gently around my shoulder, endearing me to turn around.

"Then... what?" he asked.

I faced him. Blood rushed to my cheeks as I took in his tired face, his forehead lined with confusion. The stubble around his jaw had grown noticeably since the last time I'd seen him a few days ago, adding to his jaded appearance.

His confusion stabbed me with guilt. But more than confused... he looked concerned. Concerned, just as he had been after finding me wandering the streets alone, the second night of my arrival in Patrus. As he had been when he'd held my arm tightly after our encounter with the gang members outside the Rosen-Cruz fight. As he had been when saving me from Porteque and covering up my murder. After I'd woken up to him in the helicopter. And just now, as I'd arrived outside his house with a motorcycle in the pouring rain.

Viggo Croft was a good man.

Better than my Matrian upbringing had ever allowed me to imagine existed on this side of the river, or on my side.

He was the best I'd known on either side.

As he sighed, apparently giving up hope of ever receiving an answer from me, I no longer needed to wonder how to respond.

When I gazed at his face, adrenaline surged in me. My pulse raced. For the first time, I knew exactly what to do. It didn't require any thinking. Any weighing of the pros and cons. Just instinct. Pure, inescapable instinct.

"If you're not going to talk, then I need to take you—"

Viggo's voice trailed off as I closed the small distance between us. My arms acted of their own accord as they wound around his neck and shoulders. Then they were pulling me upward, closer, until I was standing on my tiptoes. My brows furrowed, my eyelids shut… and then my lips were on his. Heat rolled through my body.

His lips were firm. Voluminous. Lips that cushioned mine in a way that made me want to take them in my mouth one at a time, experience their fullness slowly, thoroughly. Lips that could engulf mine if he responded. But I didn't expect him to respond. He had frozen, arms stiff at his sides, every muscle beneath his bare shoulders and chest tensed against me.

Any second, I expected him to grab my arms and push me away. Insist that I leave.

But he didn't pry me off. Although he remained static… he was allowing me to kiss him. My chest fluttering, I dared raise my eyelids half open. His eyes were closed tight. A deep frown marring his features, he looked stricken with conflict.

Still, he didn't push me away.

He must have sensed I'd opened my eyes, for his opened a few seconds later—only halfway, like mine. We gazed at each other like two people drowning, neither of us having the strength to surface, even in the face of sinking deeper.

Then, at some point during those few dazed seconds, something sparked in Viggo's green irises. Fervor. Hunger... Need. And suddenly, my lips were no longer maintaining control. His lips moved, prying from my grasp, before returning a second later to establish dominance. His mouth claimed mine, unhurriedly at first, the way he might scope out a new opponent in the cage. Then it escalated to a strength that left me struggling to breathe. His kiss forced every muscle in my mouth to awaken as the rest of his body loosened, coming alive. His hands dove into my hair, his powerful fingers threading through its length before trailing down my back. His lips refusing to unlock from mine for even a second, he lowered himself, dragging his hands down to my thighs before hoisting me up against his hips. He moved to the nearest wall and pressed me against it. His palms ran the length from my knees to my thighs. Then they slid beneath my shirt. The coarseness of his hands against my bare skin lit me up. He stopped above my navel, his fingers curving round my waist as he held me firmly in place.

He'd pinned me, and now he had me.

His tongue parted my lips, allowing me to feel it for the first time. It brushed against the tip of mine before moving deeper. Exploring. Then devouring.

My senses were lost in him. His scent, his taste, his hard breathing. He had overpowered me completely, and I was losing this fight. Willingly losing it.

When I'd moved in, I'd had no game plan, no clear idea of what I was even doing, let alone how long I'd let it last. I'd just felt the overwhelming need to release my tension around him. To finally provide him with a response he'd been hounding me for. *Perhaps even to say goodbye.*

But I didn't think it would last long.

Time had lost its meaning, however. My mind had become comfortably numb. Viggo's mouth, taut skin and forceful grip became all that existed in my world.

I was afraid now to pull apart. Having figured out a pattern to regulate my breathing against the rhythm of his passion, I found myself slipping out of defense mode. Anchoring myself higher up against him, I wrapped my legs tightly around his waist, pulling my chest flush against his. I clutched the sides of his face, relishing the prickle of his stubble beneath my fingers. Like the mountains he insisted on living among, everything about Viggo was raw. Wild. *Real.* He was unadulterated masculinity. From his thick waves of hair to his rough, cut-up fists. I hadn't thought it possible for one person to crave another as I did in this moment... least of all a woman for a man.

I feared we might drown even deeper that night, the two of us alone in this cabin. Especially as his hands moved higher beneath my shirt, his thumbs tracing the top of my breasts, his palms grazing my bra cups.

But we never got the chance to test our self-restraint.

As a sharp rapping sounded at the door, Viggo and I were torn apart.

We stood, frozen, lips and cheeks flushed red, our hearts thumping. Reality slammed into us, and our delicate illusion shattered. We stared at each other as strangers would, stunned by what had happened. By what we had *allowed* to happen.

There was no time for words. Viggo, trailing a quick hand through his hair, snatched up a shirt hanging over the back of his armchair and jerked it over his head. While I—with no mirror to assist me—attempted to pat down my hair, straighten my clothes and look as though Viggo's hands hadn't just been up my shirt.

Searching my face, Viggo's eyes were still glassy, shining with desire, as I suspected mine were.

His expression was questioning. I nodded, even as I tried to tame my erratic breathing, still my trembling hands.

I was as ready to face Lee now as I ever would be.

CHAPTER 31

Viggo opened the front door to reveal Lee standing on the porch in a long black anorak with an umbrella tucked beneath one arm, dark circles beneath his eyes. "Viggo," he said. I could hardly hold Lee's gaze as he glanced my way. "I'm so sorry for this." Lee held out a hand to me and I had no choice but to brush past Viggo and take it, like an obedient child, allowing Lee to pull me next to him on the porch. His arm found my waist and he held me against him. "Violet has been unstable since Porteque. The doctor said it could be a long time before she recovers from the trauma. She's been sleep-walking, going blank when I ask her questions... I didn't think she'd ever do something as crazy as this."

Viggo didn't say a word. He stood, his face stoic, his eyes remaining determinedly on Lee. I averted my own gaze to the floor. It was torture to look Viggo in the eye now. Every fiber of my being still burned for him. My lips still tingled from his kiss. The scent and feel of his bare skin still tantalized me. Standing there in his doorway, his hair loose and mussed, eyes alight with a gleam that told me his consciousness, too, was still trapped living in the moments before Lee's arrival... he was temptation personified to me. I guessed I was the same for Viggo, given his refusal to look at me.

"I understand that you are bound to report my wife for this transgression," Lee said, giving my waist a tense squeeze. "But given everything she's been through... Would you be able to wait at least a few days? I fear what being taken to court will do for her mental health."

There was a pause before Viggo's baritone voice replied, "I cannot promise anything, Mr. Bertrand."

"Of course not," Lee said quickly. I was sure that even requesting Viggo to engage in "obstruction of justice" would put Lee on the line for punishment too, if Viggo decided to report us.

"Once again," Lee went on. "I'm deeply sorry for the inconvenience. I will deposit all the money I owe you to date. Just let me know the number of hours—you've been keeping track, I assume? As for the motorcycle she came with, can I figure out a way to pick it up tomorrow? If you wouldn't mind my leaving it here..."

"You can leave the bike here," was all Viggo said. His response made me wonder if he was even planning to accept Lee's money in the end.

Lee thanked Viggo again before pulling me away from the porch, down the stairs and into the rain—much lighter than when I had arrived—toward his second motorcycle, a dark red one.

I resisted the urge to look back at Viggo as he watched us move away. Move away, when all I wanted was to race back and throw myself into his arms. Wrap my legs around his waist and lose myself in him all over again.

But this wasn't a fairytale.

Viggo's and my story was everything but.

I couldn't be sure how long Viggo remained watching us leave, but the light from the gas lamp on his porch still cast shadows as we arrived at the end of the dirt track.

Only once we had joined the road and picked up speed did Lee break the silence.

"I think you owe me an explanation."

I felt his tenseness beneath my hands as I was forced to hold on to him for support.

I wasn't sure what to say. I had betrayed his trust and been caught red-handed. I figured there was nothing to say other than the truth.

"I couldn't help it."

"Couldn't help *what*?"

"I had to see him. I wanted to stop him from showing up tomorrow. I didn't..." My voice faltered. "I *don't* want to do this to him."

I expected a barrage from Lee, but instead he remained silent.

And he stayed silent until we reached his home. Entering the hallway, he removed his anorak and hung it over the coat holder before slowly turning around. His face was ashen. His eyes flickered to meet mine.

"Do you..." He hesitated, drawing in a breath. "Do you have feelings for him?"

I swallowed. "You could say that."

"What happened when you were alone in the cabin? Before I arrived? I need you to tell me."

"I didn't say anything, and I never planned to tell him anything about the mission. As I said, my only intention was to keep him away from the lab. But then... I shut up completely because of that damn message you sent me."

From pain and frustration rose anger.

"What did you mean by that message?" I asked him, my gaze turning into a glare. "Why would you assassinate him?"

"You know the seriousness of this mission. I don't need to remind you all that hangs in the balance. For Matrus. For you. For me. We can't afford any leaky holes." Lee's tone had become quite flat, past anger, and drenched in disappointment.

"Why do we need to use Viggo at all?" I demanded. "Why can't we pin this on Porteque?"

"It's too late to change the plan now. The banquet is tomorrow! There's no way we could pull that off in a believable manner with such short notice."

"I'll do it!" I stormed. "I'll find a way!"

"No, you won't," Lee said. "There is no time! And besides, it would be against our queen's orders. Before you even arrived, she and Alastair agreed that Viggo would be the best person. Porteque is too easy and obvious a scapegoat. If you defy them, I doubt they'll fulfill their end of your deal when you return."

My hands balled into fists. "It doesn't make sense! Porteque might be easier to set up, but there would be fewer potential holes with them than with Viggo. Hell, those sick bastards might even be happy to step up and claim credit for the deed."

Lee's nostrils flared. I could tell that it was taking a lot of effort to keep his voice calm as he replied, "Violet. I repeat: it is too late to be having this conversation. Alastair has relayed the queen's wishes. We cannot change everything at such a late hour. If you want her to keep her promise to you, you're going to have to go through with this."

Exhaling in aggravation, I drove my fists against the wall. The sound made Samuel bark and scamper into the hallway.

"Now I need you to answer a question," Lee went on. "How can I trust that you didn't tell Viggo anything? How do you expect me to believe you now?"

It took more than a minute before I could bring myself to reply.

"Well"—I breathed heavily—"if we're going through with this, you'll see tomorrow, won't you? You can listen to the conversation. You'll hear his response to my request and you'll know that I told him nothing."

Still, his gaze remained on me, searching me.

I dropped down to rip off my shoes, brushing Samuel away as he moved in to sniff me.

"So what actually happened?" Lee asked. "How did you explain your appearance?"

The way he was eyeing me, it was as if he sensed something deeper had gone on. Almost like he suspected me of kissing Viggo. Was that jealousy that twitched his jaw?

But I was tired of this conversation now. Tired of anger. Tired of everything. I wanted to lose myself in sleep. After the workout Viggo had given me, I probably could even coax myself into slumber.

"Nothing happened that would be of any interest to you," I said. "I made up a stupid excuse for why I was there and we waited until you arrived."

Avoiding his gaze, I moved to push past him. But he gripped my arm and pulled me back, forcing me to face him.

"Did he touch you?" Lee's expression was serious, his blue eyes glimmering in the soft hallway light.

"No," I replied through gritted teeth.

But Lee wasn't buying it.

"Are you sure?"

"*I* kissed him!" I exploded. "What does it matter to you?"

His lips parted at my admission. "It matters to me more than you think."

"Well, it shouldn't," I shot back, brushing him aside and running to the stairwell. I felt hot tears brimming in my eyes. I did not want Lee to see them. I rarely cried, and much more rarely showed it.

"Violet, wait," Lee called to me, but I ignored him. I thundered up the stairs to my room and slammed the door behind me.

I threw myself against the mattress and buried my head in the pillows, letting them absorb my tears. My body shook in silent sobs. I squeezed my eyes tight. I felt ashamed to cry, even on my own.

I wished that I was a robot. That I could simply do, and not think or feel. That was what Lee required on this mission. A robot. Not a girl.

I staggered to the bathroom and splashed my face with cold water in an attempt to calm myself, then crawled back into bed and willed myself to sleep.

But my door slid open before I could manage it.

I groaned internally, wishing Lee would leave me alone, at least until the morning.

To my surprise, he had brought in a tray and he set it down on my bedside table. Upon it sat a jug of water, a glass, and a small white sachet.

He knelt by my bedside. I met his eyes through the gloom.

"Have some water," he said.

I was actually grateful for it. I felt dehydrated and I finished the glass and replaced it on the tray. He refilled it, then picked up the sachet.

"I've brought you something that will help you push through tomorrow," he said, his voice somber.

I sat up in bed, staring at the sachet cradled in his fingers. "What?" I asked.

"A diluted dose of the drug we talked about. The emotion-suppressing drug - Benuxupane. This is enough to make an impact for the next twenty-four hours."

My eyes widened. This drug wasn't supposed to be publicly available yet. Lee must have gotten it from the lab. As wary as I was about this mysterious new drug, there was only one logical way to respond to Lee's offer.

I nodded. Indirectly, it was exactly what I had been wishing for only minutes before his arrival. I would usually be the last person to want to give up control over my feelings and emotions. But now, I needed to. If I was to survive tomorrow without breaking down, I had to swallow this thing.

Lee nodded back curtly before tearing open the sachet and handing it to me. I squeezed it over my mouth and out popped a small powdery pill, landing on the center of my tongue. Lee handed me a glass of water and I quickly downed it.

I sank back against the pillows. Lee stood up and gazed over me. "You see," he said quietly, "I had a reason for asking what went on with Viggo." He cleared his throat. "Now, there are some known side effects like a mild headache, heartburn, and, occasionally, anxiety. But they won't last. You should be fine."

I closed my eyes. *I'll be fine…*

Lee's palm brushed over my forehead briefly before he collected the tray and left the room.

Benuxupane… What a good idea of King Maxen's after all.

CHAPTER 32

An additional side effect of the drug seemed to be sleep-iness. I must've drifted off within ten minutes of swal-lowing the pill, and by the time I woke up, it was almost midday.

I sat up slowly in bed, rubbing my head and trying to make sense of what, if anything, was different about me. My head throbbed mildly. I also felt a slight churning in my stomach, though that was not necessarily a result of the pill.

I thought of last night. Of my visit to Viggo's cabin. Of our kiss. And I experienced the strangest feeling, if it could even be described as a feeling. I remembered every-thing, of course—every detail and every emotion that I had experienced then—yet recalling them did not bring the same pain they had last night.

Where longing and guilt had thrived was now a sense of hollowness. Of numbness. A dull, monotonous ache.

That pill was like a painkiller for the brain. My emotions were still there, somewhere beneath the surface, but I was not close enough to them for them to hamper my objectiveness. The pill didn't eradicate emotions, but smothered them. At least, at the dosage Lee had fed me.

My brain felt sharp. Clear. Alarmingly clear.

I thought of the day ahead of me. Of tonight. And I saw the goal with clarity. For the first time, I was able to separate feelings from duty. Something Lee had urged me to do all along.

I slipped out of bed and took a shower, then headed out of my room. I found Lee, sitting in front of the computer in his bedroom, fully dressed.

Our eyes locked.

He raised a brow, expectant. "Well? How are you feeling?"

I shrugged. "Not a lot."

"That's good," he said. "Very good."

He offered me a chair next to him at his desk. He had been staring at the map of Patrus City and he pointed to one of the red dots. "That's Viggo. He's at Head Office. Let's hope he's not reporting you for last night."

I knew that Viggo wouldn't.

"So," Lee went on briskly, "Let's go over the plan." He reached into his pocket and drew out his phone, placing it on the table. "During Viggo's lunch break, you need to call him and set the appointment for this evening. You're going to say that you want to talk to him about last night.

Don't give him too many details—the point is to pique his interest. You will say that you are going to be accompanying me to the lab's banquet tonight, and that you want to meet him outside the camera room. He knows where that is. There's a quiet, private space outside the camera room, so he won't find it strange that you are asking him to head there."

I nodded.

"You need to tell him that you will try to slip away from me and be there at seven-fifteen p.m. But request him to wait for up to thirty minutes in case you can't leave me that quickly. Promise him that you will meet him."

Again, I nodded.

"The cameras will catch him heading to the security room. Soon after that, the cameras on the ground floor will stall. And fifteen minutes later, the first round of bombs will detonate at the back of the banquet hall."

"*First* round of bombs?" I asked, frowning.

"Yes," Lee said. "Plans changed in the last week—we will be blowing not just the ground floor, but also upstairs. Not only will this create an additional distraction, but it will choke the sky more thickly with smoke which, as you'll see, will be important."

"And where will we be?"

"Up until the bombs go off, we will be attending the banquet, of course. We will arrive at the lab at about six-thirty. Everyone will be chatting and relaxing in the lounge until about seven-ten, when we'll head to the dining hall. The banquet will be served at seven-thirty—which is when the first bombs are due to explode. I'll be watching the clock, and four minutes before, at seven twenty-six, I will receive a blank call. We'll be in the main hall, which is large. The bombs have been installed within the walls of the furthest end of the room from the door. We'll use the blank call as an excuse to stand by the exit, on the opposite corner of the explosives. I'll tell them that your aunt, who is sick, has called and you need to take a few minutes to talk to her. I'll accompany you to the door, where we'll hold an imaginary conversation in view of everyone.

"Then, as soon as the bombs go off, you'll rush to the egg's lab using the staircase, while I'll head off in a different direction to arrange transport for us…" I listened carefully as he began to explain how to set up the bombs around the glass casing of the egg and have them implode without blowing myself up.

He made me repeat the process three times until he was satisfied that every detail had sunk in, though I would've appreciated a practice run.

"Then," he went on, "all you'll have to do is retrieve the egg, hurry to the stairs, and head up to the roof. You will find the door leading out to the rooftop open, and I'll be waiting for you there. From the time you leave me downstairs, you'll have exactly fifteen minutes. You mustn't be any later than that."

Fifteen minutes was tight for all that. The light fitting hiding the package was fiddly. At least I'd opened it once already. I had to hope the second time wouldn't take me as long.

"So," Lee said, clasping his hands together, "that's all you'll have to do. Alastair is due to call to check in on us in about fifteen minutes. And we'll make the call to Viggo in an hour."

I sat in the kitchen opposite Lee, clutching his phone in my hands and staring down at Viggo's number. I pressed dial. My palms grew sweaty as it rang.

"Mr. Bertrand?" Viggo's deep voice spoke in my ear after five rings.

"Mrs. Bertrand," I replied.

Viggo went quiet. So did I.

Lee widened his eyes at me.

"I'm sorry to disturb you," I said, wetting my lower lip, "but I need to talk to you about last night."

There was a beat before he replied, "I'm not sure that's a good idea."

"It probably isn't," I said. "But I need to speak to you. I'll be at the lab's banquet with Lee tonight. I need to... get something off my chest."

"Where is your husband now?"

"Taking the dog for a walk. He's off work today."

"Then why can't you tell me now?" Viggo posed.

"It's something best said in person."

Another span of silence. Then I heard him drawing a breath. "All right," he muttered. "I'll meet you, but after that, I think it's best that we don't see each other again. I doubt your husband will ask me to have a lot more to do with you."

"Okay," I said, my voice going a tad scratchy.

"Where do you want to meet?"

"In the lab building. Outside the camera room."

"Hm. Okay."

"At seven-fifteen. I'll do my best to arrive at that time, but if I have some trouble getting away from Lee, could you wait for up to thirty minutes? If I don't arrive by seven forty-five, feel free to leave."

Asking anybody to hang around for thirty minutes was disrespectful. I could hear his reluctance, but he agreed. He was probably regretting ever having gotten involved with me in the first place.

"Okay, I'll see you later," I concluded. "Goodbye, Viggo."

"Goodbye, Mrs. Bertrand."

CHAPTER 33

Lee was pleased by my performance.

"Now you can relax for the next few hours," he said. "We will be leaving here at five-thirty to allow us some leeway with the traffic, but I suggest you get ready in good time. And wear something nice."

I wished that we didn't have hours to wait. I wished that we could leave now and get it all over with.

But the time passed quickly. Before I knew it, I was in my room getting ready. I chose the same blue dress that I had worn for Lee's and my wedding. When I ran, I would have to hike it up, but the only thing suitable for an occasion such as a banquet would be a long dress, according to Lee. I would wear my heels too. Those would definitely have to come off.

After I finished dressing and trying to make my hair look presentable, I left my room and found Lee sitting at his computer again. He was already dressed in a black tuxedo. His hair was gelled back, his face clean-shaven. He looked bland, nondescript. The polar opposite of Viggo's rugged style.

He looked me over as I eyed him, then reached into a drawer and handed me the same pack of tools that I'd used the last time I'd ventured into the egg's lab. Screwdrivers for the light fitting. He also retrieved a small lady's handbag and gave it to me.

"Got this for you in anticipation."

I couldn't quite bring myself to say thanks. I took the bag from him and stuffed the tools into it.

Lee returned his focus to the screen. "We still have about fifteen minutes before we're due to leave," he said. "Viggo is there." He pointed to a red dot near Crescent River. I couldn't find the other four dots, though I spotted my own. I hadn't questioned Lee about the tracker he'd given me and he hadn't mentioned it either. There wasn't much to say, given that I'd be dead by now if he hadn't thought to do it.

Lee shut down the map. "We won't need this after tonight," he said. "I'm going to be uninstalling it from my system and wiping all traces of it."

After he'd finished getting rid of the map, we headed downstairs.

"I've called a car service," he explained as he led me out of the house.

It was a warm evening, the clear sky streaked with hues of orange. A shiny black vehicle rolled up on the gravel five minutes later. The chauffeur got out to let us into the back of the car.

As we drove off, I glanced back at Lee's pyramid house. It was strange to think that this would be the last time I ever laid eyes on it. My sanctuary since I'd arrived. I felt a dull tug of guilt that I hadn't bidden farewell to Samuel.

Even though it was rush hour, the journey went quickly. Time seemed to have sped up, and I was grateful for it.

Soon, the car was drawing into the parking lot of the laboratory, and Lee was helping me out. I checked my watch. Six twenty-eight.

Entering the building's reception, I could hear the sound of male chatter. Lee led me past the lobby, along a corridor, and into the same lounge I had visited during my first trip to the lab. Extra seating had been placed in here, along with two extra billiards tables. The room was packed. I spotted a couple of familiar faces from my first visit: Simon, and then Richard, Lee's boss. It was as my eyes fell on the latter that I realized I wasn't the only woman here. There were two other wives, both apparently belonging to Richard—a blonde and a brunette. Wearing tightly fitted gowns, teetering heels, and long earrings that tangled with their curled hair, they didn't look much older than me. They stood on either side of him, clutching his arms. I looked away as they caught my eye.

Lee began to mingle with the crowd, introducing me to people as we passed. My mind was too distant to retain names. I merely smiled and nodded my head politely, which was all they expected from me anyway.

I kept glancing at my watch as Lee engaged in conversation. At six forty-five, Lee made his way with me over to an empty snack table as an excuse to get a bit of breathing—or rather, talking—space. "You heard what Simon said?" he asked me beneath his breath as he popped a salt-encrusted nut into his mouth.

"No." I wasn't able to concentrate on the conversations.

"He said King Maxen confirmed his plan to come. He's expected at seven-ten, about the time we're due to head into the banquet hall."

Five minutes before Viggo.

"So does that change anything?" I murmured.

"We just have to hope he's not late."

We returned to the sofas. The next twenty-five minutes slipped away in a blur of dark-colored suits and jovial chatter. As seven-ten drew in, the room became noticeably quieter, everyone anticipating the king's arrival. Then a man poked his head through the door to announce that the king would be delayed by five minutes.

Lee's face noticeably tightened at the information. That would give everyone ten minutes to settle into the banquet hall before the bombs imploded at half past. Assuming King Maxen didn't arrive even later—the banquet wouldn't start without him. If the bombs went off before we made it to the hall, they would still cause a distraction, of course, but Lee and I wouldn't be able to slip away so easily and discreetly to do what we needed to do.

But none of this worry was necessary. At seven-sixteen, the same man who'd come to announce King Maxen's lateness returned to announce his arrival. About a minute later, a tall, broad-shouldered man wearing a light gray—almost silvery—suit appeared in the doorway. He had thick sandy brown hair that extended to his jawline, which sported an immaculately groomed goatee. Clutched in his right hand was some kind of walking stick, though to call it that would be an injustice. It looked more like a scepter, forged of what appeared to be solid silver, its rounded clutch engraved with gold. Behind him stood two burly-looking men who hardly fit into their straight tuxedos. Bodyguards, no doubt.

A smile peeled across King Maxen's face, flashing a set of pearly white teeth. I had seen his picture before, but it was quite a different experience meeting him in the flesh. I could understand why people called him charismatic. There was an energy he brought to a room. "Gentlemen," he said, his voice smooth and deep. "I do apologize for keeping you waiting. Apparently, even the king is susceptible to rush hour in Patrus City."

Chuckles swept around the room.

"Shall we proceed to the hall?" he posed.

Everybody who had been seated rose immediately and bowed. The king turned and headed down the hallway with his bodyguards, while the rest of us filed after him.

The banquet hall was several doors along and the aroma of food filled my nostrils as we entered. The hall contained a huge table spanning the entire length of the room. Shiny steel warmers and platters were already laid out down the middle of the table, along with plates and cutlery. I pitied the man who ended up at the opposite end of the table. It was so close to the furthest wall. That person ended up being Richard, his two wives seating themselves on either side of him, while King Maxen sat at the head on the opposite end, his bodyguards occupying the chairs immediately next to him. The rest of us chose our seats. Everybody was obviously hungry. We were all seated and settled by seven-twenty… Leaving us ten minutes.

The king rose to his feet. He didn't need to tap a glass to call for silence. Everyone's eyes were already fixed on him.

He beamed around the table. "I am delighted to be here for this momentous occasion. More than anything, tonight is a celebration of you fine gentlemen. With your intelligence and determination, we have made progress this year many predicted impossible. It is you who are the building blocks of our society. You are the future. The lives of our future generations are in your hands. This year, you have all demonstrated that you are fully capable of bearing such a responsibility, and I anticipate you will do your nation proud for years to come. Thank you for your service to mankind."

Everybody clapped. The king, raising his glass, sat down. "Now, let us feast!"

His speech hadn't lasted long. It was seven twenty-four now. Dinner was to be served early. Servers piled into the room and began to assist the guests in laying appetizers on their plates... and then Lee's phone went off.

Now seven twenty-six.

Lee pulled the phone from his pocket, making a show of embarrassment. "Violet, it's your aunt. She couldn't have called at a worse time." He turned to Simon—who sat on the other side of him—apologetically, as well as the other men looking our way. "Excuse us for a minute."

Lee betrayed his nerves as he gripped my hand far more firmly than necessary to lead me toward the exit. We stopped at the door, still in clear view of everyone, where he "accepted" the call and handed me the phone.

"Are you out of the hospital yet?" I asked of my imaginary aunt. "Oh. Since when? Did you ask the doctor about that?"

My heart was in my throat as I spent the next minute conversing with myself. Then two minutes. Then three minutes...

And then came the blast.

I felt the heat as Lee jerked me through the doors and out of the room. Shouts and screams erupted amidst the explosion, chilling me to the bone. Lee raced faster down the hallway than I'd thought him capable of. I yanked off my heels and strapped them to an arm in order to keep up. We reached the reception area. Now it was time to part ways. Lee pointed to the stairwell and I darted for it, not even checking to see which direction Lee headed in. I didn't have a split second to waste. I had only fifteen minutes to blow open the casing around the egg and then reach the roof.

I raced up the staircase as fast as my legs could carry me. By the time I'd reached the top, I had burned through almost two minutes.

Panting, I raced along the corridor to the egg room. I stopped outside it, staring at the closed door.

Crap.

Before I'd had to page Lee for it to open, but now... I stopped panicking as I pushed at the door. It was already open. Of course, Lee had thought of this.

Emerging in the familiar lab, I hurtled across the room toward the egg. I stood on the nearest table beneath the light fitting and, reaching into the small handbag that had remained hanging from my arm since I left the taxi, I drew out the tools. My hands were shaking as I began to work on the screws. Even though I was several floors up, I could hear the noise from below. *Block it out. Focus.*

I loosened the first bolt, then the second and third, until I arrived at the last one. I quickly realized that I had made a grave mistake when replacing this fitting last time. The teeth of the screw were damaged, chipped. Which meant that none of my tools could gain a grip on it, and I had no leverage to open it.

But I had already opened the others successfully. Inserting my fingers at the edge of the fitting, I pulled downward and managed to create a gap large enough to fit a hand through. I felt for the package and found it where I'd left it. Gripping it, I coaxed it out, pressing downward against the fitting to make the gap wider. As I slipped it through, the edge of the fitting must have been too sharp and it caused a tear in the foil package—two small red cylinders fell to the floor.

I leapt off the table and scooped them up, praying that they hadn't been damaged. I planted them on the table where I emptied the rest of the bag's contents. There were five red cylinders altogether, a wire that split into five at one end, with a black button-like object at the other end, and a small black device with a round red button in the center of it: the activator.

I checked my watch.

Eight minutes.

I can do this.

Recalling Lee's detailed instructions, I began to set up the bomb. Each cylinder contained a sticky pad which allowed it to attach to the glass around the egg. Then I clipped the split wire into the ends of each of the cylinders before switching on a button at the base. It began to flash.

I took the activator in my hands, and pressed a switch on this one too. It also began to flash.

Six minutes.

I hurried backward to the other end of the room, as far as I could, and ducked beneath a table. Then, closing my eyes, I pressed the activator.

Nothing happened.

I waited for ten seconds—even though Lee said that it was supposed to go off within three. The ten seconds turned into twenty, and then I could wait no longer.

Dammit.

Whether the cylinders were faulty to begin with, or the fault had something to do with the two cylinders that I'd dropped, I didn't know.

I hurried back to the explosives and examined the wires, thinking that perhaps I hadn't inserted some properly. I thought I'd been so careful to check them, but now that I scrutinized them, one looked slightly out of place. On one of the cylinders that I'd dropped, the fitting had become loose. I needed to push the wire further inward, but that could cause the explosives to detonate too soon.

I had no choice now. I gazed around the lab, looking for some—any—kind of utensil that could assist me. I found a pair of longish tongs and grabbed them. Gripping the wire, I pushed inward.

A beep sounded.

It had worked.

"3" flashed up on my activator's tiny screen.

Adrenaline surging through my veins, I threw myself against the floor and tried to get beneath a table as the bombs erupted. Although I'd managed to duck beneath a steel table which bore the brunt of the blast and shattering glass, the billowing heat scorched my face and inflamed my Porteque injuries. An alarm blared.

Three minutes.

Coughing, I gripped the hem of my dress and pulled it up to cover my mouth and nose. I stood up and gazed at the explosion's aftermath. Setting off something like this in a lab was extremely dangerous—Lee had warned me of that. Any number of flammable substances could ignite at any moment now. That was why I had to grab the egg and get the hell out.

I picked up a chair and planted it a few feet in front of me, using it as an island to draw closer to the unprotected egg, still perched in its stand, until I could lean over and close my hands around it, touching it for the first time. It was cool and sleek and heavier than I had expected it to be. My palms being sweaty didn't exactly help my grip around it, but I held on to it for dear life as I raced to the lab's exit.

I dashed along the corridor, back to the stairwell. I scaled the first flight of stairs, and as I reached the second I heard the second round of explosions, higher up in the building. Lee hadn't been joking when he'd said I needed to get out in time.

The door at the top of the stairwell was like a gateway to heaven as I reached it. I pulled down hard on the handle, pushing it open, and staggered out into the cool night breeze.

I'd done it. I'd made it out alive. *And now… where was Lee?*

I gazed around the rooftop, whose atmosphere was quickly clogging with smoke. Lee wasn't up here.

Did something go wrong?

Rotors whirred above me. My immediate fear was that it was one of Patrus' helicopters called to the incident.

I was sure that they would arrive soon, but this… this was not one of them. This was something… I wasn't even sure how to describe. It was a bizarre hybrid aircraft. Its body was a large motorcycle, long enough to fit four people. Above it, fixed to a thick pole that ran down the center of the motorcycle, were spinning rotors. And on either end of it—where the wheels should have been— were two square wooden boxes, big enough to fit two men: I guessed some kind of balancing mechanism. Sitting on the seat and clutching the handles was Lee. He was twist- ing the latter to navigate the aircraft.

This must have been what he had been working on all along in his garage. "Fixing" his third spare motorcycle. I had assumed that by "arranging transport" for us, Lee had meant that Matrus would have provided something. But no. All this time he had been building an illegal aircraft in his basement. His engineer Chris had also broken the law. Lee must've bribed him well... and hidden the aircraft somewhere nearby in anticipation of tonight.

Lee looked relieved to see me, to say the least. He lowered the aircraft within two feet of the ground. Clutching the egg with one arm, I hauled myself up onto the seat and sat behind him.

"Hand me the egg," Lee said.

I placed it on his lap. He carefully slid it into a basket at the base of his seat, keeping it protected with both feet.

I wrapped my arms firmly around his waist as we took off. As we moved past the rooftop of the lab, my stomach flipped. As we flew over a sheer drop, I couldn't even see the ground because of the smoke, and certainly nobody could see us.

Lee sped up—we had to get out of here before Patrian aid arrived.

We headed firmly eastward, leaving the smoke-infested area. The river came into view, and Matrus' border loomed in the distance. Screams and shouts still echoed in my head as I glanced back over my shoulder at the destruction we had left behind. Then my eyes dragged over the rest of the city, and the looming mountains beyond.

So long, Patrus... So long.

CHAPTER 34

Lee and I had been quiet the whole journey. As we reached Matrus' border, he hovered a little lower, closer to the tops of the building. When I realized we were headed straight for Queen Rina's palace, I asked, "Are you going to finally tell me what's in the egg or not?"

"Not," Lee replied, clipped. "I don't have permission. That doesn't change because we've crossed borders. You'll have to ask the queen or Alastair and see if they'll reveal it to you. Alastair will have the key, and no doubt he'll want to verify the egg's contents are intact."

I ground my teeth. After everything I'd been through, I felt I was owed an explanation. I would ask Alastair when I next saw him. When I'd spoken to him before we left for the banquet earlier this evening, he'd said that he and the queen would be waiting to receive us on the highest floor of the palace—which was where the queen's private residential quarters were.

Passing over the wall of the palace compound, we flew to a circular landing pad on its roof and, with a shudder, touched down. My knees felt weak as I slipped off the seat, my bare soles touching the concrete. I still had my heels strung around my right arm. I shook them off, letting them fall to the floor.

"You don't have any spare shoes with you, do you?" I asked Lee. My shoulder bag was too small to hold much other than the tools.

Lee got off the motorbike and opened up the seat, pulling out a black backpack with a pair of shoes inside. "I did bring these, actually. In case anything went wrong and we had to do some extra running." They were my old shoes, the ones I'd arrived in Patrus with. I gave my handbag—which I had no further use for—to Lee, who dropped it into the underseat compartment before I slipped the shoes on and tied up the laces.

After snapping the seat shut, Lee turned his focus to a door fifteen feet away. I was about to start walking toward it, but he caught my hand and held me back.

"Wait here with the egg," he said. "I need a private word with them first."

I stayed put as Lee disappeared through the door. I breathed in deep, gazing around at the sparkling lights of Matrus City. It felt so strange to be back. I suspected it would take a few days to erase Patrus from my brain. To remember that I didn't legally require a man for anything anymore. That men were the ones who submitted to us.

But I didn't feel as liberated as I should have.

I was still feeling numb. I had several hours to wait until the Benuxupane wore off. I would see what emotions flooded back to me then.

Lee was longer than I had expected him to be. I wondered what he was talking about. *Something about me?*

Finally I heard footsteps returning up the stairwell. He emerged from the doorway, his bunched tuxedo jacket and bag over one shoulder, while stuffing black gloves into one pocket.

His expression was serious as he said, "Okay, you can go down now. First door on your right after leaving the staircase. I'll fetch the egg."

I ventured down the stairwell, which consisted of two flights of steps, through an open reinforced door, and into a long quiet hallway. It was lined with embroidered silk carpets, and the high walls were bedecked with portraits of Queen Rina's family and lineage. I paused to gaze at her seven daughters. They shared her features prominently: slanted brows and sharp cheeks. Their ages ranged from seven to twenty-six. All conceived via insemination—all female. Matrus' doctors had methods of maximizing the chances of conceiving a female, but they weren't always accurate. Abortion wasn't permitted in Matrus, however—not even of male children—so I supposed the queen must have gotten lucky. (To my knowledge, abortion wasn't allowed in Patrus either.)

I continued and stopped outside the first door on my right. It was half open. I knocked briefly before stepping inside a warmly-lit library, bordered by towering cherry-wood bookcases. My eyes fell on the round table in the center of the room, surrounded by high-backed chairs. I could make out the queen and Alastair sitting next to each other, backs toward me.

I approached the table and circled it to greet them... only to lay eyes on two corpses.

Their heads lolled over their chests, their backs slumped, their fronts drenched in blood. Etched across their throats were wide, still-oozing gashes.

I stood, paralyzed. I blinked hard and fast, wondering if it was a hallucination brought on by the drug. I touched Queen Rina's stiff shoulder.

It wasn't a hallucination.

It was real.

A bloodstained knife lay in front of the bodies, a few centimeters away from a message that had been scratched into the wooden table surface:

"FOR THE BOYS OF MATRUS."

My veins turned to ice.

"Lee," I choked. "Lee!" I staggered out of the room and rushed to the staircase as I continued to call for him. My voice gained volume as I ascended the steps... and caught the sound of whirring rotors.

"LEE!" I screamed, leaping the final steps and bursting out onto the roof.

Lee and his aircraft were already four feet in the air, and soaring toward the edge of the building.

"LEE! NO!"

His head tilted toward me, an almost apologetic expression on his face as he called down in a steady, steely voice, "I'm sorry, Violet. If we want truth in our world, some things must be done, and sacrifices must be made."

His words barely registered in my brain. My mind couldn't make sense of what was happening.

I had just walked in on the queen and Alastair murdered. And now Lee was flying away. With the egg.

In a haze of panic, my throat clamped up. I could no longer even scream.

Adrenaline then took over. His aircraft still being within reach, I lunged forward and, with a jump I'd hardly thought I was capable of, I grabbed hold of one of the bars that lined the aircraft's undercarriage just three seconds before it crossed the roof's perimeter. Thrust over a sheer drop of over thirteen floors, I fought to maintain my grip on the bars as the aircraft dipped with my weight.

Pulling my legs upward, I hooked them over another bar on the other side of the carriage, gaining a better hold while the aircraft continued to speed away from the palace.

As I was on the verge of attempting to pull myself higher, Lee's heavy boot crashed down against my right hand. Bone cracked. Pain erupted from my middle finger and seared up my wrist. My right hand slipped.

Hanging now by only one hand and my legs, I thrust my right arm toward a bar near the center of the under-carriage and forced my throbbing hand to wrap around it.

As Lee moved to drive his boot down against my left hand, I could afford to relinquish my grip. I let go a second prior to his boot hitting the metal. Before he could with-draw it again, I clamped my fingers around his ankle and jerked downward with all the strength I possessed.

I heard the scraping of his second boot against the motorcycle's uneven metal floor. He was sliding. Then he was shrieking. He was falling. Past me. Way past me. Down, down, down. And then, within the blink of an eye, he was lying spread-eagled on the pretty brick path that ran through the queen's back garden. Rigid and still.

CHAPTER 35

The dose of Benuxupane Lee had given me wasn't strong enough to suppress the fear ripping through my chest. Clinging to the base of the aircraft, the blood rushing to my head as I gaped down at Lee's dead body, I felt paralyzed. I was barely even aware that the aircraft was continuing to soar ahead unmanned. I was lost in the past, reliving every second of the last ten minutes.

What just happened?

Why?

Why did he do it?

My sweating right hand sliding on the bar snapped me back to the present. I felt numb all over from shock, but I had to climb up onto the motorcycle unless I wanted to join Lee in the queen's ornamental grounds.

Gradually, I managed to maneuver my way upward, making use of my left hand over my right as much as I could, until I was perched on the motorcycle's seat, my feet planted firmly on either side of me. I gripped the base of my seat and gazed back at the increasingly distant palace. Lee's form fell out of my vision, the high wall bordering the palace concealing him. The aircraft no longer seemed to be ascending much, but it was hurtling forward with unnerving speed. I looked ahead of me, over the sprawling city, and the suburbs beyond. Terror clawed at me. I had not the first clue how to navigate this thing. It was a wonder to me that it was even still flying, that it hadn't crashed to the ground the moment Lee fell out.

Where am I going?

What. Just. Happened?

I didn't know how to start making sense of it. But what I did know was that I had to put as much distance between myself and that palace as possible, as fast as possible. I didn't know how long it would take for the queen and Alastair's bodies to be discovered. I cursed myself for making so much noise when shouting for Lee. After discovering their corpses, I'd fallen into a stupor of disbelief and been so stupid as to place a hand upon the queen's shoulder. A bare hand. I'd left behind my trace. And whoever discovered them would notice that the door that led up to the rooftop had been left open. They'd search the roof, notice Lee's body, if that hadn't been discovered beforehand. And realize I would be missing.

I didn't know whether anyone else in that palace was aware of the mission Lee and I were supposed to be carrying out in Patrus. Whether they knew that we were due to return in Lee's makeshift aircraft. But if anyone did know, surely the first thing they would assume was that I had gone flying off with it. They'd send a horde of helicopters after me.

This could be happening at any moment.

My heart quivering, I fixed my eyes ahead and dared place my hands on the handlebars for support.

How does this thing work?

I'd caught a glimpse of Lee twisting the throttle while riding it, the way you would twist the throttle of a regular motorcycle. Was that action spurring the aircraft forward? Were any of the bike's other parts used for similar functions? The brakes for slowing?

God. This is insane.

Sweat dripped from my forehead as I mustered the courage to twist the throttle. The engine chugged. The rotors spun faster. The aircraft's speed increased. I blew out unsteadily. I'd figured out how to accelerate. Stopping— and eventually landing—would be another terrifying experience entirely. But I had no idea when I could stop or land. I couldn't anywhere in the city, or in the suburbs. With the queen's death, this entire area would soon be swarming with wardens. I had to go further. Beyond the suburbs.... The Green. That was where I would reach if I kept moving. And then? Once I reached The Green? Then what?

What had Lee been thinking? Where had he been planning to head? Back to Patrus? Was that where his loyalties really lay?

Then why the hell would he agree to blow up the lab and attempt to kill the king in the process?

He couldn't have been loyal to Patrus. And I couldn't believe that he would head back there. He had been navigating northward. In the same direction I was going now. The Green.

Where was Lee's backpack? I couldn't see it hanging anywhere. And, for that matter, where was the egg? *That blasted egg.* They must be in the compartment beneath my seat.

Before I could even begin trying to formulate my next step, I had to attempt to figure Lee out. How could he have been playing both sides all along? And why? For the egg? Why did he want it? It struck me that he must have taken the key from Alastair before he murdered him. Hopefully it hadn't still been on Lee's person when he'd fallen.

I threw another anxious glance over my shoulder. I could barely even make out the palace anymore.

The city was slipping away beneath me, and soon, so were the suburbs. I twisted the throttle, increasing the aircraft's speed further.

Daring to stand, I unlatched the seat to reveal a much larger compartment than I'd expected to find. Shafts of moonlight escaping through the clouds revealed Lee's backpack, dozens of tins of food, bottles of water, three guns, four knives, five aerosol sprays (the same variety that Ms. Dale had brought with us to The Green), spare clothing, a flashlight, a breathing mask, thick gloves… and the egg, safely stowed in one corner. He had come prepared for The Green.

I grabbed the flashlight and the backpack before closing the seat and resuming my sitting position. Switching on the light, I unzipped the main compartment and began to rummage in search of the key. Within it was another knife, a box of matches, a loop of rope, an unlabeled white tube of pills that looked suspiciously like Benuxupane, a compass, a camera… and then two photographs. I removed the compass and placed it in a small holder that was fixed beneath the gears. Then I picked up the photographs and shone my light down on them. My breath hitched. One of them displayed an all-too-familiar sight: the table in the queen's library, etched with the words *"FOR THE BOYS OF MATRUS"*. The second displayed a different message. *"FOR THE MEN YOU WILL DECEIVE"* was scratched into the tinted windshield of a shiny gold sedan. It looked like King Maxen's vehicle. Perhaps Lee had scratched that message while it was pulled up in the lab's parking lot, after the blast. We had parted ways on the ground floor.

What does all this mean?

What about the boys of Matrus?

Fear surged through me as I recalled Viggo's speculation. *No. They can't be killing the marked ones. They can't be.*

As I dove deeper into the backpack, my fingers closed around a crumpled piece of paper. I pulled it out and flattened it. It was covered with smudged black handwriting. My mouth fell open as I began to read.

"Desmond,

I regret what I will have to do. To Violet Bates the criminal. Chris Patton the engineer. Duncan Friedman the arms specialist. Seb Morrissey the camera technician. Jacob Venn the immigration officer. But when we have the egg and its key, I will remember that each served their purpose.

Sacrifices must be made.

I imagine the furor I will have created in both nations tonight. I can't be sure that King Maxen will be killed, but Patrus' prize lab will be shaken, and on Matrus' side, the queen and Alastair will be wiped out.

And neither nation will have the egg.

It's possible Patrus will piece together the puzzle and discover that the terrorist was not Viggo Croft. Even if they consider my and Violet's sudden absence a casualty of the explosion, we will have hardly left a hole-free trail. It doesn't matter. I don't give a damn whether a war sparks between the two nations on the back of my actions.

Every step I've taken to "conceal" Violet's and my tracks and place the blame on Viggo has been mostly a front for Violet so that she continues to trust that I'm in line with Matrus' wishes, as well as to satisfy Alastair, who continues to hound me for updates.

Alastair intends for me to assassinate Viggo after he shows up at the lab. Make it look like he committed the crime and then claimed his own life as some kind of statement. That would ensure Matrus' involvement being ruled out of the picture. But I won't bother with that.

Because, again, I don't care.

As I've sensed Violet beginning to get more out of control, however, it's been important that I rein her in. She is still of use to me, and I need her obedience. I've tried to command it with affection (albeit half-heartedly). That's had no effect on her. I've had to control her by other means, like monitoring her with the tracker. And I'll feed her a pill. I think that will be needed in order for the night to run smoothly.

God knows, I've had enough obstacles already. But it will all come through in the end. I know it will.

Patrus believes me to be Patrian. Matrus believes me to be Matrian. They don't know that I belong to neither.

I am a man of no nation.

Many people see that as a curse. But for me, it's a gift. It's allowed me to perceive the world in a way that others can't. Others who are too embedded in the two systems to even consider a life beyond that which has been chalked out for them.

I'm not sure how far back my discontent has dated with the two societies. Perhaps as early as eight. But I remember the day I finally decided I needed to escape.

It was only recently, soon after King Maxen's ascent to the throne. By some twist of providence, two incidents I haven't been able to ignore occurred within the space of a few days. I discovered the real reason King Maxen commissioned Benuxupane, and the truth about the marked boys of Matrus.

Since the two incidents, it's simply been a matter of waiting for the right opportunity. If I am going to escape, I want to leave with a bang, so to speak. I want to leave a mark on both nations—one neither will forget in a hurry.

When the egg went missing from Matrus, I saw my opportunity and seized it.

The truth is, even I don't know what's within that sleek metal egg. All I know is that anything both governments want can't be a good thing for anyone, no matter how many self-serving lies they spout.

And so, with this mission, I will be able to accomplish both objectives in one strike. Mark, and flee.

Just as I will leave a note for Matrus, I will also leave one for Patrus.

I don't know where I will head, or if I will survive. If there is anything at all beyond that mass of forest.

But even if The Green is indeed as endless as people believe, if my aircraft gives way before I manage to cross it and I never live to discover what lies beyond the trees… I don't care.

I will have lived a fuller life in the past twenty-four hours than in all of my twenty-five years of living.

I will die a free man.

Not a pawn in someone's game.

Lee."

As I finished reading, my hands were trembling so hard I could no longer hold the paper straight. This strange letter exploded a dozen questions in my mind, but I could focus on only one.

The boys. What had Lee discovered about the boys?

Folding up the paper, I slipped it back into the bag. My heart palpitating, I continued to search through its contents. I discovered a small silver key in one of the side pockets. Retrieving it, I stood up again and opened the seat. I planted the backpack inside before reaching down to scoop up the egg. I placed it on my lap as I resettled.

The keyhole was near the base. Attempting to still my hands, I managed to insert the key into the hole and twisted it clockwise. It moved two hundred and seventy degrees before stopping. There was a click, and then a smooth crack appeared around the center of the egg. Drying my hands of perspiration against my ripped dress, I eased open the egg's lid… and stared.

Only the top half of the silver casing would unlatch and it lifted to expose a second, smaller egg that fit snugly inside it. Its walls appeared to be made of some kind of extremely thick glass, and within it swirled… a sack of liquid. The sack's wall was thick, spongy and transparent. It stuck flush to the glass like it had been glued there. The liquid's texture was gooey and semi-transparent, its color brownish-amber. I touched the exterior with my finger. It was warm. Shockingly warm. The very bottom of the egg was taken up by a black plate whose base was concave, to fit the shape of the egg. I guessed that was some sort of temperature-controlling device. Shining my flashlight directly through the murky liquid, I spotted something else. It was small, smaller than the center of my palm.

It looked like an embryo.

What type of embryo, exactly, I wasn't knowledgeable enough about biology to tell. It was still in early stages of development. I could make out the bulge of a head, the curve of a back, several bumps which I guessed would be limbs. A translucent cord was attached to its midriff. The cord connected the fetus to the center of the egg's base, that strange plate thing.

What is this?

Why do Matrus and Patrus want it so badly?

What did Lee want with it?

It could be an animal… It could be a human.

A sudden gust of wind shook me out of my stupor. It was strong enough to wobble the aircraft. Given that I hadn't been holding on to anything for support—and I still couldn't with the egg in my hands—my feet shot outward over the floor to steady myself. In the process, my heel shifted a lever at the base of my seat that I hadn't even noticed.

Two alarmingly loud creaks emanated from the wooden boxes fixed to either end of the motorcycle. I tensed up, petrified I'd done something fatal.

What I was not expecting was for the bases of the wooden boxes to suddenly flap open, and for four bodies to tumble out.

Four male bodies.

I almost choked on my tongue as I realized I recognized one of them: his faded dungarees, his gray-speckled hair. His frozen, stubbled face. It was Chris the mechanic.

Hurtling down with the other three men to a quiet suburban street, they made contact with the concrete with a sickening splat.

The other three men. They had to be the other three red dots on Lee's monitor. Duncan, Seb, and Jacob.

Lee was a madman. What was he doing carrying them in his aircraft? He must have murdered them shortly before the banquet, and stored them in the boxes out of convenience. Maybe he'd been planning to dump them in The Green. Clearly, I'd never known the real Lee. The flat, Matrian-male persona he'd put forward throughout my stay with him had been an act.

Unable to focus on the egg any longer, I closed and locked it up before replacing it in the seat compartment with more care than I'd previously handled it. There was a life in that thing.

After zipping up the key in the backpack, I sat down and faced forward. I gripped the handles for support. I felt like throwing up.

Lee's letter replayed in my mind.

Desmond.

Why was it addressed to Desmond? That was one of the strangest things about the letter.

Desmond was Lee's middle name. Perhaps the letter was some kind of journal entry, an upheaval of guilt before the night. But still, it didn't make any sense to me that he would use his middle name. Why not address it to Lee? He'd called himself only Lee around me, and I hadn't heard a single person address him as Desmond either.

As I recalled the explanation Lee had given me for the name, the very first night I had arrived in Patrus, a thought struck me.

"My full name is Lee Desmond Bertrand. Named Lee by my father, Desmond by my mother… I'm native to neither Matrus nor Patrus. In fact, I was born in the middle."

It drew my mind back to a question I had mulled over and posed to Viggo the evening we'd sat atop the roof in his backyard.

What happens to someone who doesn't feel they belong in either nation?

Lee's father was a Patrian. His mother a Matrian.

Lee of Patrus.

Desmond of Matrus.

A chill ran down my spine as I wondered if Lee truly was insane.

Maybe he had some kind of split-personality disorder. Maybe his childhood had messed him up.

Maybe I finally had an answer to my question and Lee was an extreme case of what could happen to a person who felt they belonged in neither nation. They rebelled against both.

Suddenly, the night seemed to grow much colder. I shivered.

I was beginning to near The Green.

Ms. Dale had been right. She'd told me, not far away from where I soared now, that once I reached the other side of the river I should trust no one. I just hadn't considered Lee to be a member of the other side.

Now, whether I liked it or not, I didn't belong to either side, either. I was a fugitive from both nations.

And I was sitting exactly where Lee would be sitting right now. On an illegal aircraft, accompanied by the egg, some meager supplies, and a few pieces of survival equipment.

My eyes fell to the compass I'd placed in the holder.

Lee had intended to head north. But my heart felt torn in two directions. North and west. My brother and Viggo. They were the only two people who mattered to me anymore. It felt like the world could implode (which it might do anyway after tonight's events), but if I could find those two alive, I would be content.

But now I feared that both of them were already dead. Although Lee had decided not to kill Viggo earlier, for all I knew, he could have gotten caught up in the blast. Maybe

Lee had set off more bombs on the ground floor than I was aware of. He'd seemed keen to destroy the building as much as possible.

And my brother. After Viggo's suspicion and now Lee's words, I feared that Queen Rina had lied to me all along about a reunion. I had only a sliver of hope left in my heart that Tim was still alive.

But, somehow, I had to find out. My soul would not rest until I had.

However many days or hours I had left to live after tonight's disaster, I had to make them count. I had nothing left to lose.

I didn't know how I would pull any of this off, or in what order. I still barely knew how to navigate this darn aircraft. I didn't know how to change its direction, and I sure didn't know how to land.

But whatever I ended up doing, and however I ended up doing it, there was one thing I knew for certain:

From this moment on, like Lee Desmond Bertrand, I had to be a player of my own rules.

No longer a pawn in someone's game.

READY FOR THE NEXT PART OF VIOLET'S STORY?

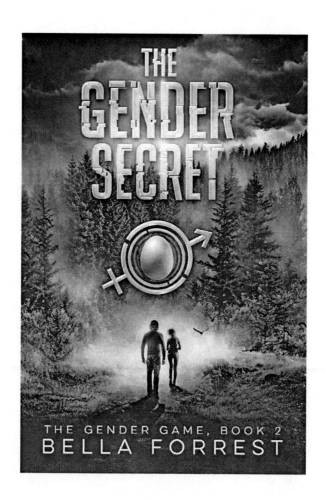

Dear Reader,

Thank you so much for reading. I hope you enjoyed The Gender Game.

Book 2, The Gender Secret releases November 21st 2016!

If you visit WWW.MOREBELLAFORREST.COM and join my email list, I will send you an email as soon as The Gender Secret is available.

You can also visit my website for the most updated information about my books: www.bellaforrest.net

Until we meet again between the pages,

—Bella Forrest *x*

ALSO BY BELLA FORREST:

A SHADE OF
VAMPIRE SERIES:

SERIES 1:
Derek & Sofia's story:

A Shade of Vampire (Book 1)
A Shade of Blood (Book 2)
A Castle of Sand (Book 3)
A Shadow of Light (Book 4)
A Blaze of Sun (Book 5)
A Gate of Night (Book 6)
A Break of Day (Book 7)

SERIES 2:
Rose & Caleb's story:

A Shade of Novak (Book 8)
A Bond of Blood (Book 9)
A Spell of Time (Book 10)
A Chase of Prey (Book 11)
A Shade of Doubt (Book 12)
A Turn of Tides (Book 13)
A Dawn of Strength (Book 14)
A Fall of Secrets (Book 15)
An End of Night (Book 16)

BEAUTIFUL MONSTER DUOLOGY:
Beautiful Monster 1
Beautiful Monster 2

FOR AN UPDATED LIST OF BELLA'S BOOKS,

please visit www.bellaforrest.net

Join Bella's VIP email list and she'll personally send you an email reminder as soon as her next book is out.

Visit to sign up: www.morebellaforrest.com

CPSIA information can be obtained
at www.ICGtesting.com
Printed in the USA
LVOW12*1834070318
568994LV00010B/140/P

Twelve
Contemporary Russian
Stories

Translated by Vytas Dukas

Rutherford • Madison • Teaneck
Fairleigh Dickinson University Press
London: Associated University Presses

© 1977 by Associated University Presses, Inc.

Associated University Presses, Inc.
Cranbury, New Jersey 08512

Associated University Presses
Magdalen House
136–148 Tooley Street
London SE1 2TT, England

Library of Congress Cataloging in Publication Data

Main entry under title:

Twelve contemporary Russian stories.
CONTENTS: Klenov, A. The son.—Gorin, G. What to open the
beer with.—Gorin, G. Stop Potapov. |etc.|
1. Short stories, Russian—Translations into English.
2. Short stories, English—Translations from Russian.
I. Dukas, Vytas, 1923–
PZ1.T9 [PG3286]   891.7′3′01   74-4969
ISBN 0-8386-1491-4

PRINTED IN THE UNITED STATES OF AMERICA

Contents

Introduction by the Translator

Introduction

Since neither Marx, Engels, nor Lenin wrote a complete or systematic account of their views on literature and the arts, one must turn elsewhere for an answer to the question: What is the underlying philosophy of today's Soviet literature and what problems does it face in order to define the dimensions of the Soviet man? Although today's official Soviet literary criticism claims that its position has not changed and asserts that the working class still remains the fundamental force in the development of its society, it also stresses the fact that it is not enough to write merely about truck drivers and fishermen (see Anashenkov, B., "Den vcherashnii, den nyneshnii," *Voprosy literatury* 16 [March 1972]: 6–38). The literary critics stress the fact that it is a great task to redefine the ever-changing qualities of a new hero. They also stress the need for continuous "differentiation in the generalization of imagery in socialist realism" (see D. Markov, "O formakh khudozhestvennogo obobshcheniya v sotsialisticheskom realizme," *Voprosy literatury* 16 [Jan. 1972]: 71–108).

Despite the fact that many Soviet literary critics persist in quoting Marx, Engels, and the nineteenth-century pre-Marxist "enlighteners" such as Belinsky, Chernyshevsky, and Dobrolyubov, contemporary attempts toward the modernization of the concept of the Soviet hero began only after the 1956 "thaw" period. Later, in 1963, Khruschev and L. Ilichev (the Party-line theoretician) accused many Soviet writers (including Yevtushenko) of modernistic deviations from established literary norms. This, however, did not stop such new poets as Voznesensky, Rozhdestvensky, and Vinokurov from writing! At the same time prose also began to show its independence of the official positions. This lonely and perhaps dangerous path was taken by A. Solzhenitsyn and new writers such as Kazakov, Aksenov, Nagibin, and Gorin. They represent the cream of today's short-story writers, whose first commitment is to their own strong individuality and to their freedom to make their heroes not from the old official pattern, but something new—lonesome men usually living away from the big cities and involved in their own search for happiness. They show that human life is a very complex phenomenon without any easily discernible pattern. Love is again treated as a highly individualistic matter that is neither holy nor evil. Despite the official pronouncement of Ilichev, Kedrina, Iezuitov, and others that the center of the literary ideological battle is nevertheless "realism," such writers as Kazakov, Aksenov, Sadovnikov, and Gorin seldom write under the banner of what one could call Socialist realism in the old sense.

There is some evidence that the new ideas may be reaching a wide audience. Just recently Bocharov (see *Voprosy literatury* 16 [Feb. 1972]: 3–30) underscored the fact that even Marx proclaimed that "a goal which requires wrong means cannot be the right one"—and goes on to encourage writers to explore all the depths of reality in order to reflect the Soviet people in its total dialectical complexity and richness. This, of course, gives a writer wider possibilities for dealing with the universal themes of love and hate, compassion and jealousy. Though the contemporary Soviet heroes have not reached the distinction of Olesha's Kavalerov (in his novel *Envy*), men who admire Bach, Mahler, Kandinsky, Dali, and Giacometti cannot be totally without interest. And Gorin's rascally hero Potapov is perhaps on the way to becoming another Russian Chichikov (in Gogol's *Dead Souls*) or Ostap Bender (in Ilf and Petrov's *The Little Golden Calf*)!

Vytas Dukas

Andrei Klenov

Although Andrei Klenov, born in 1920, is an established poet, he began to write prose only in 1961. He tends to ignore the straitjacket of Socialist realism and his prose does not always fit the party requirements. His stories often depict suffering and his characters express their personal power, individuality, and desire for self-fulfillment.

Klenov's story "The Son" develops obviously Tolstoyan ideas of a father's responsibility to his own child. Also, the individualistic treatment of young people without any *partiinost* is a refreshing change from the usual Komsomol philosophy.

11

Andrei Klenov

The Son

Translated by Vytas Dukas

AFTER MY SENIOR YEAR at the university I spent some time on the job at a factory in Kosogorsk, a few miles from Yasnaya Polyana. And it is there that my fellow students and I used to go after work and on week-ends to swim, lie in the sun, or simply stroll through the meadows and woods with their strange, old-fashioned names.

Since we were in Yasnaya every day, we willingly or unwillingly took close notice of the museum workers, the guides and scholars, and of course, above all, the girls.

I wanted to get acquainted with a certain full-time worker —I liked her. Fair, slim, with eyes almost the color of a green bottle, pug nose, face touched by the sun, and soft faded lips. She looked about twenty, no more especially from a distance. I looked for her for a long time. Then I found her in the park. She, a book in her hand, was sitting on a bench near the very edge of the woods. I sat next to her on the same bench and finding nothing better, asked her the most ordinary question:

"Excuse me, what are you reading?"

"Chekhov's Letters," she replied. "Have you read them?"

"No."

"You should," she said. "They're a good cure for a bad mood."

"That means, you're in a bad mood?" I asked, but she either didn't hear my question or didn't feel like answering it, and returned to her book.

But I kept on sitting there watching. I noticed wrinkles around her eyes and on her neck, and I realized that she was not as young as she seemed from a distance. But that didn't matter

13

—close up I liked her even better than from afar. Usually, you'll agree, it's just the opposite.

She kept on reading and paid no attention to me. Probably I should have stood up and left. But to get up and leave would mean to give up without a fight. I would not approach her a second time. I should say something else to her. Anything at all— on any subject. But I couldn't get my tongue to move and nothing worthwhile came into my head. Starlings came to my rescue.

Dark brown like chocolate pears, small and well formed, with yellowish-white markings under their wings they fell into the hawthorns and onto the meadow behind the trees, flying from place to place, making a lot of noise, squeaking, squealing, whistling. And somehow I burst out:

"Nice going!"

She left Chekhov, looked at the starlings, then at me, then again at the starlings and laughed softly.

"You, yourself," she said, "you look like a starling—dark brown, only big."

I started to laugh too. The ice was broken. I was encouraged and going from a dead stop into a gallop I introduced myself.

"My name is Kostya. And yours?"

"Mine? Dasha Mikhaylovna," she answered.

"Glad to meet you."

She didn't tell me to go to hell. But she wanted polite respect. At any rate, we got acquainted.

For some reason I began with questions—as if I were reading a questionnaire to her. But she answered.

Yes, she works in the museum . . . Yes, she graduated in literature . . . Where? In Tula . . . Stayed in the department, through correspondence studied as a post-graduate . . . Dissertation? Not yet, she became ill and dropped out. Thesis topic? On Tolstoy, of course—rough drafts and variations of *War and Peace* . . . Yes, it's difficult, but interesting . . . What was her illness? She doesn't want to talk about it, and it isn't interesting anyway . . . Doctors told her to spend some time in the country. She moved to Yasnaya only for a year, but she stayed on and

this is her third year. And she doesn't want to return to
Tula . . .

She fell silent. Then added:

"Let's take a walk."

It was a long walk. We walked about six miles, if not more.
But she didn't get tired—her steps were light and free. We
walked through forests and groves I had never seen before. And
I got to know their names: Fir Tree Woods, Plotsky Upper
Woods, Abramovsky Woods, Cut off and Mitrofanovsky Planta-
tions. Dasha knew the Tolstoy country like the palm of her hand.
Then we returned to Yasnaya, not to the estate but to the village of the same name, and stopped by a small house. She went
in the wicketgate, and I left. I wanted to turn around and look
back, but I didn't look back, and when I did, she was already
gone.

I headed toward the highway. I didn't hurry. From time to
time I would stop. I thought about Dasha. But I couldn't remember what she looked like. I mean I could see in detail her
light hair, her green, bottle-colored eyes, and her pug nose, but
her image as a whole dissipated and disappeared, I couldn't
understand it. I have a good visual memory.

When I returned to the dormitory, to the room filled with
cots where we, the student workers lived, my friends were already sleeping. I quietly undressed and slipped under the covers. But I couldn't fall asleep. I tossed and turned from one side
to the other. And that's another thing I couldn't understand—
I'm the kind that falls asleep instantly and sleeps like a bear.
And I said to myself: "You've fallen for her!" And confirming
it: "What a mess you've got yourself into!" Then having clarified my situation, I fell easily into a sweet and deep sleep.

❖   ❖   ❖

It would be difficult, in fact impossible, to recount every date
that we had—we saw each other every day, rather every evening,
three weeks in a row.

We walked and we talked. Dasha knew a lot, much more than I.

She loved birds.

"In their song," she would say, "there is some kind of secret. Any music, even the most beautiful, if you hear it often enough will eventually become tiresome, but birds never become tiresome . . ."

And the birds, it seemed, knew her. I especially remember one finch. We would no sooner sit down or stop, and he would begin to sing. His trill was brief and liquid, cut off at the end as if unfinished, yet so clear and sonorous, so joyous, that a person could actually listen to it forever.

Once we came out onto a meadow, round as a saucer, flowered and colorful with thick waving grass that had never felt a man's footprint. I fell down into it, and facing the setting rays of the sun I closed my eyes and the grass touched me pleasantly: affectionately like a caress. I lay blissfully while Dasha gathered flowers and made a bouquet.

"There is," she said, "quite a lovely selection of flowers for this time of the year—reds, whites, pink sweet-scented ones, and fluffy clovers. Look, here's a milk-white one with a bright yellow center. 'He-loves-me, loves-me-not.'"

Out of her bouquet she picked a daisy whose petals were turned down at the ends. A yellow colza with its smell of honey; tall white and purple open faced campanula, sweet-peas—all were there in the bouquet; there was neat purple plantain with its rosy puffs and faint pleasant scent—"If you cut your hand, put some on the wound—it will help"; there were cornflowers bright blue in the sun and when fresh they would become pale blue and reddish in the evening and in old age; and there were dodders, delicate, which smelled like almonds and faded soon.

"Here they are. See, they're a little faded already . . . I gathered a big bouquet of different flowers."

I guessed what she would do next. She would read to me someone's poetry that had no rhyme. She often read poetry to me.

"That's poetry?" I asked.

"Not really," she smiled. It's a paragraph from Tolstoy's *Hadji Murat*. I must admit I left some things out. You mean you haven't read it?" she asked.

"No," I said.

"You're an ignorant person," said Dasha, neither seriously nor without malice. "It's a beautiful story, maybe even the most beautiful he ever wrote. Read it."

"Ignorant but honest," I answered. "I don't tell lies. I haven't read it and I admit it."

"Honest?" she asked again. "Always and in everything?"

"Hmm," I became confused and thinking a while said, "I prefer honesty. It doesn't always work out that way, but in general I try."

"Well, I'd say that was pretty good," she said. "Keep trying."

I had no idea that this fleeting, casual conversation would have any significance, but afterwards Dasha began to act nicer toward me—or rather, closer, more trustful.

"What sort of person are you, Kostya?"

I shrugged my shoulders.

"Ordinary. Like everybody."

"And what does that mean—'like everybody?' I don't understand that . . ."

But most often as a rule, I asked the questions—and rather often direct ones. Once I asked Dasha if she had ever been married. I had wanted to know for a long time.

"I was," she answered me.

"For a long time?"

"Not long. Five years."

"Nowadays that's a long time," I said. "Divorced?"

"No. He was killed in an accident."

"In a plane?"

"On a motorcycle. It was toward the end of November. It was night. We were leaving Shchekim when we collided with a truck. It had no lights and was parked on the roadway. I got by with bruises. He was killed. After that I became sick . . . We had been going together since we were sixteen in school."

She became silent. I should have kept my mouth shut, but I continued to ask questions.

"You didn't have any children?"

"Unfortunately, no . . ."

"Why unfortunately?" I asked. "It would have been hard on you with a child."

"I don't know," she said vaguely and again became silent.

I also remember the following conversation.

For some reason I told Dasha about one of my friends, a shy modest guy who saw a girl on an escalator in the subway, and, attracted by an unknown force, followed her, started up a conversation with her, got acquainted, and the same evening proposed to her.

"And she accepted?" Dasha asked.

"Yes," I answered. "But actually, she gave herself, and him, a week to think it over."

"And how did it end?"

"They got married, and so far aren't divorced."

"And do you have a girl?" Dasha asked.

I was surprised. Up to then she had not been very interested in my personal life.

"No," I answered.

"Never?" Dasha asked.

"In general no," I said, and then correcting myself, "Not any single steady one."

"Why?" she asked.

"It doesn't work out," I said. "I don't get involved."

"Don't worry," she said smiling. "You will."

The days flew by. On the thirty-first of July our period of training came to an end, and on the first of August we left for home. Well, not actually home. I had a tourist pass to Teberda and went there, not even stopping in Moscow. As usual in such situations, I was filled with mixed emotions. On the one hand no one really wants to leave a place he likes,—I had gotten used to the factory, to Yasnaya Polyana, and to Dasha. On the other hand, I was beginning to get travel fever. It would be my first trip to the Caucasus . . . At any rate, I began to count the days, and the days, as usual, flew by. And the last day of my stay in Yasnaya arrived.

I went to the Kosogorsk department store, to the toy section, and right there decided to buy Dasha a plastic musical doll, an old woman round and red, like a fat clown, but a woman. I also got a box of candies called "Nuts from the South" and a bottle of champagne. Putting everything in my knapsack, I headed for Yasnaya.

Dasha was waiting for me on our bench.

"What do you have in the sack?" she asked.

"It's a secret," I answered. "It will be revealed in the dark woods under the thickest and tallest fir tree."

"Well let's go to Podkapustnik," she suggested.

The day was hot, sultry, but in the evening storm clouds gathered. It freshened, and the sun, leaving the clouds, descended lower and lower. I felt sad. How Dasha felt, I don't know . . .

We turned into the edge of the woods and sat down on the bank of a stream. The woods—called Podkapustnik—were very green. We were under a thick and tall fir tree. I took from the knapsack the champagne, the box of "Nuts from the South" and two cut-glass goblets which I had bought in the same department store, and said:

"Either turn around or close your eyes, no cheating now. When I tell you to look under the thickest and tallest of the fir trees, you'll find something kind of nice."

Dasha closed her eyes. I took the doll out of the knapsack and set it down between us.

"You can open them," I said.

She opened her eyes and asked:

"For me?"

"Yes," I answered.

"Thank you," she said, taking the doll in both hands and rocking slowly. The doll began to play its melody. Dasha smiled. But out of nowhere tears appeared and began to roll down her cheeks.

"What's the matter?" I asked.

"Nothing," she smiled. "I haven't received any gifts for a long time. I haven't had champagne for a long time either. Pour some for us."

The cork popped out and, like an echo, as though on cue, thunder rolled in the distance.

"To our friendship," I said. "Although a bit late, we must drink to it anyway."

Our glasses touched, and again it thundered, even louder than before.

We sat in the dark woods, on the soft warm moss under the thickest and tallest fir tree. The woods became quiet. Even the birds, sensing the storm, settled down and became silent. Only one lone little bird from time to time would chirp "dr-ink, dr-ink" as if it was thirsty before the rain.

The wind probably began to blow through the woods, as usually happens before a storm. We didn't notice it. And probably above the thickest and tallest fir tree lightning hit and thunder rumbled. But we didn't see the lightning and we didn't hear the thunder . . .

Despite the smoky black storm clouds still roaming in the sky, the stars began to appear. Fog moved in. It became chilly. I took off my jacket and threw it over Dasha's shoulders and we left.

I wasn't myself. Dasha probably wasn't herself either. We knew that something good that had started to bind us together had ended—probably never to return. I was leaving.

"I will write you," I said as if apologizing to her. At that moment I really thought that I would write, but I don't like to write letters and don't know how to write them.

Dasha didn't answer, and still apologizing, I asked:

"On the way back, on the twentieth or twenty-second, do you want me to stop by?"

"What for?" she said. "You don't have to."

Dasha opened the gate, nodded to me and left. But while going around the corner (the porch was around the corner) she reached out her hand with the doll and rocked it several times. The doll started to play—she was saying good-bye to me too.

The next day on the train taking me to Kharkov I wasn't so gloomy when I thought about Dasha. I thought: Nothing terrible happened either to her or to me. It's a pity of course that we parted so soon. But it's all right, on the way back I'll definitely stop by and see her. And if I can't stop by (I already foresaw the possibility), Dasha could come to Moscow. I left her my phone number. But nevertheless I felt lonesome. It would have been so nice if she could have come with me!

On the way back I didn't stop to see Dasha. I only looked at the countryside near Yasnaya Polyana that flashed by the windows of the train. I really couldn't stop—I was so broke that I barely had subway fare home.

Toward the October holidays I received a small package bearing Dasha's return address. Even before I knew what Dasha had sent me, I was pleased. Opening the carefully wrapped package, I found inside, in a green folder, a series of color post-cards with views of Yasnaya Polyana, and on the inside cover of the folder there was an inscription :"To my dear Kostya, with whom I shared several weeks of leisure, I send holiday greetings and some views of Yasnaya Polyana so that he will remember us once in a while—Yasnaya and me." And the initial "D", and below a postscript that was not completely clear to me: " 'Man is a contradiction' said Tolstoy once and he proved it his whole life." What did Dasha mean by that?, I thought, and whom did she have in mind? Me or herself? It means she hasn't forgotten me!

I didn't answer Dasha. I put it off until the next day, then until the next day, and then the day after, until finally it would have been an insult to write. But I placed the postcard with the white drums under the green domes on my bookshelf and looked at it often, imagining that I was on my way to Yasnaya.

I did nothing to remind Dasha about my existence, but I didn't forget her. I wanted to see her again. And maybe this was the reason that when the distribution commission had a vacancy open at the Kosogorsk factory I asked to be sent there —to the good old factory not far from Moscow, near Yasnaya Polyana.

*　 ۰ 　*

The weather was pretty bad—drizzling rain. But the rain didn't bother me—I wanted to see Dasha. I tried not to think about my not answering her and not thanking her for the gift. And I completely forgot that it was Tuesday, and on Tuesdays the museum is closed.

On the main street, Tolstoy Avenue, I saw one of the women from the museum who in some ways looked like Dasha, fair, same pug nose. What's her name?

"Hi there," I said joyfully. "How are things?"

As I neared the apartment house I began to walk more slowly and at the entrance I stopped completely. There was her door and the plate with the number "1". To enter or not to enter? I entered.

There was a rubber mat near the entrance covered with a damp rag. I diligently wiped my feet, and listened to what was going on behind the door. Behind the door it was quiet but I couldn't bring myself to knock.

Then I knocked—no one answered. I knocked again, louder, and heard Dasha's voice.

"Who's there? Just a minute."

I could hear light footsteps. The door opened. Behind the door stood Dasha.

I couldn't even see her, she stood so close. I could only see her great green eyes, opened like windows and dark as wells. They looked at me as if to say, "Who do you want? You have the wrong door." But Dasha said:

"Come in."

I stepped into a small hallway, took off my raincoat, followed Dasha into the room and saw him at once.

He, for it was clearly a boy, was lying in a barred wooden crib dressed in a buttoned shirt pulled up to his navel.

He reached out with his fat little arms bent at the elbows; his feet were located approximately where his arms were, on the same level.

He looked at me and I looked at him and honest to God! —I recognized him right away.

He already had hair on his head, not just hair but black hair just like mine, and his huge eyes were like mine—set wide and a bit slanting, only their color was somewhat indefinite. His jaw was like mine—hard set and he had my chin with a dimple in the middle. Generally speaking, it was me, only diminished in size.

We looked at each other and Dasha looked at us, and I don't know how long this gazing session would have lasted if Dasha hadn't said:

"Do you like him?"

"Yes," I answered.

"That's my son," she reported not without pride. "But why are you standing? Sit down."

I sat down. Dasha remained standing.

She was still the same as before—maybe she had put on a little weight but she hadn't become fat. It even became her.

"How are you?" she asked. She acted as if nothing had happened, as if it had only been a week or so ago since we had last seen one another.

"Well," I said. "And you?"

"You can see for yourself," she said.

And we again became silent.

The conversation obviously didn't get off the ground. Either she didn't place any significance on my visit, or she just didn't show it. And just what, actually, could she show? She could only show one thing—that she showed only total contempt for me.

Dasha broke the silence by offering me some tea.

In the meantime the little boy fell asleep. He threw his arms over his head and slept. Dasha covered him with a blanket. And only then I thought to ask his name.

"Yours", Dasha answered. "Wait a minute, I'll be right back." And she went to the kitchen.

I went up to the little boy. He was sleeping with his little hands thrown over his head. Suddenly he jerked his foot and threw off his blanket.

"Thata boy," I praised him. "That's how to do it."

He was so tiny and at the same time not so tiny. He was so weak and helpless and at the same time not so helpless—a male, even to a certain extent an individual. Yes, that's it exactly—an individual. And whose last name did she give to this individual? I asked myself. Hers or mine? Hers of course. I hadn't married her.

Damnit! Could it be that I too was once so defenseless and tiny? What a miracle it is! The most amazing miracle in the world! The most inconceivable! Two people meet, a man and a woman, their roads unite for a couple of days, and there you have it—a person is born. And he lives and grows and outlives those who gave him life, and he himself in his time will give life to someone, and so without end or beginning . . .

Consider an individual like myself. I walk this land giving no thought to any child because I just passed the childhood stage myself. Then suddenly, almost inevitably there it is again —I find I have become a father . . . Could I really be the father of this individual?

Dasha returned with two teacups—a big one and a small one, and I had to cut off my philosophizing about the mysteries of life. Dasha sat down opposite me. She's the same, I thought, and at the same time different. And it's not because she's put on some weight. She looks calm, confident. Her eyes have changed. They are still the same dark green, but they've become warmer and maybe deeper.

Dasha asked me what wind brought me to Yasnaya, and upon learning that I had received an appointment to the Kosogorsk factory, she looked depressed.

"I don't like it," she said.

"Why?" I said in surprise.

"That's where my husband worked, and on the way to the factory we had the accident."

"I understand," I said, and then, probably at the most inopportune moment, asked, "And who is his father?"

"Whose?" said Dasha not understanding.

I nodded toward the crib.

"He has no father," she answered. "I found him in **Podka-pustnik.**"

"That means I'm guilty."

"Guilty?" she repeated. "No, you're not guilty. On the contrary, I'm grateful to you. Therefore I give you tea. So drink it."

She didn't seem to be upset, and maybe she wasn't.

"That means he's my son," I said not looking to Dasha.

"Yours?" she asked. "Now that's not so! He's my son," she emphasized. "Only mine and no one else's. He has a mother and no father. Can't you understand that?"

"No I can't," I answered.

"No? And do you know how the dictionary defines the word "father"? "A man in relationship to his children". Not a very clear phrase, but I understand it this way—good or bad, a father must in some way relate to his children, and he must be a man, he must be a human being."

I sat there with my fists propped under my chin looking into my cup with its undrunk tea, and in it I could see the reflection of my face—purple-red, indistinct, covered with steam —and I said nothing.

"You of course can raise the objection," she continued calmly and firmly, "that you could in no way relate to the child, and could take on no responsibilities in relationship to him because you didn't know about him. That's completely correct! More than that, I thought that you would never know about him. So understand me, please. You are not guilty of anything. Not for him, not for me. I went into it all consciously and I'll answer for it all myself."

I was watching her surreptitiously. Red shone in her cheeks —she was upset.

"I have lived through a lot and have understood a lot, but I didn't know and I didn't believe how happy I could be when he was born! A man can do without children, but not a woman. It's not the women who have lost their husbands who are unhappy, or those who have been left by their husbands or who don't have husbands. The unhappy ones are those without children."

"And so," she continued, "all that's left is to clear up whether I thought about you or not. I thought about you. I didn't want to think about you, but I thought about you anyway. And I wanted to see you. And so I wrote to you about myself and sent you postcards. But you didn't answer me. So I blotted you out of my memory. Don't think that I named my son in your honor. I simply like the name."

She got up, went to the boy and again covered him up. She returned to the table, but she didn't sit down. She remained standing with her arms crossed on her chest. I was still sitting.

"Well, I have told you everything. Any questions?"

I was silent.

"Then you must excuse me," she said, "It's time for me to go to bed. Kostya often wakes me up and I have to go to work tomorrow."

I rose. It was clear. I was kindly being asked to leave. I went into the hall, put on my raincoat—(it was still wet)—and opened the door.

"Your hat?" Dasha asked.

"I didn't have one," I said. "Good-bye."

"Good-bye!"

The door closed. I wasn't even asked to come back.

The light rain was still falling. The wet clay made smacking noises under my feet. I went onto the highway and plodded toward Kosogorsk.

The weather coincided with my mood. Something inside me was contracting. It let up and then contracted—let up and then contracted. It was that same feeling you get in childhood when you are painfully offended.

From time to time I would remember that empty, unnecessary phrase: "A man in relationship to his children." Perhaps I even said it aloud. I don't know why I kept remembering it. And I didn't understand its meaning.

I descended small hills and climbed small hills and saw a purple-red flame above Kosogorsk. I was almost there, but I

turned back. Why I did it, I don't know. I was soaked through
and cold and I walked faster on the way back. I returned to
the house and turned into the yard.

Everyone was asleep—not one window was lighted. And
Dasha's seemed to me to be darker than the rest. I went up to
the porch and sat down on the steps.

Probably I fell asleep, or rather, into a half sleep—thick and
wet as the night so rainy it belonged more to November than
to September. The roar and the rustle of passing flattened tires
came through the cheerless noise of the rain. I sat face turned
upward to the sky. Once the sky over Yasnaya Polyana lighted
up momentarily with a glow like lightning and I heard thunder.
But maybe it wasn't thunder after all, maybe it was only a night
plane somewhere up above the clouds making the sound of letter "R".

More than likely, I fell asleep again. But soon I awoke. A
door squeaked sharply. Dasha stood behind me. She said:

"You're all wet."

And she invited me into the house.

Grigorii Gorin

Grigorii Gorin, born in 1940, began to write in 1960 and is a satirist par excellence. In many ways he surpasses such masters as Zoshchenko with his timely, witty, and covertly sarcastic satire of Soviet philistines, Soviet boredom, and especially the new Soviet bureaucracy and its bureaucrats. He is a prolific writer and his stories appear in numerous established journals. In 1968 he received a first-prize "Golden Calf" for his stories "What to Open Beer With" and "Comrade Sikintsin's Trousers." He has published a book of his short stories and one can with assurance predict a bright literary future for Gorin, since the awards committee included such famous men as the composer Veselovsky, chief editor of *Krokodil;* Likhodeev; and writer-critics Ryklin, Sazonov, and Iskander.

Grigorii Gorin

What to Open the Beer With . . .

Evening, Saturday. The end of July.

We are sitting in a room of the Ukraine Hotel. We—that is Natasha, Gizo, Victor, Nathan, Mila, and I. The room belongs to Gizo. Every time Gizo arrives in Moscow to enter the All-Union State Institute of Cinematography, he stays in this hotel, and we, his friends, gather in his room in the evenings.

"I don't understand," says Gizo, "why you don't like *A Man and a Woman*! In my opinion it's an exceptionally remarkable film. You won't begin to deny that director Lelouch performs astonishing miracles!"

"And I say it's a trivial picture!" Nathan blows small smoke rings toward the ceiling—he does this, one must say, skillfully—"A splendid fraud . . . The cover of an illustrated magazine! Beautiful, but it has no relation whatsoever to art!"

"And I say that it is art!" Gizo angrily bites off a piece of sausage. "And art of an intellectual quality. You're simply a snob! Everyone likes it, therefore you disliked it! And no one has ever worked in such a way with color . . . I know that if I enter the All-Union State Institute of Cinematography"—Gizo spits over his left shoulder—"then I definitely will work with color."

"Right!" agrees Mila. "Anouk Aimee has a pretty double in the film. They promised to get one for me . . . and a white fur . . ."

"By the way, a yogi performed yesterday in the clubhouse at Moscow State University," remarked Natasha. Then she hesitated and added, "from India!"

"How was he?" asks Mila.

"So-so. He drank a wineglass of champagne through his nose

29

. . . . Then cognac, but this through his mouth . . . amusing!"

"Are we going to drink?" Victor asks everyone and no one. "Let's drink!" Mila is the first one to agree. "Someone open the beer."

"But where's the opener?" I look questioningly at Gizo. "Do you have an opener in the room?"

"There was one somewhere. I lost it," answers Gizo, and he transfers his gaze to Nathan. Gizo loves to talk with Nathan. Everyone loves to talk with Nathan. Nathan knows a great deal and has even somehow written a small article for the journal *Science and Religion.*

"There's no opener!" I said to Mila.

"Go ask the woman on duty on our floor," suggests Mila. "I want some beer."

Indeed, she wants some beer. I get up, and go out into the corridor. At its end, sitting behind a little table, the woman on duty is knitting a scarf.

"Excuse me, do you have an opener for beer?" I ask.

"There might be one in the room," answers the woman on duty, not ceasing to knit.

"There isn't any in the room . . . It got lost, evidently."

"I don't have one either," says the woman, "Ask on the second floor in the lunchroom."

"We're only open until six!" the waitress shouts again from the lunchroom. "Always! We're only open until six."

"I would like an opener," I say uncertainly. "To open beer. . . . I will immediately bring it . . ."

"We're only open until six!" the waitress shouts again. "We're only open until six! The restaurant is open until twelve."

I knock on the glass door of the restaurant. The doorman gives me an indifferent look and spreads his arms.

"I only need it a minute!" I yell. "I have to have an opener . . . . For beer!"

The doorman does not understand and his expression indicates that he does not want to understand.

"They are selling them in a booth on the street," someone standing in the line suddenly says to me.

"What are they selling?"

"Well, these openers. . . . Twenty kopecks apiece."

The man saying this has a malicious look. Evidently he doubts that I need an opener.

"Where is this booth?" I ask angrily.

"There, around the corner of the hotel."

"Thanks!" I say, and move out of the line and go out onto the street. There are no openers for beer. Obviously that character in the line was confused. I go along the street one hundred yards, then I stop. I turn back.

Unexpectedly, right beside me, a taxi puts on its brakes. In it is Valka Belyaev. He is a little drunk and has a suitcase.

"Greetings!" he shouts. "What are you here for?"

"I want to buy an opener . . . for beer. . . . And where are you going?"

"To Vnukovo airport. I'm flying to Yalta. Get in!"

"Why should I get in?"

"Get in. I'll take you to some store along the way. There you can buy the thing."

"No," I refuse. "They're waiting for me."

"Oh, get in!" Valka takes me by the arm. It's starting to rain. Get in!"

We are on our way. Valka smokes a great deal and moves around a lot. He tells about his beautiful wife, about his son, Wunderkind, who at eighteen months can count to ten, about the new apartment that he obtained in Mnevniki, and about how he is fed up with all this and has decided to take a fling in the south to rest.

I am listening and forget about the store.

"Wait a minute!" I shout when we drive out on the highway. "Where the devil are you taking me? I just came for an opener."

"When we reach the airport," Valka says confidently. "In the buffet. I have an hour and a half before takeoff. I'm so glad to see you, old man . . ."

We sit in the bar and drink cognac.

"You don't understand how terrible this is—to lose confidence in oneself," cries Valka, and he spitefully rumples his hair. "You cannot understand this. You're single! But I'm in a mess! She's vicious! God, why is she so vicious? She doesn't even like cats. And as for me, she even said that she wished that I was dead!"

"Get a divorce!" I say decidedly. "It's best now when the kid is still little . . . while he only counts to ten . . ."

"This is all very difficult!" Valka's eyes were full of tears. "I love her . . . I love everyone! I'm a glass clinker! Listen, we'll fly together to Yalta, all right? You'll rest, you'll get tanned . . . What are you hanging around Moscow for? It's stupid."

"What's the matter with you!" I laugh. "Are you crazy? My friends are waiting for me there. And mama will get frightened."

"We'll send her a telegram!" says Valka. "It's groovy that way, without preparation. I have money I'll lend you . . ."

We order still another bottle of cognac.

It is hot and crowded in Simferopol. After drinking and a nap on the airplane, my head hurts a little. While Valka busily searches for a taxi to Yalta, I make the rounds of the trade stalls. I ask for an opener for beer. There are none anywhere. More correctly, there are some in one stall, but no one can change a ten.

"You can buy one in Yalta," shouts Valka. "Let's go now. The taxi is waiting."

We reach Yalta late at night.

The first week flies by imperceptibly. I become tan, a little thinner. The absence of necessities irritates me, but somehow I get along. Valka loans me some things and I buy some things-- fins, a shirt, dark glasses. An opener for beer, however, I can not get. But it's nothing. I am not upset.

On the beach I get acquainted with a salesgirl from a local department store. A brunette, twenty years old. Her name— Nina. She says that in several days some kind of imported opener-souvenirs are coming to her department. One can open beer with them and wear them on the chest instead of a badge.

One day when we are sitting together in the Magnolia Café, Nina suddenly begins to cry and says, "Today the openers came in. . . . Now you will go away, won't you?"

I am silent. To tell the truth, I don't want to go away.

"We'll go to Odessa," says Nina. "Father works there for a steamship line. We have a house by the twelfth pier. Cherries grow there. Let's go!"

We arrive in Odessa at the end of August.

We arrange a modest wedding. From Nina's side five or six relatives—from mine, a congratulatory telegram from mama and me.

I find work as a radio operator on a sightseeing boat. I run the tape-recorder while the contented tourists dance on the upper deck. I wear a uniform. The salary is eighty rubles. Nina is enrolled in a Polytechnic Institute—she has received a scholarship. In any case, we have enough. The purchase of an opener for beer is not a problem.

In the fall my father-in-law helped me to get a job on a steamship—the *A. P. Chekhov*, a four-decked giant that sails on international sea-lanes. In January I took a trip on it to Africa. In the port of Alexandria an Arab urchin with white teeth was selling beer openers, cute openers—the Pharaoh Ramses with an open mouth for pulling out the corks. I did not buy one. I didn't want to spend foreign currency. Later we sailed to Madagascar. Then to India, and finally a long journey to Japan. In the Japanese Sea we came across a burning Australian tanker and helped to put out the fire. My luck ran out; I fell from the bridge and broke my leg. The Captain of the tanker came to me in the hospital, shook my hand, and thanked me. He asked me what kind of present I wanted.

"I don't need anything," I said with dignity. "Only perhaps an opener for beer . . ."

The captain sent two sailors, and they rummaged around the tanker, but they couldn't find any openers. He promised to send one from Australia.

All July I was bedridden in a hospital in Vladivostok. I received a letter from Nina—my son was born. They named him Sergei. Well then, his full name is Sergei Sergeevich. That is charming.

At the end of July I was discharged from the hospital. I got into an airplane and flew to Moscow. In Domodedovo I bought an opener for beer in a shop, took a taxi, and went to the Ukraine Hotel.

They were all there: Natasha, Gizo, Nathan, Victor, Mila.

"Hi, gang," I shout from the doorway.

"Hi," Gizo greets me. "It's fine that you arrived. Just listen to what Nathan is saying here. . . . He says that color has exhausted itself in the cinema world. . . . But I say this will never happen."

"If I enter the All-Union State Institute of Cinematography" —Gizo spits over his left shoulder—"then I definitely will work exclusively with color!"

"Well, it will be trivial," says Nathan, and he blows smoke rings toward the ceiling.

"Does the yogi still appear at Moscow State University?" I ask Natasha.

"He performed a short time ago," says Natasha. "Were you there?"

"No."

"And where have you been? No one has seen you."

"I went after an opener for beer," I say.

"Did you find it?" Mila asks with interest.

"I found one."

"So why the delay?" Victor is exasperated. "We're waiting, but he, it seems, has brought the opener and doesn't say anything. Come on, come on, I want some beer."

I dug around in my pockets for a long time.

"No!" I say, "It isn't here. I probably dropped it in the taxi."

"Ask the woman on duty," Gizo advises me, and he turns to Nathan. "Well, then, in your opinion, Nathan, nothing that Lelouch does is art either?"

"Serezha, dear, bring an opener," Mila begs mournfully. "I want some beer awfully."

Indeed she wants beer. I get up and leave the room. . . .

Grigorii Gorin

Stop Potapov

Translated by Vytas Dukas

EXACTLY AT SEVEN O'CLOCK in the morning the alarm clock yanked Potapov from his dream. The dream was in technicolor, and very pleasant. Potapov dreamed about the sea, and a cafe on the cliffs where he was sitting under a striped umbrella and waiting for someone. The wait was both agonizing and exquisite.

The clock read five minutes past seven. Potapov thrust his feet into his slippers and went into the hallway. He picked up the paper, checked yesterday's hockey scores, went to the kitchen, put some coffee into the percolator, poured water into it, placed it on the gas and began to do his exercises.

Afterwards Potapov got some sausage from the refrigerator, took Alesha's report card from the window sill and began to examine it, munching a piece of bread and butter.

Yesterday his son had gotten two D's. Potapov shook his head in dismay, signed the card and finished his coffee.

"If you don't drop by the school today I don't know what I will do with you!"—his wife said coming into the kitchen and looking at Potapov with angry and sleepy eyes.

"The assistant principal has asked you to come three times now. Are you his father or not?"

"Father!" said Potapov and glanced at his watch. It was already twenty minutes till eight.

"Let's not fight, Lyubasha," said Potapov, putting his right arm around his wife, and with his left hand picking up the electric razor from the shelf.

"Stop it," she said pushing his arm away. "If you don't drop by the school today I'll stop talking to you."

"Word of honor, I'll drop by! I swear, honey!" **Potapov** pressed his left hand to his chest and with his right **hand** plugged in the razor.

"Andrey, this is serious, as far as . . ." his wife's next words were drowned out by the hum of the electric shaver. Potapov looked at his face in the mirror and nodded to his wife at the same time. Then he pulled the cord out of the shaver. ". . . or aren't you a real father?" finished Lyuba.

"Father!" Potapov said again. "But in everything else, my dear, you are absolutely right."

He smacked his wife's cheek and walked quickly through the hallway tying his tie. Sleepy Alesha came out of his room. Potapov, putting on his jacket, slapped Alesha's buttocks and putting on his coat said, "I'll have a talk with you yet!" Then grabbing his briefcase and hat, he left.

At the bus stop as usual there were many people. Potapov, skipping two buses, breathed in the fresh air.

And at this moment, Potapov, for some reason remembered Natasha. He had seen her a week ago while he was riding along in a taxi on Tversky boulevard. Natasha wore a tan leather hooded jacket. Potapov had wanted to stop her right then, but changed his mind because he was in such a hurry.

"I'll call her today," thought Potapov. "Or, even better, I'll drop by without calling . . . no, better call first . . ."

Another bus arrived and he didn't have the time to decide what to do—call her or just simply drop by—here came the bus. Stepping into the center of the bus Potapov shouted: "Commuter," then having made himself comfortable, he thrust his hand into his briefcase and pulled out *Literature Abroad*. The magazine was currently serializing Remarque's novel. Potapov opened the journal to where he had marked it on page 144, and read: "During the day I went to Cannes. He invited me to dine with him at a restaurant . . ." The bus jerked; the journal fell from Potapov's hands, but he caught it in the air and continued to read: "Mrs. Wimper made a vodka martini for me when I arrived." This, he noted was on page 163. Potapov tried to find his place on page 144, but the bus was crowded, and besides Potapov remembered that the journal had to be returned on the next day anyway, so he decided to continue reading on page 163. "We talked with her about the visit to Silvers . . ." read Potapov, but just then the driver announced his stop. Potapov closed the magazine, put it into the briefcase and began to make his way to the exit.

At nine o'clock sharp, Potapov went up to his department. Having greeted his co-workers, he sat at his own desk, pulled the folder about standardization toward himself and began to study it. All the papers were in order, except for the title page.

"Where is the title page from this folder?" he asked Mikhailov, who sat at the next desk.

"No idea," said Mikhailov. "Could it be at the production department?"

"That's a helluva thing!" said Potapov, annoyed and went to the production department.

The title page was important to him for two reasons: firstly, Potapov loved all his folders to be in order, and, secondly, on the back of his title page, he had copied a chess problem from *Science and Life*, which he now intended to solve.

In the production department they told Potapov that the title page had been sent to the accounting department; in the accounting department the secretary told him that the title page had been returned to his department. Returning to his office Potapov found the title page on his desk, but somebody had already solved the chess problem.

With a deep sigh Potapov put the page into the folder, placed the folder into the drawer and glanced at the clock. It was twelve o'clock.

"In an hour . . . lunch," Potapov thought, and for some reason he remembered Natasha. "I'll call her," he decided, and pulled the telephone closer. However, the telephone rang before he could pick up the receiver.

"Potapov?" A powerful masculine voice sounded in the receiver. "This is Kondratev!"

"Hi, old man," answered Potapov, trying painfully to remember who Kondratev was.

"We have a problem," said Kondratev, "Sashka died."

"It couldn't be!" gasped Potapov, trying painfully to re-member who Sashka was.

"Burned up in two months, burned up . . ." Kondratev said gloomily. "That's the way it is, brother! We're going to bury him today at Vostryakovsky Cemetery at three o'clock. Are you coming?"

"Of course!" said Potapov, trying painfully to remember where Vostryakovsky Cemetery was.

After such sad news it was impossible to work at all. Pota-pov gathered all the papers from his desk and went to the hall-way for a smoke. Noticing Potapov, the director's secretary bummed a cigarette from him and announced: "Today the boss is calling a departmental conference at four o'clock. It's a com-mand performance."

"Of course," said Potapov, lighting her cigarette. "You're getting prettier all the time, Sonichka!"

"Oh, come on!" flirtatiously retorted Sonya and blew out a stream of smoke. "All you do is just pay compliments, but no one wants to take me to *Hamlet*."

"And who has tickets?"

"Ermolenko has them at the Party Bureau, but he won't give them away."

"That depends who it is." Potapov, said, and nodding sig-nificantly he went to the Party Bureau.

"Listen, Ermolenko," said Potapov, walking into the Bu-reau. "You were looking for volunteer patrolmen."

"Well?" Ermolenko looked suspiciously at Potapov.

"You give me two tickets to *Hamlet* and I'll go on patrol."

"Can't be done, the patrol is tonight and *Hamlet* is tonight."

"But," said Potapov, "*Hamlet* starts at seven and the hooli-gans start later—after the performance. I could patrol after-wards, word of honor!"

"You will have to patrol till midnight," warned Ermolenko.

"Just like a soldier," promised Potapov. He took the tickets and went to lunch . . . During lunch he remembered Natasha again. "I'll go see her without phoning," decided Potapov. "I'll just drop by, that's all—I haven't seen the little darling for half a year. But how can I?"

He didn't complete his ruminations. The radio began to broadcast old Russian songs and Potapov listened to them until the end of his lunch hour.

Upon returning to his department, Potapov looked at his watch. It was a quarter past two. He picked up the telephone and called the ministry.

"Hello, Sergachev," began Potapov. "This is Potapov. Leo, let me have a car for a couple of hours."

"Listen old man, enough of this!" replied Sergachev unhappily. "The administration is already complaining about you—you may even get fired!"

"This is the last time, Leo, word of honor," said Potapov. "Friend of mine died, I have to go to the funeral!"

Sergachev was silent for a moment, then asked in a low voice:

"Is this the truth?"

"Would I lie?" sighed Potapov.

"O.K." said Sergachev, "But this is the last time."

"Of course," said Potapov. "I'll be right back. I have to pay my last respects. That's all . . ."

The ministry car was waiting for Potapov at the entry. Potapov got into the front seat, lit a cigarette and offered one to the driver.

"To the cemetery?" asked the driver.

"Yes," sighed Potapov. "But first to Khimki, to the 21st school."

He was lucky. He caught the assistant principal between classes. The break was ending and she was hurrying back to her class.

"Hello," said Potapov. "I am Potapov. I am here regarding my son's behavior. What's your name?"

"Vera Mikhailovna," the assistant principal said introducing herself.

"I am very pleased," smiled Potapov. "My mother's name was also Vera Mikhailovna. What a beautiful name . . ."

"Thank you," said the assistant principal and for some reason she blushed.

"Did I stop at the wrong time? Are you in a hurry?"

"Yes," nodded Vera Mikhailovna. "The children are waiting . . . could you come this evening, around seven o'clock?"

"Impossible, my dear," sighed Potapov. "Today I have an urgent official trip to Taymir. Could you tell me in two words?"

"It is impossible in two words," replied Mikhailovna. "The boy's a poor student, he's insolent, he lies on every hand . . ."

"I will kill him!" decisively retorted Potapov.

"Oh no, why do you say that?" the assistant principal again blushed. "You have to talk to him seriously, to think . . ."

"O.K.," interjected Potapov. "In two months I will return from Taymir, and then I will come to see you. And in the meantime, Vera Mikhailovna, please take my blockhead under your personal care. Agreed? What shoe-size do you wear?"

"Why?" The assistant principal blushed again. She was a very young assistant principal and blushed all the time.

"I want to bring you some Siberian fur-lined boots as a present," said Potapov. "Boots made from fur."

"You shouldn't." the assistant principal became crimson.

"No, no, don't argue," Potapov said firmly. "Agreed. I will not hold you any longer, the children are waiting!" He kissed her hand and ran out of the school.

It took them a long time to reach Vostryakovsky Cemetery and then Potapov wandered around for a long time among the snow-covered graves looking for the funeral. Finally noticing a small group of people and, having recognized a professor from his institute, he came to the conclusion that some friend of his student days had died, but who exactly, he didn't find out because the coffin was already closed and had been lowered into the frozen ground. Potapov recalled that in their group there had been several Alexanders, but now, as if in spite, all of them were absent. Therefore, it was impossible to find out exactly who was lying *there*, and to ask—that was not proper. Potapov took off his hat, slowly walked among the assembled mourners, shook hands and spoke sadly:

"Oh Sashka, Sashka! How could it be, brothers?"

Then, unexpected even to himself, he cried. This made Potapov feel very miserable and he wiped his tears with his palm,
lighted a cigarette and silently walked to his car.

When he returned to his office building, his watch said exactly four o'clock. The conference began in the director's office.
On the way, Potapov stopped by his office, took a pocket chess
set from his drawer, walked silently to the conference room
and found a seat in the last row. Immediately Mikhailov took
the seat next to him . . .

The match looked like it would be interesting. In the beginning Potapov made a mistake and lost two pawns, but in
the middle of the game he attacked and won a bishop.

"Give up, dad," said Potapov confidently.

"No way!" retorted Mikhailov. "I still have a chance."

"So, comrades," the director began to sum up the conference, "If no one has any questions, we can end the meeting!"
Potapov looked at the chess board. Mikhailov made a risky
move with a castle, Potapov answered the move with his queen.
The *endspiel* was becoming tempestuous.

"I have a question!" loudly said Potapov, standing up. "I
would like to know how the board of directors is prepared to
solve the problem of recycling the waste with the resulting rise
in production under the new standardization?"

"The question is well formulated," replied the director. "It
seems to me that the problem of recycling waste . . ."

"Your move," said Potapov quietly sitting down. "Now we
have another half an hour . . ."

Before the performance began, Potapov invited Sonya to
dine in a cafe; they had a couple of drinks, chatted and delayed
until they were late for the opening curtain. By the time Potapov, bending over, stepping on someone's feet and apologizing every second, got to his seat, Hamlet was talking already
about something with Horatio.

Finally, Sonya and Potapov settled down and looked at the
stage. A great woven curtain was closed slowly and fearsomely
over the stage, crushing the figures below it.

"Swell," whispered Sonya.

When Hamlet, having killed Polonius, becomes conscience stricken because of his irreparable deed and bends over the corpse, Potapov shuddered, and to his own amazement he felt a shiver go down his spine. Potapov had seen the film *Hamlet,* but only the second part and therefore the death of Polonius was a surprise to him.

Potapov watched the rest of the play as if bewitched, enjoying both his compassion for the Danish prince and the strange icy sensation which every word pronounced on the stage created in his chest.

During the intermission, he went to the buffet, ate a sandwich, and the icy feeling in his chest disappeared. Potapov looked at his watch. It was a quarter to nine.

"The play's dragging," thought Potapov. "Good acting! But too slow."

Then he suddenly thought about Natasha and his heart began to ache unbearably.

"Let's go," Potapov told himself under his breath.

He offered candy to Sonya, went out for a smoke and returned with a face full of concern.

"Sonya," said Potapov, "I just called home. Alesha has become ill. The boy has a high temperature—102.6°!"

"Oh," cried out Sonya.

"Nothing scary," said Potapov. "Evidently flu. I have to go home. You'll have to excuse the shining knight."

"No more of this nonsense! Of course you have to go!" Sonya pressed Potapov's hand warmly and kissed his cheek.

Potapov reached his office via the subway, and went to the headquarters of the volunteer patrol. He received a red armband and signed in.

"Your area is the square in the vicinity of the movie theater," some young fellow sitting behind the table told him. "You have to be on duty until twelve o'clock."

"I will patrol until one o'clock, since I came late," replied Potapov.

"Don't have to," smiled the fellow. "Till twelve o'clock will suffice."

Potapov fastened on the armband, left the headquarters and set off slowly towards a taxi stand. Walking along he inhaled the spring air and thought about Natasha. When his turn came, Potapov got into a green Volga, offered a cigarette to the driver and in an unsteady voice said:

"To the Polyanka, boss!"

He rang the doorbell for some time, and fearfully listened for a rustle behind the door, trying to make out if she were home alone or not. Finally the door opened and he saw Natasha. She had just taken a bath, apparently—she wore a striped housecoat, her hair was damp and a few drops of water were still on her forehead.

"You?"!!"

"It's me," said Potapov, and took off his hat. "You may kick me out or you may let me in."

For a few seconds Natasha peered at Potapov, then wiped the drops of water from her forehead with her palm and in a low voice said:

"Come in."

In a half a year Natasha's apartment had not changed at all. Only new blinds on the windows and a large new T.V. in a corner had made their appearance. The T.V. was on. It was tuned to Kapler's "Kinopanorama," and he, with his soft voice, was telling something about French movies.

Potapov took off his coat, came in and stopped in the middle of the room. Natasha turned off the T.V., took a cigarette from a pack on the table, and lighted it.

"Natasha," said Potapov quietly, "Punch me in the nose."

She barely smiled.

"Hit me!" asked Potapov again, "And if you wish, spread me out on the floor in the hallway, instead of the rug . . ."

He took a step forward and embraced her. She thrust her face into his jacket and sighed.

"Why did you disappear? Why haven't you dropped by even once, why haven't you called?" said Natasha and sobbed.

"Be quiet, my dear," said Potapov and kissed her head. "Don't say anything now . . ."

Later, lying in the dark, they smoked and made small talk.

"Are you leaving already?" quietly asked Natasha.

"Yes!" tersely replied Potapov.

"Stay awhile," begged Natasha.

"Can't, my dear," said Potapov. "The taxi's waiting for me downstairs."

At once he knew he had blundered. Natasha jumped up, and even in the darkness he could see that her face had become pale.

"You scoundrel!" she exclaimed, "You good for nothing!"

"Take it easy, take it easy." Potapov, tying his shoe laces, felt that he was blushing. "I was only joking, silly. It's only a joke."

"Get lost!" shouted Natasha.

"If you want, hit me," said Potapov, putting on his jacket.

"Go to hell!" shouted Natasha and hid her face in a pillow.

"It's a pity!" sighed Potapov, putting on his coat. "It's a pity that we have to part this way . . ."

The green Volga was standing at the entrance.

"It's been a long time, comrade. I have to go back to the garage."

"Everything will be O.K., boss." said Potapov, lighting a cigarette and offering one to the driver. "Everything will be compensated for. Step on it to Khimki!"

He arrived home at quarter after eleven. Lyuba and Alesha were already asleep. Potapov went to the kitchen, turned on the gas, put the tea kettle on. Eating the supper prepared by his wife, he glanced over the evening paper. Then smoking, he listened to the latest sports news.

Then he undressed and got into bed. Lyuba woke up and looked at him glumly.

"They made me go on patrol," said Potapov. "I wanted to forewarn you and called a few times, but every time the phone was busy—something wrong with the telephone. Haven't you called the repair service?"

Lyuba looked at him glumly once more and turned to the wall.

Potapov pulled the alarm clock closer—it said five minutes to twelve. He lay for a few minutes with his eyes open, looking at the ceiling, thinking about nothing. Then he turned on his right side and closed his eyes.

Exactly at twelve o'clock midnight, Potapov began to dream . . .

Grigorii Gorin

The Lecture

NOT LONG AGO at the factory we had a lecture about Derzhavin . . . About Gavrila Romanovich . . . About a poet from the last century. The lecturer said the poet knew Pushkin and even gave him his blessing when he was dying.

We all remained after our shift was over. We gathered in the recreation room and waited. The president of our factory committee, Chibirev, presented the lecturer to us—a professor-specialist in literature. Then such a sympathetic little old professor appeared on the platform and began to tell us about the poet Derzhavin. I have to say that he spoke in an exceptionally interesting way. He told how Derzhavin was born in 1743, how he grew up, how he formed his ideology, how he began to write odes.

He also mentioned the poet's relationship with Catherine. Then he recited verses by heart. To state it briefly, it was a fascinating lecture. We listened with delight and didn't notice how two hours flew by.

Finally the professor concluded the lecture and sat down. The president of our factory committee, Chibirev, stood up and said, "Dear comrades, allow me on your behalf to thank the respected professor for the informative lecture."

We broke out into applause. The professor bowed and said, "Thank you, comrades! Maybe some kind of a question has occurred to someone?"

Chibirev said, "Yes, comrades, if someone wants to ask about something, then don't stand on ceremony . . ."

We were silent—thinking. But a master from the second department, Samsonov, stood up and said, "I have the following question—When will they finally open the dining room at our factory?"

The professor was taken aback. Chibirev winced and said, "What's the matter with you, Samsonov? What are you asking about? That is an immaterial question!"

"Why is it so immaterial?" asked Samsonov. "For the last four months we have had only promises, and at the dinner break we run five blocks to eat and we lose time. There is no time to read Derzhavin."

Chibirev got nervous. He shouted, "Sit down, Samsonov! Don't put us in an embarrassing position in front of the Comrade Professor." Then he said, turning to everyone, "Comrades, I ask you to raise only genuine questions, that is, just questions related to the poet Derzhavin."

Again we sat and were silent. Samsonov raised his hand.

Chibirev suspiciously asked, "Do you have a question about Derzhavin?"

"About Derzhavin," says Samsonov.

"Well, then ask!" says Chibirev.

Samsonov stood up and said, "I'm interested in how he planned his writer's working day. How was his dinner break? Did he have a lunchroom nearby, or did he have to ride twenty minutes in a bus to it?"

Chibirev turned purple and yelled, "What, Samsonov, are you joking? How could there be buses two hundred years ago?"

"And if there were no automobiles, then I am sure that Derzhavin thought this question over thoroughly and he ate well, quickly, and not far from his work place, and thereby he enjoyed a higher productivity for his labor."

Here the professor stood up and said, "Comrade Samsonov is absolutely right. The poet Derzhavin was not a gourmet, but he respected his dinner time very much, and he loved to sit down to a beautifully set table. Here, for example, is how he described it in the poem 'Hedonistic Life.'"

> Crimson ham, green soup with egg yokes,
> Rosy-yellow pie, pale cheese, red crayfish
> The caviar, so amber-colored, and with a blue feather
> There a many-colored pike—

"—Wonderful!"

"Thanks, Comrade Professor, for backing me up," said Samsonov. "I think, Comrade Chibirev, that after these lines, the delay with a dining room at the factory—is simply disrespect to the memory of the famous Russian poet Derzhavin."

Here Chibirev became flustered and then he said, "That will do, Samsonov. Everything's clear. Tomorrow at the factory committee meeting we will decide the question of the dining room. There is no reason to bring in Derzhavin here. No other questions?"

"No," said Samsonov. "Everything's clear."

And on this note the lecture came to an end. We all went away very much satisfied.

Samsonov said, "See what it means to unite poetry with life at such an opportune time? See what kind of an effect you can get! They say in a week we'll be having a lecture by another professor about the poet Tyutchev, so in conjunction with this affair I'll ask a question about nursery schools . . ."

Victoria Tokareva

Victoria Tokareva, born in 1937 in Leningrad, is a contemporary Russian writer. She studied piano and, later, cinematography in Moscow, wrote scenarios, and in 1964 her first book, *About That Which Never Took Place*, appeared.

In 1968 she received a "Golden Calf" second prize for her story "Nothing Comes Easy at First," where the motive of "Hauptmann von Köpenick" "no work, no passport; no passport, no work" is a strong indictment of contemporary Soviet bureaucracy. She also derides the bureaucrats who, caught in their own maze, cannot fire even a fool because they fear a chain reaction. Tokareva, in the manner of Zoshchenko, gives us vignettes, caustic social commentaries; her succinct and staccato sentences and her zero endings require no additional comment.

Reprinted by permission from *Mundus Artium* 2 (1969): 12-16.

Victoria Tokareva

One, Two, Three

MY WIFE RESEMBLES SASKIA, Rembrandt's wife. Imagine Saskia with short hair in a leather skirt and a shopping bag in her hands—that's my wife.

I am as accustomed to her face as I am to the view through my own window. Through my window there is a mixture of genres: a village of ten homes squeezed in by block houses—contemporary houses, as if they were glued at the seams. But the village is old-fashioned, with leafy front gardens, haughty cows, roosters by the well, and mud in the spring. I'm standing at the window and looking at the construction cranes which, like gigantic herons, pensively hover above the little village.

I know everything that will happen in the next hour, the next twenty-four hours, the next ten years. Within the hour the door will open, my wife will enter with her shopping bag, and she will ask:

"Do you love me?"

"No," I will say.

"What—no?" my wife will say in surprise.

"It's very simple. I don't love you and that's all."

"You promised that you would love me all your life. Were you lying?"

"No."

"Does it mean that you are lying now?"

"I'm not lying now."

"I don't understand anything."

I will have to explain to my wife what she doesn't under-

50

stand. If I manage to explain it properly, she will take offense and
tell me about her girl friend, deformed and immoral, who lives
downtown and is dearly loved by a great number of people. And
my wife, beautiful and moral, lives among hens and she isn't even
loved by such an insignificant person as I because nowadays no
one needs morality and beauty. Everyone needs an external and
internal deformity. Later my wife, instead of her own qualities,
will begin to discuss mine, and she will say that I stand in front
of the window for whole days at a time, that I have a face that
looks as if it had gone to sleep, that doesn't show even an ele-
mentary curiosity about life.

I will take offense and we will argue. And afterwards, naturally, we will become reconciled. But why argue, if one will become reconciled anyway? Therefore I prefer another dialogue:

"Do you love me?" my wife asks.

"I do."

"Very much?"

"Very much."

"How much?"

"Very, very, very much."

"Good heavens, what a tone of voice," my wife will sigh dis-
appointedly and will carry the bag into the kitchen.

A single man differs from a married man in that he doesn't
know what he will do in an hour, a day, or ten years. When a
man doesn't know, he fantasizes. Fantasy is a creation and creation is a flight above the ordinary condition. A single man can
periodically fly above his own ordinary condition.

And why can't a married man do this, even for a short while?

There is a children's counting game: "One, two, three,—the
game begins with me."

One—I put on a white shirt.

Two—I get a telephone book and sit down near the telephone.

Three—I dial the number and hear ringing.

What a remarkable invention, a telephone! The earth is criss-
crossed with telephone wires like nerves. And all the people are
interconnected, one with another. And it is not complicated; one
has simply to go to a telephone and dial the required number—

a combination of figures; it's such an inexplicable and mysterious thing, like fate.

"Ira? Greetings!"

"Who is it?" Ira doesn't understand.

I give her my first name, last name, and patronymic as in a questionnaire. Then the year of birth and distinguishing traits. Then she remembers.

"Where have you been?" questions Ira.

"In Franz Joseph land. I was mining manganese. Let's get together."

"What will we do?"

"We shall fly above our ordinary condition."

"Fly alone; I can't."

"Why not?"

"I have a dissertation."

"What kind?"

"The electromagnetic effect in germanium crystals."

While I was in Franz Joseph land, Ira didn't waste her time.

"Why are you interested in this effect? It is important to you?"

"Not to me. To mankind."

"Well, suit yourself," I say.

Whenever somebody is concerned about the fate of humanity, one should not distract him. It is a very rare quality to think about someone besides oneself.

I leaf through my notebook alphabetically and read the names. The notebook is life with its main and secondary directions, holidays, cemeteries. Just like the crosses in the new Riga cemetery, the names appeared in the notebook. Behind some of them something rises, behind others nothing rises at all. People with these names continue to live and exist, but they are not in your life, therefore they do not exist. To call such people by phone is to summon a voice from another world, like at a spiritualist seance.

"Galya? Greetings." I shout cheerfully.

"Who is it?" asks Galya.

"Guess."

"Borya."

"No, not Borya."

"Sasha . . ."

"No, not Sasha."

"Alya."

"Do you think I'm a woman?"

"No, I think you are a man."

"Then let's get together."

"I can't. I have to pick up my child at mother's."

"You can send your husband."

"Right. I'm going to send my husband after my child and I will take a walk with somebody I don't know."

It all makes sense. People want to walk only with those whom they know. I also will take a walk with someone whom I have known since kindergarten.

I don't look at the notebook anymore, since I remember the number by heart.

"Andrey," I shout. "Greetings."

My wife thinks that Andrey resembles the announcer on television, Kirillov. If Kirillov's hair had fallen out, his nose become short and his face round—then he and my friend Andrey would look as much alike as two drops of water.

"Greetings," answers Andrey.

"Let's fly above our ordinary condition."

"Shall we drink?" Andrey specifies.

"We will see," I answer vaguely.

"Today I can't because I'm going to a birthday party at a relative's."

"Are you interested in going to visit your relatives?"

"It's a tradition."

"Spit on it."

"Can't. A person without tradition is naked."

Thus, one has business; the second, a family; and the third, tradition. The earth is full of telephone wires like nerves. One can dial any combination of numbers and call any place. It is possible to call, but to communicate—impossible. Is there a number by which it is possible to reach a human being?"

The telephones are occupied and the people are occupied—each with his own business and traditions. And I, by the way, have relatives. And I even have a wife who resembles Rembrandt's wife. It's possible that she also wants to fly, but she went to the store. She will be back shortly.

Together she and I can go out of the house and then fly together. But why fly over our ordinary condition if you have to return to it all the same?

One—I take off my white shirt.

Two—I return to the window and look at the view.

Three—the door opens and my wife appears with her shopping bag.

"Do you love me?" My wife, frightened, asks as if this were the only reason she had returned.

"I love you."

"Very much?"

"Very much."

"And how much?"

"Very, very, very much."

"You say it in such a tone." My wife sighs and takes the bag into the kitchen.

Viktoria Tokareva

Nothing Comes Easy At First

Translated by Vytas Dukas

FEDKIN WOKE UP during the night because he felt that he was a fool. He lay and stared at the ceiling. The ceiling was as white as a sheet of paper; he, himself, painted it twice a month. Fedkin loved to paint ceilings more than anything in his life—to stand on something high and move the brush from one side to another.

Outside it was becoming light.

Fedkin washed and sat down at the table and his wife served him breakfast. Everyone eats breakfast, and everyone also has a wife. Fedkin's wife was not too bright, but, at the same time, she was not a fool. She moved about the kitchen with a face shining from cream, and her hair done in a tail with a rubber band from a drug store package.

"Zina," said Fedkin, "You shouldn't have married me. I am a fool."

"It's O.K.," said Zina.

"What's O.K.?" said Fedkin, puzzled.

"The most important thing in this life is to find your place in it; to find equilibrium between desires and capabilities."

When Fedkin went out on the streets that day, he knew everything about himself. He walked slowly, breathed, and looked around. If he were more clever, he probably would have recited poetry, something like: "October came, the trees discarding the last leaves from their bare branches. . . ." But Fedkin didn't know Pushkin, and he just thought, "God, it's nice . . ."

In the waiting room of the office building people were sitting, smoking, and nonchalantly swinging their arms. They always came here to chat and to keep trying. At first all were worried and even suffered from nerves. But after a year they relaxed and even found pleasure in their indefinite state.

Fedkin had no secretary and therefore people entered his office directly from the hall. He sent everyone to his supervisor, and the supervisor sent them to the next one, a higher supervisor, who had two doors and a secretary. There the client was detained and sent back to Fedkin. This was like the water cycle in nature: water evaporates, rises to the sky, falls from sky to earth, etc.

Fedkin entered his office. The door opened slightly, and a skinny and nervous young man looked in. He always nibbled matches and his fingers were brown from them.

"Hello," said the young man. "Do you remember me?"

"Of course," said Fedkin, "What is your name?"

"Lesin."

"Can you interpret dreams?" Fedkin asked suddenly.

"My grandmother used to say, that if you had a bad dream, you should say 'Where went the night, there went the dream'. . ."

"Where went the night, there went the dream," repeated Fedkin. "No, not now. Too late now."

"Have a seat," said Fedkin. He tore off a page from the calendar and began to paint it evenly with ink. It seemed to him that he was painting a ceiling.

Lesin looked on and waited until it would be possible to present his problem, but Fedkin had heard about this problem many times and was not interested.

"You have parents?" he asked.

"Of course," said Lesin, surprised.

"Very good," praised Fedkin. "Aren't you ashamed you haven't worked for the last two years?"

"But you don't give me . . ."

"I?"

"Of course. In order for me to start work, a paper must be signed and you've refused to sign for the last two years."

"I cannot help you at all," confessed Fedkin.

"Why?"

"Because I am a fool."

"In what sense?" Lesin was lost.

"Intellectually."

"I understand." Lesin's instant credence offended Fedkin. "But it is you who is a fool."

"And what do I have to do with it?"

"Take up something else."

"Why do I have to do something I don't like?"

"All my life I have been occupied with things I don't like," said Fedkin.

"And how do you feel?"

Fedkin thought a minute and clucked his tongue in a tone of disappointment.

"Bored."

"And what did you want to be?"

"A house painter."

"I think that's a mechanical job," Lesin said cautiously.

"You try it," Fedkin was offended, "try to paint a ceiling white and I am sure it will come out patchy. I also want you to know my paint brush is from France." Fedkin began to talk about his paint brush; it was very interesting. Lesin listened and nodded, then he advised,

"Then drop everything and be a house painter."

"Drop what?" Fedkin asked for clarification.

"Everybody."

"I can't drop everybody. I can't drop my wife. In her youth she had many proposals, but she married me. How would she feel in her old age to be a house painter's wife? What would her friends think . . ."

"If she loves you, she will understand." Lesin's face became sad, and his voice broke. Apparently, someone didn't understand Lesin.

"She would understand, but my friends . . . they will see right away that I am a fool. From an executive down to a house painter . . ."

"But you can arrange it so they will fire you . . ."

"They won't fire me," said Fedkin thoughtfully, "I am not a thief, not an alcoholic . . ."

"You fool, this is very serious! You just underestimate . . ."

"All the same," Fedkin was upset, "they won't fire me for that . . ."

Fedkin's supervisor was a woman. Women, as Fedkin saw it, were created for love and family, and not for a job. Since the supervisor was created for both, she therefore helped her grandson with his homework over the phone. She called this caring for him from a distance.

The door to the office was left open a bit. You could hear the supervisor screaming, "Equals mass times speed squared, divided by two. Why do you call me at work rather than looking in your textbook? What will happen when I die?"

"Hello," said Fedkin politely.

"What a madhouse." The supervisor said in confusion and threw down the receiver.

Fedkin lifted his eyebrows understandingly. Fifteen years ago she had screamed at her children in the same fashion, called her home a madhouse, and asked what would happen when she died. Nothing had changed in that period. And in general, Fedkin noticed, people don't change with age.

"What's your problem?" asked the supervisor, thinking about taking care of her grandson from a distance.

"I would like to leave the job."

"You got your feelings hurt?"

"No."

"Then what happened?"

"Simply I am not up to it intellectually."

"Who said?" The supervisor was edgy.

"No one. I discovered it myself."

"Did you discover it a long time ago?"

"Today. Since this morning . . ."

"And I've known about it all the fifteen years that you've worked for me. And I beg you not to tell this to anyone. Otherwise, I will be the fool, not you."

"You think about yourself?" Fedkin got offended. "You're thinking about yourself when the matter is definitely official business."

"One fool can't hurt official business."

Fedkin went to another supervisor. This boss was gray and handsome, but short. He resembled Napoleon Bonaparte and behind his back he was called not Mikhail Ivanych, but Michel.

Michel was constantly in a hurry and constantly fell behind in everything. When he had visitors he rose from his chair and smiled. In Stanislavsky's system there are approaches, lower and upper. Michel took the one in between so that the visitors sometimes became confused as to who really was the boss.

"Hello, Mikhail Ivanych," Fedkin began.

Michel smiled. "In two words, please," he asked, "I have only a minute and a half."

And Fedkin counted two fingers on his hand and said, "I—fool." Exactly two words.

"Continue," demanded Michel.

"That's all."

"If you understand that you are a fool, that already proves that you are not a fool."

Fedkin wanted to argue, but Michel had no more time.

"That's all," he said, "I must fly to India."

Fedkin walked slowly along the corridor, and thought how repulsively the walls had been painted, how sloppily the ceilings had been done. And if this had been done as it should have been, then the bosses and all who come by would probably have been in a better mood—beauty improves a mood. And during the fifteen years—spent on who knows what—he could have painted many ceilings. But that time was gone now.

In the corridor behind low tables on small red wicker chairs, sat people smoking and talking, nonchalantly swinging their arms. Some of them he had seen here for a year or more.

Fedkin wanted to go in his office, but somehow he didn't, instead he sat down on the red wicker chair.

"You told them?" quickly asked Lesin, now addressing him in as a close friend.

"Yes."

"So?" The others asked with sympathy.

Fedkin made a cluck with his tongue in a tone of disappointment. He looked upset.

"Nothing comes easy at first," they had warned Fedkin.

"Nothing comes easy at first," confirmed Lesin.

"Don't give up!"

Georgii Sadovnikov

Georgii Sadovnikov, born in 1933, a graduate of the famous Suvorov Military Academy, has appeared in print since 1957, when he received a first prize for his story "Aunt Yura," awarded by the journal *World Youth* in conjunction with the Fourth World Youth Festival.

Sadovnikov began to write youthful impressionistic stories such as "On the Horizon—Mars," and "I Wish I Had Wings," but he also dealt with working people.

In his story *Old Man Vadik*, Sadovnikov describes an old man who tries to recapture his youth in his final and fateful walk on the Prospect. The kaleidoscopic events take place on the street— real and dreamlike scenes vividly and effectively describes old man Vadik. In these passages we are able to sense his old age and his inability to recapture his youth. Social commentary and political satire are cleverly couched in the description of the battle of the sparrows. In the story Sadovnikov shows his skill and refined techniques by masterfully juxtaposing the present and the past; the pathos of the old man ends in his complete alienation from the present. Sadovnikov's strength is in his original style and his feeling for architectonics.

Georgii Sadovnikov

Vadik, the Old Man

BEFORE UNDERTAKING his venture he carefully looked out of the room and listened to the voices flying from the kitchen; the reconnaissance confirmed his calculations. Except for himself and his mother, the whole family was sitting in the kitchen. Sunday breakfast was over a long time ago, but they were caught up in a family argument and paid no attention to him.

With such favorable odds, he wasted no time. He pulled off his pajamas and pushed them behind the couch, fidgeting, as if before a camera, in front of his mother. He winked at her, and his mother's lips slowly stretched into a smile. When she smiled her eyes beamed gaily.

She understood him. His mother followed his hasty preparations through the open door. The use of her legs had been denied her and now she sat on the balcony where she had been brought in her wheelchair; she breathed the fresh air and followed all his movements with her glance.

With a previously selected key, he opened the bureau and took out his brand-new suit and white shirt. A smell of naphthalene came from the suit. He was hurrying and scratched his neck with the stiff collar of the shirt. He straightened the accursed collar and looked for a tie on the shelf. He put his head into the bureau. His own ties were saturated with naphthalene. "What the hell," he thought, "I still have a sense of humor," and he thrust his hands into Vasili's collection. Making sly faces, he chose the very best tie and tied it with a thin knot.

Putting out the tip of his tongue and glancing at the door, he put on his jacket and turned around in front of the mirror.

"Where are you going?" asked his mother. "To the art exhibit?"

"I am going for a stroll along the Prospect. I'll just look around," he confessed. He never thought of lying to her. She was his ally.

"To the art exhibit. I knew it," his mother agreed with satisfaction. She was deaf and interpreted everyone else's speech to her own taste.

He placed his finger to his lips, calling upon her to be silent. Then he looked out the door and, tiptoeing, walked through the corridor. The hinges of the door—yesterday he had greased them with sunflower-seed oil—turned noiselessly, abetting his escape.

And immediately, in accordance with the laws of adventure, his three-year-old grandson, Sasha, ran out of the kitchen. Sasha was like a jet fighter flying on a straight course to intercept the escapee. Grandfather had to remain at the door, submissively awaiting Sasha's departure. Sasha would immediately ask, "Where are you going, Grandad? Outside?" Then everyone would appear from the kitchen, the inflexible Vasili in the lead.

But the boy took a different course. He turned sharply into a side room, giving the fugitive one more chance. The runaway, without delay, slipped out onto the front steps.

The September sun still shone as he stepped out of the shadow of the porch and it seemed to him as if everything on the street had become white: the walls, asphalt, and trees.

He looked around authoritatively and saw Kolya, who was his own age. His crony was sitting on a bench in the sun, warming his legs, hunched over and reading a book. He had pulled his ever-present cap over his eyes down to his ears and the cap's visor cast an almost black shadow. The shadow covered his face down to his chin, making the fair-skinned Kolya look like a mulatto.

"Kolya, Greetings!"

Wholeheartedly rejoicing, he slapped his crony on his sun-warmed back. Kolya shuddered, let go of the book, and it slipped onto the asphalt.

"Hello Vadim," answered Kolya. He bent down for the book and at the same time tipped his cap slightly by way of greeting.

"Why the ceremony?" Vadim said reproachfully. He felt a surge of surplus strength in his muscles, and felt like really letting himself go.

"This is a book by Lev Nikolaevich Tolstoy," Kolya reproached him in turn and wiped the cover of the book with his sleeve.

"Excuse me," said Vadim. He greedily looked around and, surprising even himself, he suddenly blurted out, "Well, Kolya!"

He grasped his crony under the arms, made him stand up, and began to wrestle with him. Kolya's cap slipped back onto the crown of his head and, as in a lunar eclipse, the shadow disappeared, revealing Kolya's pale face to the world.

"What are you doing! Have you gone crazy? There are people here." Kolya was embarrassed. He listlessly struggled to break the grip. He chuckled, but was still fearful of what people would think.

"Well, what about the people—" Vadim said in surprise, continuing to squeeze Kolya.

"It's embarrassing. We are too old to be wrestling."

"Phoo—what an important person," Vadim began to laugh. "Now then, hold on, most honorable one! All right, lad!" And trying to upset him, he lifted him from the ground.

"I give up. Leave me alone, for God's sake," mumbled the blushing Kolya, twisting his long legs. "The whole street is looking."

Kolya wasn't shy by birth and proof of this, perhaps, is still kept in the police archives. But now the presence of spectators broke his will.

"Well, at least accept the challenge. I won't argue," said Vadim, almost entreating him.

"Release me immediately. This very minute," his friend hissed.

He left Kolya and walked along the street. He was happy with himself. He was happy, even though he knew his crony—that old man—was muttering behind his back that Vadim should know better, while making excuses to the spectators.

Vadim began to walk downtown. Like a devoted little dog, his shadow gaily ran along near his legs. When he was two blocks from the main street, a kind of feverish excitement seized him. It was as if he had returned to his native land after a long separation.

"Well, well," said Vadim, exciting himself even more. In this city only one street was ever considered the main one. It was much more beautiful than the others and was even called Beautiful Prospect. Perhaps the city needed only one main street. All the best stores and movie theaters were located here—as if to make it more convenient for the city people. Everything was at hand, everything was together.

And in the evenings and on holidays the Prospect became a place for walking. There on the sidewalks two continuous crowds flowed, from one end to the other.

It seemed as if he hadn't been there for a century. This thought occurred to him just as he reached the corner where the street he was on crossed the Prospect. From then on, each subsequent minute was filled with a special significance. For a beginning, he reached into the inner pocket of his jacket and got a cigarette taken secretly from Vasili's reserves. The matches had been on the gas stove when he had happened to glance into the kitchen and no one else was around.

Vadim began to smoke, inhaling with delight. He slowly exhaled a continuous stream of smoke, observing carefully how it gradually dissolved into the air. A shoulder brushed him. Then he was hit on his leg by a hard heavy bag and somebody said in a startled soprano: "Oh, excuse me."

Then a baritone said: "Well, why is that post in the way?"

But it was if he could not feel anything, as if he had grown deaf; his only reaction was to retreat mechanically toward the wall. He wasn't on the Prospect yet, he was still on the threshold.

Having finished his cigarette, he looked around for an urn. It was on the opposite corner. He carried the cigarette butt across the street, aimed and tossed it, and waited until it disappeared into the dark mouth of the urn. Immediately the noise of the Prospect filled his ears. It was as if up until then the Prospect, with its pedestrians and packs of flying automobiles, had been separated from him by thick, soundproof glass.

Finally, trembling with uneasy hopes, he set out along the

Prospect. Buildings opened out in front of him as though the Prospect were opening its stone gates one after the other. The street lured Vadim further and further, carrying him along as if it were a corridor into the unknown. He plunged into the current of people, turning his head from side to side, trying to embrace everything with his glance.

Above his head the foliage of the trees was stirring in the summer heat. It was calm, and a current arising from the hot breathing of the people stirred the foliage.

When he came alongside the little store where local wines were sold, a man with a closely shaven face stepped back from the shop window and obstructed his way. Hanging at his side was a plump document case, held in an official manner.

"W-will you b-be third?" he asked, stuttering, and closed his eyes involuntarily, pausing as if he were collecting his thoughts.

It seemed ridiculous to Vadim and at the same time somehow pleasant. Really pleasant. From so many people walking along the street and from among all of them, he precisely had been singled out. Apparently it was because he called forth such trust.

"And where is the second one?" Vadim asked, ready for anything.

"There is a second one. He is a good conversationalist. Incidentally, he is an artist—a painter of seascapes," said the man in a weighty manner and he pointed over his shoulder with his index finger.

A stocky man in a gray bouclé jacket waited near the wall. He understood that they were speaking about him and politely nodded his closely clipped head.

"I can't," said Vadim uncertainly.

He wanted to drink and chat with good people. He wavered. The stocky man noticed this and approached slowly.

"In the first place, you are dealing with orderly people and we're not inviting you just anywhere into the gutter. Let's drop into a coffee shop," said the second one reasonably.

"No, I can't," repeated Vadim. He reached into his pocket and found four coins in all.

He excused himself and walked further, annoyed by the fact that he couldn't dine in the company of such good mixers as these men. He would really have been upset but, to balance his regrets, another idea came to him: today the whole day lay ahead of him.

He came to the corner where Ivanov Street crossed the Prospect. In bygone days he used to meet Boris here. They merged together as if they were sunbeams. He used to walk along the Prospect and Boris would arrive from Ivanov Street. While Boris was still in the distance, Vadim could always see his wide smile that reached up to his ears. He would even be able to see the black glowing coals of his eyes. In the old days, his bosom friend would arrive in a snow-white shirt that still smelled of having just been ironed. His skin would still be cold from tap water, and his damp black hair invariably showed traces of a comb. After work, Boris used to sleep an hour and a half and always woke up looking brand new. When they met, they always shook each other's hand vigorously, and Boris would always say something of this sort:

"Well, old man. How about a tango today at the Teachers' House?"

"Information received," Vadim would answer.

For awhile they would play tricks on the corner. This had a special meaning for them. Afterwards they would set out along the Prospect, each step making them feel at home, since every now and then they stopped to speak to acquaintances or they themselves were stopped by friends. Thus they would blissfully walk for a long time, and their stroll was so entertaining that it appeared there could be nothing else so diverting. But then, among the passersby, a beautiful face would sail past, and that always made everything that had happened earlier become less significant.

"Vadik!" Boris used to exclaim desperately, and they would start the chase.

"Vadik, this is *She* with a capital letter! We have waited our whole lives for this one," muttered Boris.

But *She,* with some kind of tenth sense, having detected the chase, minced forward in panic, praying to houses, trees, and passersby for mercy. After recovering his breath, Boris would begin to weave a fatal net behind her back. He used the usual patter of nonsense. But somehow, all those banalities of the type: "Girl, girl, what a warm day," coming from Boris's mouth sounded different. Sometimes he inspired intuitive trust or the devil knows what. The girl would slow her step and glance back as if searching for someone. And still she never knew that, in fact, she was displaying the white flag of complete capitulation.

"Have I seen you somewhere?" exclaimed Boris, coming alongside the girl.

"Could it be on Lake Ritsa?" the girl naively helped.

"Oh, Lake Ritsa! Luxuriant flora! Did you walk along Lago-Naki?" Boris inquired, warmly.

No, she didn't have the opportunity, unfortunately. Up to now she only had been taken to well-known health resorts where there were white buildings, palm trees or at the worst only blue firs.

"Too bad," said Boris firmly. "Lago-Naki is a great little place." After having conducted her home, they would begin saying goodbye. Actually it was Boris who was saying goodbye, with Vadim following blindly after him.

"Well, best luck!" Boris would say, suddenly indifferent.

The girl would marvel at such a turn and wait for something more. Vadim would marvel too, and nudge Boris quietly in the side, thereby hoping to change Boris's mind. But the physiognomy of his friend would become impenetrable.

Afterwards, when they were returning to the Prospect, Vadim would ask: "What are you—some kind of blockhead of the celestial czar? You should have made a date. I nudged and nudged you."

"What for? Dull girl, true philistine. Doesn't know anything about Lago-Naki—that's terrible," answered Boris, making a face.

And they set off for the dances.

Boris hadn't come here for a long time; Vadim knew this well. He waited out fifteen minutes, according to etiquette, and then went on his search for adventures alone.

He went toward the ancient chestnut trees. Their branchy crowns covered half a block. In the thick mazes of this green canopy a sparrow kingdom was settled. Even on calm days, from dawn to dusk, sparrows shrilly sang and stirred the foliage. Bird droppings poured like white rain from the top of the foliage onto the heads of the passersby, and pedestrians detoured around the ancient chestnut trees, thereby giving complete possession of this part of the Prospect to the birds.

But the city fathers couldn't resign themselves to the fact that the birds held a piece of territory within their jurisdiction. For as long as Vadim could remember, they had carried on a fierce struggle with the small occupants. And at that very moment a fire engine bolted away from under the trees with a howl of panic, decorated by the birds so that it looked exactly like a camouflaged armed transport.

Vadim mingled with the idlers who surrounded the trees in a semicircle, looking upwards. There the sparrows were shaking themselves, wet and disheveled, and therefore looking emaciated. They were excitedly making a hubbub, as if they were discussing the troubles of the past battle.

"When they opened the hose, the birds at first submitted," said one of the eyewitnesses.

"It's obvious," said a man standing near Vadim. Then he pursed his lips, and attentively looked over the general picture. He was tall and portly, with a deep furrow on the bridge of his nose, which made him look very stern.

"Aha, when they decided that they were losing, they turned off the water, and that's when it began," said the man pensively, accompanying his deliberations with gestures.

"At first, they frightened the sparrows with a hawk. It's just a stuffed hawk. There it is. And below they placed a tape recorder with a hawk's cry on it. But to the birds the hawk's cries were only whimpers," said with delight the same eyewitness, who was hidden from Vadim by the backs of the idlers.

"Do you understand?" asked Vadim's new-found companion, smiling mysteriously.

"What precisely?"

"Sparrows are city dwellers—C-i-t-y!"

"Of course," said Vadim affably.

"You still don't understand?" asked his companion, happy because Vadim didn't understand.

"Well, look. They don't know who and what this hawk is. Not the slightest idea. Therefore they absolutely don't give a damn about the hawk." He looked at Vadim, smiling as if to say, "How original this is, and at the same time how simple."

"Well, really, how could they know?" Vadim agreed willingly. It turned out that they walked on together. His companion compelled respect; Vadim was flattered and, walking alongside, he felt like a pupil singled out for the personal confidence of the teacher.

"So one has to say, each of us possess something," said the companion, confidently taking Vadim by the elbow. "Either instinct or constant striving. Therefore we must control . . . ourselves! Every minute! Do you agree with me?"

He took off his cap and, without stopping, greeted someone.

"What do you think?" he asked, putting on his cap.

"Perhaps that's so." Vadim became evasive and timid. "I don't think about things like that. You see, I simply live. I live, to be sure, quite naturally."

"No! No! Not like that!" protested his companion and, waving his hands fiercely, he added with bitter irony, "Anyone can say—'One lives as the bird sings and the grass grows.'"

"You don't understand. It is possible I didn't explain it properly," said Vadim, confused. "I don't mean biologically, exactly . . . humanly . . . well, how one would say in a word . . . I mean free, well . . ."

But his companion suddenly began to laugh inappropriately and then stopped in the middle of the sidewalk.

"Who is this I see!" he exclaimed, as he blocked the path of a woman coming from the opposite direction.

"Bah—how many years—" said the woman, smiling only with her lips.

Vadim, not knowing whether to wait or to continue on, moved

politely aside. It would be somewhat awkward, he felt, to leave without saying goodbye. But his companion chattered on with his acquaintance, forgetting Vadim's existence. He stood with his back to Vadim. Vadim saw how his companion's neck was filled with blood from time to time. Periodically the blood subsided and the neck regained its usual color. It was as if his blood were urged into the vessels at intervals.

The age of the female acquaintance was hidden under a magnificent layer of makeup. Her fresh, pale rose skin tightly covered her narrow face, her oval cheekbones were still delicate, her full lips were adequately sensual, and under her elevated upper lip her strong teeth glistened white. Her beautifully done coiffure darkened to a blue hue. But her eyes, which harbored a fear of old age, were silent. And it seemed to Vadim that soon some kind of personal secret of hers would be revealed to him. However, the woman herself still didn't suspect the existence of her own unhappy secret. And believing that her eyes were still sparkling and alluringly impudent, she stealthily glanced at Vadim. And he, standing on the threshold of her secret, unexpectedly caught himself striving to assume a dignified air. He pulled in his stomach and, in general adopting a devil-may-care attitude, tried to appear gallant. Although he straightened his back, he couldn't square his shoulders and he felt very uncomfortable in such an awkward pose.

Vadim's interlocutor offered his pretzel-shaped elbow to the woman. After a moment's hesitation, she took him by the arm, and they left, not even glancing back at Vadim.

"Goodbye," said Vadim in a whisper, to both of them.

He shook himself from the spell and again felt alone. He didn't have much time anyway, therefore he began to hurry, became anxious, and ran along the street, stumbling into the pedestrians. His eyes seemed dazzled—unable to see and therefore now and then he turned his head around as if looking for someone.

Along the way he came across a group of fellows standing relaxed along the edge of the sidewalk or near the wall. Watch-

ing them, he turned their way, cut through them, and stepped
on their feet. The fellows, with their Beatle haircuts, parted, and
somebody shouted derisively after him:

"Olla, open your eyes! Cool it!"

He selected a trio of kids and joined them. The kids sat side
by side on the metal handrails that divided the sidewalk from
the street. They were joking in eager rivalry. Perhaps this didn't
always turn out well, but still they were laughing enthusiastically, to the point of tears. Even while one of them was still talking, the others were ready to burst into laughter. Their eyes were
even closed ahead of time.

For a long time Vadim sought an opportunity and finally he
asked for a cigarette. The one who sat nearest him thrust out a
pack of "Shipki," not, however, very enthusiastically. He barely
gave Vadim a glance. As soon as Vadim got the cigarette, the
boy turned back to his friends. He had the broken nose of a boxer
and his eyes were deep set. They twinkled from under powerful, heavy temples.

Then Vadim began his act; he pressed the cigarette between
his lips and in deliberate pantomime began to slap his pockets.

"Hey, Nose, give the guy a light," said one fellow. He had a
face so broad and asymmetrical that it made his smile appear
ironic. He sat, this ironic one—as Vadim in his thoughts had
named him—third in line.

Nose handed over his lighter, not even looking at Vadim this
time. But Vadim decided not to give up. He pretended that the
lighter was not functioning and, again trying to draw attention to
himself, he spun the little wheel freely and moved his head as
if he were puzzled.

"Nose, help the fellow—" said the ironic one, frowning.

Nose patiently took the lighter, struck up the light, and
brought it toward Vadim's cigarette. Afterward, he artistically
clicked the lid and put the lighter in his pocket.

"That's the way to do it," he said, his teeth gleaming.

"Well, what's new?" asked Vadim, releasing his first cloud
of smoke.

"It depends. Some of the new things are old already," the

one seated in the middle answered affably. He was a big fellow, with a long narrow face like a continuation of his neck, and big round ears, which he turned in one direction and then in the other as if he were a radar scanner.

Vadim made a face, as if the joke were indeed a clever one, and nodded his approval.

"Not bad, but I think I'll move on," Vadim declared his intention.

"A useful pursuit. On the street there is oxygen," noted the one whose smile appeared crooked. It was a good thing that Vadim already knew about this asymmetric smile, otherwise he would have taken offense.

"Well, we don't know each other—" Vadim said uneasily, and introduced himself: "Vadim, in a word, Vadik."

"Very pleased to meet . . . Nikolai," said the fellow with the broken nose.

"Mikhail," said the second one.

"Hippolyte, Hippolyte as a matter of fact," said the ironic one.

Vadim in turn shook three hands, scrambled upon the handrail, and asked:

"Well, what shall we do?"

His new friends exchanged glances. Nikolai slipped down from the railing and said, shifting awkwardly: "Personally, we should go home. We are still minors. Mothers get angry."

As soon as he said this, the remaining two slipped off the railing.

"Strict mothers. Why are mothers so strict?" asked Vadim sympathetically.

"Old-fashioned," answered Hippolyte for everyone, and stretched.

"Goodbye, Vadik." Mikhail took his leave.

"Vadik, goodbye," chimed in Nikolai.

"'Bye, old man Vadik," added Hippolyte.

"Goodbye, boys," said Vadim goodheartedly.

They went away talking among themselves. Vadik was melancholy for a moment. "What kind of company is that? It broke up just when everything was taking shape so well," he said to himself, feeling somewhat grieved.

He didn't notice that he had reached the end of the street. It ended at the gate of the city hospital. Near the gate sat a dark-complexioned old man in a railroad field shirt with lackluster buttons. A thick silver crew cut covered his head. The old man leaned on a long, crooked crutch and, together with the crutch, he cast a black shadow like a cast-iron monument.

The sun was at its zenith and burned his head. Vadim mechanically covered the top of his head with the palm of his hand and looked around on all sides. No people, empty. He and the old man—they were the only entities.

"Hurry, brother," said the old man, and pounded demandingly with his crutch. "Dinner will be soon and then we won't let anybody in."

He shifted around on his stool and opened the view to the festive shell-paved avenue. The avenue wound between broad trunks of white acacias and led to the yellow buildings of the hospital.

"Thank you, thank you," answered Vadim, squinting at the sun.

"And later there will be a quiet hour, and again we will not allow anybody in," added the old man. His swarthy face was in sharp contrast to his white crew cut. The old man looked like a photographic negative.

"Thank you, thank you," repeated Vadim. "I have no one there, thank God. In my family, thank God, everyone is healthy."

At that moment he looked intently into the glass door of the telephone booth. It had just seemed to him that only two people were present, but in reality there were three. In the booth stood a blonde. The glass walls played in the sun, and because of this he hadn't noticed the girl at first. Now she materialized before his eyes from a sparkling nothing.

From time to time, because of the bewitched glass, she dissolved and then sprang up again, luminous and shimmering.

The girl saw him and made a sorrowful grimace. She raised

her little finger—she was asking for a minute to continue her conversation.

"Go ahead, go ahead. I don't need the telephone." Vadim began to stir. He hit himself in the chest and energetically began to wave his hands.

The girl pressed herself to the telephone receiver and her lips moved soundlessly as if she were in an aquarium.

A presentiment urged him on; he lowered his eyes to the base of the booth and saw a folded fan of yellow plastic. He bent over with a quickness that was unusual for him, and raised the lady's trinket. The fan whirred in his hands with an electric crackle, and its blades formed a Japanese landscape. Something in this simple thing touched Vadim's heart. Probably it was the unsophisticated taste of its owner.

He showed the fan to the girl—"Why are you staring?" He fanned himself, delightedly. But the girl looked through him. She was listening to what was being said to her from the other end of the wire. At times she roused, giggled, and shouted: "You don't say! Tell me!" Finally she hung up. For awhile she just stood in the transparent box, coming to her senses. Afterwards she opened the door and fluttered out, pale from happiness.

In reality, she turned out to be plain, with a flat nose and sparse eyelashes.

"Please," said Vadim. Succumbing to the desire to make her happy, he tendered the folded fan to her.

The girl looked at the fan, not understanding anything.

"A fan," whispered Vadim, laughing at her protracted return to the real world.

"A fan?" she asked, and suddenly said with unexpected hoarseness, "So what, give it to your wife, dad"; and having tilted up her sharp little chin, she made her way past Vadim.

"But, allow me! This . . . this is a fan! It's your fan!" he called after her.

His embarrassment softened the angry girl, and she turned around and said reproachfully: "Why do you say that? This fan isn't mine. Nobody carries them anymore."

"Indeed, knothead, nobody carries them anymore. Indeed," recollected Vadim. "Fans are not in style. My late wife, Nina, yes, she had a fan twenty years ago."

Suddenly he realized how wrongly his action had been interpreted by the girl and he was horrified. He should have stopped her to say: "Little girl, I could be your father."

But the girl had turned the corner and the offended tap of her heels had died away, and now he couldn't run after her.

Dejected, he wandered back downtown and stopped opposite the first shop window. He looked at his own reflection, trying to see himself with the eyes of the girl. He saw a bald skull with a pitiful fringe of gray hair, and a network of wrinkles surrounding his eyes, soft sloping shoulders, and a pot belly, which his son Vasili called "a naval chest." And to crown it all, he unexpectedly remembered his encounter with the kids, and how he had called himself Vadik at his age. Now he understood why they left for no apparent reason. They felt sorry for him.

He crossed the street and at the nearest stop he got on a trolley.

The trolley rocked along a narrow green street. Vadim looked indifferently in front of him and only once looked out the window. The trolley crossed Ivanov Street, where Boris lived. Now his old friend was resting in bed after his second stroke.

But his friend Kolya was still sitting near the entryway of the building, dozing on the bench, and gritting his teeth with delight. His book lay on his knees as before. Having noticed Vadim, he regained full consciousness and, grabbing the book, attempted to slip away.

"Sit still. I don't do anything," Vadim said to him. He approached the entryway and waved his hand as if severing something unknown to Kolya.

But all the same Kolya worried about what Vadim might do and he started to explain how he felt.

"I'm not really against horseplay. But there are people around and they might think we're foolish. Besides, if we were somewhere in a vacant lot, let's say . . ."

But Vadim had already gone to the stairs. He climbed to his

own floor and pushed the doorbell. The bell began to drone dully, penetrating to the depths of the apartment. Then he heard the worn-down heels of his daughter-in-law's slippers hurriedly slapping along the hall and she opened the door.

"Finally you've come back, thank God. We have looked everywhere. They wanted to call the police. Perhaps something happened," his daughter-in-law reproached him, letting him pass into the entrance hall.

He took off his jacket and hung it on the rack between the coats. His daughter-in-law didn't leave him, continuing to mutter, "After an illness you should walk? What do you think you are—young?"

"Why do you say that?" he muttered, trying not to look her in the eye.

His grandson, Sasha, ran out of the room and began to shout piercingly: "Hurrah—grandfather has been found—grandfather has been found."

With a grammar book in his hands, Vasili came out of the bathroom. He fixed his glasses determinedly on the bridge of his nose and announced almost officially: "Well, Dad, we have decided—you must go to the mineral springs sanitarium. Your age, father, your age. It's time to rest."

Vadim hastily nodded. They all stared at him. And he, avoiding their glances, moved sideways along the wall and dived into his mother's room. Mother was already moving onto the couch. She looked at him approvingly, convinced of the fact that he hadn't been wandering aimlessly, but had been at the opening day of an exhibition.

"Mama," he asked, nearing her.

"It's all right, my little son, it's all right," she said, and affectionately stroked his head.

Arkadii Arkanov

Arkadii Arkanov, born in 1933 in Kiev, is a physician who began to write while he was in medical school. In 1960 he began his literary career with stories on comic and satirical subjects. His stories deal with today's Soviet citizen, whose dreams and desires are petty and vulgar. Often his stories depict characters who, even when facing death, seek ordinary comforts. As a humanist Arkanov is strongly influenced by Gogol and Zoshchenko.

Arkadii Arkanov

Before Departure

I REMEMBER THAT after eating a roll with cabbage I felt I was going to die.

And I said to the woman with whom I lived—I'll never know how—all my life,

"Listen! It seems that according to all probability I'll die soon."

"When," she asked.

"It might be Thursday."

"What day is today?"

"Today is Monday."

She became gloomy and mournful. Then, having overcome her heaviness of heart, she said firmly:

"Do you have your pay?"

"Yes."

"Hand it over!"

I gave it to her. She counted the money and looked at me sadly:

"What happened to the six rubles?"

"I kept them for myself," I answered quietly. "Who knows . . . beer, ice cream . . . Maybe we'll go to the movies; after all, there are still two days left."

"Egotist!" she said. "You can't even spend two days with your family! . . . Hand over the rest of it! . . ."

"Am I spending it on myself? Don't worry, it will be spent on you!"

I gave her my last six rubles!

"This is the time to talk about it. I'd like to be buried like a normal human being . . ."

"Don't count on an orchestra!" she said.

"Don't exaggerate, please. I didn't even consider ordering an orchestra . . . I've already made a deal with Kolya from apartment number 12. He'll be glad to play his accordion for five rubles. It just happens that he has a day off on Thursday. The main thing is to decide whom we're going to invite."

She smiled:

"True friends don't need to be invited; they'll remember to come on their own."

"Yes, but how will they find out?"

"Call 'em up!"

"That's what I'm trying to say . . . so, on my side—mother and father, Petya with Zina, Lucia and her husband; Nina Ivanovna should be called from Kiev, and the co-workers . . . On your side —mother, Veronica, the Satanovskis, Uncle Abessalom from Sukhumi . . ."

"It would be rude not to invite the Kozovskis," she interjected.

"I can't stand the sight of them."

"You won't see them, anyway."

"Oh, yes . . . sorry."

"The procession will begin about five o'clock, because later it will be very hot . . ."

"By the way, don't forget to invite Kruplova and her wrestler," she said.

"What for?"

"Do you think I'm going to lug the coffin by myself?"

"They'll know why we invited them. . . !"

"Don't tell them why—just invite them and let it be a surprise."

She took a piece of paper and began to make a list.

"It comes out to 42 people! . . . We've got to cut it down!" she said irritably.

"Aren't you ashamed of yourself! People will come, as it were, to say farewell . . ."

Now she was beside herself:

"To say farewell? That's fine for you! But afterwards I'll have to serve food and drink to the whole troop! . . ." And she began to cry.

"Calm down," I said, "I'm not dying just to inconvenience you.

. . . It may seem like it . . . Calm down . . . let's draw up a menu."

She stopped crying:

"Don't you trust me?"

"I trust you, but I wouldn't want only cheese sandwiches again."

"What do you mean, again?"

"Like on my birthday . . . I'd like a rich table, catered wth taste."

"I know what I'll do," she said. "I'll cook beans Georgian style . . ."

"I get a heartburn from beans," I said, making a wry face.

"'I' again. What does it have to do with you?!"

We spent a lot of time settling the question of the menu, and then I asked to be laid out in my navy blue suit with the sparkling flecks.

"That's your only decent suit," she muttered. "Of course, it's your business, but I don't understand why you want to look like a fop."

"And what do you think I should wear?"

"Anything! Like a sweater and a simple pair of slacks . . . What does it matter?!"

"For you of course it doesn't matter! It's not your funeral! . . ."

I went to the closet. "I mustn't forget anything." She kept her eye on me . . . Well, I took a handkerchief, tie, I.D., cigarette lighter . . .

"You don't need the lighter, it's not a business trip! . . ." she commented.

I put the lighter back.

"You'll have to turn in your I.D."

I handed her my I.D.

"I implore you, don't take it so hard," I said. "Don't cry, everything will be fine . . . but I warn you, if during the service your brother says again that all my life I lived off you, I'll simply get up and spit in his face!"

"You are capable of doing anything," she said.

I put my arm around her shoulders: "Listen, my dear . . . it's only two days till Thursday; let's live in peace."

She lifted her frightened eyes to me:

"Wait, wait . . . till Thursday? . . . But on Thursday, I have a fitting. Can't you pull through till Friday?"

"Unfortunately, I feel that it will take place on Thursday."

We began to squabble again . . . and I knew that everything would take place not on Thursday, but on Wednesday—after all, this was more convenient for her.

The kids came in. Many kids. Ours, somebody else's, and the neighbors' . . .

"And how about the Zoo?!" . . . they began to jump around me.

"And the bike . . . and what about the wooden sabre! . . ."

"Children!" I cried out.

"Stop the hubbub! . . . We have a whole day in front of us! . . . We'll have time for everything! . . ."

What can one do . . .

Often we arrive at serious conclusions only at the end of our lives . . . That's what I had done.

One should not put off things to the last minute. Family misunderstandings shorten our lives.

Maybe only by one day, but they shorten it.

Yurii M. Nagibin

Yurii M. Nagibin was born in 1920 and was educated in Moscow. His family were well educated and from them he inherited his love for literature and the arts. He studied cinematography at the State Cinema Institute of Moscow. After a brief period in the military service (he was wounded and demobilized) and a stint as a war correspondent, Nagibin became a full-time writer. He has written a number of short autobiographical stories that deal with his own childhood, as well as war stories. Nagibin effectively describes the inner world of young people and is known for excellent description of children such as Savushkin in "Zimnii dub," Vit'ka in "Echo," and Vasya in "An Old Turtle," the present story. Although Nagibin officially agrees with the orthodox Soviet view of arts, he is free of the usual Soviet clichés and successfully continues to write about the inner life of the complex human beings in today's Russia, which in many ways transcends narrow political and national interests.

Yurii M. Nagibin

An Old Turtle

VASYA TOOK A DEEP BREATH, his nostrils quivered, and he was penetrated to his very depths with a strong, stuffy, animal smell. He lifted his eyes. Above the door hung a small sign, faded from the southern sun, on which was written "Pet Shop." Through the dusty pane of the show window the boy could barely make out a dusty, stuffed, long-legged and long-beaked bird.

How little do we know the streets on which we walk everyday! How many times Vasya had walked to the beach through this street; he knew every house, every light, every chestnut tree and shop window, every crack in the sidewalk, and every hole in the pavement, and suddenly it was apparent that he hadn't noticed the most important thing on the street.

But it wasn't worth thinking about now; it was more important to hurry into the enchanting, mysterious semi-darkness . . .

His mother, with her usual submissiveness, followed her son. The cramped, dark store was deserted, but like an abandoned lair it preserved the warm, living spirit of its recent inhabitants. On the shelves there was dry fish food, under the ceiling hung empty bird cages, and in the middle of the room there was an aquarium, lit by a dim electric light, covered with shells; long sinuous seaweeds, trembling slightly, entwined the slimy stone grotto. All this undersea kingdom belonged to an indifferent gnat larva, resembling a small blood vessel which, writhing silently, was attached to the ribbed surface of a shell.

Vasya stood for a long time before the aquarium, as if hoping that the lifeless splendor of the sea kingdom would suddenly become alive, and then, downcast, he moved into the darkness of the store. But then his triumphant shout resounded:

"Mama, look!"

The mother understood immediately: the same oblivious shout had preceded the arrival of an aquarium in their home with its marvelous fish, a cage with singing birds, collections of butterflies, a bicycle, a box with carpenter tools . . .

She came close to her son. In the corner of the store, on the straw-covered bottom of a box, crawled two tiny turtles. They were smaller than Vasya's fist and were astoundingly fresh and clean. The little turtles were calmly climbing the sides of the box, then slipping; they fell to the bottom and, once more, dexterously moving their light-colored feet with handlike claws, they climbed up.

"Mama!" said Vasya piercingly, not even bothering to add the crude words "buy them."

"We have enough trouble with Mashka," wearily replied his mother.

"But, Mama, just look at their little faces!"

Vasya didn't know what it meant to be denied anything; everything came to him with a wave of a wand. This is all right in a fairy tale, but in Vasya's case the fairy tale had lasted too long. In the fall Vasya would go to school. How would he feel when he discovered that the spell had lost all its power and that life has to be approached with hard work and patience? The Mother shook her head disapprovingly:

"No, three turtles at home—it's too much!"

"O.K.," said Vasya with a challenging submissiveness. "If that's what you want, let's give away Mashka; she is very old anyway."

"You know very well you don't mean that."

The boy was hurt, turned away from his mother, and said in a low voice:

"You just don't want to spend the money . . ."

"Of course he is little and he does not know what's right and what's wrong," thought his mother—"one has only to explain that he is wrong." But instead of these calm, wise words of advice, she said curtly:

"Enough! Let's leave at once!"

This was a strange morning for Vasya. On the beach each pebble seemed to be a little golden turtle. The jellyfish and seaweeds that touched his feet while he was swimming close to shore were also little turtles, affectionately offering their friendship. The boy, distracted, was totally oblivious to the usual pleasures of swimming, and he left the water indifferently at his mother's first call, slowly walking behind her. On the way home his mother bought his favorite grapes and handed him the heavy cluster, but Vasya took only one grape and didn't even eat that. He had only one wish and idea, which weighed him down, and when he arrived home he knew well what he was going to do about it.

During the day the old turtle always hid in quiet and cozy places—in the clothes closet or under the couch, or she crawled into a dark corner full of junk. But now Vasya was lucky; he found Mashka at once, under his bed.

"Mashka, Mashka!" he called her, on all fours, but the dark, round lump for a long time didn't show any signs of life. Finally, in the hole, something moved between its shell, then something emerged that looked like a bird's beak, and then the whole naked, flat head with its filmy eyes like those of a dead bird came out. On the side of the lump grew stumpy paws. And then one of the front paws slowly and pensively lifted itself, slowly extended, and, with a muffled noise, descended to the floor. After it, just as slowly, pensively, and awkwardly, the second paw began to move and, in about three minutes, Mashka crawled out from under the bed.

Vasya placed a piece of apricot on the floor. Mashka stretched out her wrinkled, stringy neck, which exposed tiny and similarly wrinkled membranes that held it to the shell, and in a birdlike fashion pecked at the piece of apricot and then swallowed it at once. Mashka refused the second piece of apricot and crawled away. In rare moments when Mashka had the desire to move, her protruding eyes didn't see obstacles, and, in her dreamy but obstinate fumbling step, she moved forward, forward, seeking some kind of a distant goal known only to her.

There was no more superfluous creature in the world than Mashka, but even she was good for something: one could sit on her or even stand on her. Vasya moved to Mashka and pressed her with his hand; under his palm she kept on scratching the floor with her extended legs. Her shell, consisting of asymmetrical squares and rhomboids, had come loose in old age; deep furrows appeared at the joints and Vasya for some reason decided to sit on her. Then he picked Mashka up and looked outside the window. His mother was lying in the hammock; her light head barely pressed the pillow, and the book she was reading had fallen from her open hand. His mother was sleeping. Vasya hid Mashka under his shirt and quickly went out.

Over the nearly deserted, sleepy bazaar one could hear the high-pitched and sad voice of a child:

"A turtle! A turtle for sale!"

It seemed to Vasya that he had stood for a long time, and the direct, merciless rays of sun were baking his poor bare head, the sweat was dripping from his forehead and obscuring his vision, and Mashka, who now seemed made out of stone, weighed down his arms. In all his body he felt oppressive, aching weakness, and he was tempted to sit down on the dusty ground.

"A turtle! A turtle for sale"

Vasya shouted these words with less force, as though he was afraid but at the same time wanted to be heard. But people preoccupied with their own business walked by him indifferently; they didn't see anything unusual in what was for Vasya almost the hardest trial in his short life. Oh, if he could only find himself in his own, forsaken world, where he had been so happy under the loyal protection of his mother.

Whenever Vasya thought of that, his own home at once lost its charm, becoming unpleasant and dull: for then he would have to give up forever the happy, golden, little turtles.

"Oh, a turtle! Now that's just what I want!"

Vasya was so lost in revery that he started and almost dropped

Mashka. In front of him stood a tall, broad-shouldered man, evidently a longshoreman who was looking at the old turtle with childish delight.

"Are you selling it, lad?"

"Yes . . ."

"How much?"

"Nine . . ." Vasya said in confusion, remembering the price of the two turtles in the pet shop.

"Nine? Won't you take a little less?"

"Can't. . . ," whispered Vasya; it was embarrassing.

"If you can't, then I'll pay in full. You know, my son is going home to Tambov tomorrow and I'd like to give him something special."

The longshoreman dug into his pockets and came up with seven rubles.

"I don't have nine on me, as you see," he said, frowning. "Only seven."

Vasya was in despair; he didn't know how to help this big and evidently good man. "Never, never will I sell anything again."

"Just a moment, lad," said the longshoreman happily. "I live close by; let's go to my place, and I will give you the money!"

And they left the market together. Vasya was very happy; all had turned out so well, he was proud of his first actual accomplishment, and besides it was a pleasure to walk along with this big man as an equal. To the right at the end of the street the midday sea was visible, and against its glistening backdrop Vasya saw how the iron arms of the cranes worked above a little ship moored at the pier. The huge, soft bales, one after another, descended from the sky onto the deck, and it seemed strange to the boy that the little ship didn't sink from all that load. He was going to ask his companion to which countries this ship would sail, but he didn't.

"Here we are, lad. I'll be back in no time!"

Vasya stood in front of the white, one-story house surrounded by thick-growing acacias. It seemed strange to him that such a huge fellow lived in such a small house, but this thought left him immediately and he began to look at the front windows attentively. He wanted to see the boy who would get Mashka.

"Oh, it's a pity my boy isn't home," said the longshoreman when he appeared, "otherwise you could have met him. He's just like you—independent . . . Here you are—the money—count it. Money likes to be counted."

"It's O.K.," mumbled Vasya, and handed Mashka to the buyer.

The latter took it in his huge palms and put it to his ear as if it were a watch.

"She isn't empty inside, is she?"

Mashka, as if to spite him, didn't show herself in her stone house, and Vasya was even hurt that she was parting with him in such an indifferent manner. The longshoreman held her in front of his eyes and peered into the crack between the shells.

"No, there's something moving. Well good-by, lad, thank you."

"I have to tell you, her name is Mashka . . ." Vasya suddenly and excitedly spoke up. "She loves fruit very much and she also drinks milk; some people think that turtles don't drink milk, but she does, really she does . . ."

"Just imagine! . . ." laughed the longshoreman, "such a humble creature and yet she makes herself out to be a person of importance!"

He thrust Mashka into the wide pocket of his jacket and went into the house. Vasya watched him in perplexity. He wanted to say much more about Mashka, about her habits, caprices, and weaknesses, that she was a good and kind turtle, and that he, Vasya, didn't know any wrong she had ever done. There was a funny tickling in his nose, but he frowned, held his breath for a moment, and the tickling stopped. Then he pressed the money hard in his hand and rushed to the pet shop.

When Vasya brought home the two little turtles and joyfully told his mother about all his adventures, she was displeased for some reason, but didn't know what to say or what to do in this case. And so it would be better to wait and to think; the

truth is that children are such complicated and difficult creatures . . .

"Yes, yes," she only said, pensively and sadly, "but such
sweet little animals."

Vasya didn't notice how the second half of the day went by.
The little turtles were extraordinarily amusing, daring, and
inquisitive. They crawled all over the room, moving in circles
to meet each other, and having met they didn't turn aside but
one would go up over the other's back, their shells striking. Unlike gloomy old Mashka, they did not try to get to some secret
corner, and if they hid occasionally, it was more like a game of
hide and seek. They weren't particular either; whatever Vasya
offered them—apples or potatoes, grapes, milk, hamburger, cu-
cumbers—they ate everything eagerly and, goggling their beady
eyes, seemed to ask for more and more.

Vasya put them into a box with sand for the night and placed
them where he could see them in front of his bed. Going to sleep
he said to his mother in a happy, sleepy, and tired voice:

"You know mama, I love these turtles so much!"

"So after all, one old friend is not better than two new
ones. . ." remarked the mother pulling his blanket up.

There are some words that, no matter how simple and harm-
less they are when to the point, reappear in your mind and make
your life miserable. After all, Mashka wasn't even a friend, that
is, Vasya's friend, but just an old, decrepit turtle, and he didn't
even want to think about her. However, he was not now thinking about what a clever fellow he had been in obtaining those
two happy little turtles with which it would be so interesting
to play tomorrow, but his thoughts were with the good-for-
nothing Mashka. His thoughts were unsettling and disturbing.

Why didn't he tell that man that Mashka had to be hidden
in a dark place for the night? And now, for sure, the green light
of the moon was shining straight into her old eyes. Further, he
didn't tell him that for the winter one has to build a little den
out of a quilt, otherwise she would wake up from her hibernation, as had happened the first year they had had her, which
could cause her death, because during hibernation turtles don't

eat. He didn't even explain properly what one should feed Mashka. You know, she is so particular . . .

Of course, he could go there tomorrow and tell him all these
things, but would the new owners take as much trouble with
the old Mashka? Indeed, the man seemed very kind, Vasya reassured himself, and certainly his son is kind too. But his anxiety
didn't disappear. Then he pulled the blanket over his head in
order to fall asleep, but once again he could see Mashka's bare,
unblinking, birdlike eyes in which was reflected the merciless
green light of the moon.

Vasya threw off the blanket and sat up in bed. At this moment he felt neither pity for Mashka nor any irritation toward
his mother, who refused to keep all three turtles in the house.
All of his was overshadowed by some kind of incomprehensible
painful feeling, one of dissatisfaction with himself, and by guilty
feelings. These feelings were so enormous and strange that they
could not be contained; they had to be given vent and Vasya
tried to cry. But nothing came of it—these bitter and painful
feelings had dried up all the tears.

For the first time in his life Vasya began to feel that he wasn't
the best boy in the world, deserving to have the best mother,
the best toys, the best comforts. "But what have I done?" he
asked himself, grieved. —"I sold an old useless turtle." "Yes, you
don't need her, came the reply, but she needs you. Everything
good in this world served you; whom did you help?" —"I feed
birds and fish, I change their water." —"Yes, as long as they entertain you, and when that's over, you will do the same thing
you did with Mashka." —"And why shouldn't I do it? . . ."

Vasya couldn't find the answer, but the answer was in his
agitated heart, which for the first time discovered a simple but
previously unknown truth: that the world exists not only for you,
but that you exist also for the world. And with this new feeling
there arose in him a new, inevitable mandate, whose name—
duty—Vasya was to discover only much later. And this mandate
made Vasya jump from the bed and dress quickly.

There were two squares of moonlight on the floor, each divided by a black cross. In the darkness his mother's tiny watch

was ticking distinctly. Should he wake up his mother? No, Vasya
was told by his new, kind, and burning heart: his mother was
tired and it's difficult for her to fall asleep. You have to do it
alone . . .

Vasya felt the box that contained the little turtles—two
smooth, heavy balls, as heavy as if they were filled with quick-
silver. But that might not be enough, and he had to act decisively.
Having thrust the little turtles under his shirt, Vasya also placed
there a box with pewter soldiers; then he thought and took down
a rifle from its nail and slung it over his shoulder.

Having stepped outside, the boy quietly closed the door. He
had suspected before that the world at night creates strange
things, and now with breathtaking triumph he said to himself
"I knew it," having noticed that the apple orchard had crawled
almost to the porch and that the cottage near the house where
the landlord lived had collapsed into the black, shadowy depth of
the yard.

In the yard old Naina's puppies were running about, each
one rolling before him the black ball of his shadow. They were
affectionate and friendly to him during the day, but now they
didn't pay the slightest attention to Vasya, being occupied with
their own nocturnal concerns. Only Naina herself, having inhaled Vasya's odor, growled dully and rattled her chain. The
sensation of the unknown hostility in the world pressed sadly
on the boy's heart.

With a heavy step Vasya approached the trees blanched by
the moonlight. There was not the slightest wind, but the leaves
on the trees nevertheless were stirring; a rustle and a faint scraping sound hovered above the orchard, as if the trees were conversing about something of their own, something nocturnal.
And Vasya recalled his idea that the trees go to swim in the sea
at night. He imagined this half-seriously, having been amazed
that, during all this time here, not once had rain fallen, and trees
cannot live without moisture. But now this fantasy brought an
unpleasant shiver in his spine.

Something flew by his face, touching his cheek lightly with
the flutter of wings. A bat? No, a bat burns up the darkness with

such a speed that one only can guess it, not see it. Now he did manage to notice a fat, spindleshaped body through the quick flutter of the wings.

"A death's-head moth," guessed Vasya, and immediately he saw it—a big moth with triangular-shaped wings, as it descended on the trunk of a little apple tree that was bright as in daytime. On the moth's wide back he could distinctly see the design of a skull, with its eye sockets and mouth cavity. This indefatigable night flyer was almost in his hands, and now his collection would be augmented by another important item! Vasya felt immediately how the gigantic moth would thrash under his palm, tickling it. But having been infused with some kind of a new, prudent respect for all living things, Vasya suppressed his hunter's instinct and only stroked the waxy back of the reveler with his little finger. As if trusting Vasya, the night visitor did not try to fly away, but only moved his antennae sluggishly and crawled a bit higher. On his way he aroused a sleeping beetle on the same trunk. The beetle lifted his pincers, rubbed his little hind legs and, not entering into any argument—there is room enough for all—clumsily moved a bit, stepping on a leg of his neighbor, another long and slender beetle. And a multitude of minute creatures stirred on the trunk of the apple tree and went to sleep again.

Vasya looked with a smile at this sleepy assemblage, for he never expected to find so many of them here, especially on such a slender trunk. They are cautious and hide during the day; how much effort they spend in order to protect themselves from him, Vasya! and now—there you are!—they lay about in all their helplessness. And he wished them good night in his thoughts as if he were an older comrade. Vasya emerged on the street calmly and assuredly, with the step of a strong and good man, but he was still far from being a master of the night. The moon was high in the sky. The wide street was unfriendly and filled with pale moonlight. In its distant corner a silent black wall rose, pierced by a silver crack. "The sea!" surmised Vasya, somewhat frightened. Flat during the day as water in a dish, the sea now was standing on its hind legs, hovering menacingly over the

city. It seemed as if an icy finger were counting Vasya's verte-
brae. He looked at the gate. How cosy and tranquil now seemed
the dear night in his own orchard.

"Don't dare!" he said to himself, forcing himself to think
where and why he was going, and he concentrated until his body
listened not to the fear but to the great and important idea . . .

It is possible that his mother in her sleep caught some unusual sound or felt the disturbing emptiness of the room with
her son missing. She got up, put on her dress, thrust her bare
feet into slippers, and went to Vasya's bed. The blanket was in
a bundle and the sheet showed the small impression of his body.
She looked at the box with turtles; the little turtles were no longer there, and she at once understood everything. Putting her
coat over the shoulders, she left the house and began to walk to
where, according to Vasya, there was a tiny white house with a
little orchard. Soon the little figure of her son appeared.

Vasya was walking in the middle of the street, which was
surrounded by thick, dark chestnut trees. He seemed so little
on the street, under the tall trees, that her heart sank. In order
to overcome this disheartening idea, especially at this moment,
she began to look at his long, almost adult's shadow, at the shadow of a soldier with a gun. She walked, and thought that it was
difficult to raise a human being, for this one must live a complete
and difficult life. And what happiness it would be if her son
should grow up with a strong and true heart! The mother therefore did not call Vasya, but decided to watch over him from a
distance in order not to interfere with her son's first good deed.

Yurii Kazakov

Yurii Kazakov was born in 1927 in Moscow and is well known not only in the Soviet Union, but also in the West. He is sometimes compared to Chekhov and Turgenev. He began to publish his stories in journals in 1952 and in 1957 his first book of short stories, *Teddy*, appeared. In 1964 a collection of Kazakov's short stories was published in the U.S.A., translated by Gabriella Azarel (Boston: Houghton Mifflin and Co.). The book contained over 20 stories, including *Autumn in the Oak Woods* (in a translation with too many errors and omissions). *New Writings in Russia*, translated and with an introduction by T. P. Whitney, also includes the same tale, entitled *Autumn in an Oak Forest*, but omits almost eight pages of the story; without these passages, the story is clumsy and difficult to understand and its idyllic atmosphere is diluted.

Yurii Kazakov

Autumn in the Oak Woods

I TOOK THE BUCKET in order to fetch some water from the spring. This night I was happy, because she was arriving on tonight's launch. But I know how untrustworthy fate is, and so I took the bucket as if I did not expect her arrival at all and were simply going to fetch water. Somehow everything had gone just too well this autumn.

This late-autumn night was slate gray, and I really did not want to leave the house, but I left it anyhow. It took me a long time to adjust the wick in the lantern and when I adjusted and lit it, the glass for a moment became foggy. A faint patch of light flickered, flickered, until the wick flamed up, and the glass became dry and clear.

I left the light on in the house, and the bright window was clearly visible while I was descending the leafy path to the Oka. My lantern cast a trembling light forward and to the sides, and I might have been a switchman except that under my boots the damp piles of maple leaves and pine needles softly rustled, reflecting, even under the dull light of the lantern, a golden glow. On the naked bushes the red barberries were visible.

One feels uneasy at night walking alone with a lantern! Alone, your boots rustling through the leaves, you are the only thing lighted up and visible; everything else is hidden and silently watching.

The path descended steeply, the light in the window of my house soon disappeared, and the path ended in a confusion of bushes, oaks, and fir trees. The last tall camomiles, pussy wil-

96

lows, and other bare branches tapped against my bucket, now louder—now softer, and the sound "bam, bam" was lost in the distance.

The path was becoming steeper and more twisting and now there were numerous birch trees, and their white trunks constantly emerged from the darkness. Then the birch trees ended too, and stones appeared on the path and the air became fresher. Although beyond the light of the lantern nothing was visible, I felt an open space in front of me. I had come to the river.

Now I could see a distant, lighted buoy in the night. Its red glow was reflecting double on the water. Then, much closer and to my side, another buoy twinkled, giving form to the river.

I walked on the wet grass between the willow bushes along the river to the spot where the launch usually stops—where it stops, that is, if someone disembarks at our remote corner. In the darkness the spring gurgled and rumbled monotonously. I set the lantern down, came up to the spring, dipped some water, drank, and wiped my mouth on my sleeve. Then I put the wet bucket next to the lantern and began to watch the distant pier.

The launch was already at the pier, its green and red running lights barely visible. I sat down and lit a cigarette. My hands were trembling and cold. Suddenly I thought that, if she were not on the launch and they noticed my lantern, they might think that I wished to get on. They might stop at the shore. I put out the lantern.

At once it became dark and only the buoys, as though punctured by a needle, burned along the length of the river. The silence was deafening. At this late hour, without a doubt, I was the only one on the shore for many miles. Above, beyond the oak grove, there was a dark little village where every one had been asleep for a long time and only in my house, which was at the edge of the hill, was there a light.

Suddenly I imagined the long trip she had made for me; how she traveled from Archangel, how she slept or sat at the window of the train, how she talked with someone. How she, just like me, had thought all these days about this meeting. How now she traveled on the Oka and watched the shores—the ones

I described to her when I invited her to visit me. I imagined her stepping off the deck, with the wind blowing in her face, carrying to her the scent of the damp oak groves. I thought about the conversation below deck, in the warmth, behind the steamy windows, and how everybody would explain to her where to get off, and where to spend the night if no one met her.

I remembered the North, and my wanderings there, and how I lived in a fishery, and how she and I killed wolf-fish during the white nights. At ebbtide we went to sea in a boat, while ashore the fishermen slept hard, snoring from time to time. She rowed noiselessly while I looked through the seaweed into the deep water, trying to discern the outlines of the fish. I quietly aimed the harpoon and drove the white point into the back of a wolf-fish. Leaning over, I pulled it out of the water, while it splashed water in our faces and ferociously fought the harpoon, opening its terrible jaws, now coiling itself into a ring, now straightening out like a spring, so that it resembled a triton. Finally, on the bottom of the boat it rustled, trembled, and seized upon everything with a last dying grasp.

I recalled the whole year—how happy I was—how I managed to write many stories, and of course I would write more during these remaining quiet days on this river, in the midst of a countryside that was already fading into fall . . .

The night surrounded me, and the cigarette, when I puffed on it, clearly lighted my hands, my face, and my boots, but it did not interfere with my view of the stars. This fall there were such multitudes of bright stars that they speckled the sky, and one could see their glow reflecting in the river, on the trees and white stones on the shore, while on the dark, square, field strips on the hillocks and in the ravines, it was much darker and more fragrant than in the fields.

It went through my mind then, that the most important thing is not how long one lives; thirty, fifty, or eighty years—because that is still too little, and to die anyway will be frightful—but the most important thing is how many nights like this each man has.

The launch had already moved away from the pier. It was

too far away to discern its movement. It seemed to be standing peacefully, but I knew it had moved away from the pier, and that meant it was moving up the river toward me. Soon the high-pitched noise of the diesel could be heard, and I suddenly became afraid that she would not arrive, that she was not on the launch, and that I was waiting in vain. All of a sudden I recalled the distance and the time that she had to overcome in order to reach me, and it came to me that all was not quite right—that my plans of a happy life of love for the two of us were too vague.

"What's the matter?"—I said aloud and stood up. I couldn't sit any longer and began to walk along the shore. "What's the matter?"—I repeated over and over helplessly. I watched the launch, thinking to myself how strange I would feel going back with only the water and how empty my house would seem. It was possible that we would not succeed, and in the end, after so many days and failures we would not meet again. Would it all turn into nothing?

I recalled how she, unsuspectingly, came from the village to see me off when I was leaving the North three months ago. I remembered her standing on the pier while I boarded the motor-boat that was to take me to a steamship for the long voyage. She said the same thing over and over: "Where are you going? You don't understand anything! You don't understand! Where are you going?" And I—already standing in the motorboat, amidst farewells, women's tears, children's shouts, and all kinds of noises—felt that I was doing something cowardly because I was leaving. Still, I had a faint hope that somehow in the future all would be better.

The launch was now quite near. I stopped close to the black water, at the very edge of the bank, and looked at the launch, blinking and breathing heavily from excitement and hope.

The sound of the motor suddenly dropped, the searchlights flashed on the clearing, and the smoky, slanting rays crossed the shore, jumping from tree to tree. The launch was searching for a spot to stop. It kept turning to the right, its powerful searchlight hitting me in the face. I turned away and then looked back. On the upper deck a sailor was standing ready to open the railings in order to descend and throw the trap ladder to the shore. Next to him, in something light-colored, she was standing.

The prow of the launch dug softly but deeply into the bank; the sailor threw down the trap ladder and helped her to descend. I grabbed her suitcase, put it back next to the bucket, and slowly turned around. The searchlight was blinding me; it was impossible for me to see her. Casting a huge sharp shadow on the wooded slope, she came close. I wanted to kiss her, but then I changed my mind because of the searchlight. We came closer, shielding our eyes from the searchlight, and with forced smiles we began to look at the launch. It began to back up; the beam of the searchlight moved slowly to the side, then completely disappeared. The diesel again began to hum from below deck, and the launch with its long lines of lighted windows in the lower cabins quickly began to move away up the river. We were left alone.

"Well, hi!"—I said in confusion. She got up on tiptoes, put her arms around my shoulders, and kissed my eyes.

"Let's go!" I said, coughing. "Darn, it's so dark. Wait, I will light the lantern."

I lit the lantern, again it fogged up, and we had to wait until the flame grew bigger and the glass became dry and transparent. Then we left, I in front with the lantern and the suitcase, and she in back with the bucket of water.

"Isn't it too heavy for you?" I asked after awhile.

"Just keep going," she said hoarsely.

Her voice always was hoarse and low and it took me a long time to become used to it. I prefer gentleness in women. But now, here on the bank at night, as we walked one behind the other, after so many days of anger, separation, letters, and strange, ominous dreams, her voice and strong body, her rough hands, and her northern speech were like the breathing of a bird—wild, and gray, and left behind after the autumn migration.

We turned to the right into the ravine, where there was a short paved road leading up the hill; nobody knew when or by whom it was built. The road was narrow, winding, and overgrown with brush, pines, and mountain ash. We began to climb in the dark, barely able to see the road by the light of the lantern, and above us was a narrow river of stars, in which the black pine branches were swimming, now and then covering and uncovering the stars.

Panting, we emerged onto a road lined with larches, where we could walk side by side.

Suddenly I felt like showing her everything, telling her everything about the people here and all the little happenings.

"Smell," I said. "It's so fragrant!"

"Like wine," she answered, slowly catching her breath from the walk. "I smelled it long ago, while I was still on the launch . . ."

"Here are some bushes, come through this way!"

We left our things on the path, jumped over a ditch, and went into the bushes, lighting our way with the lantern.

"This . . . somewhere . . . must be here . . ." I mumbled. "Mushrooms," she said in amazement behind me. "Russulas."

Finally I found what I was looking for. It was white chicken feathers, scattered on the grass among the branches and yellow leaves.

"Look"—I said, trying to produce more light from the lantern. "We have a chicken farm in this village. When the chicks grow a little, they let them out. Every day a fox comes into the bushes and sits. When the chicks spread out in the forest, the fox catches one. He devours it on the spot."

I pictured the fox with a gray spot on his dark snout, how he licked his chops and snorted to blow the down off his nose.

"He should be killed," she said.

"I have a gun; we'll both go to the forest. We might be lucky."

We returned to the path and resumed our walk. My lighted window became visible and I began to think what would take place when we got there. I knew I'd want to have a drink right away and I had some brandy. I made it myself. It was a pleasure to gather the mountain-ash berries, bring them home, press them until a yellow foaming stuff came out, and then strain the juice into a bottle with vodka.

"Back home it's winter now," she said as if surprised. "The

Dvina is all frozen, only in the center the ice breakers have cleared a passageway. The whole river is white, but the passage is black . . . and it steams. When a steamer comes through the black water, the dogs always run alongside on the ice. And for some reason they run in threes." She said "threes" in the Northern dialect and I imagined the Dvina, the steamers, Archangel, and the village on the White Sea where she came from. The village had tall, empty, two-story houses with black walls, and silence and solitude.

"Did it freeze?" I asked. "The sea, that is?"

"Oh, it's getting there," she said and became thoughtful—maybe about the things she had left behind. "On the way back I might have to take a reindeer sled—if . . ."

She became silent. I waited, listening to her breathing and her steps, then I asked:

"What do you mean—if?"

She said in a hoarse, slow voice, "Nothing, in particular. The sea will freeze over, that's all."

Stamping our feet on the porch, we went in.

"O—oo!" she said, looking around and taking off her scarf. She always said "O—oo" in a low and drawn-out voice when she was surprised or happy.

The house was small and old. I rented it from a Muscovite, who lived here only in the summer. There wasn't much furniture, only old beds, a table and chairs . . . The walls were eaten by borers and were all white, as if sprinkled with flour. However, the house had electricity, a radio, a stove, and a few fat books, which I read with pleasure in the evenings.

"Take your coat off," I said. "I will make a fire right away."

I went outside to chop some wood for the stove. I was a little beside myself from happiness, my head was ringing, my hands were trembling, I felt somewhat weak, and I wanted to sit awhile. The stars were small and bright. It will freeze, I thought, and that means in the morning the last leaves will be gone. Soon it will be winter.

From the Oka slowly came the sonorous three-toned sound

of a horn, which echoed for a long time on the hills. It was from a tugboat somewhere below, one of those rare, old, steam tugboats. The new cutters and jet tugs make short, high, nasal sounds. Awakened by the sound of the horn, a few roosters cried in falsetto voices in the chickenhouse.

I chopped some branches, gathered a few pieces of wood, and went into the house. She had taken off her coat, and was standing with her back to me, rustling in newspapers; she was getting something out of her suitcase. She wore a light-colored dress that fitted her snugly, and if anyone were to take her out in Moscow or to a fashionable club, those around would surely hide their smiles, but this, without any doubt, was her best dress. I recalled that she usually wore slacks, tucked into boots, and over them, an old, faded skirt—that had been splendid.

I put the kettle on and began to light a fire. Soon the branches began to crackle, and one could smell wood smoke.

"This is for you," she said behind me.

I turned and saw a salmon on the table—wonderful, silvery-white, with a broad, dark back and turned-up lower jaw. The house smelled of fish, and wanderlust swept over me.

She was a sea dweller, she was even born on a motorboat during the golden night of summertime. She was, however, indifferent to the white Arctic nights. Only a visitor notices them, and becomes crazy from the loneliness and silence. And only when you are there as a guest, separated from all and presumably forgotten by all—only then do you lie awake at night, constantly thinking and talking to yourself. "O.K., O.K., this is nothing, it is simply a night, and you won't be here forever! Don't worry about the night, let the sun crawl on the rim of the sea and you sleep, sleep . . ."

But she? She slept soundly during the night, behind a calico curtain, in the fishery. Because at sunrise she had, along with dozens of fishermen, to arise, to row, to lift the fish from traps, and afterwards to cook fish soup and wash the dishes . . . This was her life every summer—until I came.

And now, on the Oka, we drank homemade brandy, ate salmon, and talked, reminiscing of the past. We talked about how we used to go harpooning wolf-fish in the white nights; how, during the storms, we pulled up the traps with the fishermen; how the bitter water choked and made us sick; how we would go to the lighthouse to get some bread; and how we sat in a village library at night and, taking off our shoes and coats, read all the newspapers and journals that had been published during the time we were fishing.

I threw my fur coat on the floor next to the stove, we put the tea kettle and candles next to us, and we took our cups and lay down on the fur coat, looking now at each other, now at the red mouth of the stove and the coals, noticing how the little flames ran through them. And in order to make it last longer, I would get up from time to time and put more wood into the stove and the flames crackled and we had to turn away from the heat.

At about two o'clock, in the darkness, I got up because I could not sleep. It seemed to me, if I fell asleep, that she would leave me and I would not be able to feel her and I wanted her to be next to me and I wanted to be aware of the fact. I wanted to tell her, "Take me into your dreams, so I can be with you all the time!—One is not supposed to be separated for long." I thought how when people leave us, and we never meet them again, they die to us. And we die to them. Strange thoughts come to one's mind at night when one cannot sleep because of happiness or sadness.

"Are you asleep?" I asked quietly. "No," came an answer from the bed. "I feel fine. Don't look, I'll get dressed."

I went to the corner where a radio was hanging on the wall by straps, and turned it on. Among the static and the mumblings of the announcers, I searched for music. I knew that there must be music and I would find it. A velvety male voice said something in English, then there was a pause and I knew that the music would start right away.

I was startled because I recognized the melody from the first sound. When I feel great, or on the contrary very sad, I always remember that jazz tune. It was foreign, and it sounded as if it had some hidden meaning, and one could not sense whether it was sad or happy. It often came back to me when I was traveling somewhere and when something made me happy or depressed. That tune made me think of that night in Moscow when we rode and rode, walked and walked, lonely and unhappy, and I didn't hear a single word of reproach from her and I was ashamed. She was leaving for Archangel after five empty days spent in Moscow. Everything was as it always is in Moscow's railroad station: the porters were wheeling their baggage carts, the automatic carts were hissing, and since only a few minutes were left, everyone was in a hurry to say goodbye . . . She was leaving, although she didn't have to—she still had some time—a few more free days. And I was disappointed, bitter, and angry with myself and with her. I thought, how empty life would become without her. Again I would drink to cope with my grief.

"Don't leave!" I said.

She just smiled and with trembling eyes looked up at me. She has dark eyes, with green sparks in them, and it's impossible to make out whether they are green or black. But when she looked up at me that time, they were black; that I remember distinctly.

"This is stupid," I said. "First I left the North without any understanding, and now you're leaving, and again nothing . . . How stupid! Don't leave!"

"What more is there to say," she muttered bitterly.

"You shouldn't have stayed with your relatives who are always at home!"

"Who with, then? At your place, maybe? What's the difference?" she said stubbornly. "What more is there to say?"

"Let's go to a hotel; you can stay there these last days."

"The train will leave soon," she said and turned away.

"No, wait, think for a minute. Soon, after so many letters, we could be together, by ourselves; just think."

She was silent for a long time, biting her lips; then, her eyes moving across my face, finally, sad and hurt, she asked:

"And will you be glad if I stay?"

It was difficult for me to breathe I had such a lump in my throat, and I turned and quickly entered her car. Bumping someone, pushing myself through, I found her compartment, took her suitcase, and left. I still remember to this day how the conductors and all the people in the car looked at us.

"Let's go," I said.

"And the ticket?"—she asked me, her eyes shimmering.

"To hell with it!" I said, and took her by the hand.

We went out to the square and took a taxi. "A hotel," I said.

"Which one?" the driver asked.

"I don't care which one."

The car started and dashed through the traffic lights, past the neon lights, the railroad station, the people, and buildings.

"Stop, old man," I said to the driver at a store, and I got out and bought a bottle of wine. I returned with the bottle in my coat pocket. I pictured us drinking this wine all by ourselves, raising glasses and looking into each other's eyes. I felt the taste already in my mouth when we arrived at a hotel and I went to see the desk clerk.

"No vacancy," he calmly informed me.

"Any room will do, you understand, any room—the worst or the very best."

"No vacancy," he repeated sourly, and with irritation picked up the incessantly ringing telephone.

She was waiting for me in the lobby, timidly looking at the splendid columns and mirrors. She even looked at me timidly, as if I were the lord of all this! We went to the taxi stand.

"We will go to another hotel," I said bitterly.

She got into the taxi without saying a word, and we began driving through Moscow. I dropped in on a friend to borrow some money and I came close to asking him to give us shelter, but his sister had guests, and I looked at them, the table with wine, the sofa, the raised feet in narrow mocassins, and I didn't ask him. Instead, I took more money.

"Have a drink," he said suddenly, intercepting my glance.

"No, thank you, they are waiting for me."

An hour or two passed and we were still driving and driving, and everywhere they told us the same thing: "No vacancy!" Coming out on the street and looking at the huge hotels and apartment buildings, all those multi-story rows of windows, so many of them already dark, I thought of everyone who at this hour was peacefully sitting or lying, listening to the radio, or reading themselves to sleep, or embracing their wives, and my heart began to ache.

Finally, very tired, we took her suitcase to the railroad station, checked it, and slowly began to walk to Sokolniki. It was twelve o'clock midnight.

"What are we going to do?" I asked with a laugh.

"I don't know," she said listlessly. "Maybe we could go to a restaurant? I am hungry . . ."

"The restaurants are closed," I said, looking at my watch, and again I laughed stupidly. "Let's go to the middle of town, and the boulevards."

We walked briskly, the way we used to walk in the North on the seashore when we could not to afford to be late for the movie at the club, which was twenty kilometers away. The street lights were out except for every second one, and at that only one side of the street was lighted. There were almost no people on the streets. Finally we came to Tversky Boulevard and sat down on a bench.

"Is it impossible to go to your place?" she asked hopefully.

"Why else would I have walked with you! My father, my mother—impossible!"

"Well, O.K.," she said, "don't be bitter; tomorrow I will leave. There is a train in the morning. Then. . . ," she sighed, "then you will come to see us again sometime."

I embraced her; she pressed close to me and closed her eyes.

"Can we sit like this for awhile?" she murmured, shifting into a more comfortable position on the bench. "You are kind, I love you, you little boy. I fell in love with you up North; you just didn't know, you poor you!"

Sitting quietly for a minute, she slipped off her shoes and tucked her feet under her skirt.

"My feet hurt," she murmured sleepily. "These shoes . . . I'm not used to them."

Two policemen appeared from the side alley. Seeing us, one of them stepped into the light and came toward us.

"Please move on, citizen!" For some reason he spoke only to me. "That's not allowed."

"What is not allowed?" I asked, while she in embarrassment was putting her shoes back on her swollen feet.

"There is nothing to discuss! You heard me—move along!"

We got up and left. I began to look at the houses and windows again, and I kept seeing a room with a low sofa. There was nothing else in that room, only soft pink light and the sofa.

"Listen, let's go into a doorway," I said uncertainly.

"Let's," she agreed with a faint smile. "There we can sit on the steps and I can take my shoes off."

We entered a dark courtyard, went to the farthest doorway in the corner, and sat on the steps. She took off her shoes without any delay and began to rub her feet.

"Tired?" I asked and lit a cigarette. "Poor girl, we haven't had much luck in Moscow."

"Yes," she said and rubbed her cheek on my shoulder. "It is a very big city."

We heard footsteps, a door opened, and a yard woman looked at the doorway and noticed us.

"You get out of here!" she shouted. "Don't you have any decency, you devils. You're just like alley cats. Get out, or I will blow my whistle!"

And she pulled a shiny whistle from her apron pocket. She had a mean, high-boned face. We again walked back through the courtyard, followed by the yard woman who was cursing us. On the street, we looked at each other and laughed.

"This is not the White Sea," I said.

"It's O.K.," she again reassured me. "Let's just walk on; maybe we should go to the station and sleep on the benches."

"O.K.," I agreed and suddenly I became animated. "Listen, I'm a fool, let's take a drive out of the city! We will take a taxi. I have money and we can go out about thirty kilometers—many people do that here!"

A taxi was moving slowly down the street. I had always loved to watch these night taxis returning home late. As if bewitched, they slowly wander through the sleeping city with their green lights blinking, and looking at these lights, you feel like going to some far-away place.

We hailed a taxi.

"Out of town?" the driver asked and grew visibly insolent. "For seven and a half I will take you."

"O.K.," I said. It didn't make any difference to me.

While we were driving, I felt like sleeping. The road was deserted, the west was still dark, but the east was growing light; dawn was near. A steady wind was blowing outside, and inside there was a strong smell of gasoline.

"How about here?" the driver asked, slowing down near a grove of trees. "No one drives any further. She isn't a local girl, is she?" he asked looking at her.

We got out, and the pre-dawn cold instantly began to chill us.

"Half an hour enough?" he asked, looking at us appraisingly. "I will doze off—when you come back wake me up. Got a cigarette? Let me have one . . ."

He moved the car to the side of the road, and we set off through the coarse grass toward the woods, and the only sensation I experienced was cold and dampness. My suit became stiff and heavy, my shoes became wet, and my trousers lost their crease. There was only dusky light in the woods; I looked at her and wondered what I should do now. She looked tired, her face was drooping, and there were bags under her eyes. Suddenly she yawned openly and looked around indifferently, as if wondering what we had come here for.

"You call this a forest . . ." she half-muttered and gave me a hidden, hostile look.

I also yawned, feeling bored and angry that I was not home in my bed instead of here in the dampness and cold.

"I'm fed up," she said, yawning convulsively, her voice low and hoarse, saying "feed up" instead of "fed up." "Oh God, all this is useless. I don't want anything, let's go back . . ."

"O.K., let's go back," I said listlessly and also yawned. "But first let's have a drink; the bottle's getting heavy in my pocket."

I pulled out the bottle and tried to pull out the cork, but it was in too tight. Finally I pushed it inside with a stick.

"Drink," I said, handing her the warm bottle.

"I don't want it," she murmured, but took the bottle, and with a sigh began to drink. Two thin streams of wine, like blood, ran down her chin; she coughed and gave the bottle back to me. I finished it and threw it away.

"Let's go," I said, relieved.

Again we began to make our way through the wet woods, through ferns, and over grassy hillocks, and all this time she held her dress up so as not to get her hem wet.

"Back so soon?" the driver asked and looked at me with derision. "Personality clash?"

"Get moving!" I said maliciously, hardly able to keep from hitting him.

On the way back we dozed, bumping against each other on the curves, and, I remember, these contacts with her body were unpleasant to me, and probably to her as well. It was about four in the morning, and we had to walk somewhere for three more hours before train time. I felt bad; the wine had gone to my head, making it heavy and me depressed.

Those three hours were torture, but I couldn't go away; I had to stay with her to the end. As soon as the train arrived, I again walked her to her car, not knowing what to say, my head splitting.

"O.K., then, write me," she said, taking the handrail.

I found the strength to detain her.

"Don't be angry," I mumbled and kissed her forehead, and headed for an exit. I remember how relieved I felt when we parted. I was even surprised, but it was also sad; somewhere deep inside I hurt and I felt ashamed.

I pulled the fur coat next to the radio and we sat on it embracing. All these months I had had a feeling of loss, but now I discovered all, and what I found was even greater than I could have imagined.

The bass mumbled mournfully, searching in the dark for

his own contrapuntal movements, lost in indecisiveness, rising and falling, and the slow movement reminded me of a starry sky. And following it, a saxophone complained about something, and again and again the trumpet reached for frantic heights—and the piano now and then came in with its fivefold apocalyptic chords. And, just like a metronome, just like time, in syncopated rhythms, with soft vacant strokes, the drummer surrendered himself to the music.

"We won't turn on the light, O.K.?" she said, looking up from the floor at the greenish radio dial and its wolf's eye.

"O.K.," I agreed, and I felt that it was impossible that a night like this would ever happen to me again. And I became sad, because a full three hours of it had already passed, and I wanted all of it to start again from the beginning, and I could walk out with the lantern and wait, and we would reminisce, and again would be afraid to separate in the dark.

She got up for a minute to get something, took a look out the window, and said hoarsely:

"Snow . . ."

I rose and looked at the darkness outside the window. It was snowing silently. The first real snow of the fall. I pictured the mouse tracks there'd be tomorrow around the piles of branches in the forest, and the rabbit tracks around the acacia on which they like to nibble during the night, and I thought about hunting, was overcome by joy and even trembled. How wonderful that the snow was falling, that she had come, that we were now alone with the music, that our future would be, perhaps, better than our past, and that tomorrow I would take her to all my favorite places, I would show her the Oka, the fields, the hills, the forest, and the ravines! Night was passing, but we could not fall asleep, and we talked in whispers, embracing because we were afraid to lose each other, and we fed wood into the stove again and watched its fiery mouth while its red glow baked our faces. We fell asleep at seven o'clock in the morning, the growing dawn beginning to show in the windows, and we slept for a long time because there was no one to wake us in our house.

While we slept, the sun rose, melting the snow, but right

away everything began to freeze up again. After drinking some tea, I took my gun and we left the house. Our eyes hurt for a moment—such a white, wintry light hit our eyes and the air was so clean and sharp. The snow was gone, but everywhere there were icy crusts. They were milk-colored and only partially transparent. From the cow stall rose an odoriferous steam, and the calves were moving around and stamping loudly, as if on a wooden bridge. This was because under the clumps of ice the liquidy dung hadn't frozen yet. Some of them were grazing with delight on the winter grain, urinating frequently, raising their tails and spreading their curly-haired groins. And there, on the spot where they had urinated, emerald patches of new young rye appeared.

First we walked down the road. The ruts were frozen with gray, dull ice but there was dirty water under the ice and where our boots broke through the crust the ice was spattered with brown, muddy water. In the forest, sticking out from under the ice, were lovely yellow dandelions. Frozen leaves and pine needles were visible in the ice and the last frozen mushrooms were still standing, and when we kicked them, they broke loose and made a noise rolling over the ice. The ice under our feet was becoming gray and brittle and it cracked in front of us, behind us, and to the sides.

The fields and hills, from a distance, looked smoky-green, as if someone had sprinkled flour on them; the haystacks looked black, the forest threadbare and dark, and only the white groves of birch trees stood out sharply. The trunks of the aspen were velvety greenish, and in some places on the wooded hills the crowns of the trees that had not lost their leaves were still a burning red. The river was visible through the forest at a great distance, and it was deserted and cold. We descended into the snowy ravine, leaving behind us deep footsteps that were at first dirty, then clean, and we drank some water from the spring near the cut aspen tree. In the deep, still bottom of the spring, black maple and oak leaves had settled thick, and the felled aspen tree smelled bitter and cold, and the sap on the tree was like amber.

"Great?" I asked, and looked at her; I was surprised—her eyes were green.

"Great!" she said, looking intensely around and licking her lips!

"Better than on the White Sea?" I asked now.

She began to look at the river again and up the slope and her eyes turned even more green.

"Well, the White Sea!" she said vaguely. "We have, well . . . but here there are oak trees"—she interrupted herself. "How did you find this place?"

I was happy, but I felt a little strange and fearful. Indeed, everything had turned out fine for me this fall. In order to calm down, I lit a cigarette, and the smoke and steam enveloped me. On the Oka, from the direction of Alekesin, a tugboat appeared, rapidly going down the river, chasing a wave at its bow, and we silently followed it with our eyes. It was steaming mightily and vapor poured out to the side in a jetlike stream from an opening just above the water.

When the tugboat disappeared around the bend, we held hands and began to climb up the slope, through the sparse trees in the bright woods, to look once more at the Oka from above. We walked quietly, not talking, as if in a white dream where we were finally together.

Konstantin Finn

Konstantin Finn, born in 1904, is a well-known Soviet writer who began to write short stories and plays in 1934. His stories about World War II are especially popular. He has a tendency to adhere to the "Party spirit," that is, identification with the goals and methods of the Communist Party—*partiinost*.

"Two Encounters" is a World War II story with reminiscences of the unforgettable "Fatherland War" and its ugly scars.

Konstantin Finn

Two Encounters

Translated by Vytas Dukas

THE HOTEL ROOM, which had been assigned to Batashev, turned out to be quite decent. Batashev went to the
window and looked with interest at the street. He loved being
in a strange city.

From the eighth floor the people and cars seemed small and
they moved without haste. And it also seemed that they had no
business whatever, and that all the traffic could stop at any second, or, start moving in the opposite direction. The buildings were tall, and the sky barely showed through.

Batashev went out onto the street and jumped onto the first
bus he saw. Where the bus was headed he did not know and he
wasn't even interested. In a half hour the city came to an end,
the new, tall, buildings of light-colored stone were replaced by
low, small wooden structures. Yards. Vegetable gardens. The bus
stopped. Batashev got off and looked around. There were open
fields in the distance. A road led to them. It passed through
vacant lots, but they were not deserted. In several places men
were making surveys—measurements of some sort. In places
foundations were being dug and from all over it was evident
that no more than a year or two would pass before these lots
were transformed into new buildings.

Yes, in time the sky here, too, would be gone, but for now
it lay close above Batashev's head. Although Batashev, himself,
had built multistoried buildings that pushed the sky back further and further, sometimes it made him sad. He loved the sky.
Many times during the war, he, a scout, was close to death but
always, at the last minute his luck had changed and then he
would look at the sky because nothing gives one such confidence

115

that danger has passed and nothing can convince a person more
that he's alive—yes, alive—than the sky above one's head—the
sky one has known since childhood . . .

He looked at his watch. Half past four. Now he'll return to
the hotel and have dinner. And then what? The architect's convention will open tomorrow. But what's there to do today? He
saw a poster. The Theater of Opera and Ballet was presenting
today, "Eugene Onegin."

"Why, that's wonderful," he thought. "In Moscow I never
treat myself to the theater."

Batashev strolled through the theater foyer. Unexpectedly he
suddenly recalled the time when his childhood ended. It ended
when his father died. Batashev didn't remember his mother.
She and his little sister had died from some sort of infectious
disease when he was a year old. The father took upon himself
complete care of the child. The father didn't marry. He raised
his small son. The father wasn't old, was rarely sick, didn't
drink or even smoke, but although no one would have thought
it possible, he grew thin for no apparent reason, and began to
feel weak. In a short time he couldn't walk at all and breathing
became difficult. The day before eternal sleep came to him he
was taken outside and a mat was placed for him near the hut
and they laid the thin, shriveled-up man on it, who only a short
time ago had been a large man—almost massive. Let him
breathe the fresh air. The dying man looked upwards, searching for something in the clouds. Someone said that he was expecting an angel who, without fail, would fly down to take his
soul. Little Volodya never left his father's side the whole time,
but no matter how hard Volodya looked he did not see the
angel.

When the small mound was piled up over his father's grave,
it seemed to Volodya that everything that was dear and familiar
to him had left with his father. Their house—a little shingled,
crooked hut at the very edge of the village—got the full brunt
of all the winds and all the blizzards. The Near Zoloteevsky
woods were not far away. Now everything appeared bright and
clear before him. The years seemed to dissolve. It seemed like

only yesterday . . . What a bad habit it is to lose yourself in thought, and not notice what's going on around you. Batashev looked around. No one was in sight. A bell seemed to sound . . . once, twice, three times . . . Batashev headed quickly toward the door leading into the hall, but a woman, dressed in a dark gray dress and a white collar with programs in her hands barred his path.

"What are you doing, sir? The performance started five minutes ago. Go to the third tier."

"That's insulting," Batashev blurted out, annoyed. "I don't like to watch and listen from up there. I'll just walk around."

"Suit yourself," answered the woman in the gray dress.

Her face seemed familiar to Batashev. Where had he seen this woman? Batashev sat in a chair, took a newspaper out of his pocket and unfolded it. He wasn't able to read. He couldn't get that woman, who was now standing at the door leading into the auditorium, out of his mind. Just where had he seen her?

He got up from his chair and walked down the hall; he stopped near the woman in the dark gray dress.

"Well, are you tired of just sitting," she asked?

"She's pretty," thought Batashev. "Big gray eyes with thick eyebrows and long lashes. How old is she?"

"The first act is rather long, she continued. "I sympathize with you."

She smiled, but such an unusual smile—Her face suddenly radiant—then he recognized her . . .

✿   ✿   ✿

Three of them had set out on reconnaissance—himself, Batashev—Borisenko, and Dlugach. Borisenko was killed the very first day—blown up by a mine. Borisenko, a happy light-haired, unusually lively boy. Even in death he lay on the ground in such a way that it seemed at any moment he would jump up and start running.

"Let's go," said Dlugach, in a kind of rasping voice that didn't belong to him.

He bent over Borisenko, took the pistols out of the dead boy's pockets, and then turned the boy's face toward the sky so that it might be lighted by the sun. It seemed as if Borisenko was frowning and would soon open his eyes.

. . . Two days later Dlugach was mortally wounded in the stomach and became delirious. He and Batashev lay on some straw in a shed. It was a Russian village, but German soldiers walked in the street.

The street as well as a hut directly opposite were visible through large cracks in the wall of the shed. Children were playing in the yard in front of the cottage. Every so often one of the children ran toward the barn.

Batashev tore up all his field shirt and all his linen to make bandages for Dlugach. But the bleeding didn't stop. Dlugach was bleeding profusely, dying. And when the agony began, hoarse groans burst from his throat. They grew steadily louder and louder.

Batashev looked through a crack. Two German soldiers, who were passing by, stopped, listened, said something to one another, and left.

Dlugach began to cry out louder.

A German lieutenant and soldier appeared on the street. They were still a short way off. Dlugach was crying out. The Germans were approaching.

"Farewell, Dlugach," he said—"farewell, soldier."

He took his pistol out, and lifted his knife from the straw. Maybe he could kill this officer and soldier. That would bring other German solders on the run. They had a unit in the village. Well, anyhow, he'd kill these two at least. He started to aim. The Germans were drawing near. They still hadn't heard Dlugach's cries and were having a jovial conversation about something. But they would soon be close enough to hear the cries—perhaps in a minute—or maybe two.

All of a sudden a girl came up to the officer and said something to him. The officer and soldier stopped. Batashev lowered his hand with the pistol. The girl was beautiful. Most probably she was the village school teacher, or maybe she worked in the former village Soviet. She smiled. The officer too began to smile. The soldier apparently didn't know what to do. The officer said a few words to him and the soldier turned around and left.

The girl said something to the officer, who became more and more jovial. They came closer. Dlugach continued to groan and wheeze loudly.

Batashev again raised his pistol.

They then stopped. The officer continued to talk and the girl smiled. She and the officer were, by then, quite close. Batashev clearly saw her smile; he was surprised by her unusual gaiety.

"Enjoy yourself, scum," whispered Batashev.

Those seconds seemed like hours to Batashev, who didn't know whether the officer would come with the girl in the direction of the shed, where he and Dlugach lay, or whether they would turn back. Suddenly the girl took the officer by the hand. They started back the other way. A ray of sunlight danced on the lieutenant's silver shoulderboard and on the collar of his uniform. It was a ray from the setting sun. It seemed to stir on the shoulderboard as if it had fallen from a very high altitude and didn't have the strength to raise itself up again. It was an unhappy and dejected ray.

"Soon the sun will set," thought Batashev, "and with its setting will come evening, darkness and probably life."

It was quiet in the shed. It became dark, and there, in the darkness, he sensed the fathomless purity of the sky . . .

"Why is it quiet," thought Batashev? He looked at Dlugach. He was dead.

"What are you looking at me like that for," the woman in the dark gray dress asked Batashev?

"I recognize you," he said. "I recognize you!"

"Where have we met?"

And just then, the auditorium door opened and a man walked out.

"See, it's your fault I forgot about it," she declared, annoyed, and she quickly pulled a cord that drew back the curtain, and then she opened the auditorium doors wide.

Batashev went into the buffet and ordered a bottle of beer,

but when he left about ten minutes later, the bottle still stood untouched. Batashev repeated several times to himself what he would say to this woman. He even predicted how she would answer him. The conversation would go something like this:

BATASHEV: Just where was your conscience then?

THE WOMAN: It's fine for you to talk, but what would you have done in my shoes?

BATASHEV: You are lying. I saw the pleasure you got from that lieutenant's favor. Didn't it enter your head that that officer had killed Russian women and children?

THE WOMAN: War is war.

BATASHEV: If you had come in the direction of the shed where my dying friend, Dlugach, and I were lying, I would have shot you. First the officer and then you.

The bell rang. This was the last call. Just as before she stood by the door leading into the hall.

"Are you going into the hall?" she asked quickly. "If you'll hurry I can still let you in."

"I'm not going in."

"That's up to you," she smiled. "Well, anyway, just where was it we met?"

"Near the city of Kholm in the village of Pozhidaevo."

"Where?"

"Pozhidaevo, Pozhidaevo. Don't pretend—you know what I'm talking about."

Batashev felt hate seizing him again.

"1942," he practically shouted. "A German lieutenant and a Russian girl. Need I add any more, or is that enough?"

"That's enough. And did you see us?"

"I did. The cracks in the shed were wide."

"And do you remember the kids who were playing across from you?"

"I remember. What about them?"

"Good kids." She laughed. "Imagine, twenty-five years ago. How old are those kids now? And you, yourself, let me have a look at you, see what you're like."

She moved back a couple steps.

"A look from afar is more revealing," she said. "I better put my glasses on." She smiled again. "See how everything goes downhill. There used to be a girl that German officers would stare at, and now she's become an old woman." She took her glasses out of her purse.

"Well, let's see what you're like."

"How do you like that, how do you like that," she said, with an apparently very satisfied look. "Must be you've come for the architects' convention."

"Yes, I have."

She took off her glasses.

"After you saw that German officer, he lived for another forty, maybe fifty minutes—no longer."

"You mean you knew I was in the shed?"

"You thought I didn't? the kids who were playing across the way were watching you. They both played and stood guard. One of them ran up to me: 'Aunty, there's some kind of terrible noise in the shed!' Then I saw a lieutenant and a soldier moving in your direction. I thought to draw them away from you. But where could I take him?" Her face twisted. "And no shooting!" She closed her eyes. She went on with them closed. "We weren't allowed to shoot." She opened again her eyes and made a gesture with her hand, wanting to brush off—put out of her mind—something distressing that had held her breath. "Well, what else is there to remember? . . . After that I lived two years in the woods. When the Germans were driven from our land I returned home to Pozhidaevo. Only I didn't have the chance to teach children again." Again something disrupted her breathing.

"Do you have heart trouble?" asked Batashev.

"No, no, it's nothing really . . . I got married and left the village. My husband just started working in the head architect's office. He's a draftsman. He earns a decent salary. As for me, well, as you can see I'm here in the theater."

"So, it turns out, I owe my life to you?" said Batashev.

She smiled . . .

✿   ✿   ✿

Vasilii Aksenov

Vasilii Aksenov was born in Kazan and began to write while he was in medical school in Leningrad. In 1960 he abandoned medicine and became full-time writer. He soon became famous and at the same time controversial. His writings concerning the Soviet youth and its "stilyazhestvo"—the "Beatle generation"—upset the Soviet literary tsars and subsequently he was criticized in *Komsomolskaya Pravda*, especially for his story "Ticket to the Stars." He was attacked by Ilichev in 1961 and 1968. Aksenov was called the poet of vacationers and idle people; however, the same article stressed that Aksenov's symbolism is valid and that the author is a talented and serious writer (see *Voprosy literatury* 12 [Oct. 1968]). His poem *Ecstasy* is a typical Aksenovian short story where fantasy and symbolism transcend conventional ideas of realism.

Vasilii Aksenov

A Poem of Ecstasy

Translated by Vytas Dukas

A T THE AGE OF TWELVE I began to develop physically at a very rapid rate. My physical development began to frighten my parents. They took me to a doctor, and the doctor, a blue-eyed little lady, shuddered when I pulled my sweater off over my head.

"A phenomenal boy," she said in a very pretty voice.

Somehow I didn't feel like leaving the doctor's office, but my dad took me by the hand and led me away.

Dad was already a half head shorter than I. With each year he grew shorter and shorter, but nevertheless, I respected him and loved him, and although I had by far outrun him in physical development, I never laid a finger on him. By the way I recommend to all beginning athletes exactly the same kind of attitude to their parents.

My mental development lagged considerably behind my physical development. For the most part I was on the very same level with my classmates. I didn't strive for straight A's of course —what for?—but when it came to the Pythagorean theorem, Newton's binomial, or "Who can be happy in Russia"—all these I had on the tip of my tongue. However, my physical development went far ahead of my mental development. Sometimes I would nearly burst out laughing when I would look at kids my own age. But of course I managed to hold back my laughter, and as much as possible tried not to distinguish myself from others. It's stupid to brag about one's physical development. I don't recommend it to beginning athletes.

When I reached fourteen, I became somewhat unmanageable. I broke all the dynamometers in the physical education office; I blew (just once) into the spirometer—it came unsoldered; not to mention the muscle-building episodes in the park of culture. And once in the school corridor, without thinking, I picked up the vice-principal, Valerian Sergeevich, sat him up on my shoulders, and just like that, with the vice-principal on my shoulders, I walked into the classroom. Result: I was expelled from school for ten days.

Well, I didn't fall behind in class. Every day I spent five hours studying according to the schedule, and when I came to difficult questions, I consulted with Misha Gurfinkel over the phone. You can't fall behind in your studies, or else you'll feel like everyone is marching forward while you're still marking time.

The strange incident with the vice-principal taught me a lot. I began to think seriously about my future. I really had something to think about. The unbelievable development of my muscles and inner organs had made me a completely different person. Consider the situation yourself. Lots of boys would like to put the vice-principal on their shoulders, but few if any are able to do it. As for me, I simply got an urge to do it and did it. With such a physical development as mine, wishes common to very many, if not to all, boys, could not help but have unpleasant consequences for me and those around me.

Weighing all the pros and cons, I decided to turn to sports. I shared my plans with my parents. Dad said:

"This is the right decision. By directing your excess energy to sports, Gennady, you'll avoid any conflict with society."

And so, the decision was made. Now all I had to do was choose some sport. It would, of course, be silly for me to take up track and field when already in the sixth grade PE class I had high-jumped 6 foot, 3 inches, run the hundred meters in 10.3 seconds, shotput 63 feet and did all this without any effort, and, to be frank, without any satisfaction. Swimming, maybe? I didn't know how to swim and I didn't plan on learning. What for?

Standing on the crossroads of my life and not knowing where my destiny lay, I would stroll along streets gazing at the passersby. I would pick out some husky man, introduce myself, and then shake his hand until his eyes became frozen with pain. Then, giving him a push with my shoulder, I would run away, ashamed. I don't know how all this would have ended if I hadn't fallen into boxing.

I remember my first sparring partner—a massive champion of sport around forty.

"Don't be afraid, sonny, I'll be easy on you," he whispered to me before the beginning of the match. For the first minute I let him swing at me with everything he had, but I felt his hooks and uppercuts like an elephant feels a peashooter. The second minute I spent taking in all the skills of this field of sport. Then I feinted and then I smacked him one dead on. The old man fell. And that's how I began to make my career.

I liked boxing very much. I used to like to stand in my corner a second before the bell, modestly lowering my long, fluffy eyelashes, with a blush on my gentle cheeks, but when the bell rang, I would raise my long, fluffy eyelashes, open my big blue eyes, and smile a big, bright smile into my opponent's eyes, which were narrowed with fear, and pour a hurricane of blows on him. It usually didn't go as far as the second round.

Fame came to me. Daily I received from fifty to sixty letters from fans. I diligently answered them all. Question: How can one become as strong as you? Answer: Only through hard work. Question: How did you become so successful in sports? Answer: Only through hard work. A girl asks: Why are you so handsome? Answer to her: Only through hard work.

I should add that I did not allow my sports to interfere with my studying and did not fall behind in my class. I utilized every spare minute to keep up with my work schedule.

Once, before a fight, I was sitting in my dressing room, all ready in trunks and boxing gloves, memorizing quotations from "A Ray of Light in the Realm of Darkness" for a composition. In walked a journalist, Ilya Slonov, with a photographer. The photographer circled around me snapping pictures. "Get lost, Edulya," Slonov told him, and then sat down next to me and said, "I like your boxing, Mabukin."

I even blushed. I was always modest and at that moment my modesty showed. In this respect I also set a good example for beginning athletes.

"I like it but not all of it," said Slonov. Then, I began to get upset.

"You've got everything," Slonov continued—"Strength, reaction, high level of technique. You lack only creative spirit."

"How so?", I asked.

"Take, for example, Cassius Clay . . ." said Ilya Slonov.

At the mere mention of Cassius Clay's name even my spleen began to quiver. Oh, how I wanted to get acquainted with this friend, for the sake of my spirit!

". . . the absolute champion of the world and at the same time a sensitive lyrical poet," continued Slonov. "I assure you it was his intellect above all that crushed Sonny Liston" . . . A present day boxer is above all a creative individual," continued Slonov . . . "Boxing is poetry. A poem of ecstasy. Boxing is a symphony or, if you wish, symphojazz. Boxing is the canvas of a surrealist. Boxing is inspiration, rapture, a sculptural fugue, assonance or dissonance."

Having said this he looked up at the ceiling and small fires flitted in his dark velvet eyes.

"Do you read much, Mabukin?" he asked.

"Yes, I'd say I do . . . here, "A Ray of Light in the Realm of Darkness" . . . I showed him.

"Well, and besides anthologies? . . . Have you read *The Trial* by Kafka? . . . Are you familiar with the poems of Velimir Khlebnikov?"

This is how our friendship began and it continues to this very day.

Soon my picture appeared on the front cover of "Flame", in boxing gloves and holding an Anthology: "Champion of sports, Gennady Mabukin, passionate book-lover."

At that time our team was preparing for the major competition for the Syracuse Cup in South America. Slonov came every day to our out-of-town training camp; he brought books, records, and art books. In a short time, under his supervision,

I mastered *The Trial* by Kafka; *Master and Margarita* by Bulgakov; *Grass of Oblivion* by Kataev; read *Kentavr* and *Children of Captain Grant* (now there's a book!); became familiar with the French anti-novel, *Sartre* (of course, I studied that thoroughly—that's a must nowadays); memorized several poems by Appollinaire, Velimir Khlebnikov—"camp at night Genghis Khan! . . . and the sky is blue, . . ."; listened with immense pleasure to Bach, Mahler, Prokofiev, the Modern Jazz Quartet; I familiarized myself with the art of Vasily Kandinsky, Salvador Dali, Giacometti, and many others. I especially liked the still lifes of Morandi. As Ehrenburg said, ". . . for all their philosophical depth there is neither rationality nor aridity—they appeal to the realm of the emotions."

Gradually the true face of present day boxing revealed itself to me. Strolling through the woods surrounding Moscow, —the groves, forests' edges, hills and valleys,—I composed verses. I remember my first poem:

> My face
> from dark swamps gazing
> Tired, lonely,
> unrelenting.
> My eyes, my brow,
> the stronghold of my love . . .
> I'm not Narcissus,
> yet I am still in love.

Once our head coach said to Slonov, "What are you stuffing that guy's head with? . . . he may have to fight in the finals with George-Louis Barracuda, and you know what a right he has!"

To this Slonov retorted, "How come you don't understand? Gennady is practically invincible, the Syracuse Cup is in the bag like all the other cups, but I want to mold him into a new type of boxer,—a creator, an artist."

"Could you be a spy, Slonov?" the coach asked gloomily.

And so we came to South America to a very big city, maybe

Buenos Aires, maybe Rio de Janeiro—I can't remember now. The competition started for the Syracuse Cup. Things were really jumping there. From fifty to sixty photographers photographed my training sessions, my face appeared on television from morning to night, on all twelve channels. Every day I received fifty or sixty letters from fans in South America. How does one get as strong as you? Only through hard work. How does one become as handsome as you? Only through hard work. Is it true you're a poet? Yes, it's true.

In the first preliminary I was up against a Hungarian. His coach pulled him out. "He is the Olympic hope of our country and we can't risk him," the coach announced to the newspapers. In the second preliminary an Englishman declined to fight. "I'm a father of five children—I can't afford to become a cripple," he informed the newspapers. In the quarter finals an Italian also refused to enter the ring: "Life is worth more to me than that." In the semi-finals a Japanese explained: "I have a bronze medal and that's enough."

I had plenty of free time and Ilya and I spent it at art exhibitions, symphony concerts, and in the cellars of the local Bohemia. In this way we continued to develop me into a new type of boxer personality. In the meantime my rival, George-Louis Barracuda was approaching the finals, one fierce battle after another.

The time for the finals had come. Before the fight Adolf Selestina Syracuse himself came to see me. He, a millionaire cattle rancher, was a huge man with the neck of a bull and a patch of gray hair on his pointed head, in a scarlet vest, a diamond on his finger, and in his ear a ruby. Looking at me with satisfaction he said to the representatives of the press:

"Yes, I can see it. I see in him my youth."

And now I entered the ring and for the first time saw Barracuda. A very big, very dark, already middle-aged man around thirty stood in the opposite corner. He was very nervous, and it even seemed as though his knees were shaking. I stood modestly in my corner, with my long, fluffy eyelashes lowered, and through my long, fluffy eyelashes I looked at him and smiled

"He has long arms. Try to fight up close. Watch out for his right," my coach whispered.

My coach is a strange one. He didn't know that I had decided to execute this fight as I would a symphonic poem, a sculptural fugue in a surrealistic key in assonances and dissonances. Close-in fighting, or from a distance—what nonsense! Boxing is a poem of ecstasy!

I played everything according to the music. Barracuda, with his daring and persistent stubbornness, was a perfect instrument in my hands—just like a Stradivarius. This fight for the first time was a true, highly aesthetic pleasure because now I was a boxer of the new type: "a boxer-intellectual."

In the third round, with an unexpected uppercut, he knocked me to the canvas. In the emptiness and silence a ringing, divine pain ran through me. Choking with admiration I looked at Barracuda's approaching face, at his trembling jaw, and his eyes gleaming like diamonds. The moment of truth. The last stroke, the last touch, the last vibrating note. The head of Barracuda struck the floor like a bowling ball.

Having answered fifty to sixty questions, I asked the journalists to leave me alone. I also asked my friend, Ilya, to vacate the quarters. When everyone had left, I put one of Rachmaninoff's concertos on the tape recorder, opened an album of Morandi, and a small volume of poetry by Innokentij Annenskij.

Deep in the night, when silence reigned, I left the Sports Palace. On the steps sat George-Louis Barracuda. He was crying.

"Why are you crying, Barracuda? Could it really be because of your defeat," I asked?

"What else?" he answered.

"Do you do much reading, Barracuda?"

"I read, I read."

"It must be you don't read enough. You need to read more, listen to music, look at paintings."

"Yes, I know. I know everything about you. I try to imitate you, but what's the use?"

"Do you like Morandi, Barracuda?"

"Yes, I like him, I like him."

"And the Modern Jazz Quartet?"

"Yeah."

"Then you have everything to look forward to. Don't cry. See you later."

"Go, while you're still in one piece," he snarled.

I didn't argue with him.

What can I say about my meals? In the morning I have a glass of juice, and two eggs. For lunch a small piece of herring and a bowl of chicken boullion. Afternoon snack: glass of milk and sweet roll. At supper I eat to my heart's content: caviar, fresh and smoked salmon, mushrooms in sour cream, a double shishkebob, cream-brule, berries in sour cream, cake, ice-cream and so on. I recommend this diet to all beginning athletes.

Who was I before? A pneumatic drill.

Who am I now? An artist with a sledge hammer.